GOLEM

BOOK FOUR OF THE CHRONICLES OF PARTHALAN

JENNIFER ALLIS PROVOST

BELLATRIX PRESS

Bellatrix Press

Cast of Characters

Aeolmar—First Hunter of Parthalan and commander of the Palace Contingent, mate of Latera, father of Mara, Ember, and Tor.

Alia—commander of the Northern Contingent.

Alluria—mate of Caol'nir, mother of Aeolmar.

Alyon—priestess of Asherah in the mortal realm.

Argent—prior First Hunter. Killed at the Battle of Esguth.

Asgeloth—*mordeth-gall*, Ehkron's whelp. Killed by Latera.

Asherah—Queen of Parthalan and Lady of Tingu, mate of Finlay, mother of Finlay Torim.

Atreynha—High Priestess of Teg'urnan.

Attia—royal *saffira-nell* and Asherah's confidant.

Avinor—King Markham's youngest son, brother to Iruna.

Bron—hunter in the Palace Contingent, brother of Luth.

Caol'nir—mate of Alluria, father of Aeolmar.

Cydia—Moon Goddess, former mate of Olluhm, mother of the fae.

Ehkron—former *mordeth-gall*, Asgeloth's sire. Killed by Elvasla.

Elkin—Second Hunter, mate of Innetha.

Elvasla—former Lady of Thurnda and ancestor of Latera. Killed Ehkron in the mortal realm.

Ember—younger daughter of Latera and Aeolmar.

Esguth—*mordeth* who attacked Teg'urnan. Killed by Aeolmar.

Finlay—King of Parthalan, mate of Asherah, father of Finlay Torim.

Finlay Torim—Asherah and Finlay's son.

Grelk—King of the Trolls, master blacksmith.

Harek—former Prelate. Executed for treason.

Innetha—huntress in the Palace Contingent, mate of Elkin.

Iruna—youngest child of Markham, sister of Avinor.

Ish h'ra—The Deliverer. A member of the old gods, she was persecuted by Olluhm.

Kemen—hunter in the Palace Contingent, son of Krylle.

Krylle—priest of The Deliver and the old gods. Father of Kemen.

Leran—Lord of Tingu, son of Lormac.

Latera—First Huntress of Parthalan, *deva'shi*, mate of Aeolmar, mother of Mara, Ember, and Tor. Killed the last *mordeth-gall*, Asgeloth.

Lormac—former Lord of Tingu, father of Leran, mate of Asherah. Killed on the Day of Sadness.

Luth—hunter in the Palace Contingent, brother of Bron.

Mallia—matriarch of the palace's healers.

Mara—eldest daughter of Latera and Aeolmar.

Markham—last king of Parthalan directly descended from Olluhm and Cydia, father of Iruna and Avinor. Killed by a usurper who was then killed by Sahlgren.

Mersgoth—*mordeth* who marked Alluria, and went on to kill her, Caol'nir, and six of their children. Eventually killed by Aeolmar.

Natreus—former king of the dark fae. Defeated in battle by Asherah.

Nyshanti—goddess of dawn, lover of The Deliverer, Ish h'ra.

Olluhm—Sun God, former mate of Cydia, father of the fae. He cast the old gods from the sky and installed himself as the All Father.

Rahlle—former royal sorcerer, and one of Cydia and Olluhm's original twelve children. Hasn't been seen since shortly after Asherah took the throne.

Sahlgren—former king of Parthalan who betrayed his people. Executed by Asherah.

Sarelle—former High Priestess of Teg'urnan who acted in collusion with Sahlgren.

Sarfek—sorcerer, brother of Harek. Killed by Latera.

Solon—the child sun, first born of Olluhm and Cydia.

Surya—huntress in the Palace Contingent. Surya's eyesight rivals a hawk's.

Tor—Latera and Aeolmar's youngest child. Named for his grandsire, who was a former Prelate of Parthalan.

Torim—Asherah's companion, killed on the Day of Sadness.

Wren—an herbalist, and Latera's oldest sister.

PROLOGUE

Olluhm hadn't always been a god in Parthalan.

Long before Olluhm ruled the skies as the elder sun, two older pantheons of gods warred for the right to Parthalan's worshippers. As time went on one faction would gain the upper hand, and then the other, but throughout the centuries of strife one thing was constant: Ish hr'a, the Deliverer. So long as her temples remained clear and her idols untouched, the people knew they would be cared for.

Olluhm cared not for Parthalan's people. All Olluhm wanted was to be a god, the more powerful the better. He accomplished that by murdering the sun god, and then his family, and laying claim to the fiery day chariot. Olluhm enjoyed his new status, but the other gods laughed at him. The last sun god had been called the All Father and had spent his days surrounded by his many bright children, yet Olluhm had no mate, and no progeny. What sort of weak god had no heir?

And so the new sun sought a mate, but none of the remaining goddesses, regardless of whether they belonged to his allies or adversaries, appealed to him. He had heard tell of one goddess who might do, the moon goddess whose beauty was immortalized in song and poem, but she was a creature of the night and near impossible to find during the day. As Olluhm feared he might never have children and thus not truly become the All Father, he began his flight one morn and saw her resting in a meadow below him.

Cydia, the moon herself.

After Olluhm had claimed Cydia, and gotten her with child, he set his sights on the gods that yet conflicted with him. All who opposed his rule were cast from the sky and banished to the underworld, where they remain to this day.

The last to be defeated were Ish hr'a and her lover, Nyshanti, the goddess of dawn. Ish h'ra fought long against Olluhm, for she was loath to leave her people to be ruled by such a tyrant. Then Olluhm committed his most abhorrent act, and decreed that no woman less lovely than Cydia may walk Parthian soil. Since none could claim the moon goddess's beauty, every mother, sister, and daughter in Parthalan perished.

Two did not perish. Ish h'ra and Nyshanti watched helplessly as women fell dead across the land. And when Olluhm learned that the lovers yet lived, he turned his fury toward them.

No one, not even those of the temples, knew what became of the lovers. Some claimed that Ish h'ra spirited Nyshanti to safety in one of the other realms, far away where Olluhm could not reach her. Others speculated that Olluhm tortured Ish h'ra and Nyshanti most of all, so jealous he was of how the people loved them.

The land now cleansed, Olluhm and Cydia repopulated Parthalan with their children. Such was their beauty they were called the fair folk, and, in time, the fae. But all did not worship the All Father. Some, knowing well of Olluhm's past deeds, sought to restore the old gods to their rightful place. They prayed to Ish hr'a, made offerings, and pledged their hearts and soul to the goddess while beseeching her to deliver them once more.

She hasn't yet, but her followers do not despair. They are nothing if not patient.

Chapter One

Asherah Speaks

I am the worst ruler Parthalan has ever known.

For nearly a millennia I'd counted as my closest friend and advisor a man who had only used me. Harek, my former Prelate, and his brother, Sarfek, had sought power, were prepared to grab it by any means necessary, and I was nothing more than their witless, willing pawn. They used me as soundly as Sahlgren had used all of us imprisoned in those *dojas,* though the king's betrayal had been a different sort.

Sahlgren hadn't known me. Harek's betrayal, that had been personal.

A good ruler never would have allowed such treachery. A good ruler would have seen Harek and Sarfek for what they were, and a good ruler would have dealt with them long before they made a pact with the mordeth-gall.

Lormac would not have allowed such traitors to stand so close to his throne.

Lormac...

Lormac is not here, and—gods!—how I miss him still. I will never be the sort of ruler he was, not if I reign for another thousand years.

When Latera had returned from the mortal realm bearing Sarfek's freshly severed head, every fear I'd ever had was dragged out into the harsh light of day. I'd never felt so unsure, unsafe... unfit. Then I'd severed Harek's head myself on the steps of Teg'urnan, much as I had taken Sahlgren's head so long ago. Again, the people cheered; again, I was drenched in a traitor's blood. Before, it was the blood of he who would have traded us all for his own ends. The second time, it was the blood of one I'd thought was my friend.

After Harek's execution I hid in my chambers for nigh on a sennight, not that I'd meant to. I'd only intended to wash away the blood and gore and then return to my people, but as the bathwater swirled pink my carefully arranged emotions crashed about me, shattering like a fine crystal vase flung against the wall. So I crawled into my bed and hid, wailing away like a child. You would think that after Harek's death—my Prelate's death, he who was guilty of the vilest acts of treason—I would have settled somewhat, but in truth I felt like an utter fool. A sham. Nothing more than a pathetic former slave masquerading as queen, with neither the right nor the ability to lead Parthalan. Gods. I could hardly manage to lead myself around Teg'urnan without incident.

And so I remained, until Finlay coaxed me out of my bed, and then my chamber, and eventually back to the daily rigors of life.

Finlay, Finlay. My man from the desert. If it hadn't been for him, I truly would have gone mad in those days after Harek's execution. Finlay convinced me that it wasn't my fault I'd been duped, that both Harek and Sarfek were thoroughly adept in their evilness and I was naught but an innocent. Then Alia told the whole of Teg'urnan that the man who shared the queen's bed was also her bound mate, and against my better judgment I made Finlay my king. That remains the best decision I've ever made.

With my mate-king and my First Hunter to lean upon, the burden of ruling wasn't so taxing anymore. I could breathe again, for with both Finlay and Aeolmar as my staunch supporters I felt that nothing bad could happen. They were there to protect me from myself.

Once all the land knew that the Virgin Queen was virgin no more, talk turned to the inevitable royal child. I demurred, ignored, and outright resisted such talk; then Aeolmar's daughter was born. Mara was a beautiful babe, just like her parents and yet so clearly herself, and her big blue eyes and gurgling laugh swayed my heart a bit. Not much, but a bit. Then Finlay held Mara for the first time, and his summer blue eyes shone like they never had before.

"Would you like one of your own?" I'd asked after an evening spent with Aeolmar, Latera, and a newly walking Mara.

"A hell beast like that one?" he joked. During the short visit Mara had knocked over several chairs, a table, and while we righted the furniture she ate one of my maps. *Ate it like it was a piece of cheese, not a priceless vellum depicting the ancient boundary of Ysr. "I don't know if Teg'urnan could stand it."*

"Me, either," I'd agreed, and we left it for a time. Then he started making comments, and after a time I stopped ignoring them, the end result being that when I celebrated my thousandth winter as queen I was heavy with child. We named our son Finlay Torim, his first name honoring his father for if it wasn't for the prodding of my mate I never would have attempted to bring another being into this world. Even if I did, I never would have made a wreck like me responsible for his well-being.

My child's second name honored my first love, she who died for me, and then saved me again from beyond the veil. Gods, even those in the afterlife understood that I could barely manage.

Always seeking to do me one better, our First Huntress bore her second daughter on the same day I bore Finlay. Latera had always made motherhood seem effortless; whereas I'd been clumsy as an ox and twice as large while I'd carried my son, Latera remained the petite, graceful being she'd always been. She'd even borne her children with no one present save Aeolmar, unlike me who had been fussed over by an army of healers doing all manner of undignified things to me.

It wasn't just that Latera excelled at motherhood. The little elf had accomplished everything she'd ever set out to do with hardly a bead of sweat upon her brow. She'd killed the mordeth-gall, *found and eliminated those responsible for kidnapping her from the mortal world, and reduced the fortress around Aeolmar's heart to so much rubble. I didn't know which of her feats I was most jealous of.*

Before you could blink, Latera was heavy with her third babe, though she didn't breeze through that event as she had with the rest. The birth had been difficult for our life-bearer, and Aeolmar had been beside himself with worry. We all were, really; if Latera didn't survive, I feared for Aeolmar's sanity. I feared for my own sanity, were Aeolmar's stalwart shoulder taken from me.

I reached for my tea, bitter and hot, and drank deeply. It made my eyes heavy and soft, my limbs warm and liquid. I lay back against the cushions, and hoped I'd find myself in my usual calm, darkened dreamscape. It was nice there, no hard decisions or past regrets. Soft. Warm. Nice.

Gods. I hope my son grows quickly, for Parthalan may need him soon.

Chapter Two

Finlay eased the door shut and nodded a silent greeting to their *saffira-nell*, Attia. Asherah had taken to napping in the early afternoon, and he didn't want to wake her before she was ready. He'd made that mistake more than once. More than anything, he wished that sleep was the cure she so desperately needed.

When he considered the more significant events of his life since he came to Teg'urnan, he noted that Asherah began slipping away from him almost immediately after Harek's execution. It was no surprise that Harek's treason had affected Asherah deeply, and Finlay had tried to support her as best he could; still, there were nights she sobbed in his arms, convinced she was a failure as a woman and a queen. For the torment Harek still caused his mate Finlay would kill him again a thousand times over, and ensure that each death was more painful than the last.

After Finlay had been crowned king, something he, a simple merchant's son turned hunter, had never anticipated, Asherah calmed for a time. Asherah still worried for his safety—she'd long been convinced someone had put a price on Finlay's head—then Latera decided to end the speculation once and for all, and searched Harek's chambers. Ransack would be a better description, and she'd come across sufficient evidence to prove that Harek had been the direct cause of Asherah's former lovers' deaths; all of them, from Argent to Brendan and worst of all, Lormac. Harek's obsession with a woman he could never have had driven him to madness and murder.

This knowledge had opened up many of Asherah's old wounds, and it was all Finlay could do to distract her. Soon enough Mallia, the matriarch of the palace's healers, had offered her own brand of help, and concocted teas of dreamwort and flaedyne so Asherah could sleep without nightmares. Of course, the teas were of little help during her waking hours, but at least she could rest peacefully.

Then their son, the younger Finlay, was born, and the elder Finlay hoped his mate would finally shake herself free of the black thoughts that had so plagued her. Instead, she requested more and more of Mallia's remedies, seeking the dark oblivion of her dreamless sleeps. Finlay didn't know how he could help her; now that Asherah slept for the bulk of the day, she seemed happier while she was awake, but their son needed her. Parthalan needed her.

Finlay needed her.

I'll burn those herbs if I have to.

With grim resolve he pushed open their bedchamber door and found Asherah sitting up in bed brushing out her long, almost-white hair. Her back was toward him, and Finlay watched her through the gauzy bed curtains. Even after the many winters they'd been together, her beauty was so striking his breath caught in his throat. Her skin was pale as cream, yet her lips were blood red and her eyes black as night, coloring that was unique among the fae. What he wouldn't give to see the sparkle in her dark eyes again.

He cleared his throat, and Asherah twisted around. "Finlay," she greeted with a smile.

"My love." He ascended the steps and sat beside his mate. "You look wonderful today," he said, if for no other reason than she was awake. She smiled wanly, her eyes downcast. "What is it?"

"Finlay was just here," she replied. "He asked me why I'm always so tired."

"And what did you tell him?"

"I told him the truth," she whispered. "I don't know why I want to sleep so much. I just don't know." Finlay wrapped his arm around her and kissed her forehead.

"Perhaps those herbs have done their good," he suggested. "Perhaps they've healed what they can."

"Even if they haven't, I can't go on like this," she said bitterly. "Gods, when did Finlay get so tall? I feel like I've missed half his life."

"He grows quickly. All boys do." He held her for a moment, enjoying the feel of her alert form in his arms. "If it will help, I'll prepare some of that spiced wine you like. It's always kept you awake in the past."

"Only because I've had to listen to you complain about how much you hate it," she retorted. Finlay laughed and held her a little tighter. His mate was going to be fine. They were going to raise their son together and rule Parthalan together.

Together. Just as they were meant to be.

Chapter Three

Aeolmar entered his family's chamber, tired and frustrated from the hunt. Earlier that day he'd gotten word that a clutch of lesser demons was harrying a shepherd and her flock just past the eastern foothills, and Aeolmar decided to ride out and deal with them alone. Overall the hunt was a success, but one demon had escaped. That was one demon too many for his pride.

They're getting too bold. He unbuckled his sword belt and hung it on its peg, then Aeolmar sat and yanked off his boots, meaning to throw them against the wall. His gaze fixed on the steps at the far end of the room, and his frustration melted into concern. Though the red silk hangings obscured the sleeping area that lay beyond, he knew his mate and son were nestled in bed. He dropped the boots, muttering curses at the sound they made when they hit the floor, and approached the bed.

With a soft tread that belied his anxiety Aeolmar climbed the steps and drew back the curtains; only when he saw both of their chests rise and fall did he smile. He had hoped Latera would be awake so they could discuss the botched hunt, but she was fast asleep, her arm wrapped around the baby. Even in sleep Tor pressed his face against his mother's breast, his mouth working as if he nursed in his dreams.

With a soft laugh, Aeolmar gently took Tor from Latera's arms. While he dearly loved his daughters and would not trade them for all the jewels in Tingu, nothing matched the pride he felt when he held his son. He would teach Tor all of the things Mara and Ember had never shown an interest in, such as swordplay, and tracking, and...

And Tor let out an impressive wail, his way of letting Aeolmar know that he wanted the one thing his father couldn't provide. "Hush, little one," Aeolmar said as he sat on the bed. He unlaced Latera's bodice one-handed and placed the boy at her breast, smiling as Tor greedily sucked. Latera's eyes fluttered open, and she offered Aeolmar a weak smile.

"Undressing me while I sleep?" she teased. "After all this time, I thought you'd be bored with me."

"You remain the loveliest woman I've ever seen," he said, smoothing back her fiery hair. Even through her long recovery, Latera's red hair hadn't lost its luster, and her eyes remained a clear crystal blue.

Latera yawned, and Aeolmar tucked the blankets around her and Tor. "Sleep, beloved," he whispered as he kissed her cheek, "rest for me." By the time the words were spoken, she was again asleep, her breath matching the baby's gentle pulls.

Aeolmar rose from the bed, his smile fading as he regarded his mate and son. Tor's birth had been hard on Latera, much harder than either of their daughters had been, and her recovery was much, much slower. When their eldest daughter, Mara, had been born, she'd come in the space of a few heartbeats, and Ember's birth was faster yet. With both children, Latera had been up and around within days. Tor was near two moons, and Latera had yet to regain her strength.

When Latera had felt the birth pains for their third child, neither she nor Aeolmar sent for a healer. They even kept Mara and Ember nearby, since all four were eager to meet the newest member of their family. Latera had hinted that the third would be a boy, but Aeolmar was indifferent, outwardly at least. Inwardly, he could hardly contain himself.

The shadows had grown long while Latera labored. Night fell without the baby coming, and the chamber was eerily quiet; Latera was exhausted, so much so she couldn't cry or even whimper as her belly contorted. And she bled, more blood than Aeolmar had ever seen come from one who did not die. He was terrified that his mate and son might perish, terrified that his daughters were there to watch.

But Aeolmar was First Hunter, the strongest and most cunning warrior in Parthalan. More, his mate was the *deva'shi*, and the slayer of the *mordeth-gall*. If Latera could survive the most terrible of demons, surely she wouldn't meet her end in childbed. His mate was more than strong enough to survive this latest trial. What she, and Aeolmar, needed was a plan.

Aeolmar had yelled for Mara to take Ember from the room and fetch a healer, for he would not—no, he *refused*—to allow death to take his mate. Mara had done as he asked and removed Ember, but the girl had a mind like her mother and fetched Wren, Latera's sister, instead of one of the healers, knowing that Latera would only want to be attended by her.

With Wren's assistance, the boy finally made his way into the world, as blood-soaked and exhausted as his mother. His first weak cries roused Latera, and she held out her arms to her son. Aeolmar tried to dissuade her, stating that he would find a wet nurse for the boy and that she should rest, but Latera knew that no babies had been born recently in Teg'urnan. Reluctantly, Aeolmar placed the boy in his mate's arms, then watched over her as she did nothing more than sleep for days, only occasionally waking to take a bit of broth or to care for the baby. Those days stretched into a sennight, and then two; once a moon had passed Aeolmar let himself breathe again, and hoped that both would be well.

Aeolmar exhaled heavily as he remembered those harrowing first days of Tor's life, then he bent down and kissed first Latera's, and then Tor's, forehead. He had never been so scared in his life as when he thought Latera might not survive; he'd heard of women dying in childbed but had thought those instances were rare. Now that he had seen with his own eyes how dangerous birth could be, he wanted to forbid Latera from bearing a fourth child. He understood that the time to discuss that would be later, once she'd fully recovered. He also held his tongue because he was well aware that Latera would not agree with him.

I can't lose her, not to childbirth, not to anything. If I make her understand that I can't live without her, she will agree.

As Aeolmar descended from the sleeping area to the main floor of the chamber, his sharp gaze caught a tiny movement out on the balcony. He found his younger daughter, Ember, wrapped in a blanket as she huddled against the short stone wall.

"*Dea comora*, why are you all alone out here?" Aeolmar asked as he scooped her onto his lap. She rubbed her eyes as she snuggled against her father's chest, a tiny fire-haired nestling. Aeolmar frequently wondered if only Mara had inherited his height, and if his younger children would be small like their elfin mother.

"I was tired, and there's no room for me in the bed," Ember replied.

Her simple words tore at Aeolmar's heart. Since Tor's birth, Aeolmar had been preoccupied with caring for Latera and the baby, and Ember had been shuttled between Wren and Mara. While both were more than capable of seeing to her needs, they were poor substitutes for her parents. He held Ember a little tighter, hating that his daughter had been neglected to the point that she felt she had to sleep on the balcony, hating himself for being too distracted to notice.

Aeolmar absently fingered the fringed edge of her blanket and realized that it was the shawl Latera had been wearing the day Ember was born. Nine winters past, Latera had smiled coyly at her mate, and shared that their little family would soon get bigger. The happy news quickly spread across the palace and to the sharp ears of Mallia, the matriarch of Teg'urnan's healers. She was still nursing her wounded pride over having missed Mara's birth, for there were precious few chances in Teg'urnan for her to show off her midwifery skills. By chance or perhaps by divine design, before Mallia could rush to Latera's side Queen Asherah announced that she and King Finlay were expecting their firstborn, who would also be the first royal child of Parthalan since before the old king's rule.

Her efforts now doubled, Mallia was determined to keep a close eye on both expectant mothers. Well-meaning or no, she levied so many restrictions on Latera Aeolmar feared she would go mad from confinement. In an effort to preserve her sanity, Aeolmar located the slowest, most gentle mule in all of Parthalan and surprised Latera by planning an outdoor lunch at Esguth's Rock for just the two of them.

Latera had been overjoyed, and hardly complained about the slow pace he set as they rode out to the secluded spot. Once they arrived at the rocky outcrop Aeolmar helped her from the saddle, but as soon as Latera's feet touched the ground she gasped, and looked at Aeolmar in way she only had once before. A short time later they held their second daughter, who had made her arrival almost an entire moon earlier than anticipated. Aeolmar immediately called her his little ember, as much for her small size as the cap of red fuzz she bore. Being that they hadn't expected to be in company with a baby they hadn't brought along any swaddling clothes, so Latera wrapped the baby in her shawl, which in time became Ember's favorite blanket. As soon as they returned to Teg'urnan Aeolmar sent for Mara, who was excited to meet her sister. Mara also shared that the queen had given birth to the Prince of Parthalan that day.

Aeolmar smiled fondly as he remembered that day, not only for the joy over a second healthy daughter but also for Mallia's sour face when she learned that she had missed out on yet another birth. She insisted on examining the baby, and huffed and clucked while she admonished them for moving Ember too quickly after birth; everyone knew that a babe needed rest and quiet after the stresses of birth, otherwise there could be permanent damage. Aeolmar had balked at her accusation, and asked if he was just supposed to leave his mate and newborn out at Esguth's Rock? Besides, any fool could see that Ember was perfect.

Eventually Mallia's mood calmed, or at least she stopped bothering them, and Ember grew into a smart, inquisitive girl none the worse for her early adventures. However, Latera had not wanted Mallia to attend her while she carried Tor, to which Aeolmar agreed. After the mess that became of Tor's birth, he suspected that they'd both been a bit rash.

All these thoughts coursed through Aeolmar's mind as he smoothed back Ember's hair, much as he had smoothed Latera's a few moments ago. "There is always room for you, my little Ember," Aeolmar said.

"Really?" she asked as her eyes lit up. With her curly, bright red hair and pale blue eyes, Aeolmar imagined that Ember was the very picture of his mate as a child.

"Really," he confirmed. With that Aeolmar rose and carried the girl out of the chill air and toward the sleeping platform.

"Which side would you like?" Aeolmar asked. "Next to Mama, or your brother?"

"Mama," Ember replied. "She needs me."

"All right, then."

Aeolmar nestled the girl in the warm furs and took his place beside her, and both were soon asleep. Latera, surrounded by her family, smiled in her sleep, for she was content.

Chapter Four

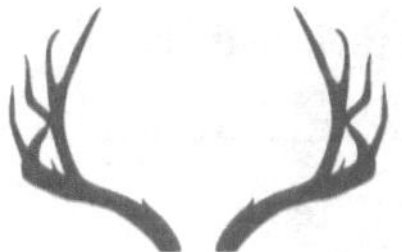

When Aeolmar woke, he and Ember were alone in the bed. Frantic, he bolted upright, then tamped down his fear. Surely if anything was amiss Latera would have woken him. Surely she and Tor were well. Still, only Ember sleeping beside him kept Aeolmar from shouting Latera's name; instead, he reached out with his mind.

Their binding had always been such that they were able to read one another's moods, the empathic bond linking Aeolmar and Latera together, even when their bodies were separated by a great distance. Aeolmar hadn't thought much about it, assuming that all bound mates shared the same attributes, until one day when Latera was heavy with Mara. He'd felt a few hunger pangs that weren't his, and mentioned them to Asherah.

"Latera's hungry," he'd said with a grin. "Our babe demands we feed her."

"Aren't women with child always hungry?" Asherah asked, as she swirled her tea in its bowl.

"True," Aeolmar conceded, "but she wants brambleberries." Asherah had questioned how he knew that, and Aeolmar explained that he felt Latera's cravings just as strongly as if they were his own. The queen was silent, but her pursed lips told Aeolmar that Asherah and Finlay had a different sort of bond than he and Latera. He said nothing, for what sort of advice could he really offer? What he had done was procure a sack of berries for his hungry mate, and quickly.

During Mara's birth, their mate bond had progressed further. He could have sworn he'd heard Latera cry out, though the room had remained silent, and attributed it to his own anxious mind. Then he'd heard the soundless shriek again, but he'd been staring at Latera's face and was certain her mouth hadn't moved. Understanding that he was hearing her thoughts rather than her voice, he'd focused his gaze and pushed his own thoughts at her.

Latera. Beloved. Her eyes had snapped open, but before she could speak she cried out again, this time aloud. *She'll be here soon. Just a bit longer. Be strong for me.*

And then Mara was there, as tiny and perfect a babe as Aeolmar had ever seen, and while the three of them rested, Aeolmar had practiced his newfound talent, much to his delight and Latera's irritation. Latera had compared the touch of his mind to hers as if he had thrown open the shutters at midday after she'd spent a moon in total darkness; the light was welcome and warm, but it made her eyes squint and her head throb. So he worked to make his thoughts as light as a whisper, and in time Aeolmar learned how to silently call Latera without making her feel like he'd shoved a hot poker in her eye.

Beloved.

Hearth.

Even in his mind, Latera's voice was weary. Aeolmar rose and parted the curtains, and saw Latera sitting in front of the fire with Tor in her arms. He let go of his latest worry, and joined her.

"I didn't think I'd find you up and about," he said, sitting on the floor at her feet. "You were so tired earlier."

"And now I am rested," Latera said. Her light comment did nothing to unknot Aeolmar's brow, or sway his concerns. "Mar, I wish you wouldn't worry so. I grow stronger every day, as does our son."

"I can see that," he said, taking her foot in his lap and stroking her ankle. He'd never been able to resist her smooth skin. "Still, I can't help worrying about you. It didn't take you this long to recover after either of the girls. You were up within ten days after Mara, and even less after Ember."

"I would have been up much sooner after Mara, if only you'd have let me out of bed," she said with a smirk. Aeolmar laughed at the memory; he had confined Latera to his chamber at the peak of the southern tower on the pretense of allowing her to rest, until she'd threatened to throw herself from the balcony unless he helped her down the tower's steep stairs. "And as for Ember, there wasn't much to be done about that."

"There wasn't," he agreed, now tracing small circles on the top of her foot.

"Look at our son," Latera continued. She sat Tor on her knee and indicated his robust form. "He's not yet two moons, but he's bigger than Ember was at six. Of course it will take me longer to recover after a larger baby, it only makes sense."

Aeolmar tickled the baby's toes. "I suppose."

Latera nudged him with her foot. "Oh, you suppose, do you?"

"I just want you to be well," Aeolmar said. "Both of you." Latera leaned forward, and stroked her mate's cheek.

"I know," she said. Tor felt the skin of Latera's breast against his cheek and turned toward his mother, whimpering softly. "And your son is hungry again." Latera steadied the baby on her knee with one hand and unlaced her bodice with the other, then pulled her arms free and let her gown fall to her waist. A moment later, and the baby was at her breast. Aeolmar grabbed the shawl that had been flung haphazardly on the bench behind him, then he rose up on his knees and tucked it around Latera's shoulders.

"I wonder if your milk tastes the same," he mused, his thumb stroking the soft skin over her heart. After Mara's birth, Aeolmar had felt that one of his paternal duties was to know what his children were consuming; no, that wasn't quite it. He'd just wanted a new way to kiss her. Latera had suspected as much, but Aeolmar's persuasion had worn away her resolve until she relented and let him take her breast. He'd thought his mate's milk was like sampling her very soul; it was light, and sweet, and warm, just like the woman he loved.

Once Mara had been weaned, Aeolmar waited a small eternity for Ember to come along, and to taste Latera's milk again. He'd been pleased to learn that it had lost none of its wonderful characteristics. He hadn't broached the subject after Tor's birth, partly because he wanted Latera to rebuild her strength, partly because their son was always hungry.

"Go ahead," Latera said, once again reading his thoughts. "You've done it before."

"I worry that you don't have enough, what with his appetite," he replied with a nod at Tor.

"I have enough," she said, her lidded eyes an invitation for something more than a quick kiss, "certainly enough for my beloved."

Aeolmar pushed her shawl aside as his hand gently cupped her breast; he stroked his thumb over the tip before he bent his head and bestowed a sucking kiss. Latera's milk flowed into his mouth, as warm and sweet as he remembered, and once again he felt as if he was drinking in the essence of her. His mouth travelled upward, leaving a trail of wet kisses on her breast and neck before he claimed her lips.

"Tastes the same to me," she said once they parted.

"Me, too." Aeolmar kissed her again, then resumed his seat on the floor and settled her foot on his lap. He stroked her ankle, slowly expanding the lazy circles to her calf. They hadn't made love since before Tor's birth, the longest they had gone since they were bound. Aeolmar missed the feel of her skin against his, her sweet scent and taste, but he had avoided their bed while she recovered. But if Latera was as well as she claimed...

Aeolmar kissed her ankle, enjoying her soft laughter as he pushed up her skirt and caressed her shins, then her knees as he moved toward what he truly sought. Finally he reached her thighs, Latera relaxing into a sigh as he kissed her deeply. So happy he was to have his lover returned to him, he almost didn't hear her.

"Aeolmar! You'll make me drop the baby!"

He raised his head, and saw Latera hanging on to the edge of the chair, clutching the arm of it with one hand and Tor with the other. Aeolmar had nearly pulled her onto the floor beside him. He chuckled as he pulled down Latera's skirts, then took the baby while she righted herself.

"You know the effect you have on me," Aeolmar said with a sheepish grin. Latera didn't answer; instead, she reclaimed Tor and wrapped the baby in her shawl. Aeolmar hoped that he hadn't angered her, but before he could defend himself (she must know he'd never let them fall!) she tucked the now-sleeping Tor onto the chair's cushions. Once she was certain that the baby was secure, she cast a quick glance toward the bed. Thus assured that Ember remained asleep, Latera stood and let her gown fall around her feet.

Aeolmar's first thought was that she was lovely, though her skin was pale and stark against the rich turquoise silk puddled at her ankles, and her belly soft thanks to the three children she'd borne him. Even so, her brazenness shocked him. A moment ago he'd wanted her so much he could think of nothing else, but now he merely stared at her.

"What?" Latera knelt before him and unlaced his shirt. "Don't want to finish what you started?" She pushed Aeolmar's shirt up and over his head; that done, she thrust her hands into his hair and kissed him.

"Beloved, I'll be gentle with you."

"I'd rather you weren't."

Aeolmar wrapped his arms around his mate, and took everything she gave him.

***

A short yet satisfying time later, Aeolmar was once again sitting on the floor before the hearth, this time with Tor in his arms. Latera leaned against him, her bare feet tucked underneath her. Aside from two contented smiles, there was no evidence of their interlude.

"You really did shock me, dropping your dress like that," Aeolmar said, as he tucked a lock of hair behind her ear. "I wondered if my lovely maiden had been taken from me, and an evil sylph left behind in her place."

"Hardly a maiden," Latera retorted. "And, I've done that before."

"So you have," he conceded, kissing the top of her head. "All of once, I believe."

"Perhaps I'll endeavor to entice you more often," she suggested, leaning up to nip at his earlobe. Before things could progress, they heard the soft rustle of the bed curtains, and a sleepy-eyed Ember descended to the main floor.

"Sweetheart," Latera called. Ember bounded toward her mother and snuggled deep into her arms; Aeolmar hadn't been the only one who'd felt lost without Latera these past few moons. Latera asked Ember what she'd been up to of late, and the girl launched into a tale of each and every incident, however mundane, that her mother had missed out on. Toward the end of the third sennight's recounting, Tor squealed and demanded some attention of his own.

Ember watched in mute fascination as Latera scooped up the baby and put him to her breast. "Is that the only way he eats?" she asked.

"It's how all babies eat," Latera replied. When Ember wrinkled her nose, Latera added, "It's how you ate when you were small."

Ember leaned forward, apparently to get a better view of the proceedings, then asked, "Do you feed Papa this way?"

"Ember, your father is a grown man," Latera answered. "He eats regular food, like you and I do. You know that."

"Oh."

"Wherever would you get such a silly notion?"

"I saw his face on you, just like Tor's," Ember replied.

"That was only the one time," Latera replied, blushing furiously. Aeolmar laughed, and Latera elbowed him so hard he nearly toppled over.

"Oh. May I go play with Finlay?" Ember asked, and Latera murmured that was fine. As Ember ran off to find her friend, Latera glared at her mate.

"Laugh all you'd like, you oaf," she said, giving him another shove. "Next time, you may answer her questions."

"Next time, I'll tell her—Well, I don't know what," he said as he wrapped his arms around Latera, careful of her sharp elbows. "But I'll tell her the truth." Latera grumbled, and Aeolmar shifted so he could look into her crystal blue eyes. "Why do her questions make you so uncomfortable? I don't think it's wrong for our children to know how much we love each other."

"It's not that," Latera said. "But we should be more careful around our inquisitive one. I don't want her to be constantly embarrassed by us, the way Mara is." Aeolmar laughed; he doubted anything could embarrass Ember.

"I was always very much aware of how much my parents loved each other," he countered. "My father never missed a chance to pull my mother onto his lap, or steal a few kisses."

Latera laughed shortly. "The most affection I've ever witnessed between my parents was when my father took my mother's hand," she said. "And that was all of once."

"Then where did you think all those sisters came from?" Aeolmar teased. "A traveling tinker?" Latera went on about the differences between sleeping in a royal nursery as opposed to a small cottage, and unsuccessfully stifled a yawn.

"Come, beloved," he said as he scooped her up, feeding baby and all, "I fear I've worn you out." Latera gave his chest a halfhearted thump, but otherwise didn't protest being carried off to bed. "Perhaps tomorrow we'll all take a walk in the sunshine."

Chapter Five

Mara darted around the hawkers and stalls clustered along the outer edge of the palace complex, and narrowly avoided being run down by a cart or two. The congestion in the merchants' quarter was as sure a sign of spring as the warm breeze that ruffled her auburn hair, for once winter relaxed her icy grip on the land anyone with something to sell made their way to Teg'urnan. Livestock, bolts of soft silk and heaps of rough burlap, fine foods, exotic liquors, and more were sold at the stalls, but if one turned the corner just past the Raven's Nest, one would be standing on Magician's Row. Among those sellers a buyer could exchange a few coins for a love spell, a canister of dragon's fire, or an enchanted plough guaranteed to make your crops grow tall and quickly, though why someone who lived in a palace would need a plough was beyond Mara's ken. Not to mention, everyone knew that dragons were just a children's story.

Mythical beasts notwithstanding, Magician's Row was where Mara needed to make her purchases. Wren's stores had gotten low of late, what with the many draughts and poultices she'd been preparing for Latera, and replenishing her supplies at the healers' ward was no longer an option. After Mallia had missed the third of Latera's births she became well and truly offended, and her rancor spread to anyone even remotely associated with the *deva'shi*. Why, the woman had even attempted to scold Aeolmar for not having a healer present at the birth, possibly the most foolish act she, or anyone else, had ever committed.

To everyone's relief, Aeolmar hadn't killed the matriarch when she insinuated that he had knowingly placed Latera and Tor's lives in jeopardy. Instead, he banished her from his side of the palace ("The side I'm in is mine, and you'll stay on the opposite end!" was what he'd bellowed). Wren had thus accepted the task of being Latera's sole caregiver, not that there had been many options. In a show of solidarity the rest of the hunters avoided the healers ward as well, and instead went to Wren for everything from blood burns to upset stomachs. Mara wondered if they should all start calling her aunt the Hunters' Healer.

I should have brought a list. And a basket. Mara had readily offered to obtain Wren's supplies for her, knowing how her aunt disliked venturing outside of Teg'urnan without Latera. Even after her many winters in Parthalan Wren still hadn't shed her human characteristics, though Latera claimed to have looked fully elfin after a few seasons of being exposed to the realm's magic. But then, Wren was Latera's half-sister, and their shared father had very little elfin blood to speak of. That abundance of mortal blood also accounted for the silver threads that wound through Wren's hair, and the soft lines around her eyes and mouth. Mostly-mortal Wren appeared far older than Asherah, though she was hardly a tenth of the queen's age.

"Looking for work?" a gravelly voice inquired. Mara had been so lost in her thoughts about Wren's supplies she'd taken a wrong turn.

Instead of ending up on Magician's Row, she was on Scullery Row, an area filled with taverns and brothels. The woman who had spoken seemed to be affiliated with the latter.

"I am not," Mara replied. "I have business with the apothecary."

"Mmm, a shame." The speaker, a woman who had yellow hair piled atop her head and a brightly painted mouth, was clad in a green skirt and tight black bodice that left her shoulders and arms indecently bare. She stepped forward and gestured as if to caress Mara's cheek. Mara jerked away, but otherwise remained frozen in place, largely due to the dagger sheathed at the woman's waist.

"Skittish, are you?" the woman purred. "I've a few who'll pay extra for that." She made a few other comments about Mara's appearance, mostly about her clothing. Mara tended toward the tunics and leggings her mother favored rather than dresses, and though she was still young by faerie standards she had truly grown into her beauty. She had her father's sapphire eyes and height, along with her mother's delicate features and slender limbs. Her hair, long and thick and shiny, was a deep auburn that she usually left loose, as she had done today. Now, she twisted the ends of it around her fingers, unsure if she should wait for the woman to move on, or take her chances and run.

"Simma, you truly are a foolish whore," said a man's voice. Mara was too frightened to turn around, but was relieved when Kemen strode up beside her. "You do realize that you're propositioning the First Hunter's daughter?"

If Simma felt that this was in any way an inappropriate action, she hid it well. "As I said, I've some who'll pay extra," she said, toying with the stays of her bodice. Mara worried that the strings, which were putting up a valiant effort at restraining her bosom, would fail at any moment.

"Olluhm's Balls, woman, she's but a child," Kemen spat. "Every day you sink lower into your own muck." He didn't wait for Simma's reply, and grabbed Mara's elbow and led her away from the brothel.

"Why are you out here alone?" Kemen demanded once they were out of Simma's sight. "This is no place for you."

"I came to get supplies for Wren," Mara replied, then she realized that she should be offended. "And I can come and go as I please, alone or no!"

"This is no place for children," Kemen retorted.

"I am not a child," Mara shouted, garnering some interested looks that she deliberately ignored. "My mother killed the *mordeth-gall* when she was younger than I am now!"

Kemen raised an eyebrow and Mara felt like a fool; of course Kemen knew exactly when Asgeloth had fallen, being that it was due in no small part to Kemen's selfless act. While Kemen had initially betrayed Parthalan by putting one of the old Prelate's schemes into play, after he'd been captured Latera had offered him a chance to redeem himself: bait the *mordeth-gall* to attack Teg'urnan and fall into the fae's trap, and all would be forgiven.

Kemen had done the impossible, by both carrying out the plan and not getting killed in the process. Since his return to Teg'urnan a few short moons after Asgeloth's death, he'd been lauded as a hero. Even Aeolmar had admitted that Kemen had done well, and deserved his place among the palace hunters. Which meant that Kemen had little patience for half-fae children that got themselves into trouble.

"Whether you're elf or fae, grown or still suckling, matters not," he said. "Do you know who that woman was?" Mara shook her head. "When Simma ran her brothels in the east, she would enchant young girls into a deep, deep sleep, then sell their bodies to whoever had the most coin. The girls never woke, never knew, never even got paid for the loss of their maidenhead. Do you want that to be your fate?"

"If she's so terrible, why is she here, in Teg'urnan?" Mara asked. "She should have been punished."

"She was," Kemen replied. "She was stripped of her magic, then she was peeled and whipped in the town square. My father's the man that did the whipping."

"If she has no magic, then she can't capture me," Mara pointed out. Kemen shook his head, and moved closer to Mara. She backed up until she bumped into a wall.

"There are other ways to capture young girls," he said. "I've no magic, and look where I've gotten you." Mara shuddered, and remembered all the stories she'd heard about Kemen before his return to the palace, none of which had painted him in a pleasant light. But she couldn't reconcile those stories of a selfish rake with the man before her. Even though the fate he'd rescued her from was likely no more than a bit of embarrassment, he'd still rescued her.

Not to mention that Mara had been fascinated by Kemen for as long as she could remember. She recalled the jubilee held to honor Asherah's one thousandth winter as queen; Mara's mother had been heavy with Ember at the time, and since her father had been occupied with his mate's care Mara had the freedom to roam about the celebration. Most men shied away from her, being that she was the First Hunter and *deva'shi's* daughter, so she had had precious few opportunities to dance. Then Kemen had arrived, his eyes shining like green glass and his black hair pulled away from his strong, angular features, and she realized that the rest of the men present paled in comparison to him. She hadn't managed to dance with him that night, but she'd admired him ever since.

And now he was here, and they were talking, and... And why was Kemen in this section of the merchants' quarter?

"W-Why were you near the brothels?" she asked. *Gods, gods, gods, please don't tell me you frequent these places. Lie if you have to, just please don't say you do.*

"I was headed to The Swan when I saw you turn down Scullery Row," he replied. "I assumed you'd lost your way, so I followed you."

"Why?" Mara pressed.

"Your mother saved my life. The least I can do is keep her child from harm."

"I'm not a child," Mara said again, rather more petulantly than she'd intended. *Wonderful. I've just proven that I act like a baby.*

"I can see that," Kemen replied as he looked over Mara's form, his heavy gaze nearly palpable. She felt hot blood rise in her cheeks, but if Kemen noticed he made no mention of it. He moved away from her and into the street, and gestured for Mara to do the same.

"Now, you were headed to the apothecary?" Kemen asked, his hand firm on her back. Mara nodded. "The one Wren prefers is this way."

"Are you going to wait for me while I make my purchases?" Mara asked.

"Yes, and then I'll see you safely inside the palace," he replied without looking at her. "Unless you'd prefer to visit a few more houses of ill repute?"

"Maybe I will next time I'm here, when I don't have a self-appointed chaperone following me around."

"By all the living gods, if you think I will allow you to come here again unescorted, you're mad."

Kemen offered her his arm, and Mara took it. As they picked their way among the flower sellers and ribbon weavers, she found herself hoping that Wren's supplies would run low again, and soon.

CHAPTER SIX

The outer hall of Teg'urnan was crowded with peasants and nobility alike, as was typical of Reckoning Day. Parthalan as a whole relished these occasions, which were held at the turn of every season, when Queen Asherah and King Finlay personally presided over any quarrel, whether it be over a disputed inheritance, a contested border, or a missing chicken. They were fair and just with their people, with those that were found against frequently feeling that they'd also gained something during the discourse with their sovereigns.

Iruna hated Reckoning Day, almost as much as she hated the queen.

She could hardly remember her father, King Markham, who had been the last true royal monarch of Parthalan. Iruna had seen less than twenty winters when the usurper (Iruna refused to speak the name of her father's killer, even in her thoughts) had managed to kill the then-Prelate and capture the royal family. Iruna had never learned all of the details, but the original dispute had had something to do with farmland in the east. Avinor, her older brother, knew more about it than she ever had, and she'd never once asked him about those times. Some things were best left unsaid.

The usurper's intent was to threaten the king into compliance, but things had quickly gotten out of hand and Markham offered up his life to keep his family safe. Iruna still remembered the usurper's eyes, glazed over with a feverish madness as he took her father's head.

Then the madman had become the king; a king without a Prelate, since Odbin's son was still in swaddling clothes; and a king without a sorcerer, since Rahlle refused to give the madman his oath.

Without any allies, those members of the royal family that still breathed were imprisoned in the western tower. Not long afterward, the mad king confined Iruna's mother to his bedchamber, and she ended up dead. No one was certain of how she died, but Iruna's sister and two of her brothers also died in that same room; each had been alone with the usurper at their end. Then, when only Iruna and Avinor remained, the demons came, and the two youngest siblings were quite forgotten.

Unsurprisingly, the usurper had proved to be weak on the battle-field, and in the span of a sennight Teg'urnan had been captured by the *mordeth-gall* himself. Sahlgren, one of her father's trusted commanders, killed the *mordeth-gall* and then beheaded the usurper, thus claiming the kingship for himself. Iruna, and many others, counted that day as one of the greatest in Parthalan's history.

Once the demons had been routed and the palace searched, Iruna and Avinor were found locked away in their tower prison. Sahlgren, not wanting those with royal blood to endanger his new claim to the throne, quickly arranged for the siblings to be taken to one of their father's estates in Parthalan's western hills. Sahlgren had claimed no ill will toward the orphans, and Iruna had always believed this to be true. Despite his speedy removal of the royal children from both Teg'urnan and the people's memory, Iruna had always considered Sahlgren her father in more ways than Markham had ever been.

Then that young upstart Asherah had accused Sahlgren of engaging in plots with Ehkron, who was the whelp of the *mordeth-gall* Sahlgren had killed. The very thought was ludicrous, for why would Ehkron want anything to do with his father's killer? And the Faerie King in league with a demon? Never, not once in all the nine realms, not once in all eternity, had such a partnership ever been formed.

Iruna would have personally defended Sahlgren, but by the time those lies had made their way to her ears Asherah had already taken both his head and his crown. In due course she and Avinor had gone to pay their respects to the new monarch, and Iruna had been disgusted by the simpering, pathetic woman that was now her queen.

"She's distraught over the death of her mate," Avinor had explained after that disastrous first meeting. Not only had Asherah not known who Iruna and Avinor were, nor could she properly explain her own parentage.

"The elf?" Iruna scoffed. "To think, the Queen of Parthalan is also Lady of Tingu. Surely, Olluhm will right this wrong."

Iruna had the utmost conviction that the patriarch of the fae wouldn't let the mess that was Asherah remain on the throne for long, yet here they were, more than a millennia after Sahlgren's death, waiting on Asherah in a palace that should have been their home. Worse, Iruna and Avinor were packed into Teg'urnan's atrium along with the rest of the peasants who'd arrived to air their grievances, waiting their turn to be announced. By all rights, Avinor should have been king after their father, not a former slave who took elves and other lesser creatures to her bed. (Rumor was that the king was part troll. At least they tended toward gemstones and the like.) Oh, she knew Solon's edict, that whoever beheads the sitting king also claims the throne, as well as anyone, but surely Solon had never meant for this to happen. She imagined the child sun looking down on Teg'urnan during his daily journey, and regretting that proclamation more than any other act.

Finally, a steward called out their names, and Avinor guided Iruna toward the great hall with his hand on her elbow. Those closest to the pair gasped and backed away, which pleased Iruna. The common folk should give way to their betters, just as Asherah should have relinquished her throne to them long ago. But now that Asherah had a son, maybe Iruna's wait had finally gotten shorter.

The siblings were ushered before the king and queen, though Iruna hardly glanced at Finlay; he was seated upon the golden throne that was once her father's, and she couldn't bear to look upon it. Instead, she fixed Asherah in her disapproving stare, and wondered yet again why no one had yet sought to eliminate the fraud. Her disdain for her ruler was known far and wide, yet Iruna managed a respectful tone when she spoke.

"Your Majesties," she intoned, bowing low before the dais, her hand clasped with Avinor's.

"Lady Iruna, Lord Avinor," Finlay greeted. "What brings you to Teg'urnan on this Reckoning Day? Surely no one has spoken words against you." He affected a jovial tone, but Asherah hadn't moved or acknowledged them in any way. Her stiff countenance, coupled with her white gown and nearly white hair, made her resemble a statue carved from ice.

"We have no squabbles to be sorted," Avinor replied, his sonorous voice reaching all corners of the vast hall. A true king's voice, Avinor had. "We have come to invite you, my king and queen, and your son the prince, to our estate."

"My son?" Asherah repeated, her voice like cracking ice.

"Yes," Avinor continued. "Our estate holds many artifacts from the early days of Parthalan. We thought that your son, being that he will someday be our king, would want to familiarize himself with the rich heritage of this great land."

Asherah smiled tightly, then conferred quietly with her king and a man who stood to next to the thrones and looked to be some sort of a warrior; Iruna thought he was the First Hunter, but she couldn't be certain. All of these peasants looked alike to her. Then the man turned, and Iruna felt a spark of recognition, but not because she'd ever met the man. He had the look of Olluhm.

Being that the royal family was directly descended from the sun god, Iruna and Avinor also looked like Olluhm, what with their silky chestnut hair and bright blue eyes. The man on the dais shared those features, along with a stature reminiscent of the god. If Iruna was honest with herself, which she usually wasn't, she would admit that the man on the dais looked more like Olluhm than either she or Avinor.

"Who is that man?" Iruna whispered to Avinor. "The one on Asherah's left."

"First Hunter," Avinor replied. "Aeolmar, they call him. A western-er."

"What do you know of his lineage?"

"Nothing. Why? You fancy him?"

Iruna looked over Aeolmar's well-muscled limbs, noted how his blue eyes gleamed as they reflected the chandeliers' light. "Perhaps."

While Iruna conferred with her brother, the royal pair debated her request. The discussion took longer than Iruna cared for, but the discomfort on Asherah's face more than made up for the wait. In time, Aeolmar resumed his place at the queen's left as the rulers again faced their petitioners.

"We accept your most gracious invitation," Asherah said. "I assume you are ready to receive us now?"

"We are," Iruna replied quickly; she hadn't expected such easy acquiescence.

"Then we shall arrive at the next bright moon," Asherah stated in a tone better suited to directing *saffira*. "Will you do us the honor of remaining in Teg'urnan tonight, as our guests?"

"We shall, my lady," Iruna said. She clutched Avinor's hand a bit tighter, and they again bowed in unison. "My brother and I appreciate your hospitality."

And soon enough, the frigid bitch will be gone.

***

"Hospitality!" Asherah spat. "How dare she stand in my hall and manipulate me so!"

Once the remaining petitioners had been heard and sent on their way, Asherah, Finlay, and Aeolmar retreated to the vestibule behind the throne room's dais. Finlay had marveled at Asherah's composure in light of Iruna and Avinor's unscheduled appearance, more so as she continued to judge cases until the elder sun went to rest. Now, away from the eyes and ears of her Parthians, she loosed her anger.

"Is this really such a bad thing? We've only been invited to their home," Finlay said. Asherah's only response was a harsh glare. Aeolmar took a position near the door, ostensibly to keep any innocent *saffira* from feeling the queen's wrath. When both remained silent, Finlay continued, "Then why did you agree to the visit so quickly?"

"What else was I to do?" she retorted. "The gall, the *nerve* of that woman, to ask me such a thing before the whole court. And on Reckoning Day! Reckoning Day is *my day*!" Asherah sank heavily into a chair, and supported her head with her hands. "If I'd declined, I'd be refusing Finlay knowledge of Parthalan's history in front of dozens, maybe hundreds, of witnesses. She knew well that I couldn't do that, not publicly."

"I disagree," Aeolmar said quietly, for as much as his deep voice could manage quiet. "You could have taken the matter under advisement, and responded later. Hells, Asherah, you can even change your mind and decide not to go."

"And then what will she do to me?" Asherah murmured. "Such a thing never would have happened to Lormac."

Finlay clenched his fist at the sudden lurch in his chest. When he'd first come to Teg'urnan, Asherah had only mentioned her prior mate when she spoke of events that had occurred before she became queen, and during her infrequent dealings with Leran. However, since their son's birth, she uttered Lormac's name whenever she was anxious or upset. Those incidents had become much more common of late.

Finlay willed himself to believe that Iruna's rude behavior had upset Asherah, thus causing her outburst, and took her hands. "Iruna won't do anything, not to you or Finlay or any of us. Love, you're making this into something it's not."

"Lormac wouldn't have let her bully him," Asherah mumbled. "If Lormac were here—"

"He's not," Finlay reminded her, struggling to hold on to his last bit of calm. When next she spoke, it was gone.

"If only he were here to guide me—"

"And if he was? What would the great king advise you to do?" Finlay demanded. "Hells, Asherah, all Lormac ever managed to do was to get himself killed! Is that what you want? To be dead like him?"

Save for the blood pounding in Finlay's ears, the room fell silent. Asherah stared at him, her hand before her mouth as if he'd moved to strike her, her lower lip trembling. Then there was movement at the door; guards had rushed to the vestibule upon hearing the king's raised voice. Aeolmar sent them on their way, and turned back to regard the two.

Briefly, Finlay wondered if Aeolmar would come to Asherah's defense. Aeolmar had always been protective of his queen, and it wouldn't be the first time he'd stepped between them, but he said nothing. Instead, Aeolmar folded his arms across his chest, and waited. Finlay closed his fist around the royal seal of Parthalan, always worn on a chain around his neck and a symbol of his kingship.

"I'd like to speak to my mate in private," said the king.

"And I'd like to avoid quelling the thousand rumors that will spring up once you two start shouting again," Aeolmar replied. The King of Parthalan and First Hunter stared at each other, and Finlay wondered if this would be the day they'd finally go to blows over Asherah. Finlay's grip tightened on the seal; what was the point of him being king if no one ever listened to him?

"Go, Aeolmar," Asherah said. "We can always tell them I dropped a bowl of hot tea in my lap." Aeolmar's gazed flickered between the two, and without another word he left Finlay and Asherah alone. Finlay rubbed the back of his neck and stared at the far wall; in the many winters since he and Asherah had been bound they'd fought occasionally, as all mates do, but never had his words reduced her to tears. While he struggled with his apology, she spoke.

"I didn't." Her voice faltered, and she began again. "I did not mean for it to sound as if I wished Lormac was here instead of you. He just… He had a way of routing the undesirables from his court. They always left smiling, and it didn't occur to them until much later that they weren't to return. I wish I understood how he did it."

"Was he also a foolish man that bellowed at the woman he loves?" Finlay asked. "If so, he and I are more alike than I ever imagined." Then Asherah was behind him, laying her cheek on his shoulder while she twined her fingers with his. She flicked the gritty skin of his palm with her thumbnail; it had always been her way of telling him that she loved him, just as he was.

"You're nothing like him," she whispered. "With the exception of your questionable taste in women."

Finlay turned around and captured her in his arms. "Do you really think that Iruna and Avinor mean to harm Finlay?"

"Avinor is interested in gambling and Iruna's backside, nothing more," Asherah replied. "As for Iruna, I don't think she'd lower herself to harming another. No, she is the sort who convinces others to dirty their hands on her behalf."

"We can rescind our acceptance," Finlay offered, but Asherah shook her head.

"No. Let us go to the scions of the royal family, and find out what they're plotting. Perhaps we'll learn enough to disrupt their plans. Or, maybe we'll learn that I'm nothing more than a paranoid fool." She laughed mirthlessly, and Finlay tilted her chin to face him.

"Forgive me? For shouting," he amended. "I do not want forgiveness for attempting to keep those fools away from you and Finlay, or for sending Aeolmar away."

"Forgiven," she murmured, then stifled a yawn. Gods, but she was tired again.

Chapter Seven

"I truly am shocked," Avinor said. He and Iruna had been shown to a suite in Teg'urnan's northern tower. While the rooms were are fine as the royal apartments, they were also at the furthest point in the palace from where Asherah and Finlay slept. Iruna had made note of that. "I was certain Asherah would refuse our invitation."

"So was I," Iruna said. Truth be told, she'd wanted Asherah to refuse, at least initially. It was much more difficult to complain the queen was an unfit ruler when she readily agreed to Iruna's plans. "Of course, nothing is as shocking as this room."

"Mm." Avinor looked over the fine furnishings, the silk hangings and velvet cushions, and the near feast that had been laid out for him and his sister. "Good to know our stipend hasn't drained the palace's coffers."

Iruna plucked at a golden tassel. "If these are the accommodations reserved for guests, it makes you wonder what the royal rooms are like. Do they eat off golden plates?"

Avinor shrugged, then he withdrew a purse from his doublet and upended it onto the table. "And what if they do? We have golden plates."

"Yes, but ours come to us by way of our father. Perhaps Asherah is taxing our Parthians too heavily." Iruna made a mental note to find out how much the average Parthian was taxed, and how much the rate had increased since her father was king. A public outcry against unfair taxation could ruin Asherah's next Reckoning Day. "Do you think that's something Mallia would know about?"

"I don't think a healer has much say in taxes," Avinor replied. "Like as not, she hasn't thought one bit about taxes since she last oversaw the tithe to the Great Temple, and that was before Asherah's time."

"Then the Great Temple is where I'll go," Iruna said. "I haven't been in so long. Would you like to accompany me?"

"Mmm. What?" Avinor looked up from the coins he'd been counting out.

"The temple," Iruna repeated. "I am going there."

"Good, good," Avinor muttered, returning his attention to his coins. "If I recall correctly, the hunters gamble in the lesser hall before supper."

"Take all their money, brother," Iruna said. "And, let me know if you see Krylle's son."

"The hunter?" Avinor looked up from his coins. "What is this sudden interest you have in hunters?"

"I am not interested in them, but something tells me he may become useful."

Avinor nodded, then Iruna tossed her shawl about her shoulders and swept into the corridor. There was no one there to witness her grand entrance, but Iruna didn't mind. She loved being within the palace again, its polished gray walls comforting her as if it they were long-lost friends. Iruna glided her fingertips along the stone, and let her feet guide her to the Great Temple of Parthalan. She was halfway there when she altered her path and entered the healers ward.

Iruna lingered in the ward's entrance, letting the bittersweet memories wash over her. The ward was the first place she and Avinor had been taken after Sahlgren found them, both of them fussed over and cosseted by every healer still breathing. Sahlgren had been many things, but a fool wasn't one of them, and he refused to let the newly rescued children be anything less than healthy before he sent them away. Sometimes, Iruna wondered if faking a cough would have helped her hold on to her legacy more tightly.

Movement caught Iruna's eye. She stepped fully into the ward, and saw Mallia rushing toward her.

"Oh, my child," Mallia said as she embraced Iruna. If anyone else had flung their arms around Iruna she would have had them whipped, but she loved the healer as a child loved their mother. "How are you in this den of villains?"

"How am I? How are you?" Iruna countered. "I need only be here a single night. You're continually mired in this swamp of traitors."

"It's not so bad when you have your own corner to retreat to." Mallia held Iruna at arm's length. "What of your fool brother? Let me guess, dice?"

"That, or something else to lose his coin," Iruna replied good-naturedly. In addition to the sizable inheritance from her father, Sahlgren had set up generous stipend for her and Avinor, and Asherah had made no attempt to halt the funds. That, coupled with other investments, meant they had more gold than even they could spend, and Iruna didn't care how much Avinor regularly lost to his habits.

"Surely Avinor can gamble anywhere," Mallia said. "Why have you come back to Teg'urnan now?"

"I wish I'd been able to discuss this with you before we arrived," Iruna began, then she told Mallia how she and her brother had come to Teg'urnan to both invite the prince to their estate and humiliate Asherah, but had only succeeded by half.

"Asherah is much more pliable of late," Mallia said once Iruna had finished. "After the prince was born, I began making her teas."

Iruna raised an eyebrow. "One of your special blends? Isn't that risky?"

"Oh, hush, you," Mallia said. "I have my reasons. Will you be in Teg'urnan long?"

"We're leaving tomorrow," Iruna replied. "You are welcome to come with us, if you like."

"If only I could," Mallia said. "I have things in motion here, but I will visit when I can."

Iruna nodded. "Very well. I'm off to the temple, to pay my respects to Olluhm and the new High Priestess."

Mallia smiled as she touched Iruna's cheek. "You always were such a good girl. Never doubt that the All Father recognizes your devotion."

"Will you accompany me?" Iruna asked, remembering the many times Mallia had brought her and Avinor to temple as children.

"I cannot," Mallia replied. "It is difficult to maintain this form as it is. Within the temple it will be nigh on impossible."

Iruna squeezed Mallia's hand. "Even though the current rulers ignore your plight, know that I appreciate you."

Mallia patted Iruna's hand. "I know you do, child. I've always known."

Chapter Eight

Latera Speaks

"You hate that you're not accompanying her."

Aeolmar and I were standing on the royal balcony, watching the hustle and bustle of the courtyard. We'd left Tor in Wren's care for a time, something both aunt and baby enjoyed. As much as I loved Tor, and my sister, it was good to have my mate all to myself for a few hours.

The activity below us was due to the final preparations for the soldiers and hunters that would accompany Asherah and the Finlays on their journey to Iruna and Avinor's estate. Elkin, who had left the Northern Contingent and taken over as Second Hunter once the elder Finlay had been crowned, was doing an admirable job of directing the mad chaos that swirled around him. Despite Elkin's obvious control of the situation, Aeolmar gripped the balcony railing so hard his knuckles were white.

"I should be going," he said. "It is my duty to see to the king and queen's safety, not my second's."

"Then why aren't you?" I asked, though in truth there was no reason for him to make the journey. For one, the ride to Iruna and Avinor's estate could be completed in less than a day, though Asherah had planned on two for comfort's sake. Also, upon learning of this planned excursion Aeolmar had sent half the legion to secure the route, thus transforming what was already a well-traveled road into the safest place in Parthalan. It was highly unlikely that Asherah and the Finlays would encounter anything untoward on their journey, save for Iruna herself.

Despite all of those facts, I knew the real reason why Aeolmar wasn't going: me. Not that he would admit as much without a struggle.

"Demon activity had increased in the north," Aeolmar began. "The last attack was only four days north from the palace. And in the east, the border is hardly secure."

"But the borders are secure." I laid my hand on his, the tension he was carrying having made his flesh hard as stone. "And you have Brynne in the east, and Alia is doing a fine job in the north, and the west and south are as quiet as can be. Surely Parthalan won't be overrun in a few days' time." He pursed his lips and looked away, a sure sign that he was hiding something. "What haven't you told me?"

His brow furrowed, but he didn't ask how I knew. He was used to me reading him like a book. "Something... Something is wrong."

"Have you anything less vague to share with me?"

"If I knew what it was, I would tell you," he snapped. I arched a brow and waited. He blew out a breath and pulled me against his chest.

"Beloved, forgive me," he murmured against my hair. "I don't mean to speak to you so."

"It's all right," I replied, squirming against him so I could breathe while wrapped in his massive arms. "You'll feel better once you tell me what's bothering you."

Aeolmar smiled ruefully, but began his tale anyway. "In the north, there are reports of more than just demons. The attacks do come, more in number than ever before, but demons are not the only vermin that harry our border." I suppressed a shudder. When Aeolmar tightened his arms about me, I realized that I hadn't done a very good job.

"So it is my fault you aren't going," I mumbled. You would think that the death of Asgeloth, mordeth-gall and king of all demons, would have signaled the end of demon onslaughts in Parthalan, but we only had a few seasons reprieve. Mara was hardly walking when the first reports of demon attacks filtered to the palace, Aeolmar and I staring dumbfounded at the messengers.

What's worse, the lack of a leader had seemed to make them stronger. Before, Asgeloth had ruled his vermin with an iron fist, and all attacks were carefully planned and controlled. Now they were little more than ravaging bands of monsters, destroying anything and everything they came across.

"None of this is your fault," Aeolmar said. "They don't have a mordeth-gall, and that weakens them overall. They are many, yes, but if we can keep suppressing them before another rises to power, we will contain them." I relaxed against him; while they were the same words, he'd said many times before, they always reassured me.

"Well then, what's in the north besides demons?" I asked.

"What isn't?" he countered. "Mountain trolls, orcs, all manner of beasts. We've even had reports of gryphons." I leaned back and met his eyes; there was no reason for him to have kept this information to himself. From the general populace, even from most of the hunters, yes, but not from me, his mate. Again, I silently got my point across.

"Beloved, I know very, very little at this point," he said, weariness creeping into his tone. "The reports I get are few, and not well organized.

We only know about the orcs because of a few pools of ichor seen in
Urth'nn."

"But the elves surely must be aware of such monsters in their midst.
Why wouldn't they come to Asherah for assistance?" My voice trailed off
at the end, having divined the answer on my own. "Leran."

"Leran," Aeolmar confirmed.

"Does he really hate Asherah so much that he'll let his lands be overrun
and his people slaughtered?" I wondered. I remembered his unexpected
appearance at the celebration of Asherah's thousandth year as queen;
both she and I had been heavy with child, and Leran had been surprised
by both pieces of news. He'd been taken aback, but quickly settled into his
normal, brooding self. He certainly hadn't presented as a man whose
land was under constant attack from a grotesque assortment of monsters.

Unless the attacks had begun after the celebration.

"I don't think he hates her at all," Aeolmar said. "I believe it's a
matter of pride."

"Something you would know nothing about." He nipped my ear, but
I didn't mind. In fact, I enjoyed it. "What of the lands not beholden to
Tingu?"

"Ah, my wise mate," Aeolmar said, gliding his thumb over my cheek,
"you always know where to look. We already have information from one
of Leran's esteemed lords."

"Who?" I demanded. I hated his guessing games.

"Micon," he replied, his eyes gleaming in satisfaction.

"Micon of Rael?" I asked, and Aeolmar nodded. "But he has returned
to Tingu! He went willingly, so they say."

"He went because he was terrified." Aeolmar went on to tell me of
a northern trader who'd come to Teg'urnan a few moons past. Being
that the trader and Elkin were old friends, they spent the afternoon

drinking. After they'd drained a few tankards, the trader told Elkin all manner of things, most notably how Rael had been attacked by a horde of mountain trolls. Micon had run to Leran begging for aid, which Leran only offered on one condition: he recant his sire's actions and give Rael over to Tingu.

"Then Leran put down the trolls, quickly and quietly," Aeolmar concluded. "If not for that one trader, we'd have no idea that the incident ever took place."

"So, you think the mountain trolls are working with demons? And orcs?"

"No," he replied, shaking his head. "I think much bigger forces are in play." He watched the hubbub in the courtyard for a moment, stroking the back of my neck. "Remember our journey north?"

"I do," I murmured. "It was wonderful, only worrying about you and me for a time."

"It was," he agreed. "I also remember a peaceful, quiet land. The only demons there were sent to attack us."

"Thurnda was peaceful and quiet," I said. "Elkin told quite a different tale."

"True," he conceded. "But if the monsters have ranged as far west as Rael, my thought is that something—or someone—has placed them there."

"Do you think it is a new mordeth-gall?*" I asked, though who it could have been I couldn't guess. As far as we were aware, Mersgoth had been the last of the* mordeths, *and he'd died long ago. It took a great many winters for demons to gain the strength to lead and control others. "Why do they hate us so?"*

"They think they've more right to Parthalan than the fae," Aeolmar replied. "But Olluhm disagrees, so we remain."

As if it could really be that simple. I sighed, and kept my grumblings to myself. "So you're not making the journey to Iruna's estate because of the attacks in the north?"

"Yes."

"And that's the only reason?"

Aeolmar's big hand cupped the back of my head. "You know it's not."

I didn't have a chance to respond, since the Finlays chose that moment to walk out to the balcony. Well, the elder Finlay walked, while the younger erupted into our presence with the boundless energy of the young, dragging Ember along behind him.

"Everything good?" the elder asked with a glance to the courtyard. Aeolmar grunted, one of his generic responses that could mean anything from 'yes' to 'I'd rather stick a dagger in my eye than discuss this right now'. Before I could tease my mate, Attia stepped onto the balcony and announced that it was time for them to be departing.

When Attia moved aside, I saw Asherah standing behind her, clad in simple green riding gear. It was the first time I'd set eyes on my queen since before Tor's birth. She was gaunt, with dark hollows under her eyes and cheekbones, and I wondered when she'd last eaten. Despite her obvious frailty, Asherah's pale beauty still shone, and when she smiled it touched my heart.

"Latera," she cried, rushing forward to embrace me. I was careful, fearing I'd snap her like dry kindling. "I'm so glad you're up and about!"

"I'm glad to be about," I said. Her gaze alighted on my throat and her brow creased. My hand moved to my pendant, and I felt like a fool. While I'd convalesced, I'd taken to wearing Aeolmar's mother's necklace again as a way to ground myself; I'd stopped wearing it back when I'd learned that it was actually a preserved tear of Asherah's shed the day

her mate and dearest companion had died. Understandably, one didn't like to be reminded of such things.

I tried to apologize, but before I could Elkin announced all was ready and the royal family was whisked away. Aeolmar and I, now joined by Ember, watched as they entered the courtyard and mounted up for their journey.

"Mar, she looks terrible," I whispered. "Is it those teas?"

"Apparently, she's stopped drinking them," Aeolmar said bitterly. "At least that's what she told Finlay."

"I thought the queen was better," Ember said. "Is she still sick?"

"Maybe it's a new sickness," I murmured, then changed the subject. "With your playmate gone, will you help me with your brother?" I asked Ember. She nodded, then ran off to ensure that Wren was caring for Tor properly. Once she was gone, I pressed myself against Aeolmar's chest, seeking whatever comfort he could spare. I hadn't expected Asherah to look like a frail old woman; no, I'd wanted my queen. My healthy, happy queen. I shuddered again as I watched the royal procession disappear into the distance, and burrowed further into my mate's arms.

"I'm so glad you're not going," I said.

"Me too," Aeolmar said as he kissed my hair. "Me, too."

Chapter Nine

Asherah and Finlay's party traveled until after the elder sun went to rest, their intent to cover as much ground as possible on their first day of travel and thus limit time spent sleeping under Iruna's roof; they would arrive early tomorrow, spend one night with their hosts, and return home. The problem surfaced once they were on the road, and the quick pace Elkin set. Asherah was no longer used to traveling at speed, and was soon exhausted.

Asherah swayed on her horse and the younger Finlay, riding before her on her saddle, squealed and grabbed their horse's mane. She hushed her son, blaming the movement on their horse picking its way across uneven ground, and hoped that the elder Finlay hadn't noticed. She had also hoped that he wouldn't notice the small pouch of dreamwort she'd hidden in her trunk.

After they'd made camp Finlay offered to get her nightclothes, and Asherah was so tired she forgot why she'd had their things packed separately in the first place. There it had been, nestled amid the blankets and woolen stockings, a nondescript leather pouch filled with dried plants, the only thing keeping her madness at bay.

"Why are you hiding this?" he asked. They were alone in their tent, a small pocket of calm amidst the bustle of camp. Even their son was outside, pestering Elkin and Innetha for lessons in swordplay and tracking. Asherah sighed, and wished for a small crisis to distract them.

Even if demons attacked at this very moment, Elkin is so blasted capable he'd likely handle the skirmish himself. "I wasn't hiding it," she said. "I..." Asherah pursed her lips, and stared at her hands. "I don't know if I can sleep without it."

"You slept last night," he pointed out.

"No," she whispered, recalling how she'd lain awake all night, terrified she would never sleep again. Terrified she'd never dream again. She'd never been so glad for elder sun to rise, since it meant she could leave off her ruse. "I didn't."

Finlay gathered his mate against him, and gently stroked her hair. "You should have woken me," he murmured against her temple.

"One of us should be rested," she said. "Otherwise, Parthalan may crumble to dust around us."

"That won't happen." He guided her to their cot for the night, lumpy and hard and not at all likely to ease her to a gentle slumber. Finlay must have come to the same conclusion, and he pressed the small pouch into her hand. "But I can't present the Queen of Parthalan to Markham's ill-tempered children looking like she hasn't slept in a season. I'll make you the tea. Just for tonight, it will be all right."

With that, he stood and prepared the herbs; she noticed that he used less than half the amount of dreamwort Mallia prescribed, but said nothing. Even so, the brew was stronger than ever, the steam carrying a delicate sweetness that wasn't there before; Asherah remembered Mallia telling her that she'd added another herb to the blend, but she couldn't remember what the newcomer was called. After only a few sips, Asherah's eyes became heavy, and Finlay tucked the soft furs around her.

"Will you stay with me?" she mumbled.

"I'll be right here."

Finlay was beside her when she woke, as he always was, though she always navigated her dreams alone. Well, at least she used to. Last night, for the first time since Asherah had started with those blasted teas, there had been someone with her. Someone familiar, someone that she had desperately wanted to be near, but he was too far away to glean an identity. Now, more than ever, Asherah wished to sleep again, to delve once again into that dream.

But first, there were matters of the land to attend to.

***

The King and Queen of Parthalan, together with Prince Finlay and a rather large complement of hunters and soldiers, reached Avinor and Iruna's estate just before noon. Several times since they received Iruna's unexpected invitation on Reckoning Day, Asherah had almost taken Aeolmar's advice and called off the visit entirely, and she only refrained because she didn't want to give Iruna the satisfaction of her refusal. Truth be told, Asherah hated the woman, but that was the smallest of details. Throughout Asherah's reign, she'd successfully avoided the urge to hide in her bed and ruled Parthalan, and she wasn't about to let a few orphans change that.

Orphans like me. Asherah had never considered herself an orphan, not really. Rather, she was a woman who couldn't remember her past, or her family. Since she took Sahlgren's head and then his throne, parental claims had surfaced from time to time, but none had ever been considered legitimate. One thing Asherah did remember was how Harek had always been the one charged with sending those claimants on their way, and she wondered if keeping her isolated from those who may have known her true history was another aspect of his obsession with her. She sighed, and resolved to look over those early scrolls upon her return to Teg'urnan, hopeful that they may offer her a clue. After she returned to the palace and slept for a sennight, maybe two.

"You look wonderful today," Finlay said, reaching over to squeeze her hand. He'd told her as much when she first opened her eyes; this morning he had woken first, or perhaps he had remained awake all through the night, guarding her slumber. However it had happened, the first sight Asherah's eyes had beheld that morning were her mate's eyes, summer blue without a hint of gray.

"Thank you, love," she murmured, then looked toward the manor before them. It was the last bastion of the first royal family of Parthalan, those who had been ousted once the Usurper had taken Markham's head. This new king had proven weak, and through his inaction had allowed Teg'urnan to be overrun with demons, but Sahlgren had managed to banish them to the underworld. Right after he had beheaded the beheader, of course. Actually, it was Rahlle who had banished the demons, but Sahlgren had indeed led the charge against the vile beasts, and without his leadership, who knows if demon or fae would have claimed victory?

There were those who claimed that the Usurper had only failed because Rahlle, one of Olluhm and Cydia's original twelve children, had refused to swear fealty to him. Those same voices claimed that Rahlle had always been the true power behind Parthalan's throne.

Asherah didn't doubt this in the slightest; often enough, she'd felt powerless since the ancient sorcerer had departed from Teg'urnan.

"Do you think they're in contact with Rahlle?" Asherah asked, cocking her head toward the estate.

"I thought Rahlle had remained in the mortal realm," Finlay replied, raising an eyebrow.

"We don't know if he is still there," Asherah said. "Latera never saw him, only the three priestesses who now reside in the temple." *A temple dedicated to me. Mortals really are foolish creatures.*

"Rahlle who made the Hill?" asked the younger Finlay.

"Yes, Rahlle who made the Hill," she answered, "and the tunnels below Teg'urnan, and who did so many other wonderful things." Asherah tightened her arm about her son; really, this entire journey was about him. While she and King Finlay were not royalty by birth, Prince Finlay's claim to the throne stood undisputed since he was the child of the reigning monarchs.

Undisputed as long as the actual royalty doesn't challenge him. Not since Natraeus, the former king of the dark fae, had anyone dared to challenge Asherah's right to rule. Natraeus had been soundly defeated on the battlefield, and now the king and his people were little more than a bedtime story. Their numbers had never been many, and once Nibika had been dissolved, those few that had survived Leran's razing quietly assimilated into the surrounding faerie and elfin lands. Asherah couldn't remember the last time she'd heard of anyone even claiming descent from Nibika, which was just fine with her.

Despite that, and Asherah's other victories, there were factions who believed that the first royal family, those directly descended from Olluhm and Cydia, belonged upon Teg'urnan's throne. Avinor had always been polite to Asherah and had never directly suggested that she take him as her mate, and thus her king. She'd always gotten the impression that Avinor considered her beneath him; certainly, his frosty sister Iruna did. Then Asherah's binding with Finlay had been made public, and Avinor had sent a message to Teg'urnan expressing his sincere regrets over not claiming her as his own. Asherah had torn it to pieces.

Mind you, not that he cared to assist us against the mordeth-gall. For the most part, Avinor and Iruna kept to themselves, only deigning to walk amongst the common Parthians at large gatherings, where all could openly gawk at these children of the gods. Well, all fae were descended from the gods, most just weren't so full of themselves.

"Are these people nice?" Finlay asked. Asherah recalled when Avinor and Iruna had visited Teg'urnan at the first Winter's Eve jubilee held after Finlay's birth. They'd brought the prince a length of cloth-of-gold; tradition dictated his first formal tunic should be sewn from such finery. They had also bestowed upon the prince a heavy ring set with onyx and rubies, which was once worn by the last true ruler.

Asherah had nearly choked when she had heard that, though Lady Iruna smiled sweetly and explained that she'd misspoke and meant no offense, and that she'd meant to describe it as once worn by her father, and that she only wanted Finlay to have a tangible item from Parthalan's past. Asherah had responded with a cloying smile of her own, and had done everything in her power to keep Iruna and Avinor away from her son. She'd done a good job, right up until this accursed invitation had been extended.

If Asherah let herself remember such details, she would remember that her fears had magnified on that day, and that she had slowly convinced herself that others were conspiring to kill her son and mate. Those fears, coupled with the still-unhealed wound of Harek's betrayal, threatened to drive her mad. Eventually she had confided her fears to Mallia, who then offered the queen some dreamwort... It was enough to make Asherah wonder if she hadn't been right all along, and that Iruna really did have it in for her.

But that's just another conspiracy, isn't it? Asherah brushed the pale curls, so like his father's in all but color, back from Finlay's brow. "Yes, Finlay, they will be nice to you."

The crested the last rise, and Iruna and Avinor's estate, known as the Golden Knoll, was visible on the plain before them. Referring to it as an estate was a misnomer; if anything, this was a palace near as grand as Teg'urnan.

"Markham had several of these properties?" Finlay asked.

"Oh, yes," Asherah replied. "Before his death, he had a dozen or more smaller palaces scattered across Parthalan. Building summer homes, as they were called, was something he and his ancestors regularly did."

Finlay grunted. "What happened to the rest?"

"Most were dismantled during Sahlgren's reign," Asherah replied. "A few are still standing. In fact, the Northern Contingent resides in the remains of one, and I know of another in the east." Her gaze slid toward Finlay. "Why so curious?"

"Just wondering how much of our treasury is being diverted toward these two, and this estate's upkeep."

Asherah laughed. "You will never not be a merchant. When we return to Teg'urnan, I will have the archives searched and all the deeds presented for your inspection, my lord."

Finlay caught her hand and kissed her knuckles. "As you wish, my lady."

The avenue that led to the estate was a league if it was a pace, which gave Asherah plenty of time to look over the estate. Golden Knoll wasn't as tall as Teg'urnan, and only had a single tower; Asherah imagined Iruna making her rooms at the tower's peak and telling anyone who would listen of her need to be rescued. The main house stretched out on either side of the tower, and Asherah knew of the vast stretches of farmland that lay beyond, which accounted for yet more of their income.

Finlay may be right to question their wealth. Asherah kept her musings to herself, since Iruna and Avinor themselves were standing at the base of the entrance steps.

"It's a copy of the palace square," Finlay muttered. "Almost exact."

"Perhaps they were homesick," Asherah said, then she turned her attention to the siblings. They were so alike they could have been twins, with their long brown hair and matching blue eyes. Avinor wore his hair nearly as long as his sister's, something almost no men did any longer, save Aeolmar. Everything about the siblings was old-fashioned, from their style of dress that mimicked temple garb to Avinor's hair. Asherah wondered if they kept to the older ways out of habit, or if they purposefully tried keeping themselves separate from modern Parthalan. Asherah suspected the latter.

"Your majesties," Iruna greeted. She and Avinor clasped hands and bowed as one. "Prince Finlay. Thank you so much for honoring us with a visit."

"Thank you for inviting us, Lady Iruna," Asherah replied. Elkin was beside her horse in an instant, helping her son dismount. The Second Hunter had strict orders to never let the prince out of his sight. "We are eager to learn more about you, and your family."

As soon as Elkin had the prince on the ground, Avinor appeared beside Asherah. "Allow me," he said, and helped her dismount. Asherah looked toward Finlay, and saw that Iruna had offered the king her hand. Once on the ground Asherah nodded her thanks to Avinor, then she grasped her son's hand.

"Now, I am sure you're all tired from your journey," Iruna said. She looped her arm with Finlay's, then extended her other hand toward Asherah. "Please let me show you to your rooms. Supper will be ready in a few hours, and we will relax together long into the night. Won't it be wonderful?"

"Yes," Asherah said. She took Iruna's hand, and felt Avinor rest his on the small of her back. She clutched her son's hand harder. "Wonderful, indeed."

Chapter Ten

Latera stopped before Wren's door, adjusted Tor in his sling against her body, and raised her hand to knock. Instead of knocking she paused, and ran a hand over her hair, but found the braid as tight as it had been that morning.

As if Wren cares what my hair looks like. Latera again moved to knock, but Tor fussed and she stroked his forehead instead. That was when Wren opened the door.

"How long have you been standing there?" Wren demanded.

"I was about to knock." Latera entered her sister's apartment. The front room acted as Wren's still room, where she distilled herbs ad made tinctures. The smaller chambers at the rear of the apartment served as her private spaces.

Wren looked down the corridor. "Where's your tall, scowling shadow?"

sola," Latera replied. "What with both Innetha and Elkin away, the instructors turn to him for everything."

"That must be frustrating."

"Oh, no, he loves it," Latera said. "It keeps his mind off the queen being away." Latera's gaze settled on the herb bundles on Wren's worktable, and she bit her lip. "Have you seen Asherah lately?"

"Up close? No. Being the *deva'shi's* sister doesn't grant me access to the royal chamber." Wren claimed Tor from Latera and gave him a squeeze. He squealed and grabbed at his aunt's pendant. "But I do know what Mallia's been giving her."

"Well, what is it?" Latera demanded. "Poison? Rancid mushrooms? Whatever it is, it's killing her!"

"Actually, it's nothing of the sort," Wren replied. "I've checked the herbs myself. It's nothing more than regular tea, with a bit of dreamwort to help her sleep, and a sweetener to mask the taste."

"How did you manage to get some?" Latera asked, since everyone knew Mallia saw Wren as her adversary.

"Bron offered to deliver the tea to the queen, and Mallia accepted. He brought me a sample." Wren smiled, and continued, "While Mallia hates me and all of the hunters, everyone loves Bron."

"Everyone, hmm?"

Wren's cheeks pinked. "Yes, everyone. But my point is that the teas aren't harmful."

"Then what is harming her?" Latera linked her hands behind her neck and walked toward the hearth. "Asherah doesn't look like herself. She's old and frail, like Halse."

Wren chuckled, remembering the royal nursemaid that raised them. "Halse is a thousand summers if she's a day. And she did always long for a boy to care for," Wren added, as she unwound her necklace from Tor's chubby hands.

"How sad that my mother was cursed to bear only girls." Wren glanced at her sister, but said nothing. Regardless, Latera understood her meaning.

"I... I don't know if I will bring Tor to Gannera," Latera said. "I know I should. He should know his entire family, and my family deserves to know him, but after our last journey..."

Latera sat heavily on the bench before the hearth. A moment later, Wren and Tor joined her. "I know. Our father is awful."

"He never used to be."

Wren raised an eyebrow. "When was that?" she asked. Despite that Wren was King Harold's firstborn, her mother was a maid with no hope of marrying the king, and had died soon after Wren's birth. Wren had been given over to Halse and grew up, unacknowledged, in the servants' quarters. Latera hadn't even known Wren existed until she was an adult. "Because I have surely never met the kind, loving man who resides only in your memories."

Latera sighed, and held her head in her hands. "I'm sorry. I suppose he was only kind to me and my sisters, and even then only when it suited him. He certainly hasn't shown my mother much care."

"Perhaps they could come live here, with us," Wren suggested. "The girls, that is. I can't imagine your mother would ever leave Gannera."

"Neither can I." Latera reclaimed her baby and kissed his head. "Enough of that place. You're certain the teas are safe?"

"I am," Wren replied. "Whatever's harming Asherah—if anything is harming her—it's not what Mallia's giving her."

"What do you mean, if?" Latera asked. "She is not well."

"No, she isn't," Wren agreed. "Which means that something else is happening. I find it odd that the queen isn't recovering faster from whatever this illness may be, what with her being under Mallia's direct care."

"As do I. When are you seeing Bron again?"

"What makes you think I see him often?"

"Not like that," Latera said, amused by Wren's reaction. "When might he be able to bring you another sample of the teas, or perhaps have another look around the healers ward?"

"I will ask him," Wren said. "No matter what is happening in the ward and the royal chamber, we will discover it."

"Yes, sister, we will."

Chapter Eleven

Asherah Speaks

*A*ll I want to do is sleep.

If I were sleeping, I would not be subject to Iruna's false friendship and insincere words, nor Avinor's thinly veiled disdain for me and my mate. Of course, they had received us with all the pomp and circumstance as befitted the King and Queen of Parthalan, but to those real royals, Finlay and I were little more than paupers who'd filched the keys to the castle. Indeed, their eyes looked upon me with the same contempt that demons had once expressed toward a filthy, pathetic slave. And my mate, their king? He was nothing more than a common man who had the misfortune of being mated to a former slave.

However, mine and Finlay's low beginnings apparently did nothing to tarnish our son's lustrous image. Iruna fawned over Finlay as if he were royalty (which he was, but she treated him as if he was actual royalty, not like one of those who stumbled onto a throne like I had). Avinor, for his part, gave my son the deference and respect he'd long withheld from me. At one point during our stately feast, Iruna had laughed gaily at something Finlay said, the sort of laugh women used when flirting. I wondered if she was considering taking my son as her lover.

"If she lays a single talon on him, I'll kill her," I whispered in my mate's ear.

"I believe she has Avinor for that," Finlay replied. He had made no effort to conceal his disgust over Avinor and Iruna's... familiarity. Their reasoning was that customs had been different in the time of the Old Ones, and, being that Iruna and Avinor were much closer in relation to the gods due to their unbroken lineage, they weren't held to the earthly morals the fae had developed over time. Never mind that the term 'Old Ones' referred to Olluhm and Cydia's original twelve children, at least ten—maybe twenty—generations removed from Avinor's lot. It's not like their parents had been siblings.

"Pardon me?" Iruna asked sweetly. My, but she was even polite around my son. Perhaps I'll have a statue of him installed right here at the Golden Knoll, to ensure her continued good behavior.

"I was commenting to the king of how enamored you are with our son," I replied. I felt no need to mince words with her, regardless of who her long-dead father was. For all her efforts to ignore it, I am her queen.

To my surprise, Iruna was sincere in her reply. "He's a wonderful boy," she said. "Truly, with young Finlay as the land's heir, Parthalan has no worries."

I nodded, all the while biting my tongue so hard I nearly drew blood. Little did I know, Iruna's inquiries weren't over yet.

"Your warrior, the one who attends you in your hall," Iruna began. "I believe his title is First Hunter?"

"Aeolmar?" Finlay asked. "What of him?"

"What do you know of him?" Iruna asked.

"He's loyal," Finlay replied. "Easily our best hunter."

"Either him or his mate," I said.

Iruna's brow pinched. "He has a mate?"

"He does," I replied. "Why are you so interested in him?"

"I'm not," she replied, "but when I saw him in Teg'urnan he seemed familiar. I'm just a bit curious about him, that's all."

"Of course," I lied. The only thing Iruna was curious about was how she could remove me from my throne. After dinner, I told Finlay exactly how I felt about her prying questions.

"What she meant was, hopefully this wretched monarch will expire soon so we may again have some real royalty in Teg'urnan," I griped once Finlay and I were alone in our guest chamber, and our son safely tucked in bed. "And the way they went on about Finlay. Gods, have she and Avinor never seen a child before?"

"Perhaps they haven't," Finlay mused. "As far as I know, Avinor's not sired anything save his ill temper, and Iruna claims childbirth is beneath one of her stature. They seem to be the last of their kind."

"There's a bit of good news." I was rooting through a trunk, flinging bedclothes aside while I searched for my dreamwort. Blessed Cydia, after the day I had I needed sleep more than I needed air or sunlight. "And why did she question us about Aeolmar?"

"Perhaps she's tired of her unnatural relationships."

I snorted. "Perhaps Avinor can't stand her anymore."

"Didn't Avinor once have designs upon you?" Finlay asked as he stood behind me and wrapped his arms around my waist.

"He did," I replied, not turning away from my search. The pouch must be here somewhere.

"And what happened?" he asked. Foolish question, that. Finlay knew exactly what happened. I twisted free of him and moved to search the other trunk.

"I ignored him until he went away," I mumbled, now sorting through our son's things. Then Finlay's hands were on my waist again, only this time he pulled me around to face him.

"It's by the hearth," he said, and my gaze flew to the little table on which stood a kettle and two bowls, alongside my little leather pouch. I blew out a great breath, nearly giddy with relief. I moved to brew a cup, but Finlay held me fast. "Love, you just had some last night. Do you really need another bowl so soon?"

"No, I—" I dropped my gaze, unwilling to meet his eyes. I couldn't tell him that someone had been with me in my dream last night, and I needed to know who it was. Who he was. If I got just one more look, one good long look at his face, just so I could know...

But I couldn't tell Finlay any of this. For the first time, I was glad I was unable to touch his mind the way Aeolmar touched Latera's, but I was beginning to understand why I couldn't.

"Forgive me," I whispered. "I'm just in the habit of brewing it before bed. I won't, not if you don't want me to." He gathered me against him, and held me for a moment before he spoke.

"I only want you to be happy," he murmured. Gods, he is such a good man. "What if I brew us some plain tea, and we can share that before bed?"

I couldn't think of anything I wanted less, other than hurting Finlay again. "That would be wonderful," I said. Times past, a woman would have had her tongue cut out for lying to her mate, but Finlay kissed me and then settled me on the edge of the bed while he saw to our tea. The whole time I stared at his back, and wished I could recognize the man in my dream.

Chapter Twelve

The tea was brewed soon enough, and after Finlay poured it he handed his mate a bowl and sat beside her. Neither drank, and once the tea had gone from steaming to tepid, Finlay took both of the bowls and set them on the floor.

"Love, you can tell me what's bothering you," he said.

"I can't," she whispered, staring at her feet. Those simple words confirmed what Finlay had long feared: Asherah was sleeping to escape that which she felt she couldn't control. Things like Iruna. Worse, the dreamscape Asherah craved was a place he couldn't follow her, though he'd tried. Somehow, the dreamwort he'd gotten from the apothecary didn't have the same effect on him that it did on his mate; it hardly even helped him sleep. However, his dreams had been amazingly vivid.

Still, he occasionally brewed himself a bowl and lay down beside Asherah, willing himself to find her spirit, wherever it went. He'd yet to find her somewhere on the dreamscape, if it was even possible to do so, so he concentrated on his wakeful mate. When she was awake, that is.

"Can you tell me why you can't?" he asked. Asherah's frown deepened, and she twisted her hands in her lap.

"It will hurt you."

Finlay's heart felt like a leaden weight; after all this time, she still wanted to spare him the burdens she carried. *Will she ever realize that I don't need coddling?* He gathered her in his arms, nuzzling the soft spot behind her ear.

"Is it Iruna?"

"She wants my throne," Asherah snapped, surprising Finlay; he hadn't expected to ferret out her concerns so quickly. "She's always wanted it, but now she thinks she has the means to get it." Finlay followed her gaze to where their son slept peacefully, without the aid of herbs and teas.

"Finlay's but a child," he soothed. "It will be many, many winters before he has that kind of an interest in anyone."

"Which is why she's starting now." Asherah went on, listing the extravagant gifts Iruna had bestowed on Finlay since birth, the way she had fawned over him during their evening meal. When her tirade was complete, she yawned and leaned against Finlay's chest; the journey from Teg'urnan had already tired her, and he dared hope that she would fall asleep naturally.

"Did Iruna ever move against Sahlgren?" he asked.

"By all accounts, she was terrified of him," Asherah replied. "I suppose she must have been, being that he killed the man who killed her father. Perhaps she was even a bit grateful."

"What of Avinor?"

"What of him?" Asherah leaned forward, now grinding her fists against her eyes. "No, he's merely her pawn. Iruna is behind this plot. She is the one who wants me gone. Avinor is not in play, not here."

"Plot?" Finlay took her hands and tilted her chin upward; her eyes were red where she'd rubbed them, the orbs that normally sparkled like black diamonds were dull as unpolished onyx. Finlay made a mental note to ask Attia about her eyes, and also speak with Wren. Perhaps he'd also ask them if dreamwort affected one's rational thought. "Do you really think they're plotting against you?"

"You mean would I formally accuse the last remaining members of Parthalan's first royal family of treason?" she countered with a rueful smile. "No. My mind is not so far gone as that." Finlay returned her smile, more relieved than he was willing to admit, and tucked her head beneath his chin. Then Asherah spoke, and his relief vanished.

you think there is a plot?" she whispered. Finlay tightened his arms about his mate, and took a moment before he replied. Of course, there wasn't a plot, save what Asherah had imagined, but he feared her reaction to an outright denial. Instead, he did his best to reassure her.

"It doesn't matter," he said, his lips against her hair. "You have me, and I won't let anything harm you or Finlay. You have the hunters, and the strength of the legion at your back. You're the most powerful ruler in all the nine realms, and only a fool would plot against you. If Iruna and her simpleton brother talk a few schemes, what of it? If they act upon their words, they'll be put to death as traitors." He leaned down close to her face and stared into her eyes, summer blue into darkest night. It may have been his imagination, but he thought he saw a bit of the sparkle he so missed. "If there is a plot, I say, let them come. We'll destroy our enemies, and pick our teeth with their bones!"

Asherah laughed, not one the half-hearted chuckles he'd heard lately, but a true laugh that brought color to her cheeks. "Finlay, I truly don't know what I'd do without you. Cydia knows, you are the best of men." Then she was serious, gliding her fingertips across his cheek, pausing to twine them in his hair. "My king," she murmured. "My man."

"Always."

Chapter Thirteen

Iruna was unhurried as she descended to the lower floors of her estate. Really, why should she rush for Asherah and Finlay? In fact, she hadn't rushed all day; instead, she had spent the morning leisurely stretching her limbs in bed, then in her warm and scented bath. By the time she'd dressed and left her rooms, it was well past midday. When Iruna finally stepped into the large day chamber on the ground floor of her estate, she learned that the royal family had managed quite well without her.

"Iruna," Asherah said, not deigning to look up from the game of stones she played with her son. "How lovely of you to join us."

Iruna's jaw tightened, but she held her composure. Not that any of her guests had bothered to look at her. No, the false queen was seated on the floor, tossing about colored stones with her son, while the equally false king busily examined one of the wall hangings.

"Forgive me my tardiness," Iruna said, schooling her voice to an even timbre. "It has been so long since Avinor and I hosted anyone of your stature, and I—"

Abruptly, she stopped. Neither Asherah nor Prince Finlay had looked up from their pretty stones. Hells, they hadn't even acknowledged when she began or stopped speaking. Iruna wanted to stomp into the middle of their little circle, dash the stones from their patterns, fling them at Asherah's eyes... Iruna took a breath, and willed herself to be calm. Revealing her displeasure at that moment would not do. No, it would not do, not at all.

If I frighten the boy in front of his mother, he'll only ever look upon me with distrust. While she had initially been irritated when she learned how *young* the younger Finlay was—Iruna had forgotten how many winters past he'd been born, as she intentionally forgot most aspects of Asherah's reign—she soon realized that his youth fit perfectly in her plans. Instead of a few seasons or even moons, Iruna had many winters to cultivate a friendship between her and the boy. A friendship, and so much more.

Understanding that Asherah would be of no help, Iruna moved on to the weaker of the royal pair. "My lord."

"My lady," the elder Finlay replied with a nod of his head. Unlike his mate, the king didn't lack for manners.

"You have an interest in maps?" Iruna asked, noticing how he scrutinized the hanging in front of him. It was a tapestry depicting the eastern grounds of the estate.

"Asherah does, more so than I," he replied. "What caught my eye was the cloth of gold."

"And silver," Iruna said, indicating the heavy fringe. "Father always insisted on the best for us."

"I can see that," Finlay replied. "I am somewhat intrigued by this structure." Finlay's finger hovered over a symbol that, to the untrained eye (as his surely was) appeared out of place. "What does this mark represent?"

"Why, Olluhm's love for Cydia," Iruna replied. "The legends say that he once took her on that very spot." The symbol that had so confounded the king was a blossom from the melon vine; really, didn't everyone know that Olluhm had once fed his mate melon laced with sweet honey? Iruna reached out as if to caress the blossom, but stopped short of touching it. "Legends also say that the round, juicy melons reminded Olluhm of Cydia's ripening... belly. Would my lord like to see it?"

"See what?" Finlay demanded.

"The temple," Iruna replied. It pleased her that she had so easily made the king red faced and flustered, tripping over his words as he called for Asherah and their son to join them on the short walk. Of course, mother and child first finished their game of stones, and once the queen got herself up off the floor, the four of them set out toward the tiny temple.

It was really little more than a shrine, a peaked white roof held aloft by four stately marble pillars. Nestled beneath the roof was a small altar, and on it a golden bowl filled with freshly lit incense.

"You make daily offerings?" Asherah inquired with a raised brow.

"As do all temples," Iruna replied. "My brother and I strive to honor Olluhm in all matters. Why, Sarelle herself once oversaw the rites here."

"Sarelle," Asherah repeated. "I haven't heard that name in so long..." Her words trailed off. After a moment, she noticed the elder Finlay's quizzical face. "Sarelle was the High Priestess of the Great Temple before Atreynha," she explained.

"How would the High Priestess of Parthalan be able to spend time away from the Great Temple in order to officiate here?" Finlay inquired. "Surely she didn't leave her work in the hands of an acolyte."

"Oh, she never came for the greater rights, or at the dark of the moon," Iruna said quickly. "Long ago, our little temple even had a dedicated priest, so the rites were always performed by those learned in the proper methods. But Sarelle would come as often as her duties allowed. I daresay she was something of a mother to myself and Avinor."

"A pity she was in collusion with Sahlgren," Asherah said coldly. Iruna's nostrils flared in anger.

"Is that true?" asked the younger Finlay. Iruna softened her gaze when she looked at him.

"It is, though I wish it weren't so," Iruna said. "I don't know why Sarelle acted as she did. I can only assume she was duped by Sahlgren along with the rest of us."

"Then she was put to death for treason?" the elder Finlay asked.

"She was banished to the underworld, a fate she richly deserved," Asherah stated flatly.

"We don't know if that is true," began Iruna.

"I witnessed it," Asherah spoke over her, the queen's voice having regained the royal pitch she'd lost of late. "A priestess, herself wronged by Sarelle and Sahlgren's plots, banished her using the very same portal Sarelle used to loose *mordeths* in the temple." Asherah's eyes narrowed. "Do you doubt my word, Iruna?"

"Of course not, my lady," Iruna murmured, dropping her gaze. *Now is not the time,* she reminded herself.

"I daresay that the new High Priestess keeps her memory," Iruna continued. "Sarelle always wore orange robes, but all have noticed how Atreynha only garbs herself in blue. Out of respect, I daresay."

"Or perhaps, out of a desire to disassociate herself with the traitor," Asherah stated firmly. Iruna's temper boiled, but she knew better than to engage the false queen in an outright debate in front of the king and prince. "Enough talk of the past. Iruna, is that a vineyard?"

"It is." Iruna gathered up her skirts, steeling herself against the prospect of spending the days walking about the grounds with her guests.

"Lady Iruna?" the younger Finlay asked.

Iruna looked down at the prince, and smiled. "Yes, my lord?"

"What happened to your priest?" he asked.

"He no longer follows Olluhm," Iruna replied. "He and Sarelle were once quite close, and after her disappearance he accused—wrongly, in my opinion—the All Father of abandoning his charges."

"He wouldn't be the first to make that accusation," Asherah said.

"True, but Krylle's abandonment of his calling was truly without equal," Iruna continued.

"Krylle?" Asherah repeated. "It cannot be the same man."

"What man?" Finlay demanded.

"Kemen's father is a priest called Krylle," Asherah said. "He is a priest of the old gods, those cast from the sky by Olluhm."

Iruna nodded solemnly. "I am sorry to say that you are correct. When Krylle abandoned what he'd built here, he went eastward and started a new temple, one that is dedicated to they who came before."

Asherah stared at Iruna for a moment, then her mate touched her hand and shook his head slightly. "Perhaps we'd better leave off tours of the vineyards for another time," Asherah said. "The suns are hot on my neck; I don't believe Olluhm hearing enjoys talk of those who have left his worship."

"As you like," Iruna said, for once in agreement with the queen.

Chapter Fourteen

Finlay woke in the middle of the night, alone. He dressed quickly, and after checking that his son remained asleep, he went in search of Asherah. It wasn't long before he found her standing in front of Olluhm's shrine, staring at the roof.

"How did I know you'd be here?" he asked, coming to stand beside her.

"Please explain how you came to that conclusion, since I myself don't understand what I'm doing here," she replied. "Do you remember the Ish h'ra's temple? The one we went to?"

"Of course," he replied. He'd taken her to the desert shrine—one of the last remaining shrines to the old gods—shortly after they'd been bound. Finlay followed Asherah's gaze and realized what had caught her eye. She was staring at the peaked white canopy. "It's the roof, isn't it?"

"Why is that roof even here?" Asherah countered. "Olluhm's shrines are open to the sun, so he may look down and see the offerings left for him. Even the temples have an oculus. Yet this shrine, *Markham's children's shrine*, is closed off to him, just like the Ish h'ra's."

"Is it really closed?" Finlay asked. "The walls are open."

Asherah shook her head. "He would consider this closed. The beginning of the great feud between Olluhm and the Ish h'ra was after he became the sun, and she refused to open her shrines to his gaze. Ish h'ra maintained that her shrines were for her followers alone, not for Olluhm's passing pleasure." Asherah glanced at Finlay. "As you can imagine, he wasn't pleased with her."

"I've never heard that story," Finlay said. "It's different from the rest. It implies that Olluhm and the Ish h'ra were contemporaries."

"They were, in the beginning," Asherah replied. "One could have even called them friends. But then Olluhm got his first taste of power, and he no longer had any use for friends."

Finlay frowned and placed his hand on Asherah's arm. "Have a care how you speak of him at his temple," he warned. He wasn't an overly devout man, but speaking ill of a god while standing within his shrine wasn't wise.

Asherah laughed, and Finlay's grip on her tightened. "That's just it. I don't think this is a temple to Olluhm. I think Krylle set up a shrine to The Deliverer right here under Iruna's nose and she never noticed the difference." She glanced at Finlay's hand on her arm. "I didn't mean to make you nervous."

"I'm not nervous," he said. "I'm calculating how long it will take me to fetch my sword and fight off whatever gods you've angered."

Asherah slipped her arms around Finlay's neck. "You'd defend me against Olluhm?"

"Of course I would," he replied, shocked she'd even ask such a thing. "I probably wouldn't survive, but I would defend you to my dying breath." Finlay gathered her against him. "But in all honesty, I'd rather just hold you."

Asherah's gaze returned to the temple. "Then hold me, but don't fear for me. I've won every battle I've ever fought, and I'll win this one, too." She laid her head on his shoulder. "To best a god one needs two things, patience and time. I have plenty of both."

"You have experience warring with gods?"

Asherah nodded. "Yes. Something tells me I do."

Chapter Fifteen

The next morning Asherah was awake by first dawn, energized though she'd hardly slept. She roused the others and ensured her family and the rest of her party were ready to leave as soon as possible, and said goodbye to her hosts at the morning meal.

"Thank you for your hospitality," Asherah said to Avinor; much like the day prior, Iruna hadn't yet risen. "Please tell your sister on my behalf."

"I shall," Avinor said, then he turned to the king. "Iruna told me of your interest in the surrounding lands. I have collected some of our maps and had them sent on ahead to Teg'urnan. They'll be waiting for you when you arrive."

"Many thanks, Lord Avinor," Finlay said. "When next you find yourself at Teg'urnan, I'll spot your first dice game."

Avinor grinned. "I look forward to it."

The party was on their way soon afterward. "I'm so glad we're going home," Asherah said.

Finlay glanced at his mate. "Don't you mean you're glad we've left Iruna behind?"

Asherah laughed. "Yes, the lack of her has much to do with my good mood. Why did you want those maps?"

"Something isn't right," Finlay said. "They live in opulence they haven't earned. Where is their money coming from?"

"Isn't it what they inherited from Markham?" Asherah suggested, but Finlay shook his head.

"Unlikely. There's too much grandeur. I will consult Avinor's maps and the archive, as you suggested."

"What will you do if you discover their wealth is suspect?"

Finlay rubbed his chin. "I don't know. I suppose my course of action will depend on what information I find."

On the advice of a few maps, the party travelled southward until they reached a village. They sent a rider ahead to look into rooms for the night and make arrangements for supper. The rider returned shortly, and informed them that rooms were being prepared.

"More good fortune," Finlay said. "Perhaps leaving Iruna has changed our luck, indeed."

"I'm sure it has." Asherah dismounted and helped her son from the saddle. The king joined them, and the royal family entered the inn. They'd just sat down when another called for the king.

"Finlay!" Finlay looked toward the voice; Elkin had hailed him. "Can we speak for a moment?" Finlay murmured something to Asherah, then he strode over to the Second Hunter where he stood at the bar.

"Apologies," Elkin said. "I never remember to refer to you as king."

Finlay snorted. "Half the time, I forget I am one. Is something wrong?"

"No, and that's the problem." Elkin grabbed two full tankards, passed one to Finlay, and beckoned the king to follow him outside. Once they were in the common area before the inn, Elkin swept his arm to the side, as if to encompass the entire village. "Look at how quiet everything is."

Finlay looked around the square; it was quiet, but he was used to the never-ending bustle of Teg'urnan. "Is that a bad thing?"

"It's an unusual thing," Elkin replied. "What's more, those I have spoken with are afraid."

"Afraid of what exactly?" Finlay demanded. Before Elkin replied, Innetha exited the inn and walked over to them.

"The kitchen is in a flurry," Innetha said. "You'd think they never before hosted guests of some stature."

"What kind of flurry?" Finlay asked. "Are they nervous?"

"Yes, but more than that, they're scared," she replied. "Terrified is more like it."

"Perhaps they only want to make a good impression," Finlay said.

Elkin glanced at Innetha. "Beloved, can you keep an eye on the innkeeper?"

Finlay snorted. "You're as paranoid as Aeolmar."

Innetha nodded toward the inn. "Here comes the innkeeper now."

Finlay turned and saw the man approach. He was pale and trembling, with a sheen of sweat across his brow. Innetha was right. The man was terrified.

"My lord. Lords," he amended with a nod toward Finlay. "You're certain my establishment will be acceptable for the king and queen?"

"If you only knew of the many times Asherah and I have slept on bare ground, with rocks and roots for pillows," Finlay replied, hoping to reassure the man. "I'm sure you've comfort aplenty. Now then, what will you be feeding us?"

***

Supper turned out to be a roasted ox, which was fortunate for all but Asherah, who still refrained from consuming meat. Neither she nor anyone else in her retinue mentioned that to the kind yet anxious innkeeper, and she made do with bread and a few roasted vegetables. Once all had eaten their fill, the innkeeper passed around jugs of sweet eastern wine. Finlay looked at his mate over the rim of his cup.

"Remember when we used to do this?" he asked.

"Drink wine? Don't we still do that?"

He smiled; he loved it when she teased him. "I meant, remember when we would sneak out of the palace and go about the land, sleeping in tiny inns and on the floors of public houses, pretending we were ordinary?"

Asherah looked into her cup and laughed. "As if you could ever be ordinary."

"Or you, love."

Asherah nodded, then she swirled her wine and set it on the table. "Finlay, give me your wine."

"I can call for more," he said, but Asherah grabbed his cup and swirled the liquid within, then she poured both cups out onto the table. The liquid drained away, leaving a sandy residue in its wake.

"There's something in the wine." Asherah stood and shouted, "There's something in the wine! Pour it out! The innkeeper has poisoned us! Where's Finlay?"

Hunters and soldiers alike threw down their cups as Elkin hauled the prince up from his seat and carried him under his arm like a sack of laundry to Asherah.

"I'll get the innkeeper," Elkin growled as he set the prince down. A few moments later, he dragged the innkeeper out from the back room and threw him at the queen's feet.

"What did you do?" Asherah demanded. When the innkeeper only whimpered, she said, "Tell me now or lose your tongue. What did you do?"

"N-Nothing," he replied. "I've done nothing, my queen!"

"Then what is in my wine?" Asherah dragged her fingertip through the dregs she'd poured out and thrust it into the innkeeper's face. "What is this powder?"

"A sweetener. My mate makes it, from dried berries," the innkeeper replied. "The stock we had was not that good quality, and I added it to—"

"Added it when?" Finlay asked.

The innkeeper looked at the king. "When?"

"Yes. When did you add it?" When the innkeeper only gawked at Finlay, he ran his finger through the dregs as Asherah had done. "I was once a merchant, did you know that? When we received barrels of sour wine, we sweetened them. It's a common practice."

"Yes, yes," the innkeeper agreed, nodding. "I added it as soon as I spoke with your man," he added, nodding toward Elkin.

"It takes a sennight or more for the sweetener to take effect," Finlay continued. "Yet you only learned of our coming earlier today."

The blood drained from the innkeeper's face, then he fell over. Asherah ripped open his tunic and found a charm around his neck.

"He's dead," she said. "This charm was worked to kill him after he'd done whatever it was he was contracted to do." Asherah yanked the charm from his throat and stood.

"You've seen these charms before?" Elkin asked.

"Yes," Asherah replied. "We found at least a dozen in Sarfek's rooms, along with the spells to make them."

"Was this man one of Sarfek's?"

"I don't know. Search the premises," she ordered. "Bring anyone you find to me. Look for charms on their person. And dump out all the wine."

Asherah handed the charm to Elkin. Once the Second Hunter went off to search the inn, she sat and drew her son onto her lap. Finlay sat beside them.

"Do you think it is a coincidence that someone attempts a poisoning right after we leave Iruna's estate?" she asked. "Who knew we were there?"

"Gods, half of Parthalan knew," Finlay replied, remembering the announcement made in the palace square, and the many soldiers sent on ahead to secure the area. "I'm sure that word's reached Tingu by now." He looked at his son, clutching his mother's arms. "Don't be scared. We have this under control."

"I know," Finlay said. "I just wish Ember and Mara were here. They'll be so mad they missed all the fun."

Finlay smiled; only a child would think an attempted poisoning was fun. A child, or a madman.

"Asherah," he began, "who could have done this?"

"I don't know," she replied, "but I will find out. And when I do, they'll know exactly why I'm called Asherah the Ruthless."

***

Asherah ordered the entire village searched and burnt. The buildings surrounding the inn were vacant, leading them to believe that the residents had abandoned their homes. Then one of the hunters forced open the door to the ice house, and revealed the pile of corpses that had been blocking it.

"Burn them," Asherah said. "Burn everything. Their spirits have fled. There's nothing more we can do for them except honor their lives."

Elkin nodded, then he strode off and relayed the queen's orders. Asherah reached out beside her, and her mate laced his fingers with hers.

"What did this?" Finlay asked. "Never have I heard of an entire village being murdered, not for any reason."

"I have." Asherah stroked her son's hair; he hadn't left her side, not once since the innkeeper had been made. "I once lived in one of these villages. They took all that suited them, and the rest were killed."

Finlay blanched; Asherah was speaking of the village she'd lived in before she'd been captured and enslaved by demons. "Sher, you don't think—"

"I don't know what to think," she said over him. "But I will find out."

Chapter Sixteen

Latera speaks

I rushed down the corridor toward the royal apartments, Aeolmar at my side and Tor fast against me. Asherah and the rest had returned from their sojourn at Iruna's days ago, but Aeolmar had only just informed me of their near-poisoning. After I insisted on seeing them with my own two eyes, Aeolmar sent a saffira on ahead to inform the king and queen of our imminent arrival.

"You're certain that neither she nor the Finlays were harmed?" I demanded. Again.

Aeolmar glanced at me, then behind him. Ember was skipping after us, excited to see her playmate the prince. "By all accounts, Asherah's and Finlay's included, they were not," he replied. "After they'd located and destroyed all of the poisoned wine, Asherah had the village burned to the ground."

I shifted Tor against my shoulder. "They must have been terrified."

Aeolmar made a noise deep in his throat. "Asherah's the one that did the terrifying. She's not one to let a threat against hers pass."

"Nor should she." I didn't know how I'd react if anyone had laid such a trap for my family, other than quickly and without mercy.

"And, she's better?" I pressed. I was referring to Asherah's sudden and complete dependence on those strange herbs that had begun shortly after her son's birth. In the beginning, I had thought nothing of them; since they had come recommended by Mallia, I assumed they would help Asherah, not plunge her into days-long slumbers and transform her to a wretched, pale shadow of her former self. Of course, I now know that Mallia is not as selfless as one would hope the matriarch of the healers to be.

"Finlay claims she hasn't had the herbs since the night before that attempted poisoning," Aeolmar replied. "That's the longest she's gone without them in seasons. And he said that she hardly used them at all during their stay with Iruna and Avinor."

"If I was forced to spend time with the two of them, I'd resort to something stronger than dreamwort," I muttered. Horrible hosts aside, Aeolmar had said that Asherah's few days without dreamwort were the longest she'd gone in seasons. Seasons! I understood that Harek's treachery had cut Asherah deeply, and that those wounds had resurfaced not long after her son's birth. Was the black pit of sleep really her only solace? I wished Asherah had come to me, if for no other reason than to share her pain. I would have done anything to help her.

Of course, I hadn't exactly been available, had I? I'd been busy bearing child, after child, after child; I'd been made to understand that faeries tend toward one child every hundred winters or so, yet Aeolmar and I had produced three in under half that time. Even elves, who as a race are much more prolific than the fae, cannot claim such numbers. I supposed this unusual fecundity is one of the few aspects of my humanity I've managed to retain.

Regardless, Asherah was my friend, and she needed me. I may not have been there for her before, but that would change. Now that Tor and I were doing better we would spend all the time with her we could, though Aeolmar had not been very receptive to us paying the king and queen a short visit in order hear about their journey, and to finally introduce them to our son. After Tor's birth, my loving, overprotective, stubborn mate had forbidden everyone but our children and Wren from our chamber, and the palace at large had begun to wonder if our son was nothing but a myth.

"Let's prove them wrong," I'd implored, then I won Ember to my cause by promising her an afternoon playing in the queen's garden with Finlay. Younger Finlay, that is, though I suppose the elder was invited as well. Was that fair, playing Ember against her father? Certainly not, but I wasn't interested in fair. I was interested in my queen's wellness. That, and showing off my son.

At last Aeolmar had relented, and now we stood before the private entrance to the royal chambers. The door opened of its own accord, as it always has for Aeolmar and I, and I beheld my dear friend. Even though we'd seen them off on their journey to Iruna and Avinor's, this was the first time we'd been able to spend an afternoon together in more than three moons. Gods, how I'd missed her.

"Latera," she greeted, rushing to embrace me. "I'm so glad you're here! Aeolmar wouldn't let us near you after Tor's arrival," she added.

"You know how Mar gets," I said with a sidelong glance at my mate. He merely shrugged; be it royal edict or a friend's concern, Aeolmar would not have allowed access to Tor and me for anything less than a demon attack, and even then he'd probably just barricade the door, leaving

me and the children inside while he fought off an army. "Asherah, about the village."

She shook her head. "It wasn't the first time someone tried to kill me, and it likely won't be the last." She smiled, and I saw a bit of the Ruthless in her. "But I'm still here. It takes more than fouled wine to put me down."

"Scrappy old fighter that you are."

Her grin widened. "Asherah the Scrappy. I like that. Now let me introduce myself to Tor," Asherah continued as I relinquished my baby to her arms. "Oh, he's heavy!"

"He is," I agreed. Asherah glanced toward the younger Finlay, but he was unperturbed at the sight of his mother holding a baby.

"Where's Mara?" the boy asked.

"She's helping Wren," I replied.

"She never comes to play anymore," he muttered, then he grabbed Ember's hand, and they went out to the garden. Aeolmar and the elder Finlay followed the children, and Asherah and I sat near the windows. As always, Attia appeared out of nowhere, bearing a bowl of my favorite t ea.

"Many thanks," I murmured to the saffira-nell. Aeolmar had banned saffira from our chamber along with everyone else while Tor and I recovered, and he'd thus taken to brewing my teas himself. Being that he despises tea, his concoctions were barely palatable. Attia's, however, was perfect.

"Quite a fine boy you have here," Asherah declared, bouncing Tor on her knee. The sight of them reminded me of the many hours Asherah and I had spent together after Ember and Finlay's births. The four of us had been nigh on inseparable, much to our mates' chagrin, but I'd waved away Aeolmar's rumblings. I'd had precious few friends in my life that hadn't either betrayed me or ended up far removed from me, and I enjoyed my closeness with the queen.

Then our children grew, as did Parthalan's demands upon its queen, and our friendship bowed to the more pressing demands of court. Then Mallia had offered Asherah a tea to help her sleep, and I'd ended up heavy with Tor...

I shook my head, not quite ready to confront my own guilt over Asherah's descent into such a dark place. I was here for her now, and I wouldn't let her go back.

"Was your stay with Iruna as terrible as I imagine?" I asked dryly.

"More so," she replied. "I'd have rather toured the underworld." Something flitted behind her eyes, a thought or memory that troubled her. Then it was gone, and Asherah changed the subject. "Now tell me, how did you come by such an uncommon name for your little man?" Asherah asked. Tor had taken possession of two fistfuls of the queen's hair, and she was trying to reclaim it with minimal success.

"It was Aeolmar's idea," I replied. "I hadn't realized it was so unusual."

"Times past, I heard it more often," Asherah said. Tor let go of Asherah's hair and grabbed a finger, enthralled by her shiny rings. "Was it Aeolmar's father's name?"

"No, his eldest brother's," I answered. It still surprised me how little others knew of Aeolmar's life, even those who were close to him like Asherah and Finlay. I must admit, I enjoyed being the only one privy to Aeolmar's most private self. "His father was called Caol'nir. Is that uncommon, as well?" I asked.

Asherah blinked slowly, staring at Tor as if he were a ghost in her hands. "It is most uncommon," she murmured. "I haven't heard it in... gods, almost longer than I can recall."

"Oh? Is it a western name?" I asked, but Asherah didn't acknowledge my question. Panic swelled within my breast as I imagined Asherah descending once again into the dark abyss and taking my baby with her.

"Asherah? Asherah!" I repeated sharply. She blinked, almost painfully slow, and turned her attention back to me.

"Forgive me," she murmured, raising Tor up to her shoulder. "It's just... I haven't heard that name in many winters. Many, many winters." She looked toward the garden doors; Aeolmar and Finlay stood just beyond the threshold, calling out for the children to remain close to them. One could easily wander off in the queen's enchanted garden toward a mountaintop or seashore, and never be seen again. "Nor have I heard the name Tor in just as long a span." Asherah chewed her lip for a moment.

"Why are these names affecting you so?" I asked. Asherah took a deep breath, then resolve settled about her shoulders like a cloak, and her black eyes met mine.

"Before I became queen, the old king's Prelate was called Tor," Asherah began. "Did you know that the title of Prelate was once hereditary, passed along from father to son?" I shook my head, since I knew very little about the days before Asherah reigned; really, almost everything I knew of Parthalan's history had been gleaned from a book I'd found in Gannera, of all places.

Asherah went on to tell me the story of Solon, the firstborn son of Olluhm and Cydia; we still see him daily in his guise as the child sun, following his father in their daily route across the sky. He was also the first faerie warrior, and all those descended from him were honor bound to serve the royal house of Parthalan as its Prelate. Harek had not been of Solon's line, Asherah made sure to tell me. That grotesque little man certainly hadn't behaved as if he was descended from anything remotely godlike.

"That's all well and good," I said once she'd finished the tale, "but what does a Prelate from the old king's time have to do with these names?"

Asherah squeezed her eyes shut, and for a moment I didn't think she would answer. Then she said, "Tor had three sons. The eldest was called Fiornacht. He was killed by mordeths *in the Great Temple."*

"Demons in the temple?" I gasped. I knew the stories of Asherah's ascension to the throne as well as anyone, but the facts never ceased to shock me. The queen presented as such a gentle and refined lady that it was easy to forget the horrors she once endured.

"Eighteen mordeths *invaded the temple and captured all within," Asherah confirmed. "As I said, Tor's eldest died in the temple. Tor's younger sons were called Caol'nir and Caol'non. Shortly after I went to Lormac for aid, Tor and Caol'nir arrived in Tingu. Caol'nir had witnessed Sahlgren's meetings with Ehkron, the* mordeth-gall *killed by your ancestor," she said with a nod to me.* Ah, Elvasla, the many ways you've impacted us all.

Wait… Tor the Prelate had a son called Caol'nir?

"When we returned to Teg'urnan," Asherah continued, "Caol'nir crept inside the palace the day prior to our attack in order to retrieve his mate. He found the Great Temple overrun by demons, and killed seventeen of the eighteen mordeths.*"*

"Did he use the tunnels?" I asked. Aeolmar knew the network of tunnels that ran beneath the palace like the back of his hand, though most that had lived in Teg'urnan their entire lives had no idea of their existence.

"No," she replied. "Rahlle created the tunnels afterward."

We stared at each other, each afraid to speak lest our next words confirm what we both knew. "Who was the eighteenth mordeth?*" I asked, my voice little more than a hoarse whisper.*

"Mersgoth," Asherah replied. I squeezed my eyes shut, and bowed my head.

"Aeolmar had two brothers," I began slowly. "One was called Tor, and the other Fiornacht." I raised my head and looked toward the queen, but Asherah was staring at Aeolmar through the glass garden door. "Do you really think Aeolmar's father may be the man you knew?"

"They must be one and the same," Asherah said. "All three names in the same family? It cannot be a coincidence." She shook her head, and continued, "Only Caol'nir could have taught Aeolmar to wield a sword with such skill. Only Caol'nir, or Tor his father." She laughed softly. "I am queen, yet it is the First Hunter who is descended from the gods. Perhaps he should rule the land."

Her words stunned me. Surely, Asherah did not think that Aeolmar would want such a thing; he was so stubborn he'd likely refuse a kingship just for the sake of being difficult. I wondered if those words were born of Asherah's short but awful stay with Iruna, or maybe a deeper pain, but I didn't have time to deal with that right now. Now, I needed answers. Aeolmar needed answers.

"Asherah, you must tell him," I said. "He doesn't know his father was ever anything but a farmer."

Asherah nodded, her gaze still fixed upon Aeolmar's back. I understood her reticence, since Aeolmar blatantly refused to discuss his family with most people, myself often included. But this was more than a casual question that would rub salt in his wounds. This was his identity.

Beloved.

Aeolmar's head snapped around at my mindtouch, so quickly he startled Finlay. What's wrong? he demanded, with such force my head throbbed.

Nothing. I... I looked at the queen, and wondered how much I should tell him. Lies could not be shared from one mind to another, not that I *would have lied to him. Nor did I want to be the one who divulged this piece of information.* Please, sit with me?

Of course. Aeolmar called over his shoulder to Ember, instructing her to mind the king, and reentered the royal sitting room. He paused to reclaim Tor, holding the boy aloft as if to present him to the sun.

I blinked, amazed that the comparison had entered my mind, and turned my attention to what Aeolmar was saying. He lowered Tor and cradled him against his chest, our baby grabbing at his father's fingers.

"Already so strong," Aeolmar said in a prideful voice. "He will be a great swordsman, of that I have no doubt." Tor squealed, and my heart ached at the sight of them. Aeolmar was so happy, and I hated for him to be otherwise. That was really all these revelations would do, dredge up those painful memories he kept hidden away under lock and key. Still, he deserved to know. He needed to know.

I love you.

Aeolmar's dark blue eyes met mine, and though his brows peaked, he smiled. It was unusual for me to keep touching his mind, since he was well aware of how much it pained me. Then Asherah stood, and it was all I could do not to cringe.

"Of course he is strong," Asherah said, wiggling her fingers at Tor. He grabbed one, and gurgled a victory cry. "He is the scion of a great line of warriors, descended from the sun god Solon, as is his father." I felt the blood drain from my face; until Asherah said it aloud I hadn't really appreciated that the man who slept beside me was descended from a god. All with fae blood could trace their lineage back to Olluhm and Cydia, yes, but Aeolmar's connection to Solon was direct, the line unbroken over these many millennia. I'd once compared Aeolmar to the god of swordplay, never realizing how accurate my comparison was.

Aeolmar's eyes flamed, and I again reached out to his mind. Calm, beloved. *His anger flickered toward me briefly, since he was now aware that I knew something of this. Then, with visible effort he composed himself and settled his gaze upon Asherah.*

"How would you know of my ancestors?" he asked. "What's the meaning of this?"

"I was sworn to hold my tongue, and never again say your parents' names aloud," Asherah said; in a true testament to the queen's bravery, she was still looking Aeolmar in the eye. Most would have run off screaming at the fury boiling in those blue depths. "In fact, until a few moments ago when Latera told me your father's name, I had no idea that you were Caol'nir's son, himself son of Tor, the last Prelate descended from Solon."

Aeolmar flinched at the mention of his father's name, though the small movement did nothing to abate his fury; if anything, his anger had increased tenfold. Finlay chose that moment to reenter with the children in tow, and found Aeolmar poised as if he would rend the queen limb from limb.

"What are we talking about?" Finlay asked.

"Asherah believes she knew my father," Aeolmar announced.

"And your mother, though I knew Caol'nir much better than she," Asherah added. I hadn't even considered that if Asherah knew one, she was likely familiar with the other. "You look just like Alluria, you know."

Aeolmar and Asherah's eyes remained locked upon one another, the both of them seeming oblivious to the rest of us. I felt my hands tremble along with my sharp pangs of guilt; I'd wanted Asherah to tell Aeolmar what she knew, but not like this. He was looking at the queen with such anger and suspicion, and I didn't need the aid of a mindtouch to feel his pain. No, Asherah hadn't known of Aeolmar's lineage until this day, but that was just a detail. He still felt betrayed.

"Is Alluria my grandmother?" Ember asked, and with the innocence of a child's question the tension cracked like a pond's icy covering during

the spring thaw. Aeolmar smoothed Ember's fire-colored hair from her brow, and smiled at our daughter.

"Yes," Aeolmar answered. I let out the breath I'd been holding, nearly giddy from the quick release. For him to be speaking in such a calm tone, he was likely shocked more than angered. *"Yes, Alluria and Caol'nir are my parents. Your grandparents. The queen is going to tell us about them."*

Ah. So all is not forgiven quite yet. Aeolmar sat beside me while Ember and the younger Finlay climbed onto Asherah's lap, for a story told by the queen was a rare treat indeed. Asherah chewed her lip as she decided what to say in front of the children; I empathized with her, for I still had the image of *mordeths* in the Great Temple forefront in my mind, but really, she'd brought this upon herself. Asherah of all people should know better than to confront Aeolmar in such a way and not expect retribution.

You knew of this?

Only for a moment. As soon as I knew I insisted that she tell you.

He smiled and squeezed my hand as he shifted Tor on his lap. Now, Tor will learn of his namesake's namesake.

That he will.

"I think I will begin with Caol'nir," Asherah said once the rest of us were settled. "In truth, I didn't know Alluria very well; in fact, less than a moon after I met her, she and Caol'nir left Teg'urnan for the last time."

"But why did they leave?" Ember asked. "They didn't want to live in a palace?"

"No, sweetheart, they didn't," Asherah replied. "But that's a later story. Let me begin with how I met Caol'nir. You know, Aeolmar, your father taught me much in the way of swordplay."

Chapter Seventeen

Aeolmar Speaks

We spent the afternoon in the royal chambers while Asherah regaled us with tale upon tale of my father's feats of bravery. I was both amazed and humbled by the many things I'd never known about him. More than once, Asherah referred to my father as the greatest warrior to walk Parthalan's soil since Solon, and while I freely admit to embellishing my memories of him a time or two, his skill with a sword truly was without equal. I'd witnessed that skill myself, both as his frustrated student who never thought he'd measure up to his father and brothers, and as a frightened onlooker on those rare occasions when he'd defended us from bandits. No longer would I have to wonder how a poor farmer in the west had come by such skill, or a sword that was worth more than a small castle.

Speaking of my father's sword, Latera slipped away to fetch it during the third retelling of my father teaching Asherah and Torim proper grip. I don't think Ember quite believed that her grandsire had once instructed the queen in swordplay, or that Asherah had ever been a warrior. At times, it seemed that Ember's entire world revolved around *her admiration of Asherah; truly, in her eyes, our queen was held higher than Cydia.*

While Ember pestered the queen, Latera returned with the sword that almost no one but she and I had laid eyes on since my father's death. Asherah stopped speaking once she caught sight of it, while Finlay and the children murmured their appreciation of such a magnificent weapon. I took the blade from my mate and completed a few overly dramatic flourishes, the brilliant blue pommel stone catching the light and throwing tiny rainbows onto the walls and floor.

"Yes," Asherah murmured, her gaze fixed upon the sword, "that is the sword Grelk forged for Caol'nir." I balanced the sword on my palms and presented it to Asherah, as much to her surprise as my own. I'd hardly ever let Latera touch it.

"A blue stone, to match Alluria's eyes." Asherah glided her fingertips across the blade, naming each of the engraved herbs as she traced them. "Do you know why a warrior requested that flowers be engraved upon his weapon?"

"I imagine you do," I replied, unable to keep the sarcasm from my voice. Now that I was over the initial shock, I enjoyed hearing Asherah's stories about my parents. I just wished they were here to tell me those stories themselves. Asherah took no offense, and continued her explanation.

"Before they were bound, Caol'nir would sneak Alluria out of the palace. They claimed they were only picking herbs," Asherah added, still gazing at the sword as if it was a long-lost friend. In a way, I suppose it was. "These six were what they gathered the first morning he took her abroad."

"Why did they need to sneak out of the palace?" Latera wondered. I know she wasn't really expecting Asherah to answer, just as I wasn't. I assumed that any sneaking around was due to one being promised to someone who was rather disagreeable, or perhaps a father who had

wanted his daughter mated to someone other than a warrior, or other such matters of young love. What Asherah said next shocked the both of us.

"During Sahlgren's day, it was forbidden for a priestess to leave the palace complex." Asherah went on, describing the great lengths my parents had gone to in order to be together. My father had even filched a saffira's *dull dress for Mama to wear, so he could bring her outside of Teg'urnan in disguise. Because she was a priestess.*

"I thought priestesses were chaste," Latera ventured. Asherah's eyes widened as her hands fell to her sides. Apparently, she had forgotten how little I knew.

"Is that why they left the palace?" Finlay asked. "To avoid scandal?"

No, Finlay wouldn't understand the gravity of Asherah's words. He was from the south, where there were few temples and most mates weren't formally bound, and thus he didn't know that when a priestess took her vows, she became Olluhm's mate. Despite my ignorance of various aspects of my family's past, I was certain that the Caol'nir I remembered was not the sun god.

"She couldn't have been a priestess," I insisted. "If she had been bound to Olluhm, she never would have been able to bind herself to Father. She must have been a novice." Asherah chewed her lip, a habit she'd picked up from Latera. It wasn't a good sign on either of them.

"Alluria wore the blue robes of a priestess, not a white novice's dress, but she was never Olluhm's mate," Asherah said. That made no sense, though Asherah must have realized this since she turned and paced across the room, another habit she'd picked up from Latera. "Aeolmar, these are not things that I should be telling you."

"There's no one else to tell me," I countered. "They're both long dead. You're my only link."

"There is another."

"*What other?*" Just when I thought I couldn't be shocked any further, my mind leapt to unknown siblings, or perhaps a grandsire working in the kitchens. The answer wasn't as bad as I'd feared.

"The High Priestess, Atreynha," Asherah said. "She knew Alluria, and Alluria's mother. She was there the day Alluria was born, and the day she left Teg'urnan. She can tell you everything."

Atreynha, the High Priestess of the Great Temple of Teg'urnan, had known my mother. Ostensibly, the High Priestess knew all of her charges, though I'd always been under the impression that Atreynha came to the Great Temple long after Sahlgren's death. Then again, I'd also been under the impression that I was born of a farmer and baker, not a direct descendant of Solon and a rogue priestess.

I glanced toward the windows overlooking the garden; it would be a while yet before the child sun went to rest. Questions burning in my mind, I stood and hauled Latera to her feet.

"Beloved, would you like to hear more about my family?" I asked.

Latera smiled. "Of course I do."

I cupped her cheek and smiled at my mate, she who had always seen the truth of me. "To the temple, then."

Chapter Eighteen

"Amazing," Finlay murmured after Aeolmar and Latera had departed from the royal chambers. They'd taken Tor with them to the Great Temple, but Ember had insisted upon remaining behind. She and the younger Finlay sat cross-legged on the floor, flipping through one of the queen's illustrated books; ironically, based on the earlier revelations, it contained several depictions of the living gods, Solon included.

"You really had no idea about Aeolmar's parentage?" the king inquired with a sidelong glance at his mate.

"The thought never entered my mind," Asherah replied. "Although it certainly does explain a few things."

"Like what?" the younger Finlay asked, echoed by Ember.

"Oh, Aeolmar's foul temper, for one," she replied, to a resounding chorus of giggles. "Caol'nir was not an easy man to get along with. Not to mention, Aeolmar's tremendous swordsmanship. He has amazed me on more than one occasion with not only his skill, but his great knowledge of ancient technique. I must say, though, his resemblance to Alluria is uncanny."

"Alluria?"

The four of them looked toward the voice, and watched Attia usher Mallia, matriarch of the healers, into the royal sitting room. "I don't think I've ever heard such a lovely name."

"It's my grandmama's name!" Ember shouted, leaping to her feet. "She was a beautiful priestess!"

"Was she?" Mallia inquired in the indulgent tone one only uses when hearing a child's stories. "And what of your grandsire? Was he a priest?"

"He was a warrior like my papa!" Ember seized a quill and brandished it like a sword. Not to be outdone, Finlay grabbed a weapon of his own—in this case, a rolled up map—and met her swing for swing. Attia admonished them to be careful, and herded the children out to the garden. The elder Finlay then took his place beside his mate, and addressed Mallia

"What can we do for you?" he asked.

"I've come to check on my queen," Mallia replied. "I noticed that you haven't sent for more dreamwort since your return. It has made me hope that whatever illness has plagued you has finally run its course."

"I believe it has," Asherah said, her confidence strengthened by Finlay's hand in hers. "I feel wonderful. I've missed out on so much, and I don't want to sleep my life away any longer."

"You only missed things because you were unwell," Mallia soothed. "I'll return in a few days in order to assess your progress. I am glad to see you so much improved, my queen."

With that, the healer took her leave of the royal pair, and Asherah's head drooped onto Finlay's shoulder. "You wanted to ask for more dreamwort, didn't you?" he asked softly.

"I did," she replied. She noticed her knuckles were white where she gripped Finlay's hand, but couldn't bring herself to loosen her hold. "I only said no to her because you're here."

"Next time will be easier," he murmured, pressing a kiss to her forehead. "And the time after that, easier yet." She nodded, not quite believing him, but hoping that his words were true. Without Finlay's support, she truly would crumble away.

"You'll be here those times?" she asked, her tone somewhat more desperate than she'd intended.

"Every time."

Chapter Nineteen

Alluria.

When the First Hunter's daughter said that name, Mallia assumed she'd misheard. Or perhaps the child had only referred to a woman with the same name, not the one who had caused her to dedicate her life to vengeance. But then the child had confirmed it: not only had her grandmother been called Alluria, she had been a priestess. A priestess mated to a warrior.

Many, many winters past, long before Mallia became a healer. She was a seer called Relle who occasionally burned herbs for the queen, and stole the odd girl from other realms. Once she'd gotten bored with that life, she became a healer, and was soon the matriarch of Teg'urnan's wards. She'd always imagined that she would tire of that ruse in a century or so until the day Asherah herself lay in childbed.

The prince's birth had been an easy one, and once Asherah and the boy were resting comfortably, Mallia gave the queen a sleeping draught. After Asherah drifted off she began speaking, but Mallia paid her no mind. Many talk in their sleep, after all. Then Asherah began speaking about her long ago companion, Torim, how she was golden as the dawn and Asherah pale as the stars. But when Asherah said the word dawn, she said it in the old language: *nyshanti*.

Nyshanti, the goddess of dawn, belonged to the pantheon Olluhm had cast from the skies shortly after he claimed Cydia. Nyshanti's lover had been Ish h'ra, The Deliverer.

Though both goddesses had been cast out, neither had ever appeared in the underworld among their peers. Some assumed they had perished during their fall from grace, while others maintained that The Deliverer would return to lead Parthalan once more under her aegis. As Mallia gazed at the sleeping queen, she wondered who Asherah really was.

She wondered if forcing an old god to her knees and dragging her before Olluhm was the way to regain his favor.

So Mallia began experimenting with dreamwort, and plunging the queen into one magical sleep after the next. She even located the tunnels that ran beneath Teg'urnan, used them to spy on Asherah as she slept. Asherah hadn't uttered the word *nyshanti* again, at least not while Mallia was listening, but that was all right. Mallia was patient. Then the First Hunter's girl named her grandmother, and Mallia knew that her patience had at last been rewarded, albeit for a different reason.

Long before Mallia was Relle, she was a priestess called Sarelle. She hadn't told anyone that name since Alluria sent her to the underworld, and her mouth had overflowed with fire that never burned out. She wondered if the time had come for her to leave Mallia behind, much as she'd left Relle, and become Sarelle again.

Mallia laughed, cackled even, tossing back her head as tears ran freely from her eyes. If only her master was still with her, so he could share in this latest irony. That neither of them had realized that the First Hunter was one of Caol'nir and Alluria's boys was amazing enough, but who would have imagined he'd take the girl she had kidnapped from the mortal realm as his mate? Truly, the gods worked in mysterious ways.

Briefly, Mallia wondered how Aeolmar had escaped the trap she'd sprung on Alluria so long ago. It had been a fitting end for the disgraced priestess, she who had sent her to the underworld with Mersgoth's own portal, to lay dying amidst her slaughtered family.

Mallia shuddered, remembering the underworld, the fires that had burned her flesh within and without, hot then cold, icy and smoldering all at once. She remembered the day Sarfek had come for her, how his benevolent brown eyes had gazed at her through the haze and smoke, his gentle hands as he'd healed her flesh.

It did not matter how Aeolmar had escaped his parents' fate; in fact, Mallia was glad of it. She could torture Alluria's children yet again, and twist the knife so hard that the priestess would scream from her grave. So what if she never regained Olluhm's favor? Like as not The Deliverer would kill him, just as it had been foretold.

Yes. This was a good thing.

Chapter Twenty

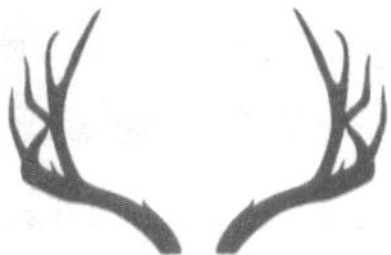

The shortest path from the royal apartments to the Great Temple ended at the temple's eastern door, a colossal silver slab that was incised with a ruby glass disc meant to represent Cydia in her guise as the full moon. Aeolmar, who could recite the varied and complex customs of Olluhm's temples as easily as his children's names, moved to push open the door. He was halted by Latera's hand on his elbow.

"What is it?" he asked.

Latera nodded toward the door. *Of course, the east is only used for bindings.*

"This way," Latera said.

She led him to the temple's southern door, that one crafted from a living oak to represent Parthalan's ever-growing knowledge. Once they were inside the main room of the temple, Aeolmar breathed deeply of the familiar smells: charcoal, incense, herbs freshly crushed for poultices and teas. His mother had brought him to the temple near their village often, though that place was nothing like the magnificent house of worship he now stood in. But of course it was splendid, being that this was the Great Temple of Parthalan. The temple and the whole of Teg'urnan had been constructed by Olluhm himself as a love token for his mate, Cydia. It was the most sacred place in all the realm, the true and everlasting home of the gods' children, and any priestess who was appointed to the Great Temple considered herself blessed.

Now I know why Mama was always offering to assist the priestesses.

Aeolmar had always thought that his mother had freely offered her services to the priestesses out of her love for herbs and flowers, and her general good nature. As he recalled the wistful expression she'd worn while grinding herbs and measuring out incense, he wondered if that little temple in the west had reminded her of home.

"I don't believe I've set foot in here since we were bound," Latera said. Aeolmar quashed his latest pang of guilt, for he was remiss in bringing his mate, and now his children, to temple. While others viewed the sun god's temples, whether it be the Great Temple in Teg'urnan or the one of the many smaller shrines scattered across the countryside, as a warm, welcoming abodes, they only reminded Aeolmar of his dead mother. It was one of the many memories he struggled with, and he dealt with it by avoiding all temples and thinking on other matters. Occasionally, those tactics even worked.

"First Hunter."

Aeolmar turned toward the voice and was greeted by the High Priestess Atreynha, thus ending any lingering thoughts of retreat.

"First Huntress," Atreynha said, and Latera nodded to the priestess. Latera and Atreynha had always gotten on well, despite their infrequent meetings.

"High Priestess," Aeolmar greeted, bowing his head. Atreynha smiled at him, a warm and loving smile that reminded Aeolmar of his mother. As he glanced over Atreynha's blue robes, he tried to imagine his mother garbed to serve the gods. Alluria had worn blue often, but

Aeolmar had always thought she tended toward the shade because it complemented her eyes. Now, he wasn't so sure.

"Have you come to present your child to the gods?" Atreynha inquired.

"His name is Tor." Latera shifted so that Atreynha could view Tor's sleeping face, and the High Priestess of Parthalan dropped all semblance of propriety and cooed at the boy. Thus heartened, Aeolmar said a silent plea to his mother's spirit, and another to Cydia for good measure, and stated his purpose.

"I have not," Aeolmar replied. "I've been told that you knew my mother."

"I've known a great many mothers," Atreynha replied, not taking her gaze off Tor, "and I've helped a great many children into the world. Where would I have encountered your mother?"

"Here." He spoke softly, but his directness gave the priestess pause. "Here in this very temple where she served Olluhm alongside you. According to the queen, I look a great deal like her." Atreynha glanced up from the baby, then gave Aeolmar a long, sweeping gaze. Atreynha stepped closer to Aeolmar, and reached up to touch his cheek.

"Blessed Cydia, you're Alluria's son," she murmured. "All these winters... But she isn't here, is she?" Atreynha shook her head. "No, she and Caol'nir swore that they would never return to Teg'urnan."

"She's gone," Aeolmar said. "And my father, and the rest of their children. I'm all that's left." Atreynha's eyes softened, and she petted his head as if he were a small boy.

"The *mordeth*?" she asked, and he nodded. "Alluria always knew he would come for her, but Caol'nir vowed to keep her safe until his dying breath. Your father was as brave and valiant as Solon himself, but I gather that you already knew that bit. You're here to learn of their life before."

"I am," he replied. "Will you help me?"

"Of course."

With that, the priestess beckoned Aeolmar and Latera to follow her, and led them to a room at the rear of the temple, one of many used by priestesses when counseling patrons. The temple tended toward silence, but this room was almost oppressively quiet, the only sound being the rustle of Atreynha's heavy silk skirts. She bade them sit around a stone table and departed without another word. Once she had been gone long enough for Aeolmar to wonder if she'd retreated to the underworld itself, she returned bearing an armload of scrolls sealed with blue wax.

"Asherah has told you that Caol'nir and Alluria's names were stricken from the records?" Atreynha asked, as she arranged the scrolls before them.

"Yes," Aeolmar snapped. Latera began an apology, but Atreynha waved it away.

"It was a deception, yes, but done with the best of intentions," Atreynha said. "All Caol'nir and Alluria ever wanted was a life free from demons and wars. They wanted a home, and a family, and happiness." She didn't wait for Aeolmar's reaction, and instead presented him with the first scroll, as indicated by the seal. "These are the original birth records, which tell of your lineage from Solon to Caol'nir. And this," she indicated a smaller scroll, "records the few known details of Alluria's parentage."

"Do her parents yet live?" Aeolmar asked hopefully.

"We see her father in the skies every day," Atreynha replied. "As for her mother, after Alluria was born Olluhm brought her to his side. I suspect that is where she remains." Aeolmar felt his last shred of sanity drift away at Atreynha's words. Luckily, Latera still had wits enough to speak.

"Olluhm?" Latera asked. "Alluria was fathered by someone named for the elder sun?"

"Alluria was fathered *by* the elder sun," Atreynha confirmed. "Alluria's mother—her name was Annalee—was the first woman other than a priestess to bear a god's child in millennia. Olluhm had been well and truly captivated by our Annalee, and shortly after Alluria was born, he took her from us. I and my sister priestesses raised Alluria at our temple in the east. Many winters passed, and then the king summoned us to Teg'urnan. After we came here, she met Caol'nir."

"You are twice born of gods," Latera murmured, resting her hand on Aeolmar's arm. Aeolmar shook his head, and wondered what else he could possibly learn about his parents. He found himself longing for the simplicity of a grandsire in the kitchens.

"That he is," Atreynha confirmed, then she turned her attention to the wax seals. "The seals may only be broken by one who bears Alluria's blood. I believe it would be best for you to read the records first, then ask me what questions you'd like. I'll fetch you some refreshment; like as not, you'll be a while." Aeolmar nodded toward the priestess, overwhelmed by the many scrolls before him. At the doorway Atreynha paused, and added, "Perhaps, once I have told you all I can, you will tell me of Alluria's life with you." Atreynha's tone held a note of sorrow strong enough to tear Aeolmar's gaze from the scroll. When he looked up, he saw not the formidable High Priestess of Teg'urnan, but a mother who missed her child.

"I will tell you everything," he promised. "My father did give her a good life. He gave all of us the best life he could."

Atreynha smiled, the corners of her eyes crinkling. "I have never doubted that, not for a moment."

The High Priestess then left them alone with a small mountain of parchments, all sealed with dark blue wax. Aeolmar dragged his thumbnail around the seal, but could find no purchase. He wondered if the wax's age had resulted in a near-impenetrable bond, when he remembered Atreynha's words: *These seals may only be broken by one who bears Alluria's blood.* He smiled, remembering his mother's many lessons on holding an item fast, and how one could later allow the magic to flow away.

"*Vral'nee.*" Aeolmar whispered the word to release the charm from a spelled door. Latera gasped as the blue wax peeled away from the parchment, falling to the floor as the scroll flattened itself against the table.

"You want to start now?" Latera asked.

"Why not? I've wanted answers for too long to turn away now." His confident words belied the trepidation he felt; there were dozens of scrolls, and Aeolmar wondered if they recorded more than his lineage; gods, there could be information in these scrolls that he'd never wanted to know. Then Latera slipped her small hand in his, and the gentle pressure of her fingers against his palm calmed the torrent inside him.

"I'm glad you're here," he said as he kissed her knuckles.

"Of course I'm here," Latera said. "You think I'd let you navigate all of this without me? You'd probably get lost."

"That I might." Reassured by her presence, Aeolmar began his quest by reading the story of Solon aloud to his mate and son.

Chapter Twenty-One

"**M**y lady, you have a visitor."

Iruna looked up from her dressing table and regarded her *saffira-nell*. "I'm not expecting anyone."

"It is Mallia, the healer."

"Interesting." Iruna rose and left her chambers, sweeping past the startled *saffira*. She could think of no reason why Mallia would make an unexpected journey from the palace, and the one thing Iruna possessed in abundance—other than coin and vitriol—was curiosity.

She found the healer not in the antechamber or one of the formal sitting rooms, but standing outside of the small shrine to Olluhm. "I can only wonder what turn of events has brought you all the way out here," Iruna said by way of greeting.

"The incense is old," Mallia snapped. "Have it replaced, and bring fresh flowers. Perhaps a bowl of cold spring water as well, for our father does work up a mighty thirst as he drives his chariot across the skies."

Iruna glanced over her shoulder and nodded toward the shrine's attendant. He bowed, and then scurried off to refresh the offerings. "My apologies. I try to keep the temple as—"

"No apology is necessary," Mallia said, waving away Iruna's words. "I know you do the best you can. You always have."

"Thank you."

The heiress and the healer stood together in quiet contemplation for a time. "I have brought you information, and a request," Mallia said at length.

"You know I will do for you anything that is within my power," Iruna said.

Mallia nodded. "You and your brother have always been good to me. Even when the rest of the world hated me, you and Avinor showed me kindness." Mallia paused. "There is one in Teg'urnan who is closer in relation to Olluhm than even you."

Iruna's eyes widened, but her sharp mind made a quick connection. "Asherah's warrior?"

"Yes, the First Hunter," Mallia confirmed.

"Does he have more of a claim than I do?"

"He is Alluria's son."

Iruna nodded; she knew of the eastern priestess who'd been fathered by Olluhm. "Then he must be removed from Teg'urnan."

"What of his children?"

Iruna shrugged. "You have the quarrel with Alluria, not I. I leave their fates up to you."

"You don't see Aeolmar as a way to return yourself to Teg'urnan? He has a son only slightly younger than Asherah's."

Iruna pursed her lips. "I can return myself to Teg'urnan. I do not need a child's assistance."

"Aeolmar's father was of the old Prelate's line," Mallia said.

"And the warrior's claim grows stronger yet," Iruna murmured. "What of his mate? He cares for her still?"

"He adores her, but she is not of Parthalan," Mallia replied. "She is of the human realm."

"Perhaps we can send her back where she came from." Iruna gazed about the shrine, hoping that Olluhm had finally heeded her prayers. "Avinor told me that the king has an interest in our lands."

"Does he?" Mallia asked. "I wonder why."

"Can you find out?" Iruna implored. "Quietly?"

"I can try, yes. About what I've told you..."

Iruna turned to Mallia and grasped her hands. "My assistance, you have it. Anything you need."

Mallia patted Iruna's cheek. "You always were good to me."

Chapter Twenty-Two

Mara leaned across the balcony wall as far as she could, stretching until only her toes touched the stone pavers. Kemen typically took up an afternoon post at the base of Teg'urnan's main stairs, sometimes joined by Luth, sometimes alone, a fact most anyone knew. On that day, Mara wanted to be certain that Kemen was alone before she walked down the steps.

She'd tried finding Kemen alone a few times over the past sennight, and each time she'd been thwarted. Once, he had been engaged in some sort of drinking competition with Luth and Bron, clearly as the loser (or winner, if drunkenness was the prize); another time, it had been a game of dice with Elkin that held him enthralled. Mostly he just wasn't there, which made Mara wonder if he was avoiding her, though how he would even be aware that she was looking for him, she didn't know. She'd told no one of her infatuation with Kemen, not her mother to whom she told her most embarrassing secrets, and certainly not Ember, who would have repeated everything, word for word, to their father. The only person she might have confided in was Alia, but she was long since gone to the Northern Contingent.

Mara stretched out even farther over the railing, and was rewarded with a glimpse of Kemen's black hair. She knew it was him, for most who claimed black hair really had very deep brown hair, not the dark as night tone of Kemen's, so dark it reflected blue in the midday sun...

Abruptly, Kemen stepped into Mara's full view and hailed her. "Good day, my lady Mara," he yelled, loud enough to be heard all the way in Tingu. "Do you seek an escort through the merchant's quarter?"

Mara scrambled back from the railing, and in her haste, landed flat on her backside. She got to her feet and into the adjacent great hall, fully intending to hide in her father's tower chamber for the next hundred winters. Spoiling her plans was Kemen striding through the entrance at the opposite end of the hall.

Wonderful. She briskly moved toward the exit, but Kemen's long stride had him before her in a matter of moments. Mara tried to evade him, but he sidestepped and blocked her path. Finally, he backed her onto the same balcony where this awkward scene had begun.

"And you are spying on me because?" He waited, but Mara remained silent. "What, will no one else take you to the village? Surely you're not that disagreeable a companion."

"I don't need an escort," she insisted. "I come and go as I please!"

"Then why are spending your time looking and watching me, instead of coming or going?" Kemen inquired. She glared at him for a moment, then looked away. Truly, Mara herself didn't know what she was after, other than she had wanted to see him. *Had.*

"You're infuriating," she grumbled, hoping he would give up and walk away. That wasn't likely, since Kemen was lauded as the most tenacious of hunters, never giving up on his prey no matter the obstacles.

"Then tell me, my lady, why would the *deva'shi's* daughter seek me out, if not for an escort through the unsavory streets of Teg'urnan?" he murmured, leaning forward to trace her cheek. "I for one cannot think of a single other reason why she'd do such a thing."

"What makes you think I was seeking you?" Mara countered, doing her best to ignore his hand, though the heat of him threatened to burn her. "All I was doing was leaning over the railing."

"As you've been doing every morning for the past two sennights." Mara bit her lip, but otherwise remained expressionless. Kemen placed his hands on her shoulders, and gently turned her toward the open square. "While you were leaning and looking, I was watching you," he said, indicating the southern watchtower; she'd never noticed the small balcony adjacent to his chamber. It was across the square, and afforded an excellent view of both Kemen's usual haunt, and where they now stood.

"You were watching me?" Mara asked.

"Lady, I watch you often," Kemen replied. Startled, and half expecting he was teasing her, Mara turned back to him. Kemen's face was sincere, his gaze so intent she looked away.

"No," he said, tilting her chin upward, "don't look at your feet. Look at me."

"Why?" she asked.

"Because I like your eyes," he answered, the corners of his mouth curling up. Mara mumbled something about her blue eyes being her father's legacy, but Kemen touched his fingertips to her lips. "Lady, I'd rather not hear about your father right now."

"Oh." Mara couldn't stop staring into his eyes, a bright and clear green like the glass bottles that contained Wren's potions. "What would you like to hear about?"

"You."

Chapter Twenty-Three

Asherah Speaks

*M*allia's put something in my tea.

Something new.

Something other than dreamwort.

The tea doesn't look or smell any different, but I know she has added something to it. If I ask her, she'll deny it, like she always does. That woman has meddled her way through Teg'urnan more than once, but I've always ignored her since her value as a healer has always far outweighed her annoyances.

I can't ignore her now, not now that she's meddling with me.

Whatever the different bit in my tea may be, I'm certain that she first put it in the supply I took to Iruna and Avinor's estate. I hadn't meant to ask her for more, but when she had arrived bearing the tiny brown pouch, my resolve had melted away. "It can be difficult to rest while traveling," she'd crooned. "Please. Just in case you need it."

Like a good patient, I'd stowed it with the rest of my luggage, and of all people Finlay had brewed up that batch of tea. That night, my dream had been different, as were all of my dreams that followed.

Until we left Iruna's horrid home, and my loving mate packed that pouch away, assuming that I no longer needed it. Ha. His faith in me may mean all of our deaths.

When we had returned to Teg'urnan, I brewed a bowl from a small amount of dreamwort I'd hidden away, and my dreams were quiet. Dark. Solitary. Just as they'd always been. Then I found where Finlay had hidden that insidious brown pouch and steeped the last bit. It happened again.

My dream was light.

Happy.

There was someone with me.

I couldn't discern who, but it was the same man as before. It definitely was a man. I liked being near him; he was a calming force, his evenness tamping down the whirlwind of my mind. I wanted to see him again.

I needed to see him again.

I was out of dreamwort.

I sent for Mallia, all the while trembling with anticipation. Then she was here, and goddess bless her she had a basket dangling on her arm and my tea must be in it, but the first words out of my mouth weren't a request, or even a greeting.

"There's something new in my tea," I said without preamble. "In the pouch you sent me for traveling."

"I thought you might enjoy more active dreams," the healer replied, in that soothing, I'm-so-sorry-you're-an-invalid voice of hers. "I know how unpleasant Iruna can be, and I thought the dreams might distract you from her nastiness."

They certainly had, but that wasn't the point just now. "Each dream is the same," I said. "Something or someone is there, just beyond my reach."

"Ah." Mallia set down her basket and took my hands; her skin was cool and moist, and I assumed she must have been washing herbs in the ward. "Is it your heart's desire come back to you?"

"Back to me?" I shook my head, denying what I somehow felt to be true. "I have everything I want."

"Then, perhaps it's someone that desires you."

Me? Who in the nine realms would desire me? Finlay does, I suppose, but the man in my dream certainly wasn't him. I'd know Finlay anywhere, what with his ebon curls, his sandy palms... No, this man felt different. Familiar. Safe.

"Who could it be?" I murmured.

"Would you like to learn?" Mallia drew one of her little leather pouches from her basket, but before she loosened the tie, Attia threw open the door, and an enraged King of Parthalan strode into the room.

"Out," Finlay barked. Attia didn't wait for Mallia's response before she gathered up her basket of whatnot and thrust it at the healer. Mallia wisely kept her mouth shut and let Attia usher her out of my chamber. Finlay shut the door loudly behind them, then he faced me.

"I thought you didn't need the teas any longer."

"I had dreams," I mumbled. Why was I mumbling? "Dreams with men in them, and the men weren't you." My vision swam, and for a moment, all the colors in the room swirled together. Then Finlay's hands were on me, grasping me about the waist, feeling my neck and forehead, his gritty palms my only link to reality.

"Are you ill?" Finlay asked. I must have swooned a bit, I deduced. I tried to tell him I was fine, but my tongue seemed to have swollen to thrice its normal size. "You're not feverish. Have you eaten?" he pressed.

Garbled bits of speech fell from my lips, though I've no idea why. I only meant to say that I'd eaten a bit of bread and a few grapes. Then Finlay was shouting for Attia, their concerned faces bleeding together as they stared at me. I tried to speak and instead found myself in darkness.

Chapter Twenty-Four

"You're sure she was bringing her more dreamwort?" Finlay asked Attia for the fourth time.

"The *saffira* was specifically told to fetch Mallia, and for her to bring the herbs," she replied. "As soon as I learned of it, I sent for you."

Finlay grunted; what Attia had left unsaid was that Asherah had deliberately sent someone other than her *saffira-nell* to the healers ward. Whether Asherah had done so because Attia would tell Finlay, or because Attia would have outright refused to fetch the matriarch of the healers, he didn't know.

"Mallia should not have come," Finlay said. "Asherah told her she wanted no more of those teas. She should have stayed away."

"She can't ignore a direct summons from the queen," Attia pointed out. "None of us can, save you." Finlay grunted again; Attia was correct, but he didn't have to like it. *Gods, I'm starting to behave like Aeolmar.* "Further, what if the queen truly had taken ill? We cannot afford to offend the one person who may hold the key to curing her. Need I remind you of what happened with the First Huntress?"

"I remember." Finlay recalled the dark days after Latera had borne her son, and how Aeolmar had honestly believed she might not survive. It was the first time he'd ever seen Aeolmar, a man who would stride up to a *mordeth* without a second thought, afraid.

Finlay grabbed the bowl Asherah favored for her tea, contemplated throwing it, and put it back down. Broken pottery scattered across the bedchamber wouldn't help anyone, least of all his often-barefoot mate.

"Do you think Mallia's herbs are what made her collapse?" he asked.

"I've never seen any herb cause what happened to her earlier."

"But you have seen the like before."

Attia sighed, and sat on the bench at the foot of the bed. "When Asherah was first queen, she struggled with her memory. Her lack of memories, really. She was relentless in the pursuit of her past, tearing apart old books and maps in her search."

"She never found anything," Finlay said when she paused.

"That's not true. She found many things." Attia stared into the hearth; the fire had been banked, and the logs were glowing red. "Whenever she found something she thought she might have recognized, it was as if her mind had left her. She forgot how to speak, how to stand, and eventually collapsed. Each and every time she collapsed, just as she did today." Attia cleared her throat, and used the edge of her sleeve to dab at her eyes.

"After many winters of this, it was determined that whatever trauma she had sustained in the *doja* would not allow her to search for her past," she continued. "In time, the attacks eased. This is the first time she's collapsed since Aeolmar came to Teg'urnan, and she started living in the present."

Finlay rubbed his jaw, and wondered why Asherah had never told him these things. Then again, she probably didn't want anyone to know that certain images could reduce her to a gibbering heap. "But she still searches for answers," he pointed out. "I've helped her search. Hells, I've brought her to the shrine of Ish h'ra, yet I've never seen her like this!"

"I cannot explain that," Attia said. "All I know is that she and Sarfek would search the archives—"

"Sarfek." Finlay scanned the chamber, wondering what item held a lingering charm or spell. "I think we have our answer. What here is from his day?"

"Nothing," Attia replied, somewhat taken aback. It wasn't often that her housekeeping skills were called into question. "Remember, we all thought he was dead centuries ago, long before Latera finally killed him in the mortal realm."

Finlay raked a hand through his curls. "Do you think Mallia could have caused what happened today?"

"If she did, I've no idea how," Attia replied. "You forget, my king, these chambers are warded against magic."

"Who warded them?"

"Atreynha, with the same wards that bind the Great Temple."

Hells. Finlay sank down next to Attia, holding his head in his hands. "If it's not an old charm, and not the teas, then what? What is happening to her?"

"I don't know," she replied, gazing at the sleeping queen. "I wish I did."

Chapter Twenty-Five

"Do you think it's a coincidence?" Aeolmar asked.

Finlay glanced at Aeolmar, then he resumed staring out over the palace square. The king and the First Hunter were standing on the royal balcony, and Finlay had just told Aeolmar about Asherah's recent collapse. To Finlay's great dismay, Aeolmar had never known that Asherah was susceptible to such occurrences.

"Do I think what is a coincidence?" Finlay countered. "That Asherah refused Mallia's herbs, and then she collapsed?"

"Not that. Iruna."

"You're as paranoid as Sher is," Finlay muttered.

"According to Attia, Asherah hasn't collapsed like that for so long everyone in Teg'urnan had forgotten about it," Aeolmar continued. "Then she spends a few days with Markham's children, and it happens again." Aeolmar's eyes narrowed. "What was added to that wine in the village?"

"Wren has a sample," Finlay replied. Innetha had managed to save an entire cask of the altered wine and had delivered it to Wren so she could study the poison. "Last I heard, she thought the residue was some kind of powdered metal. Evidently, some metals are quite lethal if ingested."

"True, but the source is more likely a plant," Aeolmar said. "The west is beautiful, but underneath that beauty lies danger. My mother knew of a hundred herbs that could sicken a man with a single leaf."

Danger beneath the beauty... "You're a westerner," Finlay said. "What do you know about the lands around Iruna's estate?"

"Not much," he replied. "I don't think anyone does, save those who work there."

"Work there? But what about the farmland?"

"That's all owned by Iruna," Aeolmar replied. "There's a stretch near the river that Avinor lost gambling in Ysr, but the rest all belongs to the Golden Knoll."

"How is that possible?" Finlay asked, then he recalled the cloth of gold tapestries that lined the walls, the gem-encrusted plates. "Have they been collecting rents on the land?"

"Shouldn't they? It's their land."

Finlay shook his head. "It's not. Since they inherited it from Markham, it's royal land. Teg'urnan does not tax them or charge rents. Hells, we pay them a stipend. But if they're working and making money from the land..."

"Are there tax records?" Aeolmar asked.

"There should be," Finlay said. "I have one of the scribes searching the archive."

"You might want to search the vaults, as well," Aeolmar said. "Atreynha would know if there had been a special edict." Aeolmar paused. "What does Asherah think of your search into Iruna's treasury?"

"She didn't think anything of it. Instead of being concerned about those two bleeding Parthalan dry, she sent for Mallia and fell ill."

Aeolmar grunted, and resumed staring and the landscape beyond the towers. "None of this makes any sense."

"Agreed." Finlay rubbed his eyes. "Sher had already thought Iruna was after her throne, and our son, and then all that happened in the village, and now..."

"Now, what?"

"Now, I don't know what to think."

"I should have gone with you."

"And what would you have done differently?"

Aeolmar shrugged. "Hit things. Searched for clues. Interrogated people."

Finlay snorted. "That's a regular day for you."

Aeolmar nodded toward the gate. "Messenger's arrived."

Finlay saw the messenger in question. He was dressed like a farmer, and was waving his arms about as he spoke to the gatekeeper. "Have you ever seen that man before?" Finlay asked.

"No, but whatever he said put a bug up Merritt's arse." Aeolmar had no sooner said the words when the gatekeeper left his post and ran across the square toward the royal balcony. Finlay straightened and squared his shoulders, and motioned for him to come closer.

Merritt halted below the balcony, and shouted, "Demons, my lord! And they have a *mordeth*!"

"Where?" Finlay demanded.

"Just past the rise," Merritt replied. "Vilja's estate."

Aeolmar was striding off the balcony and toward the exit before Merritt was done speaking.

"Send a message to the *sola*," Finlay said as he caught up with Aeolmar. "We can have every palace hunter ready, and—"

"Tell them to catch up. I'm leaving now."

Finlay grabbed Aeolmar's arm. "You don't know how many there are, and there might be a *mordeth*. Going after them alone is the same as committing suicide."

"Vilja's estate is a half day's walk from the gate," Aeolmar said. "If you think I'm letting that *mordeth* get any closer to my home, you're mad."

"You're the mad one, facing it alone!"

"You know what drove me mad?" Aeolmar demanded as he rounded on Finlay. "Watching my mate nearly die as she bore our son. Now that she and Tor are finally healing, I'll be damned before I let a demon or anything hurt them."

They stared at each other for a moment, then Finlay nodded and Aeolmar resumed walking. "What of the others?" Finlay called.

"You're the king," Aeolmar replied. "Summon them yourself."

***

Aeolmar went to the stable for Myrnnhe, then it was a short gallop to Vilja's estate. He reined in his horse, and from his vantage point, he surveyed the destruction below.

Vilja's estate wasn't exactly an estate, so much as it was a collection of outbuildings surrounding fields of grains, equally allocated for grinding into flour and brewing ale. The farm's namesake, Viljeanne, had planted the fields shortly after the Battle of Esguth. The demons had burned whatever crops they found as they approached Teg'urnan, and Viljeanne, who was shrewd and compassionate in equal portions, understood that not only did the people needed to be fed, but that she could sell them the grain and flour and turn a substantial profit.

Most of the outbuildings were for storing the harvest, but those on the eastern side were mills set along the river. The mills were essential to those who lived in and around Teg'urnan, since without flour, there was no bread.

Aeolmar remembered the mill that was near his childhood home, and how his father and brothers had seen to harvesting the grain and grinding it down to flour. He'd been too young, and too small, to be of much help, but he'd done what he could. He missed those days.

He heard a crash near the river. Aeolmar's gaze tracked the sound, and saw what was indeed a *mordeth*—in fact, the first *mordeth* sighted since Asgeloth's demise—rip the center mill's water wheel free and fling it into the fields. His grip tightened on the reins; Aeolmar had no idea why a demon would be interested in grain or flour, but he would not allow them to destroy the mills.

He flicked the reins, and Myrnnhe thundered down the slope toward the mills. Aeolmar leapt from the saddle and toward a clutch of lesser demons that didn't hold out long under his blade.

"Myrnnhe, away," he yelled. The stallion neighed in reply, and charged at the lessers. Before Aeolmar could grab Myrnnhe's reins and try to force him to leave the battle, he heard a roar that could only belong to the *mordeth*.

Aeolmar faced the beast. The *mordeth* was at least a head taller than him, and his barrel chest and thick legs told Aeolmar he weighed twice, maybe three times as much as the First Hunter.

No matter. He'd killed bigger.

"Why are you here?" Aeolmar demanded. "What interests you in this farm?"

The *mordeth* shrugged. "I go where I am sent."

"Sent by who? There is no *mordeth-gall*!"

"You are quite curious for one about to die."

The *mordeth* lunged and Aeolmar moved to the side. His sword caught the *mordeth's* shoulder, and the demon's claws raked across Aeolmar's side. He went down on one knee, his hand pressed over the wounds, and looked up at the beast.

"Did you come to kill the queen? The king?" Aeolmar pressed. "Me?"

The *mordeth* cocked his head to the side. "Who are you, other than a weakling?"

"I am First Hunter!"

The *mordeth* laughed. "I am not here for you, but if I bring back your mate's head I will be—"

Aeolmar screamed and rushed at the monster. The *mordeth* knocked him down, but as Aeolmar fell he caught his hand on the beast's lower leg and pulled it off balance. He leapt onto the *mordeth* as it landed on his back, and thrust his sword into his throat. Blood like acid sprayed upward and soaked Aeolmar's chest and neck, but he didn't care. It was dead, and that was what mattered.

Aeolmar stood and ripped off his jerkin before the blood could soak through to his skin. He heard shouting behind him, and saw hunters, led by Elkin, coming down the hill. Feeling he had a moment's reprieve, he went behind the mill, removed his gear and ducked into the pond to rinse away the caustic demon blood. When he emerged he found Elkin standing at the edge of the pond, frowning at the *mordeth's* corpse.

"We're out here fighting for our lives, and you're taking a swim?" Elkin shook his head. "Typical."

"How goes it?" Aeolmar asked as he pulled on his clothes.

"Well," Elkin replied. "We're routing them. Of course, you did most of the work." Elkin's brow wrinkled when he saw the marks scored across Aeolmar's chest and ribs. "That looks rather painful."

"It's not as bad as the one on my leg." Aeolmar hadn't even felt the wound above his knee, and had only noticed it after he'd gotten out of the pool. He assumed it was from a lesser's teeth.

He finished dressing, and called for Myrnnhe. "Oh, no," he said as the horse approached him. There was a fresh tear across Myrnnhe's flank. It was shallow, but seeped blood. "Myrnnhe, I wish you'd retreated."

Elkin leaned forward and scrutinized the wound. "He'll be all right. Takes more than a little cut to harm a war horse, right, boy?" He patted Myrnnhe's neck, and the horse whuffled in response. "Even so, Latera will have your hide for this."

Aeolmar surveyed the estate. "Yes, she will."

"We're nearly done here," Elkin said. "Rest him while we take care of what's left."

Elkin returned to the fields, where a few lessers still scurried among the crops. Aeolmar cleaned Myrnnhe's wound, and as the thrill of battle wore off he became aware of each and every one of his own hurts.

"Myrnnhe, I fear we might be getting too old for this."

***

Aeolmar led the hunters up the royal road to Teg'urnan, him walking as he led his wounded horse. How many times had he made this walk, battered and bruised yet triumphant? Though his legs ached and his skin burned, he'd done it. He'd destroyed the *mordeth*, along with a fair amount of lessers. It had been a good fight.

He crested the last rise, and saw his mate standing in the center of Teg'urnan's dark iron gates. Even at that distance he could see her arrow-straight back, feel her tension through their bond. Aeolmar had done this for her, for the tiny bundle she held against her breast, and he'd keep doing it as long as there was breath in his body.

Beloved.

Are you injured?

Yes.

Where do you hurt?

Everywhere.

Latera's next communication was more of a sensation than words, and she quite effectively expressed her displeasure with him. *Was I supposed to let demons overrun the palace?*

There are a dozen hunters and entire legion at your disposal. You're supposed to take them with you so you don't end up dead.

He laughed aloud at that, the resulting pain in his side letting him know he'd probably cracked a rib or three. Aeolmar completed the rest of the walk in silence, only stopping when he stood before his mate.

Latera looked at him with her crystal blue eyes, fiery brows low across them. Aeolmar braced himself for whatever shouting she was about to do, when she surprised him by standing on her toes and kissing him.

"Next time, tell me before you leave," she said against his lips.

He cupped the back of her head, kissed her a bit deeper. *I'm sorry.*

I know.

Latera drew back, and Aeolmar bent to kiss Tor's head. He'd barely done so when Latera tore away from him.

"What have you done to my horse?" she demanded and she examined the cut on Myrrnhe's flank.

"Your horse?" Aeolmar snapped. Latera glared at him; of course, all horses stabled at Teg'urnan were hers. She'd had words with the ostler just this past sennight about that. While Latera cooed over the nearly-perfect warhorse, Aeolmar signaled the gatekeeper. A few moments later, a stable hand approached them.

"We'll see him tended," the hand assured Latera, as the First Hunter stood there bleeding. After Latera had kissed Myrrnhe's nose and sent him on to the stables, she returned her attention to Aeolmar.

"Why didn't you send him back?" she asked, since all of Teg'urnan's horses are trained to return to the palace at the first hint of demons. "You know how those vermin like to snack on horses."

"I tried, but he wouldn't leave me," Aeolmar replied, sliding an arm around Latera's shoulders. "He was all hooves and fury. Reminded me of you."

"Hush," she said as she swatted his arm. *Do you need to lean on me?*

He smiled tightly; Latera understood that the First Hunter couldn't appear weak. *Only for a moment.*

Then you'll fall over?

Hopefully we'll be in our chambers before then.

Shouldn't you report to Asherah?

Elkin can handle that.

"Of course Myrnnhe wouldn't leave you," she said, as she adjusted the baby so she could take more of Aeolmar's weight. "He's as much a hunter as we are. A good hunter would never leave his commander in peril."

"He's the best horse I've ever had." *I love you.*

I should punish you for taking off like that. You're worse than the children. Are you bleeding on me?

Aeolmar laughed. *You're only mad because you love me, too.*

Mean man.

As I said.

Chapter Twenty-Six

Latera, with a sleeping Tor cradled in her arms, climbed the spiral staircase to the peak of the southern tower. She was intent on visiting the apartment Aeolmar had lived in while she had been stationed at the Eastern Border. The rooms had never been reassigned, and the mates occasionally retreated to the small stone chamber to escape the bustle of Teg'urnan. The rooms also held an assortment of oddities and mementos that Aeolmar had accumulated during his time as First Hunter, and before that as a farmer's son, and couldn't bear to part with.

On that day Latera sought something of her own, and once she completed the steep climb, she pushed open the chamber door and headed straight for the stacks of boxes with single-minded determination. She didn't bother looking around the room until she heard a few muffled voices behind her. Wondering who could possibly be in the chamber, she turned around and found her eldest daughter in Kemen's arms.

"Mother," Mara yelped as she untangled herself. "I-I didn't think you'd be coming up here."

"I can see that," Latera replied, taking in the sight of them. Mara and Kemen were seated on the steps that led to the bed, their flushed faces telling Latera that the heap of cushions and furs was their ultimate destination. Her gaze settled on the loosened stays of Mara's bodice. "I'll be gone in a moment," she said, turning back to the clutter.

"I should go," Kemen said as he stood and moved toward the door.

"There's no reason for you to leave," Latera said, but he waved her words away.

"I'm due to patrol soon," Kemen said. "It's past time I should be leaving." With those words and a nod toward Mara, he disappeared down the stairs. Latera looked at Mara and shrugged.

"Well then, you can help me look," Latera said. "They've got to be somewhere over here."

Mara, her bodice now tightly fastened, obediently went to her mother's side and stared at the stacks of dusty boxes. Neither Latera nor her daughters understood Aeolmar's tendency toward mementos. "What are you looking for?"

"My troll swords," Latera answered, as she picked her way toward the rear wall.

"Whatever for?" Mara asked.

"You don't think Tor's old enough to learn swordplay?" Latera asked. Mara folded her arms across her chest and stared at her mother; the girl had never appreciated sarcasm. "I've been thinking about them lately, and thought I'd bring them out."

"You're not going to run off and fight cadres of demons on your own, are you?"

"Of course not. We have your father for such foolishness. Ah!"

Having located a dark wooden box, Latera deftly popped the latch and beheld the twin short swords that had been a gift from Grelk, the troll king. Exquisitely crafted by the master of the forge himself with edges that would never dull, each hilt was set with a large yellow gem surrounded by small blue crystals. Now that she knew of her mate's lineage, Latera suspected the hilts represented the suns. She wondered how much Grelk had really known about Aeolmar's parents.

With a satisfied smile, she closed the box and fastened the catch. She stood and attempted to drag it one-handed, and quickly gave up. "Would you mind, sweetheart?"

Mara grabbed the box and brought it into the center of the room. Latera sat on the same steps her daughter and Kemen had recently vacated, and unlaced her tunic. "I need to feed your brother. Sit with me?" she asked, and Mara sat beside her mother. Mara played with Tor's chubby foot for a moment before she spoke.

"Does Father know you came all the way up here?" Mara asked. Aeolmar had told them about the altercation at Vilja's, and the *mordeth's* implication that he'd been sent after the *deva'shi*. "Without him?" she pressed.

"I don't need to ask his permission to walk around the palace," Latera replied, "but I'm very happy to find you here. I hadn't yet worked out how to carry the swords and the baby back down." She smiled sheepishly at her daughter, acknowledging that this hadn't been the best planned venture.

Mara returned her smile, then she clasped her hands in her lap. "We've never come up here before," she said suddenly. "We only wanted to sit on the balcony for the view. Then Kemen said he needed to patrol, so we came down... And then you were here."

"Mara, you don't need to explain yourself to me," Latera said gently. "You're grown. You can make your own choices."

"I know, but…" her voice trailed off, and her hands fidgeted in her lap. "How did you know that Father was your mate? How did you know you loved him?"

Latera smiled as she thought back over the years. "I knew the day I met him."

"Really?"

"Really. You know the story, how I killed the demons with your father's sword?" Mara nodded, for even if her father hadn't told the tale hundreds of times over every child in Parthalan knew the story of Latera Demon-killer: a stable girl grabbed the First Hunter's sword and slew two demons while Aeolmar lay wounded and defenseless behind her. "What the stories don't mention is that I collapsed into a sobbing mess afterward. I cried so hard I could hardly breathe."

"You did?" Mara asked, wide-eyed.

"I did," Latera confirmed. "Your father, rather than becoming annoyed with the blubbering fool that was me, scooped me into his arms and held me tightly to him, soothing me until I was calm. He gave me his word that he wouldn't let anything harm me, and I believed him." Latera smiled as she remembered that day so long ago. "I loved him in that very moment, with all my heart."

"And you two have been happy ever since," Mara declared, only to have Latera laugh shortly.

"It wasn't quite that simple. When this happened, I was just past my sixteenth winter. I was so young that I didn't realize what I felt for him was love, not until I was older."

"Sixteen winters?" Mara repeated, and Latera nodded. "So, when did you know?"

"Well," Latera began, mildly amused by her daughter's interest in the topic, "two winters after we met, and a full winter after I'd been named a huntress, I kissed him."

"And then you knew? And you were together?" Mara asked eagerly.

"I knew, but we still weren't together. I didn't see him again for two more winters, because I'd been assigned to the Eastern Border."

"Two winters," Mara repeated. "What was going through your mind when you finally saw him again? When he finally kissed you again?"

Latera shut her eyes, remembering that long-ago moment when he found her at the border. "That he was worth waiting for."

"And you never sought another, you just waited for him?"

"Yes, as he waited for me."

Mara thought for a moment. "I've only ever kissed Kemen. We have never... I have never..." Mara glanced at the bed and turned away, hiding her red cheeks.

"I thought as much," Latera said gently.

"You have only... with Father?"

"Mara, I was sixteen when I met him," she reminded her daughter. "Who else could there have been?"

Mara laughed. "There could have been others," she insisted. "But Father... He hasn't only been with you?"

"Your father is a great deal older than me. It's a different situation." She regarded her daughter for a moment, and added, "As Kemen is a great deal older than you. You cannot hold things against him that were done before he ever knew you."

"I know," Mara said softly. "I don't even know if I would want to be with him. Up there." She glanced toward the bed.

"You were born in that bed," Latera said.

"I know, you wouldn't let Father leave you to get a healer," Mara rattled off. Both Mara's parents had told her the story of her birth many times, at least as many as the story of the *mordeth-gall's* death.

"I was so scared, but Aeolmar was with me and he promised every-thing would be well," Latera said. "I clutched his arm so hard he was bruised for days. And then you were here, and I finally loved someone else as much as I love my mate." Latera smoothed a stray hair from Mara's brow. "Mara, you are smart, and strong, and I have every confidence in you. Whatever choice you make, as long as you follow your heart, you will find happiness." She squeezed Mara's hand, then detached Tor from her breast. "Now hold your brother for a moment," she said as she handed off the baby and laced up her tunic.

"Do you think Kemen is a good man?" Mara asked.

"I know he is. You know, your sister thinks he is the most handsome man in the palace, save your father."

"Ember is eight," Mara said.

"But she is an excellent judge of character," Latera said with a smile. She reclaimed the baby, and once Mara had hefted the box of swords, they started down the stairs.

"Oh, and Mara?"

"Yes?"

"If you and Kemen decide to return, be sure to knock before en-tering." She glanced at Mara's confused face and smiled. "Your father and I come up here from time to time. Not for the view."

"Mother!"

CHAPTER TWENTY-SEVEN

In the space of a sennight, Aeolmar had transformed himself from a man who avoided the Great Temple at all costs, to one who eagerly waited for its doors to open each morning. Usually he waited outside the southern door, which stood for knowledge, but occasionally he went to the northern door for strength. And strength was what he truly needed, for not only was reading about his family painful, the extra time he devoted to this new pursuit soon proved grueling.

Something else that was painful were his still-healing wounds from the battle at Vilja's estate. He'd originally thought the puncture wound above his knee was his worst injury, but that was healing cleanly. What gave him continued trouble were the deep scratches across his chest and ribs; with every motion he made, even when he was just breathing, they burned. Whenever he complained, Latera sd that maybe those wounds would teach him not to take on a clutch of demons alone. Aeolmar merely smiled, because he'd done it for her and he'd do it again. Also, she was right.

Despite his healing wounds, Aeolmar wasn't the only one feeling the strain from his research. At first Latera accompanied him on each trip to the temple, but the increased activity left her exhausted, and Aeolmar worried she'd relapse to the near-invalid state she'd been in after Tor's birth. When the eighth day after the skirmish came, and Latera and Tor had slept through both first and second dawn, Aeolmar left them to their rest and brought Ember along with him to the Great Temple. Ember quickly noticed that it wasn't only Latera who was fatigued.

"Why is everyone so tired?" Ember asked after Aeolmar yawned.

"Coming here to read the scrolls, on top of all of my other duties, has left Mama and me with very little time for rest," Aeolmar replied.

"Why can't we just bring the scrolls back to our chamber?" she asked. "Then you wouldn't have to go back and forth all the time."

"The scrolls are from the vaults," Aeolmar replied. "Such items are sacred, and must be handled with respect."

"But if they're all about our family, aren't they ours?" Ember pressed. "We should just bring them back with us. Then you and Mama won't be so tired. Don't worry," she added. "I'll make sure we're careful with them."

"I suppose you're right," Aeolmar said, and after he had obtained Atreynha's consent—for only a fool would neglect to ask the High Priestess' leave when it concerned items from her temple—he and Ember had carefully stowed the scrolls in a well-made satchel. While they did so, Ember questioned the many unbroken wax seals.

"To keep the knowledge contained within, and safe from those who shouldn't have it," Aeolmar replied. "Your grandmother was quite careful with her secrets." Ember's brows knit together as she slid her finger across the wax, and Aeolmar remembered his own frustrated childhood; he had never been able to wield magic as well as his mother, or a sword quite like his father. "Would you like to learn how to open them?"

"Yes!" Ember's face brightened, and Aeolmar crouched before her.

"In order to release something, we first must know how it was bound," he said, tracing the edge of the seal as she had done.

"But grandmamma isn't here to tell us," Ember pointed out.

"She's not," Aeolmar agreed, "but I remember a few of her tricks." He turned the scroll so the seam was lengthwise between them, and touched the blue wax oval. "Where do we keep those things that are dear to us?"

"In your tower?" Ember giggled.

"No, silly," he admonished. "What about those things that are truly dear?"

"Our hearts?"

"Good. Do you remember how to say heart in *ahm'ri?*"

"*Vral?*"

"My scholar," Aeolmar said, his voice prideful. Ember was a much better student than he had ever been. "And our hearts beat in our breasts, and our breasts lay down to slumber behind our chamber doors, and when we want to seal our chamber doors...?" He let the question hang in the air between them, watching Ember's puzzled expression as she worked out the problem.

"*Vral'ei'a,*" she said at last. Aeolmar wasn't surprised that she remembered the charm, but when she deduced the next bit he was truly impressed. "So we say *vral'nee,* and we break the seal." Ember touched the seal and the wax peeled away, revealing yet another parchment covered edge to edge with small, elegant writing.

"Very, very well done."

Aeolmar turned toward the voice and saw Atreynha standing in the doorway and watching them. "Her mind is ripe for knowledge, just as Alluria's always was," the High Priestess complimented.

"I'm like my grandmamma?" Ember asked.

"In many ways. You're just as brilliant as she was," Atreynha replied, and that was all Aeolmar or anyone else had heard from Ember as they crossed Teg'urnan and returned to their chambers. She quieted down once they were back in their chamber, and set to organizing the many scrolls. It was a daunting task, even for Ember, but luckily Latera and Mara were there to help.

While Latera and the girls put the scrolls in some kind of order, and Tor slept, Aeolmar finally found the one scroll he'd been searching for. It was the one that recorded his father's lineage. As he deciphered the ancient script, he learned more about his male family members.

"Tor's three sons," Aeolmar mumbled. He had found a family tree that reached from Solon all the way to his grandsire, and listed his grandsire's progeny. There was Caol'nir, Aeolmar's father, along with his brothers, Caol'non, and Fiornacht. Aeolmar wondered what it had cost his father to never mention his brothers.

"What's that?" Latera asked.

"Just reading out loud," he replied. He traced the family lineage with his finger; yes, the last Prelate of Solon's line had had three boys. He remembered Asherah saying as such, but seeing it on the scroll somehow made it real. What's more, his father had been a twin. He read further, and learned that Tor's mate, Iseult, had died as result of the twins' birth. Aeolmar squeezed his eyes shut for a moment, then he glanced back at his own mate. Latera looked so healthy now that one would hardly believe he'd almost lost her a scant two moons ago.

Latera caught his gaze and smiled, then she crossed the room and sat beside him. "Tell me what's so interesting that you're reading it out loud." She settled Tor on her lap, and leaned against Aeolmar's shoulder.

"I'm reading about my father's brothers," Aeolmar said. "The elder, and his twin. A twin! I never knew about either of them. He... he never said a word about them." He

read Tor's name again. *My grandsire.* The scrolls also told Aeolmar that his father, Caol'nir, had been younger than the eldest brother, Fiornacht, by many winters, and a full day younger than his twin.

"I imagine it was difficult for him to speak of them after they'd been killed," Latera said gently, but Aeolmar shook his head.

"No, only Fiornacht was killed in the temple," he said, shuffling the parchments until he located the one that recorded the eldest brother's death. "Caol'non, Father's twin, did not die that day. Or on any other day, as far as I can tell."

"Warrior's fire and warrior's strength," Latera murmured, translating the twins' names from *ahm'ri* into the common tongue. "And Alluria meant servant of the gods. I must admit, your parents' names make a great deal more sense to me now." Aeolmar nodded absently, hardly hearing her. "Do you think Caol'non still lives?"

"I wish I knew," Aeolmar muttered. Latera grasped his hand, but before she could speak, they were distracted by Ember.

"Who are all these people?" she asked. Ember had decided to put her new knowledge to use, and broke the seals on several scrolls that turned out to be a collection of portraits. Aeolmar said that he hadn't yet seen them, so Ember dutifully hauled over her find.

The first portrait was a rendering of Solon, as bright and blazing as if he were living sunlight. The next was of Solon's firstborn, Parthalan's first Prelate, and the next of that Prelate's firstborn. Realizing that this was a pictorial family tree, Aeolmar skipped to the last scroll and gazed upon his grandsire.

"The first Tor," Latera said, holding her own Tor a bit closer. "Did your father resemble him?"

"He did," Aeolmar replied. He traced the hard charcoal lines of Tor's jaw, the determined brow. "He did indeed."

"Where are the pictures of your papa?" Ember asked, delving further into the satchel.

"There probably aren't any," Aeolmar said, his voice tinged with regret. "He left Teg'urnan before he could become Prelate. Though, here is a rendering of Fiornacht. Being eldest, he would have been the next Prelate if he hadn't perished."

"Were women Prelate, too?" Ember asked.

"No, *dea comora*," Aeolmar replied. "Solon's edict says that the title passes from father to son." Latera elbowed him in the ribs, but not too hard. He nipped at her ear in retaliation.

"Then who is she?" Ember asked, once again distracting her parents from each other. She was intently studying the scroll spread before her. It was larger than the rest, and was a color portrait of a woman clothed in the blue robes of a priestess, with long chestnut hair and deep blue eyes.

"Mara looks like your mother," Latera murmured, for it was plain that the woman depicted was Alluria.

"Who looks like me?" Mara asked, then she peeked at the scroll. "Oh, she's lovely."

"She is," Latera agreed. "Sweetheart, are there any others of her?" Ember produced three more scrolls, one of which was Alluria clad in a green and gold gown, clutching a garland of yellow flowers.

"Pretty dresses," Ember murmured. "Papa, did my grandmamma always wear dresses?"

"She did," Aeolmar replied. "Every day, even if she was working in the fields or the mill. She never once dressed like a man."

"Not even for riding?" Latera asked, her brow arched.

"She disliked horses," Aeolmar replied, chuckling at his mate's disbelief. "You and she are not similar," he said, bending to kiss the corner of her mouth.

"No, your mama's like the queen," Ember gushed. "Always wearing pretty dresses, pretty hair..." Ember gave her mother's riding breeches an appraising glance. "Why don't you wear dresses like the queen, Mama?"

"Because if I did, your father would chase me relentlessly," Latera replied, ignoring how Mara huffed in indignation. "Then you'd have so many siblings we'd need to build another palace in order to house them all."

"I'd like more brothers and sisters," Ember said after a moment's thought. "When can I have more?" Aeolmar cocked an eyebrow at his mate, and Mara stalked out of the chamber.

"Not for a little while yet, sweetheart," Latera replied, bending to kiss her daughter's forehead. "The three of you are quite enough, for now."

For now. Later that day, after Ember had gone to play with Finlay, and Latera fed Tor yet again, Aeolmar stood on the balcony as those words echoed in his mind. He'd always wanted a large family, and knew that his mate desired more children, but he could not purge the images of Tor's birth from his mind. Aeolmar suspected that Latera didn't remember much aside from her intense pain, then she slipped into oblivion while he and Wren had struggled to keep her alive. He wondered if a fourth child would mean her death.

***

Those first few days after Tor's birth had been grueling for Aeolmar. First, he had had to endure watching his mate nearly die while he stood by helplessly, then he was saddled with the babe's care while Latera recovered. It wasn't that he minded caring for his son; in fact, he enjoyed it. What he had wanted was for his mate to be up and around, and to share in this new life they had created together. Really, he'd just wanted her to be well again.

Mara and Ember helped Aeolmar where they could, and Wren as well, but by the third morning, all three of them were as spent as he was. Aeolmar had sent them to rest in Wren's chambers, got himself a fresh bowl of goat milk, and settled himself and his son on the bed next to Latera. Wren had administered a sleeping draught to her sister nearly two days prior; that, coupled with the injuries Latera had sustained during birth, had kept her in a deep sleep that Aeolmar was loath to disturb, but the baby still needed to eat. Instead of waking Latera, he remembered a trick his mother had once used on one of his younger sisters that involved dipping one's finger in a bowl of warmed milk and letting the baby suck off the drops. Not the ideal nourishment for a newborn, but it would have to do.

Until that moment it had done just fine, but on that morning the boy turned his head and fussed until he and Aeolmar were both a milky mess. Both had been frustrated, and on the verge of losing their tempers, but Aeolmar would have been a poor First Hunter if he hadn't been able to think quickly.

mordeth-gall. Gently, Aeolmar propped her up in a sitting position, and took his place behind her. After a moment's thought he pulled off his tunic, and then he settled her back against his bare chest. Once Latera was settled Aeolmar grabbed the baby from his cradle and placed him at his mother's breast.

"There, that's what you wanted," Aeolmar crooned to the boy over Latera's shoulder, smiling at the funny little sounds that only a feeding child makes. Aeolmar kept talking, telling his son stories about his own older brothers, until Latera stirred.

"Did I... did I fall asleep?" Latera had asked, unsurprised at having the baby against her. Aeolmar remembered that she'd been holding him when she was last awake.

"That was days ago," Aeolmar said against her ear. "Wren gave you something to sleep, and I didn't want to disturb you. I've been giving him goat milk."

"He's been suckling from a goat?"

"My finger."

"Did he like that?"

"Not especially." Aeolmar rested his cheek against her temple, enjoying her warm skin. "I missed you."

"I've been right here." She glanced sidelong at him, and he couldn't help but smile. Trust Latera to scold him while he feared for her life. "What's his name?"

"He doesn't have one yet." In response to her arched brow, he replied, "I wanted to wait for you."

As always, Latera heard what he left unsaid. "And if I'd died, would you have named him Latera?"

"Perhaps." He kissed her cheek, then leaned forward to regard the boy. "What would you like to call him?"

"I don't know," she said as she stroked the baby's head. "Those stories you were telling him. Who were they about?"

"My older brothers." Aeolmar laughed softly. "Tor and Fiornacht. I was telling our little one how good they were to me, and how he would be as good a brother as they were."

"Tell me about them," Latera said. With her free arm, she reached back and tangled her fingers in Aeolmar's hair. "What kind of men were they?"

"Tor was the eldest of us all," Aeolmar began, adjusting their position so Latera didn't have to stretch to touch him. "He looked just like my father, except that he was taller. He and Fiornacht were both taller than Father."

"Taller than you?"

"Much taller than me. I followed them like a lost puppy, wanting to do everything they did. From the time I could walk, I didn't give them a moment's peace."

"How did they react to their little pest?" Latera asked. He nipped her shoulder before he replied.

"As one would expect. Fiornacht was too busy to put up with me. He was always trying to impress the girls in the village—"

"Mm. Something you never did, I'm sure?" That remark earned her another nip.

"As I was saying," Aeolmar continued, "they were both kind, but it was Tor who took me everywhere. Anywhere. When I was small, I rode on his shoulders; when I was but half-grown, he taught me to ride a horse."

"Tor," Latera repeated. "How did he look? Like you?"

"No. I take after my mother. Tor had straw-colored hair and green eyes, like Father. Fiornacht did as well."

"Tor," Latera murmured, stroking the pale, downy hair on the baby's head. "That means mountain?"

"Mountain," Aeolmar confirmed. "Or strength, or wisdom."

"You faeries and your silly language," Latera chided. "One word should mean one thing." Aeolmar responded by nuzzling her neck, and repeating his oft-made but never carried out threat of punishing her for her insolence. A contented gurgle had issued forth from the now-sleeping baby, and Latera shifted him so she could take in the sight of their son.

"Three beautiful children," Latera murmured. "His hair's so pale. Do you think he'll take after your father?"

Aeolmar reached forward and stroked the baby's head. "It seems he might."

"He still needs a name."

"Would you prefer an elfin name?"

"No one speaks the elf language anymore," Latera replied. "Not even elves."

"True," he agreed, pressing his lips to her shoulder. "We could name him Harold, after your father," Aeolmar suggested. Latera's only response was a frown, and Aeolmar hadn't pressed the matter.

"Tor," Latera said with finality. "We will call him Tor."

***

Aeolmar stood on the balcony, his memories of the days following Tor's arrival threatened to overtake him. Then Latera's arms were about his waist, rousing him back to the present. *Tor must be settled for now.* She rested her cheek against Aeolmar's back and asked her mate what he was thinking.

"If I tell you, you won't like it," he replied.

"I'm told lots of things I don't care for. Tell me anyway." He turned around and caught her in his arms.

"I don't want you to bear another child," he said. Latera remained silent, but Aeolmar felt her back go rigid. "Beloved, it's not that I want to deny you more children. I just want you to be safe."

"But you are denying me all the same." She turned her face up to his, and he couldn't tell if she was sad or furious. Then she spoke, and the waver in her throat removed all doubt. "Don't you think I know the risks? Any mother could die in childbed. I remember it happening often in Gannera."

"It may be a common death among humans, but not among faeries," he said. "Wren has spoken with Mallia, who claims it's not common among elves, either."

"That woman hates me," Latera grumbled. "As if I intended to birth Mara at the highest point of the palace, or Ember in the middle of a field, just to belittle her midwifery skills. And I have spoken about this at length with Asherah; she feels that Finlay's birth would have been all the smoother without the crazed healer bustling about." She went on about the many indignities Mallia had imposed upon the queen as she labored with Finlay, and Aeolmar smiled at his mate's rant.

"Be that as it may, I don't ever want to see you so close to death again," he said once she finished. "I've read more of the scrolls."

"And?" she prompted.

"My father's mother died shortly after he and his brother were born. She was small, like you," he said.

"But I am not her," Latera stated. "And your father was a twin. A rarity among faeries, to be sure."

"A rarity, yes, but not so rare he wasn't one," Aeolmar said softly. "And twins are much more common among humans. What if..." His voice trailed off as he tightened his arms about her, until she thumped his shoulder so he would ease up.

"I can't help but hold you tightly," Aeolmar said as he dropped his arms. He sat on the stone bench and pulled her to his lap. "Beloved, do you want more children so badly you'd risk your life?"

"Of course not," Latera replied. She was silent for a time, fingering the edge of Aeolmar's sleeve. "What if I don't consult with you when I want another?" His brows pinched, so she continued, "Perhaps I won't tell you once I'm with child, either. I'll just surround myself with food, and all will talk about the First Hunter's fat mate."

"Perhaps," he whispered in her ear, "I'll withhold from you that which causes the child to sprout in the first place."

"Not likely," she said around her laughter. "You're nothing if not insatiable."

"If it kept you alive, I'd gladly go without." Latera arched a delicate brow, so he amended, "Maybe not gladly, but I would. Beloved, can't you see what you mean to me? I would be lost without you. I was lost until I found you." He held her gaze until she frowned, and laid her head on his chest.

"So not one more, not ever?" she asked. "That's an awfully long time."

"It is," he agreed. "As it would be an awfully long time for me to be without you, should anything take you from me." Latera sighed, and kissed the underside of his chin.

"You really think I'd leave you?"

"No. I only know that I don't ever want to lose you."

Latera laid her cheek against his throat, her head tucked under his chin. "Mar..."

"We should leave," Aeolmar said suddenly.

"Right now?" Latera asked. "It will be dark soon. Can this journey wait till morning?"

He ignored her sarcasm. "Do you remember, before we had the children, how we once talked of leaving Teg'urnan?" he murmured, his lips against her hair. "We'd leave the palace and live in a cottage by the sea."

"I remember," she replied.

"We can still make that happen."

"Could we really abandon Asherah?"

"If she needed us, she would send a message," he replied. "I would not ignore a directive from my queen."

"And if she ordered us not to leave?"

Aeolmar exhaled heavily. "Then, I don't know. I don't think she would deny us."

"But what if she did?" Latera looked up at her mate, her pale eyes seeing his intent rather than his words. "What do you mean to accomplish by leaving Teg'urnan? If we'd been all alone in a cottage by the sea, I'd likely be dead, and Tor along with me."

Aeolmar pulled her close; he did not like to be reminded that he'd nearly lost her, despite that it was ever present in his thoughts. "I just want you to be safe. The attacks of late, and the news from the north... I want you and the children to be safe. Is that such a terrible thing?"

"No." Latera was silent for a moment, busily raking her fingers through her mate's long hair, arranging it against his shoulder. "So, no more children, no more Teg'urnan—"

"Beloved—"

"I know. I don't want to lose you, either." At that, Aeolmar took her hand and kissed the tips of her fingers. "What if we wait until Tor's grown?" she suggested. "Once he's a man, we can discuss children again. And as for leaving, let's wait until we're certain that Asherah's done with those herbs. I would never forgive myself if we abandoned her before she's truly recovered."

"I will agree to both," Aeolmar murmured as he bent to kiss her. When they parted, Latera rose and pulled him to his feet. "Where are you taking me?"

"Just because we've agreed to discuss children at a later date, doesn't mean I cannot try to sway you now," she replied with a glance over her shoulder. "And I need to make sure that you won't—what was it?—*withhold* things from me."

Chapter Twenty-Eight

Mara was terrified.

Yesterday, as she read the scrolls along with the rest of her family, her parents had started teasing each other. Aeolmar and Latera were often playful, though Mara had frequently expressed her displeasure when they took things a bit too far for her tastes, but she wasn't just annoyed at her parents for acting like young lovers rather than the mated pair they were. She had worried that her mother would turn her teasing words toward her daughter, and tell Aeolmar how she'd been making time with Kemen.

She was fairly certain that her father was unaware that she had been found in Kemen's arms—found by her mother, no less—her certainty due to the fact that Kemen was still breathing. A single careless comment could change everything, and not only send her father charging after Kemen to do or say Cydia knew what, and thus destroy Mara's new and fragile relationship with him.

So Mara had left the family chamber on the pretense of being annoyed by her parents' unending innuendos, when in truth she was certain that if she'd remained her tryst with a certain hunter would be revealed to her father at any moment. She spent the night in Wren's chamber, as she'd often done after Tor's birth, and had found a few small diversions to occupy her morning. Now noon approached, along with the midday meal which her family typically ate together. While Mara's presence wasn't exactly a requirement, she did not want to risk being away too long. What if her mother assumed that she was off somewhere with Kemen? What if she thought she was *doing something* with Kemen?

Mara gulped a lungful of air, squared her shoulders, and then strode into her family's chamber. Her mother was seated in her favorite chair before the hearth with Tor nestled upon her lap, and both of them were watching Aeolmar as he sat on the floor, the scrolls fanned about around him. He was intently studying one of the parchments, and Mara's curiosity overrode her caution. After all, it was her family history, too.

"Where's Ember?" Mara asked.

"With Finlay," Aeolmar replied. "She got bored with the scrolls."

"Have you learned anything new?" Mara asked without preamble as she sat beside her father. Latera smiled a greeting at her oldest, and Tor gurgled approvingly.

"I've learned so many things," Aeolmar replied, then he pushed a parchment toward her. "This is a copy of the king's edict, which ordered all the priestesses of Parthalan to abandon their charges and serve only in the Great Temple. It was this edict that made my mother leave her temple in the east and come to Teg'urnan. If not for this, my parents might never have met."

Mara carefully read the scroll, which was written in the formal language and stiff quill marks of all court documents. Her own script was a flowery scrawl, being that she favored a brush over a quill. Below the proclamation was a list of all the temples and the priestesses expected from each. Mara read until she found mention of her grandmother, along with two other familiar names: Atreynha, and Alyon.

"Your mother served with Atreynha in a different temple?" Mara asked.

"Yes," Aeolmar replied. "Atreynha says that my mother was born there."

"And Alyon?" Mara looked toward her mother.

"I don't believe she is the same Alyon who keeps the temple in Gannera," Latera replied. "I imagine that the Alyon mentioned in the scroll was the ancestor of the one I met."

"I suppose that's possible," Mara said. "Then Atreynha hasn't always been the High Priestess here?"

"Atreynha was the Mother Priestess at the eastern temple," Aeolmar replied. "Before Atreynha came to Teg'urnan, a priestess called," Aeolmar scanned the parchment for the priestess's name, "Sarelle oversaw the Great Temple."

"What happened to her?" Mara asked.

"I don't know," Aeolmar asked. "I've not yet found a record of her fate."

"Perhaps she fell when the demons attacked," Latera suggested, and Mara shivered. How anyone had managed to survive the *mordeths* that attacked the Great Temple was beyond her. And to think, her grandsire had killed almost all of them.

"The rest of the fallen are recorded here," Aeolmar said, shuffling through the parchments until he found the proper reference. "Why wouldn't they record the High Priestess's fate? By all the living gods, who were these inept scribes?"

"What does that even mean?" Mara grumbled under her father's string of curses. "Saying 'living gods' makes no sense. Gods are eternal." To her surprise, Aeolmar paused in his griping.

"There were many gods that ruled before Olluhm and Cydia danced together upon the green meadow," Aeolmar replied. "When Cydia became heavy with Solon, Olluhm cast the old gods from the sky and claimed the sun's path as his alone. Since then Parthalan has belonged to Olluhm, though a few scraggly priests still keep to the old ways, worshipping the fallen."

"Your grandsire once killed gods?" Latera asked with a raised brow.

"Yes," Aeolmar said. "I suppose he did."

"Those priests you mentioned, the ones keeping the old ways," Latera continued. "Isn't Kemen's father associated with them?"

"Yes," Aeolmar replied. "His father, Krylle, is the High Priest of the old pantheon. It's why Asherah didn't want Kemen assigned to the palace contingent. She once worried Krylle was trying to depose her."

"Has Krylle ever deposed a ruler in the past?"

Aeolmar snorted. "I doubt Krylle could muster the means to do so. Olluhm is strong, and has been worshipped for thousands of years. What could a few dead gods do against him?"

Latera shrugged. "Elves have no gods to speak of, and look at all we accomplish."

Aeolmar grabbed Latera's foot and kissed her ankle. "Elves also have the sense to stay away from the likes of Krylle. And elfin women are, by far, the most beautiful in all the nine realms."

"Mar, you'll make me blush."

"Can't we ask Atreynha? About Sarelle, I mean," Mara asked, her voice calm though her heart thumped away in her breast. "Surely she must know what happened to her predecessor." In truth, she couldn't care less what had befallen this Sarelle, or about any living or dead gods, but she needed her parents distracted from anything even remotely resembling a possible suitor of hers. Especially if that suitor happened to be Kemen.

"We can," Aeolmar said, then he got to his feet. "We will go to the temple and ask Atreynha directly," he said decisively. Latera looked pointedly at the heaps of scrolls he left on the floor, but said nothing. "Coming, beloved?"

"You two go along," she replied. "Tor will be hungry soon." Mara nearly laughed aloud; this was just what she'd wanted, both of her parents distracted. The fact that they'd be apart from one another was an added bonus.

Aeolmar and Mara left the chamber and headed toward the center of the palace, and soon enough, she and her father were inside the Great Temple.

"First Hunter," Atreynha greeted. "Hello, Mara. Have you come for more scrolls?"

"Actually, we're come with a question," Aeolmar replied. "Everything about the Battle for Teg'urnan is recorded, save for what happened to the High Priestess. Do you know what happened to her?"

The High Priestess's eyes darkened at their words, but she answered readily. "Sarelle's fate is not recorded because no one knows what truly happened to her. She was..." Atreynha swallowed, and looked away. "She was in collusion with Sahlgren. It was she who allowed the *mordeths* passage into the temple, and she who trapped the priestesses inside."

Mara gasped, and clutched Aeolmar's forearm. "The *mordeths* my father killed," Aeolmar stated, and Atreynha nodded. "Was my mother here when it happened?"

Atreynha looked at Aeolmar for a long moment, as if she was choosing what should and should not be revealed. Then she walked toward the altar, beckoning for Aeolmar and Mara to follow. "Did you know that the original altar, the one Cydia reclined upon while Olluhm built the temple, and then the palace, around her, was destroyed during the Battle for Teg'urnan?"

"I have heard that tale," Aeolmar replied. "Destroyed by the demons, wasn't it?"

"Caol'nir himself was the one who destroyed the altar," Atreynha said softly. "He forced his way inside the sealed temple doors—to this day, I've no idea how he managed it—searching for Alluria. He found her there," Atreynha halted before the steps to the dais, and looked up at the altar, "beset by Mersgoth."

"Beset?" Aeolmar repeated.

"Mersgoth sought Alluria out," Atreynha continued. "Your mother, being that she was Olluhm's child, was unique and valuable in the demon's eyes. Sahlgren had offered to give her to Ehkron as payment for the demon's assistance in his...his schemes. Then the *mordeth-gall* was killed in the mortal realm, and Mersgoth decided that he should claim his master's prize." Atreynha made a low sound in her throat, a sob masked with a cough.

"And Sarelle was part of this?" Mara asked.

"Sarelle, our loving High Priestess, had encouraged Sahlgren's plot," she continued. "She went so far as to offer Alluria a place in the temple after she had bound herself to Caol'nir, and dressed her in a bright green and gold robe so Mersgoth was sure to know her. She made Alluria a target."

"What did Mersgoth do to my mother?" Aeolmar asked, his gaze on the altar stone.

"Beat her nearly to death," Atreynha replied. "When Caol'nir found them, the beast was burning his mark into Alluria's leg. Caol'nir castrated the demon, then in his fury he struck the altar stone and cleaved it in two."

"She was marked," Aeolmar said. "That's how Mersgoth found her."

Atreynha nodded. "We—Rahlle and I—tried everything we knew to remove the mark, but nothing we did made any difference. Alluria even tried cutting it out of her, but when her skin healed, the mark returned." Atreynha took Aeolmar's hands. "You must believe me, Aeolmar, we did everything we could for Alluria. We did not leave her to die by the demon's hand."

"I believe you," Aeolmar replied. "From what I know of *mordeth's* marks, there likely wasn't anything to be done. That must have been terrible for her, living with such a fate."

Atreynha nodded. "It was why they left Teg'urnan. They wanted to be together for as long as possible before Mersgoth found her."

"Why didn't they track and kill Mersgoth?" Aeolmar asked. "Why did they just wait for death?"

"Caol'nir and his father wanted to, but Alluria forbade it," Atreynha replied. "She feared that if they did that, Mersgoth may prevail. Once she found Caol'nir, and left the temple for him, she couldn't imagine living her life without him."

"Like Latera and I," Aeolmar murmured.

"Yes, Alluria easily loved Caol'nir as much as you love your mate."

When both Atreynha and Aeolmar fell silent, Mara asked, "Did Caol'nir kill Sarelle?"

"No, child," Atreynha replied, Mara's words having roused her. "Alluria herself saw to Sarelle's punishment." Both Mara and Aeolmar looked at Atreynha quizzically; from all of Aeolmar and Atreynha's accounts, Alluria was the gentlest of souls, hardly the sort to dole out punishments.

"How does one punish a High Priestess?" Mara asked.

Atreynha cleared her throat. "Caol'nir had come across one of the portals used by demons. Alluria took it, and used it to send Sarelle to the underworld." Mara gasped aloud; banishment to the realm of fire and torment was a terrible fate, despite the fact that it was a fate Sarelle richly deserved.

"Amazing," Aeolmar said. "Is she there still?"

"No one knows," Atreynha replied. "I've heard nothing of her since that day."

Mara looked at the sacred altar, amazed that her grandsire had destroyed the original, further amazed that her grandmother had been marked by a *mordeth* and survived the ordeal. "Must we be descended from gods?" she murmured. "It almost seems that because of them, we are destined for terrible fates."

Aeolmar nodded, pulling his daughter closer. "At times, it does indeed."

Chapter Twenty-Nine

Finlay entered the royal chamber, smiling when he saw Asherah seated at her map table. She'd been more herself of late, behaving like Parthalan's queen instead of a sickly woman dependent on Mallia's herbs. He wondered if that was due to her realizing she knew Aeolmar's parents, and remembered what her life was like before the burden of ruling became too much.

Finlay cleared his throat. Asherah glanced up, and said, "Waiting to be announced, my lord?"

"A trumpeter would be nice." He sat next to his mate, brought her hand to his mouth, and kissed her knuckles. "What's that?" he asked, indicating a bundle of herbs on the corner of the desk.

"Oh, that." Asherah fingered the ribbon that bound the bundle. "Mallia brought it by earlier. She said if I toss it into the fire, it will release a calming scent. She claims it's similar to the incense used in the temple on feast days."

"And she thinks you need calming?"

"Apparently so." Asherah tugged on the ribbon. "She means well, Mallia does. It's not her fault I used more of the dreamwort than necessary. She was only trying to help me."

"Sher." Finlay squeezed her hand. "If you need the herbs—"

"I don't. Not anymore." She pushed the bundle to the far end of the table and drew her map closer. "Will the Raelian envoy be here soon?"

"That's what I came to tell you. They sent a herald on ahead, and he's advised they will be here before the elder sun goes to rest."

"Good, good." Asherah leaned closer to the map. Finlay did as well, and saw it depicted the border between Rael and Tingu, and their shared border with the Northern Waste.

"Wondering what's happening up there?"

"Wondering how we'll survive whatever's up there. Wondering if Leran's all right."

"If anyone can deal with the Northern Waste, it's him."

Asherah leaned against Finlay's shoulder. "You're right. And I need to ready myself to greet our guests."

Asherah stood and rolled up her map and moved to replace it with the rest; as an afterthought, she grabbed the bundle of herbs and set it above the hearth. She then set the map in its place, turned to face Finlay, and collapsed.

Chapter Thirty

Mara caught herself against the edge of the stone railing. "Afraid you'll fall?" Kemen asked.

"Among other things."

They were standing on a balcony above the south side of the palace square. It was a favorite spot of Kemen's, for even though it was a public balcony it was off an infrequently used corridor, which meant he had his privacy. It also meant that he had an unobstructed view of the square, which is how he discovered Mara had been watching him.

Now, he drew her auburn hair away from where her neck met her shoulder and kissed the gentle curve. "You're safe. I've got you."

"I know." Mara wanted to close her eyes and enjoy his attention, but she couldn't stop staring at the walkway across from them. It was an open gallery that led to the royal chambers, and she knew the moment she looked away, her father would stride down the gallery and spot her. Or worse, spot Kemen kissing her.

"You haven't given me an answer."

"I'm still thinking about it."

The answer Kemen sought was whether or not Mara would accompany him to The Swan, the tavern most favored by the hunters, that evening. Even though Mara had never been inside The Swan she'd walked by it on many occasions, and was certain it was safe. Not only was it in a quiet part of the village, at any given time one could find three or more hunters inside, and Mara knew all of them would have her back. What she didn't know was if she wanted to go there with Kemen.

Well, I do want to go. I just don't know if I should. If Kemen and Mara went to such a public place as The Swan it would be tantamount to declaring their relationship to the whole of Teg'urnan. Setting aside the fact that they didn't have a relationship—not a real one, not yet—Mara knew that it would be less than a day before the news reached her father. She'd always told her parents everything, and while her mother knew about Kemen, she knew if her father heard the news from anyone other than herself it would break his heart.

I will have to tell him myself. If he forbids me from seeing Kemen... No, I won't speak to him. I will speak to Mother first. She'll know what to do.

A banging door caught Mara's attention. She looked toward the gallery and saw two *saffira* run from the royal chamber. A moment later, Attia rushed into the rooms, the door banging shut behind her.

"What's all that about?" Kemen wondered. Before Mara could speak, she noticed activity in the square below.

"And this," she said, nodding toward the gates. A group of warriors wearing Rael's colors, but flying Tingu's flag, were entering the square.

"Envoy from Rael," Kemen said. "Aeolmar summoned them a few sennights ago."

"Why are they flying Tingu's flag?" Mara asked.

"Rumor is Leran rescued them from whatever monsters were harrying them," Kemen replied. "Aeolmar heard the rumors and wanted to hear the truth of it. I'm glad I'm not in the Raelian's place."

"Me, too." Mara glanced at the royal gallery. Her gut told her something had happened to the queen. Her father would want to know if Asherah had taken ill, and when Mara told him about the queen, she could easily mention her outing with Kemen...

"I have an errand," Mara said.

"An errand that will keep us from The Swan?"

"I... don't think so." Mara turned around and linked her hands behind Kemen's neck. "Meet me at the base of the steps in an hour?"

"An hour it is." Kemen kissed her forehead, then her cheeks, and finally her lips. "Don't be late."

***

Mara knocked on the royal chamber's main door; times past she would have gone to the private door reserved for close friends, but Mara had never done that without one of her parents, and she didn't want to learn the hard way whether or not she qualified as close. A bare moment after she'd knocked, the king himself flung the door wide.

"Mara," he said, peering into the corridor behind her. "Are you alone?"

"Yes." When Finlay looked at her expectantly, she continued, "I saw Attia rush down the gallery. Is the queen all right?"

Finlay frowned, then he stepped aside and motioned her inside. Once he'd shut the door behind her, he said, "Asherah is fine, at least for now."

"Is there anything I can do?" Mara asked. "I can fetch Mallia, or Wren, if needed."

"I don't know," Finlay began, pausing when Attia emerged from the bedchamber.

"My lord, she's asking for you," Attia said, then her gaze landed on Mara. "Oh, hello. Are you here for your sister? She and the prince are back from the lake, and are having a snack in the kitchens."

"Oh, that must be lovely," Mara murmured, feeling well and truly out of place and wishing she'd never come.

"Mara came by to ask after the queen." Finlay turned to Mara. "If you wouldn't mind waiting a moment, I'll ask Asherah if she's up for a visitor."

"No, no, let her rest," Mara said. "But please send for me if I can help."

Finlay smiled tightly, then he and Attia disappeared into the bedchamber. Mara turned to leave when she spied the queen's garden door ajar. After a quick glance toward the bedchamber door, Mara made for the garden. She knew just what she needed for her evening with Kemen.

Chapter Thirty-One

Aeolmar Speaks

I was staring up at the sky, squinting toward the glowing orbs that I was more closely related to than I'd ever imagined. Even though Olluhm and Solon were our gods, I'd never paid the suns much mind. When I'd been a child at Mama's knee, it had always been her tales of Cydia that fascinated me. Now, I couldn't stop looking at the suns, hoping to find a hint of a face, perhaps an eye turned earthward. Despite the fact that I detected nothing, and wasn't surprised at that, I couldn't bring myself to turn away.

"Tor is sleeping."

Latera whispered the words as she slid her arms around my waist, rousing me from my contemplation of the child sun. Not so long ago, I'd thought I was the son of a farmer and his patient mate. Now, I knew that my mother had once been a priestess, and that she'd been fathered by Olluhm himself, and that my own father was one of the greatest warriors Parthalan had ever known, arguably a greater warrior than Solon himself. The kingdom—no, the whole realm—could have been my father's for the asking, but he gave it all up and had his name stricken from the records, all so he could have a life with my mother.

I would do the same, and more, for Latera. But then, I'd known that bit for quite some time.

"Is he?" I asked, gathering my mate against me. Before Latera came into my life I'd been rendered to nothing by my family's murder, a hollow shell fueled by grief and vengeance. Now, I was a man who looked forward to every day, since it meant another day with her. "Where is Ember?"

"With Finlay."

"Older or younger?" I pressed.

She thought for a moment. "Probably just the younger, along with Attia. She took them swimming."

"Mmm." I bent down to nuzzle her neck, then while she was distract-ed, I picked her up and carried her inside. She thumped my chest, but I didn't carry her far, and soon we were both settled on the cushions before the hearth. "And how do you propose we pass the time?"

"However you'd like," Latera replied, doing that thing with her eyes that drove me mad. The first time she'd looked at me that way she'd been hardly more than a child, though she had a strength that belied her few seasons. She'd just accepted my offer of entering the sola *as a* nuvi. *To this day, I wonder if she realizes how happy she made me.*

***

"Tell me, what goes on there?" she had asked. "In this sola. *"*

"*Training, mostly,*" *I'd replied.* "*You'll lean various forms of combat, along with stealth and woodcraft.*"

"*Woodcraft?*" *she repeated, her delicate brows peaking.*

"*Demons don't tend to frequent cities,*" *I replied, then cursed as I shifted and pain bloomed across my leg. I'd taken a spear to the thigh earlier that day, not a deep wound, but it was the length of my hand. After I'd been struck by the spear, I'd taken a fall that had left me unconscious, and Latera had taken care of both my leg and my head wounds while I slept. I'd awakened to find the stable girl fighting off three demons. She did well.*

Upon seeing my face twist in pain, Latera leapt into action, grabbing fresh bandages and kneeling before me. Gingerly, she peeled away the blood-soaked packing, those coppery brows of hers furrowed in concern. "*I think this may need to be stitched,*" *she mumbled as she swabbed at the wound.*

"*No.*" *Gods, I hated stitches.* "*A tight dressing will be fine. Here, let me.*"

Latera watched as I wound the bandages around my leg as tight as a tourniquet, her lips pursed but silent. Of course, she'd been correct in that it should be sewn, being that the wound was rather close to my knee and would likely reopen whenever I walked, but she held her peace. Little had I known, she was only biding her time.

"*Who will train me?*" *she asked suddenly.*

"*The instructors,*" *I replied without looking up from the wound.* "*There are many of them in the sola, schooled in all sorts of—*"

"*But who will teach me the rest?*"

"*The rest of what?*" *I asked.*

"*The rest of what it means to be a Parthian. I imagine there's more to it that swordplay and demons, yet I only know how to brush horses and mend saddles.*" *I halted, bandage in mid-turn, and looked up at her.*

Even then, I hadn't quite believed that Latera was mortal, what with her delicately pointed ears and large, pale eyes, but that hadn't been her point. She felt like an outsider, a feeling I was all too familiar with.

"Latera, you already know," I'd said, taking her hands in mine. They were so small, her palms roughened by her years spent in the barn, her bones as delicate as any bird's. They were the loveliest hands I'd ever seen. Still are. "You already have all the qualities of a Parthian."

"I only wish I had more to offer the queen than the skills of a stable hand," she said.

"From what's said in Brennus, you're the best stable hand in all the nine realms. Ingvarr told me as much."

"Well, I am good at mending torn leather. Once, I mended a lord's saddle so neatly even he couldn't find the tears." She cocked her head to the side, and gave me the most innocent of faces. "If I told you of something that needed mending, would you allow me to complete the work?"

Then she'd done it, that thing with her eyes that's somewhere between a flutter and a heavy gaze, and conquered me in that moment. Latera laughs when I mention it now, but it's the truth: one look and I was hers.

"Of course," I murmured; in that moment, I would have granted her anything. What's that, you'd like me to pluck the moon from the sky and give it to you on a silver platter? Here you are, my love. While I'd been debating how to offer her my heart, she'd freed her hands from mine, and gently touched my leg.

"This needs mending." I glanced down, and she already had the bandage halfway unwound. "Don't worry. I'll make the stitches small."

***

She had, and while I still bear the scar, the wound had healed cleanly and without infection. My lovely stable girl has been caring for me ever since.

Now, Latera was fluttering her eyes at me again, and I wondered if there was something more on her agenda than a stolen afternoon. Then she kissed me, and I was pleased to be wrong. Tor sleeping and Ember away with Finlay meant that we were alone, there was the most color in Latera's cheeks since she had been heavy with child, and—

"Mother?"

And Mara, our beautiful eldest daughter, felt the need to converse with her mother at that very moment. "Here, sweetheart," Latera called, wiggling herself upright as she adjusted her bodice. Mara rounded the small partition between the entrance and the hearth, barely hiding her annoyance over finding her parents wrapped in each other's arms.

"Really, what were you two doing now?" she muttered, taking a seat across from us.

"Nothing you won't be doing with your mate someday," I replied, earning myself another round of thumps from Latera's little fists while Mara's cheeks went scarlet. I grabbed Latera's hands and kissed her knuckles, then turned my attention back to Mara. I noticed the white flowers wound in her hair, her new calfskin boots, and wondered if there was a formal event I'd forgotten about.

"Shouldn't you be with the Raelians?" Mara asked.

"What Raelians?" Latera echoed.

"They were summoned to report on the state of the north, specifically its border defenses," I replied. "And no, I'm not supposed to be there. Finlay claims I intimidate them."

"You like intimidating them," Latera said.

"I like getting answers," I said. "How did you know about the envoy?"

"I saw them arrive," Mara said, then she dropped her gaze. My daughters were both brilliant, but neither had ever shown any interest in statecraft. Mara was using the Raelian's as an excuse to start a conversation, and I needed to know why.

"And what troubles my daughter today?" I asked.

"I-I wanted to speak with Mother," she replied, her eyes darting to Latera's before they focused on her hands. Like her mother, Mara's hands trembled when she was nervous, and she was doing a good job of hiding the fact. Anyone other than her parents likely wouldn't have noticed.

"What's wrong?" I demanded as Latera asked, "Is it Kemen?"

"Kemen?" I glared from Latera to Mara; clearly, there were things happening. Things they had kept from me. "Has he done something to you?"

"No," Mara shrieked, then appealed to her mother for help. "You see? Father hates him!"

"Aeolmar does not hate him," Latera said decisively, throwing a stern glare in my direction for good measure. "Anything you can say to me, you can say in front of your father." Mara remained silent, her eyes wary. Smart girl; only a fool would believe that I held anything other than contempt for Kemen, who'd been Brynne's second while Latera had served her time at the Eastern Border. He'd taken a liking to Latera and chased her relentlessly at the border, and for a bit of time after they had returned to Teg'urnan.

He was also a large part of the reason why Asgeloth had fallen. Kemen had undertaken a suicidal quest to inform the mordeth-gall that the traitor Harek's plans were moving forward, and that the time was ripe for the demons to strike Teg'urnan. Kemen had managed to complete his mission without dying in the process, and upon his return to the palace he'd been lauded as a hero. I still didn't like him. The only thing that kept me from actively hating him was my reluctance to waste my efforts.

Latera jabbed her elbow into my ribs; clearly, not admitting to my strong dislike of Kemen was in my best interests. "She's right," I said, and Mara's shoulder's relaxed. "I won't haul off and beat Kemen. Unless that's what you're here for?" I asked hopefully.

"Why would you beat him?" Mara demanded.

"Don't listen to your father," Latera said. "He thinks he's helpful, but he's not."

"I'm not? Not ever?"

"It's all right," Latera reassured Mara. Since Latera was completely ignoring me, I pulled her onto my lap. Another eyeroll from Mara later, we were back to normal. "Have you two been in the tower room again?"

That had my attention. "Our tower room?" I murmured in Latera's ear. She hushed at me out of the corner of her mouth, her signal for me to behave.

"No," Mara admitted. "We were only there the one time." That was a relief, depending on what had happened during that single visit. "But he wants to bring me somewhere."

"What's wrong with that?" Latera inquired in that genial way of hers. Mara bit her lip and stared at the empty hearth.

"I don't know if I should go with him," she replied.

"Don't you want to get to know him?" Latera pressed.

"I think so. But..." Her voice trailed off, then she regarded Latera and I. Our affectionate nature was a constant source of embarrassment to Mara, who'd caught us in compromising positions more than once. I take full blame for the incidents; after all, I can hardly hold Latera's loveliness against her. "I don't know if he's my mate."

"What?" Latera asked, echoing my own confusion.

"I mean, how do I know if he will be my mate?" Mara clarified. "I enjoy being with him, but... What if it's not him?"

"*Does that really matter right now?*" Latera asked. "*You cannot simply enjoy his company?*"

"*I think he may want to take things further.*" Mara chanced a look in my direction, but I held my tongue. Barely. "*And I don't want to do anything with him that I only want to do with my mate.*"

Ah. My precious, perfect daughter wanted to remain chaste until she found her one true mate, and not waste her virginity on someone like Kemen. Suddenly, this conversation was a good deal more appealing to me.

"*Mara, you cannot make such distinctions,*" Latera was saying. "*It may be a long, long time before you meet a man you love, and who loves you in return.*"

"*You said you were sixteen when you met Father.*"

"*That's true,*" she conceded. "*But if he hadn't happened by that stable, I would likely be there still.*" Mara nodded, then resumed staring at the hearth. "*Something else is bothering you,*" Latera observed. Mara sighed; attempting to keep something from Latera was like trying to keep a stream from flowing. You could dam it, yes, but the water would push itself up and over, eventually washing away all your efforts.

"*Kemen has been with so many women. The saffira, they talk,*" she added, then fell silent. "*What if... what if I'm just not what he likes?*"

"*What if nothing,*" I said. From the way they jumped, I wondered if they'd both forgotten I was there. "*Do not consider, not even for a moment, that you wouldn't measure up. If a man loves you, truly loves you, it matters not if he's bedded a thousand women. Only you will matter.*" Latera smiled at me, and leaned against my chest a bit more heavily than before.

"*You see?*" Mara sat bolt upright, perching on the edge of her chair. "*I want silly, sloppy love, the sort you two have. When you look at Father, anyone can see how you adore him. And he adores you.*"

"You adore me?" I asked, and Latera's smile widened. Now she was making herself at home on my lap, and I resisted the urge to tell Mara we were done. At any rate, we needed to move this conversation along.

"You know, Ember thinks Kemen is one of the most handsome men in the palace," Latera said.

"Ember is eight," I said. "What, are we now going to ask this wise child's opinion regarding military campaigns and border skirmishes?"

"That's what I said," echoed Mara. Latera slid her gaze from our indignant daughter to me.

"The only man she claims to be more handsome is you," she said, eyeing me as if I was a horse up for auction.

"Ember thinks I'm handsome?" I leaned back against the cushions, flush with pride. "She is a smart girl."

At that, Mara shot me a withering glare worthy of her mother. "Regardless, I don't think I can judge matters of such import on whether or not Ember thinks a man is attractive."

"Besides, Mara," Latera said, still wiggling into place against me, "it would be unusual for someone of Kemen's years to be untouched. You can't eliminate people because of what happened before they knew you."

"Finlay has only been with the queen," I offered, and was rewarded with two quizzical stares. "In the High Desert, where he hails from, it's still the custom to go to one's mate chaste."

"I didn't know that," Latera murmured. I imagine not many did. "Does this mean you'll be taking a trip south?" Latera asked Mara. "It may be your only hope."

"Perhaps I shall," she replied, not letting her mother goad her, then she added, "He—Kemen—wants to take me to The Swan."

"The tavern in the village?" I asked, and she nodded. "Mara, there's nothing wrong with The Swan. I've been there with the queen."

"Was that when you were her lovemate?" Mara asked with perfect innocence. Latera went rigid in my arms, but said nothing. "Everybody knows," she added. Yes, I suppose everyone would. Everyone, but Latera.

"It was a long time ago," was all I said; thankfully, Mara didn't press the matter.

"Well? Should I go?" she implored.

"Are you fond of him?" Latera asked, and Mara nodded. "I don't see what harm spending the afternoon with him can cause, whether or not he's meant to be your mate."

"Then I have your blessing?"

"Of course you do." Latera's voice was so calm and even, I entertained the notion that she wasn't angry with me. Mara got to her feet and said her goodbyes, and I tried to draw Latera deeper into my arms. It was like trying to folding a statue in two.

"Beloved," I murmured, kissing the back of her neck, "do you think Tor will sleep for a while yet?"

"You were her lovemate?"

Gone was her gentle tone, her words now grating like a rusty hinge. I tried to turn her, but she remained as unyielding as stone. "Yes."

"When?"

"After I was named First Hunter. After Esguth." I didn't add that I'd been hurting, still reeling from the death of my family, my only desire to destroy Mersgoth and avenge them. That part, she knew.

"How long?"

For a moment, I didn't know what she meant. "Eight winters."

"Eight winters?" Latera wrested free of my arms and spun to face me. "You were sleeping with the queen for eight winters *and you never thought to tell me?"*

"You told Mara that she shouldn't to hold someone's past against them," I shouted. "This all happened before I met you! Before you were born! It doesn't matter!"

"This is different," she said, her voice wavering. And she was right, it was different. "And I had to hear of it from our daughter! Does the entire palace know?"

"I've no idea," I shot back. "Can what went on in Asherah's bedchamber more than two centuries ago really be gossip today?"

"Apparently, it is." She wrapped her arms around her stomach, and turned away from me. "Eight winters," she repeated. "I hadn't known you that long when I bore Mara."

"Beloved," I said as I reached for her.

"Don't touch me," she spat over her shoulder.

"Latera, hear me," I pleaded. "I didn't think this mattered. Truly, I didn't. Please. Talk to me." She glanced over her shoulder, and I thought I'd won her over but no, she wasn't looking at me. Tor was fidgeting in his cradle, and Latera swept by me as she went to check on our son.

I exhaled heavily, squeezing my eyes shut as I balled my hands into fists. Should I have told Latera about my past with Asherah? Honestly, I thought she'd already known. I'd assumed that Asherah had told Latera herself; the two spent so much time together, and had been nearly inseparable after Ember and Finlay were born. Was that arrogance on my part, assuming that my former lover talked about me with my mate? Probably.

I drew another breath and resolved to take whatever lashing Latera felt I deserved, verbal or otherwise, but before I opened my eyes I heard the door. I spun around, calling her name, but Latera and Tor were gone.

Chapter Thirty-Two

Mara made her way toward the great square, the conversation she'd just had with her parents having increased her confidence tenfold. She did enjoy being with Kemen, and her mother was right—who cares if he'll end up as her mate? After all, this was only one evening spent in his company. What harm could come of it?

She found Kemen alone in the palace square, leaning against the palace wall near the grand steps. His usual companions, Luth and Elkin, were nowhere to be seen. When Kemen turned his glass green eyes toward her and smiled, Mara felt like she was the only woman in the world.

"Have you made up your mind about today, lady?" he inquired. Unlike the conversations he had with his fellow hunters, Kemen's speech was always formal with Mara. She took it as yet another sign that he saw her as an adult, not a child, and not as Latera and Aeolmar's daughter. Couple that with the way he spoke to her when they were alone...

"I think I'd like to go to The Swan with you," Mara declared. Kemen smiled and kissed her hand, his eyes never leaving hers. Mara wondered if everyone felt as if their bones were melting when they were kissed, or if it was just the effect Kemen had on her.

"Let's be off then."

Chapter Thirty-Three

Asherah Speaks

My latest attack passed quickly enough, though it had managed to scare Finlay half to death. I tried explaining to him—again—that when I'd suffered them before there was no lasting damage, but my words fell on deaf ears. He demanded to know when they'd last ended (a few centuries past, while Argent was still First Hunter), how many times I'd had them (gods, I'd lost count some time ago), and why I had never told him about my tendency to have these fits.

"I thought I was done with them," I replied. We'd moved to the sitting room, and I was searching out patterns in the polished wood armrests, concentrating on focusing my eyes. One of the more annoying aftereffects of my fits was a few hours of blurred vision. "I certainly hoped that was the case."

"And now you've had two in the space of a fortnight." Finlay cleared his throat. "Attia claims that these attacks are brought on by you searching for your past."

"We never knew exactly what precipitated them," I said. "However, they always seemed to occur after I'd spent some time in the archives. I believe we concluded that I'm overly sensitive to some form of vellum, though we could never pin down which one."

"What were you searching for this time?" he asked.

"I wasn't searching for anything today," I replied. "I only reviewed my maps."

"And, the time before?"

"I wasn't searching for anything then, either. I sent for Mallia to ask her a question about my dreams..." I paused and looked away, unwilling to tell my mate about the man in my dreams, the face I so desperately wanted to see again. "Honestly, it's been so long since I collapsed, I hardly remembered them occurring. I'm sorry I never told you."

Finlay made a soft sound in the back of his throat, and took my hands in his. "I've never felt so helpless," he said. "It was as if you were fading away before my eyes."

Before I could reassure him, Attia entered the room. "The envoy from Rael is here. I have them waiting in the outer chamber."

I moved to rise with Finlay, but he bade me remain. "I will handle this," he said, kissing my temple. "Rest now, love."

With that he departed, and Attia left a short time later to do whatever it was she did while her queen recovered from yet another of her mysterious episodes. Knowing her, she was ordering the cooks to prepare some sort of a feast to ward off possession. I hope it works.

After a time, I heard my private entrance open and shut with a bang, then Aeolmar's heavy footfalls as he stalked about the chamber. The parade of thuds often told me as much as his words, sometimes more. On that day they spoke of anger, and sadness.

Rather than calling for Aeolmar to join me, I entered my bedchamber and found him sitting cross-legged on the floor before the hearth. He was holding his head in his hands, his shoulders hunched inward as if they bore a heavy weight. I hadn't seen him that despondent since Latera had been swallowed up by a portal before our very eyes and deposited in the mortal realm, though at the time we were unaware of her destination. All we had known was that she was gone, possibly forever. Dearest Cydia, I hope her recovery hasn't taken a turn for the worse.

I sat behind him, watching the orange firelight reflect off his long hair, and resisted the urge to wrap my arms around him. It would only be comfort for a friend, nothing more, but with my cursed luck Finlay would choose that moment to walk into the room and catch me in the act. I didn't need to hear that lecture again.

"She knows," Aeolmar murmured, saving me the trouble of asking about the purpose of his visit. "I thought she knew all along, but she didn't. She knows now, and she is furious."

I had no idea what he was talking about. Who was this infuriated woman, and what bit of knowledge could cause such...

"You never told her?" I gasped. Only Latera was able to generate such sadness in my stoic First Hunter, and I could only think of one incident (well, series of incidents) capable of provoking such a response. "Aeolmar, that was foolish. Even for you."

"I am well aware of that, thank you," he growled. "What I need, my queen, is to know how to fix this." He said queen as if it were a curse; likely, to him, it was. I often wondered if Aeolmar regretted the time we'd spent together, if he wished he had never wandered into my tent that night all those winters ago when we were tracking Mersgoth. In truth, even after waking with him I had expected that we would carry on as if nothing occurred, but Aeolmar had scoffed at that notion. He further surprised me by being the most caring lover I had ever known, far more caring than...

Enough of that. "How did she learn about it?" *I ventured, hoping that Latera had heard it directly from Aeolmar's lips.*

"From Mara," *he replied.*

"Oh, Aeolmar," *I said, now forgoing whatever shreds of decorum were left between us as I leaned my brow against the back of his head and draped my arms over his shoulders.* "That is truly awful." *He shifted so his head rested against my knee, and we sat that way for a time.*

"How did Mara even learn of it?" *he asked at length.* "Do the fools inside this wretched palace have nothing else to speak of other than who has bedded whom? And to say these things to my daughter, that is truly vile."

"Perhaps no one told her specifically. Perhaps someone was speaking of your many conquests, and our names were merely said in the same breath," *I suggested. It was a most plausible argument, being that Aeolmar's prowess in the bedchamber was spoken of nearly as often as his skill on the battlefield. I'd heard the rumors myself, beginning on the first day he had set foot in Teg'urnan. Despite his outwardly disagreeable nature, people had always flocked to Aeolmar like so many moths to a flame.*

"What conquests?" *he asked.* "Since I've been in Teg'urnan, there have been no conquests to speak of. There was you, then there was no one. Not until Latera."

"How can that be," *I said, shocked by his declaration.* "I remember all those nights you spent at The Swan, how all the women..." *His mirthless laughter silenced me.*

"You thought I was like Argent." *Aeolmar turned about and faced me, his eyes fixing me in that dark blue gaze that I used to so easily lose myself in.* "I went there often, yes, but only in my quest for a quiet, drunken oblivion. I always came home to you."

My hand flew to my mouth, my heart beating away wildly within my breast. I had always assumed that Aeolmar frequented to the tavern to find a girl or two for the night, just as I had always assumed that I had never been enough for him. I thought that was why he had so readily pushed me toward Finlay, to be rid of me. "I... I never knew that."

He leaned forward and took my hands. "Believe me when I say that I was never unfaithful to you, and I would have died before I allowed anything to harm you. I still would."

I bit my lip, and dropped my gaze to our interlaced fingers. Gods, if he had said such things before... I tasted blood, and decided to speak before I chewed a hole through my lip. "You are nothing like Argent," I said, ignoring the swirling mass of emotions in my breast. "Nothing at all."

He smiled tightly. "If only my mate thought so," he grumbled, releasing my hands as he did so. "Gods, what if she leaves me?"

"You're bound," I pointed out, rather unnecessarily. "She can't leave you."

"She's not fae," Aeolmar said, his head again buried in his hands. "If Latera were wholly human then my immortality would hold her to me, but she's an elf."

"But the gods accepted you," I said. "Didn't they?" I'd never asked about Aeolmar and Latera's binding, since I had assumed that the ritual was the same for all, but his words gave me pause.

"Accept us they did, but elves follow no gods," he said. "We are bound, but Latera can sever our attachment whenever she chooses to."

I mulled over this latest piece of information. I was well aware that elves worshipped Nexa, but she was the first elf, certainly no goddess. My thoughts turned, as they still often did, to Lormac, my first king, my first mate; he had asked me to bind myself to him. Had he known that I would have been the only one bound?

"Then why do elves bother with the ritual at all?" I wondered aloud, for Latera was far from the first elf to undergo a binding. Silently, I wondered what Finlay's troll blood meant to our bond.

"*For one who carries the title Lady of Tingu, you know precious little about elves,*" *Aeolmar said dryly. I ignored that statement; after all, he was right. After Lormac's death and Leran's abject hatred of me, I had distanced myself from all things elfin in an attempt to preserve my sanity. If only it had worked.*

"*Does Latera know of this?*" *I asked.*

"*Yes,*" *Aeolmar replied. "Atreynha explained everything to us shortly after we were bound. I haven't withheld everything from her." He fell silent for a moment, staring at a fixed point somewhere past my shoulder. "She looked at me as if everything I'd ever told her was a lie. I would never lie to her."*

"*But you didn't exactly tell her the truth, did you?*" *I pointed out. That earned me a sharp glance, but I wasn't about to soften my words now. "Do you need to divulge to her each and every night you've spent with another? No, I think not. But Latera lives here, in the palace, and you should have told her about us. She deserves to hear of these things from your lips, not from some tired old gossip." Aeolmar muttered a few more things that one really shouldn't say about one's queen, but I took no offense. The way Aeolmar's mind worked, muttering meant that he was listening, and the fact that he was listening to me was rare indeed. While he grumbled about the mess he'd made, I brushed the hair back from his brow.*

"*I used to love running my fingers through your hair,*" *I said, long-forgotten memories of Alluria surfacing in my mind's eye. "I can't believe I've never noticed how much you look like your mother. Her hair was just the same, dark and soft and smooth." Aeolmar cocked an eyebrow at me, and I withdrew my hand. No, I really shouldn't be stroking his hair no matter who he reminded me of, not now that we were both mated elsewhere. Especially not now that I knew such bonds could be broken. "Would you like me to speak to Latera?" I offered.*

"No," Aeolmar said. "You're right; I should have told her long ago. I need to make my amends myself. I only hope she'll hear me." He stood and turned to leave, then paused and drew a tendril of my hair between his fingers. "I always played with your hair while you slept. The color of it has always fascinated me, so pale but not quite white. I wondered if you were born of the stars."

"Lormac called me his little star," I said. Aeolmar smiled, though it stayed far from his eyes, then strode off in search of his mate. Me, I resumed staring into the flames. My First Hunter had given me much to consider, much indeed.

Chapter Thirty-Four

"I've never seen it so busy," Kemen said.

"It certainly is crowded," Mara agreed.

They were standing in the doorway to The Swan, where it seemed that half of Parthalan had stopped by for a cool drink or toss of the dice. There wasn't a vacant chair or stool in the place, and those at the bar were standing shoulder to shoulder. "You'd think they just tapped the last cask of ale in Parthalan," Kemen added.

"I suppose we'll have to try again another day," Mara said, at once disappointed and relieved. Kemen, however, was not so easily dissuaded by a crowded room.

"Giving up so soon, lady?" Kemen asked.

"N-No," Mara replied, and Kemen chuckled.

"Wait here," he said, and Mara watched as Kemen wove between the patrons and ultimately ducked under the far end of the bar, then proceeded to snatch a bottle and two clay cups. He ducked under the bar again but was met by Mara's harsh stare, hands on her hips and foot tapping away.

"You are going to pay for that," she said.

"Of course I am," he replied, as he stepped back and placed a few coins on the bar.

"Will we be drinking in the street?" Mara asked when Kemen nudged her over the threshold and into the alley.

"In the clouds," he said with a wink, then he led her around to the back of the tavern and waved the bottle toward the vine-covered wall.

Blessed Cydia, he wants me to climb that wall. Dubiously, Mara eyed the roof. It seemed awfully far up from the ground.

"The roof is sound, as are the vines, if that's what you're wondering," Kemen said in response to her peaked brows. "As to your other concern, if you find my manners lacking, those inside will certainly hear you scream."

"I wasn't thinking that," she snapped; in truth, she was wondering if she could manage the climb without making a fool of herself.

"Then after you, my lady." Kemen shoved the cups and bottle inside his jerkin, and gestured to the wall with a flourish. Mara hesitantly tugged at the vines, which proved to be well and truly anchored to the wall. She sighed, grabbed onto the vines, and began her ascent. There were handholds aplenty, and Mara was nearing a second-story window when something occurred to her.

"Did you send me up first to get a look at my bottom?" she called over her shoulder.

"Absolutely," Kemen replied. Mara laughed so hard she had to stop climbing for a moment.

"Pay attention," Kemen said. "If you fall, you'll ruin our adventure."

"Forgive me," Mara said as she laughed harder. Kemen grunted and climbed on ahead of her, so Mara teased, "Proving your noble intentions?"

Kemen hauled himself onto the roof, then he turned and held out a hand. "Always, lady," he said, helping her onto the flat roof.

"You've been here before," Mara said as she looked about the space. Signs of life were everywhere, from empty bottles and cup to a few chairs, some of them battered to the point of being little more than kindling.

"Many like to sit beneath the sky and enjoy a quiet drink up here, away from the crowds below," he said. "I've been a time or two." They sat in the sheltered nook created where The Swan's roof abutted a much taller storehouse, and Kemen set the bottle and cups between them.

"Pilfering liquor isn't beneath a man of your stature?" Mara inquired.

"I paid for it."

"Because I made you."

"Lady, if you think I have any stature at all you've been woefully misinformed," he replied with a wink. "And this is no mere liquor; this is honey mead."

"Mead?" Mara replied. She accepted the cup and sipped the sweet liquid. "I thought mead was sour, and strong," she murmured, then took a second, larger sip.

"Most is, but honey mead is special," he said, catching Mara's free hand. "The legend is that Olluhm plied Cydia with sweet honey until she consented to kiss him."

"But I've already kissed you," Mara said.

"That you have," Kemen conceded, then he pressed her fingers to his lips. Mara felt her cheeks go hot, and raised her cup in order to hide them. "Careful," he warned, "for this mead is as strong as the rest. We don't want you to leave behind anything you'd rather not part with."

"Oh." Mara set down the cup, eyeing it as if it might move of its own accord. "Did you really once chase after my mother?" Kemen raised an eyebrow, but answered her anyway.

"Everyone chased after your mother, here in Teg'urnan and at the border," he replied. "She was like no one we had ever seen, a woman as beautiful as she is deadly. She saved my life, you know." He loosened his jerkin and pulled up his shirt, exposing the knot of scars he'd gotten when he was gored by one of Asgeloth's beasts. "You must know the story."

"I do."

"If not for her, I'd have died under that beast." Mara reached forward and trailed her fingers over the slippery skin beneath Kemen's ribs, noting the contrast between the pale scars and golden flesh.

"But it mattered not who chased after Latera, for her heart belonged only to the First Hunter," Kemen continued. "I teased her mercilessly, assuming she was just an infatuated girl. Little did I know that Aeolmar loved her in return."

"Is it odd for you to be here with me, after all that?" Mara asked before sipping more of her drink.

"Somewhat," he replied. "But it's a nice sort of odd."

"You don't speak like a warrior," she said. Dimly, she realized the mead was muddling her thoughts, but she was muddled to the point where it didn't bother her.

"I wasn't meant to be one," he said. "I'm from the east, where the old gods are still held in awe. My family keeps one of their temples."

"Old gods? You don't follow Olluhm?" She recalled her father ranting on about scraggly eastern priests. Kemen didn't seem scraggly.

"How can I not, when I see him above me every day?" He smiled and pressed his hand over Mara's, and she realized she was still touching him under his shirt. "No," he murmured when she tried to withdraw it, "closer." And closer he drew her, deep into his embrace while his mouth roamed her jaw and neck and breast.

"What's under here?" he murmured, hooking his finger at the neckline of Mara's leather riding vest. Mara grabbed his hand, caught in a wave of embarrassment. Vests were meant to be worn with intricately embroidered blouses beneath them called maiden's secrets, a custom Mara normally followed. The day Latera had caught them in the tower room, Kemen had expressed his approval over a blouse emblazoned with bright red and yellow birds, but Mara had snatched this particular vest from her mother's wardrobe because she thought its tight fit enhanced her breasts. Since Latera was so much smaller than her daughter, none of Mara's blouses would fit underneath it.

"There's... There is just me," Mara whispered. Kemen smiled as he bent to kiss her cleavage, then he teased the uppermost laces free of their grommets.

"Kemen." He raised his head, but didn't withdraw his hands. "I don't know if I want to be anything other than chaste, just yet," Mara said slowly, half expecting him to yell or maybe even throw her off the roof. Instead, he smiled.

"Then you'll remain chaste until you say otherwise," he said.

"But I thought you wanted to make love to me," she blurted out.

"I intend to," he confirmed. In response to her wide eyes, he asked, "Don't you know, little one, that there are many ways of making love?" She shook her head. "Let me show you," he murmured, and Mara did not know if it was the effect of the mead or the hot suns or Kemen's even hotter skin, but her world swam together. She couldn't discern where he ended and she began, nor did she want to. What she wanted was him, all of him, no matter that they were atop a tavern roof with the streets bustling below them...

Pain exploded at the back of Mara's skull, and she was thrown onto her belly and dragged away from Kemen. The grit from the roof got between her teeth and scraped her tongue. She heard Kemen shouting, but he sounded very far away. Then he was quiet, and rough hands pushed her onto her back. A rag was tied around her eyes, then her mouth was forced open and a liquid poured down her throat, then there was pain, her throat and gut burning as if she'd been thrown atop a pyre. Blissfully, darkness took her.

CHAPTER THIRTY-FIVE

If was Latera, and I felt betrayed by my mate, where would I go?
To the one person who would never betray me.

Wren.

Aeolmar steeled himself as he knocked on his mate's sister's door. Wren was as stubborn as Latera, maybe more so, and might refuse him entrance regardless that he was First Hunter. In the midst of debating if he should stride into her chamber or perhaps break down the door, Wren opened it. To his surprise, she seemed relieved by the sight of him.

"She's positively despondent," Wren whispered without preamble as she stepped out into the corridor, carefully shutting the door behind her. "I haven't seen her so upset since we were in Gannera."

"When was she upset in Gannera?" Aeolmar asked. "Was it when your father tried to force that prince on her?"

"No. It was the last time we were there, the time you didn't come with us," Wren replied. "Father tried convincing her to remain as his heir."

"Why would Harold do that?" Aeolmar was well aware of which journey Wren was referring to; shortly after Mara's tenth winter she, Latera and Wren made the journey to Gannera without him. There had been many demon attacks in the north that season, and Aeolmar had been forced to remain in Parthalan. Latera had never mentioned anything untoward occurring during that short time away, but then again she hadn't returned to her homeland, not even to present Ember or Tor to her parents and younger sisters.

"She is firstborn," Wren reminded him. "Gannera is hers to rule, should she desire it." Wren had the same piercing blue eyes as her sister, and Aeolmar now felt as if she'd sighted his worst fear. *Gods. I've just told Latera that I don't want her to bear any more children, and now she thinks I've been lying to her about my past. She could leave me behind and live as a queen.*

"Did she tell you what happened earlier?" Aeolmar asked.

Wren nodded. "She did." With that, she turned to leave.

Aeolmar caught Wren's elbow. "Where are you going?"

"I'm leaving so you may speak with her," Wren replied, as if it were obvious.

"She'll see me?" Aeolmar had assumed that this would be a fruitless endeavor, for no one held on to their anger quite like Latera. "I worried she might hate me."

"Make no mistake, she is livid," Wren said. "She's been ranting on about you for half a day. She even threatened to go back to Gannera without telling you where she was headed."

Aeolmar's heart fell; Latera still possessed the enchanted dagger, and if she really wanted to leave Parthalan, there was nothing he could do to stop her. Without the dagger, he'd have no way to follow her, save through the underworld; portals, like the one his mother once used, had been banned long ago from Teg'urnan, and the closest sorcerer who created them (legally) was in Thurnda, a ten-day ride to the north. Without his mate, Aeolmar would once again be that hollow man that he had so despised, stone-hearted and fueled by despair.

"Well?" Startled, Aeolmar looked up. "Do you want her to leave?" Wren demanded.

"No!" He grabbed Wren's shoulders. "I love her! I nearly went mad without her! She can't—"

"Don't tell me," Wren said as she extricated herself from Aeolmar's grasp, "tell Latera." Wren patted his hand, and then she walked away, leaving Aeolmar staring at the closed door.

He pushed it open, half expecting to find Latera pacing back and forth in front of the hearth, cursing him in every language she knew. She wasn't there, nor was she seated in any of the chairs scattered about, and he wondered if she'd slipped away when she heard his voice in the corridor. Then he looked toward Wren's bed; the curtains were drawn back, and he saw a flash of bright hair.

Aeolmar smiled; so many times Latera's rants had gotten her into such a frenzy up she was exhausted afterward, and she would fall asleep against his chest. Although, those times had been different, because she hadn't been angry with him. Aeolmar crossed the room, pulled off his boots and climbed onto the bed. Latera was lying with her back toward him, Tor snuggled against her breast. Aeolmar laid against her back and slid his arm around her waist.

"I'm still angry with you."

"I know." He brushed her hair from her neck, and pressed his face against her warm skin. "You've every right to be angry." Latera remained silent, and for what felt like half of eternity they laid there. When Aeolmar could bear it no longer, he asked, "Beloved, how can I make this right?"

"Why didn't you ever tell me?" she countered.

"I didn't think it mattered."

"It does," she snapped, the hurt evident in her voice. Aeolmar propped himself up on an elbow and looked down at her; her pillow was soaked with tears. Tor cooed, happy to see his father, and Aeolmar let the baby grab his fingers.

"You must understand, I didn't think it did," Aeolmar said. "Nothing mattered, nothing I'd done, no one I'd ever been with, not once I met you. You were everything." He grazed his fingertips across her wet cheek; he hated it when she cried. "Nothing in your past would change how I feel about you. No man or deed would change anything."

"Aeolmar, you broke me," she reminded him. "Or have you forgotten that bit of information?"

"How could I?" he asked. "How could I forget finding you, after searching for so long? I'd given up long before we met that day in Brennus, and accepted I would live my life alone. Then I found you, my perfect girl, hiding in a stable. You were—you are—everything I've ever wanted. Only, you were just that—a girl, and I thought I'd go mad waiting for you to become a woman." Aeolmar lay back against the cushions, pressing his body against Latera's. "When you told me you loved me, my heart nearly burst. Then, when I claimed you..." He paused to nuzzle her neck.

"I can't live without you," he declared, his deep voice having gone hoarse. "I love you, Latera, and I'll never let you go. If you leave, I'll follow you. Even if you return to the mortal realm, I'll follow you."

"I'm not going anywhere," Latera said. "Ember would be furious with me."

"She would," Aeolmar agreed.

Besides, you could find me anywhere. For a moment, Aeolmar thought she'd spoken aloud, hardly recognizing the gentle touch of her mind to his. It was unusual for her mindtouch to be so clear, but then he remembered what his mother had always told him about magic: strong magic works best with strong emotions.

You're right. I would. Latera grimaced and rubbed her temple, his words being a bit too forceful for her. He used her distraction to his advantage and rolled her onto her back, then proceeded to kiss away her tears. *All shed for me. Never cry again, beloved, never again.*

"Not all for you," Latera whispered out loud. "Some were for me." Tor squealed, unhappy that neither of his parents were paying attention to him, so Aeolmar scooped the boy into his arms and nestled him between himself and Latera. Momentarily placated, Tor yawned and closed his eyes. Aeolmar pressed his forehead against Latera's, and stared into her eyes.

Tell me what will make this right.

"Anything?"

Anything.

"I want to know."

Know what?

"Everything you've done. Every deed, every ill-made plan, every unforgivable act. Everything, and every*one*."

Aeolmar rolled to his back, and rubbed his eyes. He thought of his youth in Savey, the many winters he had spent wandering the realms, the many despicable acts he had done in the name of vengeance. The many things he had never wanted Latera to know. He rubbed his eyes again, but it did nothing to disperse his memories.

"Are you sure this is what you want?" he asked.

Why don't you want to tell me?

You'll know what kind of a man I am.

I already do.

He cracked an eyelid and looked at her, mother to his children, his life's mate. *I suppose, since you're willing to put up with me, it's only fair.*

Latera smiled as she thumped his chest; she loved him, and she deserved to know what sort of events had made him the man she chose as her mate. Aeolmar nestled their sleeping baby on his chest and wrapped an arm around his mate, and recalled the first time beauty had caught his eye.

"When I was hardly more than a boy, there was a girl that lived near my family. A girl called Ishlia," he said. "I used to go swimming with her instead of working in the fields."

"Didn't that make Tor and Fiornacht mad?"

"Mmm. Quite mad."

Chapter Thirty-Six

Finlay was thoughtful as he made his way back to his and Asherah's chambers, and more than a bit befuddled. He had spent the rest of the day and part of the night with the envoy from Rael, and had learned absolutely nothing. When he had asked about any attacks upon Rael—demon, troll, or otherwise—the envoy's leader had taken it as a great jest and commended the king on his sense of humor. When Finlay asked again, he was quickly assured that no such attacks have occurred within the past hundred winters, maybe longer.

He was obviously ordered to convey that pack of lies rather than the truth. As far removed as he was from his shop in the desert, Finlay hadn't lost his talent for reading people. Even if he hadn't already known of the northern unrest, he'd have known the man was lying. Finlay didn't hold the man's actions against him; he was a high-ranking lord, and his silence had likely been ordered by the Lord of Tingu himself. He wondered if the man would have spoken freely to Asherah, being that she still bore the title Lady of Tingu. He'd resisted having Asherah present at this meeting in order to avoid placing undue strain upon his mate, so the truth of the northern matter, whatever it was, would just have to wait.

These thoughts were quickly set aside once he entered the royal apartment. He found Asherah in their bedchamber, seated before the hearth. Finlay was surprised that she hadn't gone to bed yet, and felt a glimmer of hope. *Perhaps she waited up for me.* Asherah was deep in thought, and hadn't noticed his entry.

"My love," Finlay greeted. "What is my beautiful queen thinking about so late at night?"

"Oh, nothing," she replied. "Just bits of things from the past." She looked up from the flames, and smiled. Finlay noticed that it didn't reach her eyes. "How did things fare with the Raelians?"

"Someone has ordered their silence," Finlay replied, taking a seat beside Asherah. After a moment, she laid her head on his shoulder. He wrapped an arm around her, and continued, "And I fear that someone was Leran himself. Perhaps he would have been more talkative with you, Lady of Tingu."

"Not likely. Only a fool would defy Leran, no matter the consequences. Perhaps we'll send a spy northward, a trader maybe. Then we might learn what's really going on." Asherah yawned. Finlay stood and pulled her up alongside him.

"You're exhausted," he said. "Come to bed with me."

Asherah smiled tightly. "You don't seem tired at all."

"I'm not."

Asherah smiled and ducked her head. "Then why ever would you want to take me to bed?"

"Oh, I don't know," he replied; nothing aroused him faster than when Asherah played coy with him. "Maybe I just want to look at you."

Asherah laughed, until Finlay silenced her with a kiss. She was pliant in his arms, and let him nudge her toward their bed. When his feet bumped the steps that led to the raised sleeping platform, he scooped his mate into his arms and carried her the rest of the way.

"So soft," he murmured as he opened her robe and his mouth traveled from her neck to her breasts. He reached the tip of her breast and took it in his mouth, his spine shivering when she gasped.

"Don't stop."

"Never."

***

The mates stayed awake all night, talking about everything and nothing as they lay nestled in their bed. It had been so long since they'd done so, and reminded Finlay of their first few seasons together after they'd been bound. Asherah was as bright eyed and energetic as she'd been all those winters ago.

"I think I fell in love with you all over again last night," Finlay said after first dawn.

"Had you fallen out?" Asherah asked. "Not that I would blame you. I haven't been much of a lover lately, have I?"

"It wasn't that," Finlay murmured. "I just missed you."

"I missed you too," Asherah whispered. Before she could continue, Attia burst into the room.

"A hunter has been attacked!" she told them.

"Attacked?" Asherah grabbed her robe and was on her feet in an instant. "Who was it?"

"I don't know. He was found badly beaten atop The Swan's roof."

"The Swan?" Finlay asked incredulously. "Was it a brawl?"

"If it was, it was all against one," Attia replied. "He can hardly move or speak. The innkeeper's sons found him. They had to bring him here in the back of a cart. He's being moved to the ward now."

"Bring him here," Asherah ordered, "and fetch Wren. I want to know, from my hunter's own lips, who dared to harm him." Attia nodded and rushed off. Finlay noticed Asherah's eyes burning like black flames, incensed over such an affront.

"Whoever did this will feel my wrath," she muttered. "No one, *no one*, harms my hunters. Whoever these fools think they are, wherever they are, they will suffer."

Finlay fought the urge to smile. This was his mate, the fiery warrior maiden he'd met in battle so long ago, the strong woman who faced her fears instead of hiding behind a curtain of herb-induced slumber. Before he could say as much the wounded hunter was carried in, his face so badly bruised he was hardly recognizable. His bent and broken hand clutched a woman's leather vest.

Chapter Thirty-Seven

Aeolmar and Latera remained in Wren's chamber for the rest of the day and night, and the First Hunter told his mate almost everything he could remember about his past. He recounted his youth in Savey, a time filled with such happiness it never occurred to him that those blissful days could end. Latera had held him while he spoke of the lonely decades after his family was murdered, and of the things he'd done during those first, vengeance-soaked winters. Throughout it all, Latera hadn't judged his actions, accepting that these were the events that made Aeolmar the man she fell in love with, and loved more every day.

When the rain began falling, they moved to sit before the window, leaving Tor nestled amidst the bed cushions. They flung the shutters wide open despite the torrent; it was a strong storm, with thunderclaps so loud the windowpanes rattled in their frames. Throughout it all, Tor snored peacefully.

Aeolmar loved to watch the lightning, a fact Latera was well aware of and why she had decided to sit before the window. Truth be told, she also loved a good storm. Some feared the fiery bolts, but she never had. She had seen for herself the scarred trees and burnt ground caused by lightning, but the lightning itself was a tool of the gods. Surely, the gods wouldn't strike someone down unless they deserved it.

At that thought she glanced sidelong at her mate, he who was twice born of gods. Aeolmar was always staring skyward, be it at clouds or stars or the lightning that now streaked across the gray skies, the last bolt being so brilliant he had stopped speaking. He had always felt the sky's pull, as if his ancestors' blood called to him.

While the storm raged, he continued doing as Latera had asked, and relating every incident he could think of, be it about a past lover, or battle, or a theft of boots and other supplies. He had skirted the issue of Asherah altogether.

"Do you plan on telling me about your time with the queen?" she asked. Before the lightning had distracted him, Aeolmar had been in the midst of recounting, for easily the hundredth time since she had met him, how he had defeated the orcs while employed by Grelk. Aeolmar pursed his lips and looked away, letting his long chestnut hair fall before his eyes.

"Are you sure you want to hear of it?" he asked.

Why are you ashamed?

I'm... He had forgotten, an untruth could not be shared mind to mind. "I'm not."

Here, she said, poking his forehead. He sighed, taking Latera's hands and clutching them to his chest.

"I was never ashamed," he said. *Never,* he repeated wordlessly. *I could have done better by her. I should have.*

"You couldn't have been that bad if she remained with you for eight winters," Latera said, for she knew well that Asherah suffered no fools.

Asherah was a different woman then. She was still distraught from the elf's death, and had been treated badly by many men.

"Were you one of those men?" Latera asked gently.

"I tried not to be," Aeolmar replied. "I only wanted to treat her as she deserved, like the queen she is." Latera leaned her cheek against his chest; less than a day ago, she had been furious to learn of her mate's tryst with the Faerie Queen, but then he had told her of his life after his family's death. He had told her bits and pieces before, but now he was telling her everything, every deed, every emotion, every fell act. He had worried that these revelations would drive Latera further away, but the tales had the opposite effect. They only endeared him to her.

Then, what happened between you?

Aeolmar's eyes darkened, and for a moment Latera regretted her attempts to pry. She nearly recanted her question, but she didn't. Couldn't. She needed to know. Never once had she doubted Aeolmar's love for her, but she needed to know what he was keeping hidden away from his mate.

"Did you break her heart?" she teased, and was rewarded with one of Aeolmar's half smiles.

"In a way, she broke mine," he replied. Latera hadn't been expecting that; in truth, she had assumed that Aeolmar had grown distant, and then Asherah had moved on to Finlay. Fear wrapped its cold fingers around Latera's heart, and she wondered if she was the only woman Aeolmar had ever loved.

A squeal distracted them, and Latera rose and parted the bed curtains. "He talks in his sleep, just like Mara," Latera murmured, a quick check having revealed that Tor was still fast asleep. She turned back to the window; not only had the storm abruptly ended, the elder sun had already risen. "It's nearly second dawn. We didn't even notice the first."

"So we didn't," Aeolmar said. Then his arms were about her waist and he pushed her onto the bed, careful to avoid the baby.

"Mar! What are you doing?" Latera struggled a bit, more to prove a point that anything else; she knew he'd never hurt her. Aeolmar laughed at her halfhearted wiggling, then bent to kiss her.

"Making sure you're not too cross with me," he replied, now tugging loose the combs that restrained her hair.

I'm not cross, I'm confused.

Aeolmar relaxed his hold as he put the combs to the side and smoothed her hair from her face, then he kissed her forehead. She was confused, and angry, but more than anything she was hurt. Her mate had his secrets, yes, but to keep such a significant part of his life from her for so long...

"I'll go to Gannera with you," Aeolmar said. Latera opened her mouth to ask why he had said that, then closed it. Perhaps she had raged a bit too loudly to her sister.

"Wren told you?" she asked, and he nodded.

"She made it seem like you'd be on your way soon," he said. Here she was, furious with him over incidents that were done and over with long before she'd drawn her first breath, yet she had never told her mate what had occurred between her and her father only a few winters past. Worse, he didn't seem angry.

"Gannera is your birthright," Aeolmar continued. "I'll help you rule, I'll lead your legion, or whatever you want me to do. You'll be a wonderful queen."

Latera laughed softly; she could hardly imagine herself as a queen, though she was in truth a princess, the rightful heir to Gannera. "You really think so?"

"I do," he replied. She let herself relax into his arms, warm and safe, and briefly wondered if Ember truly would hate the mortal realm. It was different, yes, but it wasn't a bad place. And Mara and Tor...

Latera banished the thought. Her children weren't mortal, and she wouldn't deny them their birthright the way hers had been. And Aeolmar's, she realized; after all these winters, she never thought to learn of another commonality between the two of them, that he should have been Prelate instead of a farmer's son. Before she could say as much, Wren burst into the chamber.

"Latera! Aeolmar," Wren shouted, wheezing as if she'd just run all the way from the Hill of Torim. "It's Mara."

Chapter Thirty-Eight

Latera Speaks

I have no idea how I got from Wren's chamber to the royal apartments. Nor do I remember being told where to go; all I knew was that something had happened to my daughter. I handed Tor off to my sister, then I was off and running.

I burst through the royal entrance and found others—at the time I couldn't have recognized them if my life had depended on it—surrounding someone, obviously wounded, who was lying on one of the benches in Asherah's receiving chamber. Assuming that this wounded person was Mara I shoved the rest aside, but my daughter wasn't lying there. It was Kemen.

"Where is she?" I demanded. The others remained silent, Kemen included, and as my eyes focused I realized what a terrible state he was in. He'd been badly beaten, to the point where his eyes were swollen shut, and his clothes and skin were crusted with blood. His left arm was cradled close to his body, the unnatural angle telling me it was likely broken. Kemen hadn't looked so horrible when he had been gored by a beast all those winters ago.

Then Aeolmar was in the room, bellowing at everyone all at once. Had I really crossed half the palace faster than he? I suppose I had. Kemen groaned, trying to offer some explanation as to Mara's whereabouts, but I couldn't hear him over Aeolmar's shouting. As I bent closer to Kemen, a voice cut through the room.

"We don't know where she is."

I spun around and saw Asherah speaking to Aeolmar, her fingers resting on his forearm. She noticed my gaze and dropped her hand as if she was a child caught stealing sweets, and cleared her throat before she continued. "Mara and Kemen were at The Swan yesterday. That is where they were attacked. Kemen was rendered unconscious. When he woke, Mara was gone. I fear she was taken by whomever attacked them." Asherah went on, relating how the proprietor of The Swan had found Kemen and had enlisted his sons to get him back to the palace, but none of that mattered.

She'd said that Mara was gone.

Taken.

I will get her back, find whoever dared harm her, and destroy them.

I shoved my fears aside and crouched next to Kemen, examining his wounds for clues as to whom had taken my daughter. It seemed that he had suffered a standard beating with a cudgel, or maybe a large rock. I prodded an odd wound on his arm; it was somewhere between a scrape and a burn, out of place amidst the welts and bruises. Then I noticed what he clutched in his left hand: it was one of my vests, the honey-colored leather one that Mara was always asking to borrow, to which I had always replied no. She must have taken it yesterday, after I'd gotten mad at Aeolmar and stormed off to Wren's rooms.

"*Where did you get this?*" I asked Kemen as I touched the vest. Before he could answer, a cold, clammy hand found its way on to my arm.

"*I've warned him not to speak,*" Mallia informed me. I hadn't even noticed her in the room.

"*Stand between me and information concerning my daughter and I'll kill you,*" I hissed, jerking my arm free. I brushed Kemen's matted hair back from his face, my fingertips rousing him a bit, and repeated my question.

"*It was all that was left,*" he rasped. I assumed he'd been throttled as well as beaten. "*When I woke, Mara was gone, with only this remaining.*" I took the bit of leather from Kemen's hands and smoothed it over my knees.

"*Did you see who attacked you?*" I asked. "*Did you see who took Mara?*"

"*No. They struck me from behind and dragged me away from her, then they threw a sack over my head and beat me. I couldn't get to her.*"

"*Mm. No one else in The Swan saw what happened?*"

"*We were on the roof.*"

The roof. That was where those looking to drink themselves into an especially dark patch of oblivion went so they wouldn't disturb the rest of the patrons. That was where Kemen had taken my daughter.

"*What a wonderful hunter you are, Kemen,*" I said, my voice dripping with contempt. "*Centuries of service to the queen, yet you were unable to defend my innocent daughter against someone wielding a sack and a stick.*" I stood, staring down at the man I'd foolishly told Mara wouldn't harm her. He hadn't, but the end result was the same. "*If this vest is truly all that remains of her, I will kill you.*"

Mallia gasped and Kemen shut his swollen eyes, but I ignored them as I moved to stand beside Aeolmar. My mate, not me, was the one who usually struck fear into the hearts of others, being that I'd almost never *killed anything; well, anything save demons and beasts. The only man I'd ever killed was Sarfek, and I'd only done that because he had attacked first. I wasn't a killer, yet I'd just threatened the lives of two people. More, I'd make good on those threats this very instant if those acts would bring back my Mara.*

Aeolmar was naming the hunters that would accompany us on Mara's rescue. The first hunter mentioned was Innetha, since she was the best tracker in Parthalan; she had already been sent to The Swan to scent a trail, so to speak. Also named were Bron, Luth, and Surya. I noticed, not for the first time, that Aeolmar was giving Asherah orders. For the first time, I wondered why she so easily bent to his will. Aeolmar also named Kemen, and wouldn't you know it, that stupid healer stuck her nose in my family's business once again.

"He is not to travel," Mallia chirped in that shrill, grating voice of hers. "He needs at least a sennight to recover! I'll not have you—"

"I'm going." While he was far from standing, Kemen had swung his legs around and was sitting up. Mallia tried to get him to lie back, but he refused. "You can't stop me. Mara was my responsibility, and I failed her. I will find her, even if it means my death." Mallia pursed her lips and narrowed her eyes, but remained silent. I hoped her face would stay that way, just as my nurses used to warn my sisters and me.

"Then there are seven of us," I declared, ignoring the withering glare from Mallia. "We should depart at once." Aeolmar's brow furrowed, Asherah and Finlay looked elsewhere. "What's wrong with leaving now? After last night's storms there won't be much of a trail, even for Innetha."

"Beloved, you cannot join the search." Aeolmar tried to take my hand, but I snatched it away. "What of Tor and Ember?"

"Mar, she's my daughter," I said. "I have to find her!"

"She's my daughter, too," he said in a soothing, condescending tone. "And I will find her. I won't come back without her."

He was denying me. First, he had denied me more children, he'd been denying me knowledge of his past deeds (though every other living Parthian seemed well aware of them) all along, and now he was denying me the chance to find my daughter. Asherah was watching us with a pitiable face, and her pity was more than I could stand.

"Are you taking Asherah on your grand quest?" I snapped. "Will the two of you relive your fruitless pursuit of Mersgoth? Maybe if you hadn't been so busy rogering her, you would have caught the beast, and you'd have left me alone in Brennus!"

Aeolmar winced as if I'd struck him, Asherah gasped, and Finlay looked as confused as everyone else in the room; well, then, I suppose my mate's former relationship with the queen wasn't common knowledge. I threw the vest Mara had worn in Aeolmar's face and stalked away from the lot of them and into the queen's garden, slamming the door so hard the hinges rattled. I only managed a few steps before I collapsed in a sobbing heap.

Then Aeolmar was there, gathering me in his arms as I cried. He had always been there for me, from that first day in Brennus and throughout all the other trials we'd endured, to today. He was my constant, my rock. My mate. I wanted to remain furious with him, but I couldn't. I needed him too much.

"I'm sorry," he whispered, his lips against my ear. "I'm so, so sorry. I never wanted to keep anything from you, I just didn't want to think about the past ever again. I never wanted to hurt you. Gods, nalla, I'd die to keep you from hurting."

He hardly ever called me nalla. The last time he'd done so was during Tor's birth, when he'd worried I was near death. I'd been closer than he'd known, but I held on to him then and he saw me through, just as surely as I held him now. If anyone can see me through this nightmare, it's Aeolmar.

"Mar, if she's gone I don't know what I'll do," I sobbed into his chest.

"She's not," he insisted, now speaking ahm'ri. *He only did that when his emotions ran strong, or when his strength was close to breaking. "We would know if she was dead. She lives, and I will find her."*

"We didn't know she was hurt," I pointed out. *"Mar...nall..."* I couldn't continue, my thoughts being too horrible to voice. Please bring her home.

I will. *He kissed my forehead, then tightened his arms about me. By all the living gods, I will.*

Chapter Thirty-Nine

Aeolmar had intended to leave immediately in pursuit of Mara, but preparations were frustratingly slow and took most of the day. Mindful that half a day and a full night had been lost while Kemen lay unconscious on the roof of The Swan, and that Mara could have been spirited anywhere in that time, two additional horses and were outfitted with provisions for extended travel. Lashed to their packs were the makings of a litter, as much for Kemen's possible use as Mara's.

While horses were saddled and the provisions secured, Innetha had located the remnants of Mara's trail at The Swan. The huntress reported that Mara had been dragged from the rooftop to one of the upper rooms, but she had only remained in the room for a short time. The innkeeper recalled a covered wagon that had been sitting outside The Swan close to dusk the prior day, and Innetha had already determined that the wheel ruts headed west. Latera hoped that those ruts would lead directly to Mara.

Hopefully, my daughter still breathes.

When the preparations were complete, Latera cradled Tor against her breast as she walked with the hunters toward the dark iron gates of Teg'urnan. Despite the fact that she wasn't accompanying them, she was dressed in her hunter's gear, and had almost strapped on her swords. She hadn't, but only because she worried that Tor might cut himself.

Latera stared straight ahead as she walked, not looking at those who called out well-wishes for Mara's safe return (*Gods, how does all of Teg'urnan know my business so quickly?*), not even looking at Aeolmar, carrying Ember as he walked beside her. She certainly didn't look to the opposite side, where Asherah walked with the Finlays. Latera hadn't said a word to the queen since her outburst in the royal chambers, and she fully intended to keep it that way. Once Mara was home safe Latera would sort out the rest of her emotions and decide how she felt about the queen, and not a moment sooner.

The somber group reached the gates, and the hunters began mounting up while taking a few final instructions from the king. Elkin drew Innetha aside for a private farewell, while Bron and Luth handled the pack horses. Surya helped Kemen into his saddle, the hunter looking so battered that Latera almost regretted threatening his life. Almost.

Aeolmar set Ember on her feet, then turned to his mate. He pressed his forehead against Latera's and touched her mind with his. Instead of words, Latera felt herself surrounded by Aeolmar's deep affection for her. Latera's knees nearly buckled, but his strong arms held her fast against him. No, he would never let her fall, not while there was breath in his body. It seemed incredible that she'd doubted his love for her, even for a moment.

I'm not coming back without her.

Just come back.

"So we all can hear!" Ember whined, pulling on Aeolmar's jerkin. He smiled at the girl, and wiped her cheek with his thumb.

"I was telling your mother that I love her. I love all of you," he said, crouching down and pulling Ember into his arms. "I'm going to get your sister now, and I'll need someone to look out for Tor and Mama while I'm gone. Can I count on you?" Ember nodded, for there was nothing she liked more than being in charge. "My scholar," he murmured as he kissed her brow. "You may begin your duties by taking your brother for a moment, so I may say goodbye to Mama properly."

Aeolmar straightened and took Tor from Latera's arms and kissed his downy head, then he placed him in Ember's arms. Aeolmar and Latera gazed at each other for a moment, then he embraced his mate as if she were his lifeline. They held each other for long moments, their bodies now as close as their minds.

"*Je nall'e te,*" he said.

"I love you too." Latera kissed him hard, not caring that half the palace was watching them. *You don't have to say it in* ahm'ri. *I know.*

Do you?

Since that day in Brennus.

Aeolmar drew back from Latera, then he deposited two final kisses upon his children's heads. The First Hunter of Parthalan mounted up and gave his family a farewell nod, then he rode off to find his eldest daughter.

Elkin approached Latera. "If they need the rest of the hunters or even the legion, we'll be there," he said. "The moment I feel Innetha needs me, we'll go."

"How will you find them?" Latera asked.

Elkin smiled and tapped the side of his head. "The same way you would."

"Thank you, Elkin," Latera said as she reclaimed Tor from Ember's arms. She watched the hunters file out of the gates with a sharp pang in her heart, but quickly quashed it. She had children to look after. "Don't worry, Ember. Papa will bring back Mara."

"I know," Ember said. "Why are you mad at the queen?"

"I-I'm not," Latera began.

"Yes, she is." Latera glared at Asherah, but the queen continued, speaking only to Ember, "She has every right to be."

"But you're the queen," Ember said.

"I am," Asherah agreed. "And sometimes queens do the most foolish things."

With that, Asherah turned on her heel and walked back to the palace, arm in arm with the king. The younger Finlay offered Ember his hand, and the two followed their monarch, leaving Latera and Tor to walk alone.

Chapter Forty

Asherah Speaks

*T*hings in Teg'urnan had certainly taken a turn for the worse over these past few sennights, what with Mara missing, Aeolmar and many of the hunters away trying to find her, and Latera hating me, and those three individual situations coming together in a thoroughly maddening way. I could understand Latera's hurt feelings, but really, she needed to come to her senses. Aeolmar's and my relationship was so long in the past it was practically a myth, certainly nothing for her to be so upset over.

Although I must admit that whenever Aeolmar was away from the palace, I felt the loss of him as surely as I would the loss of a limb. I leaned heavily upon my First Hunter, far more so than I'd ever leaned upon Harek or even Finlay. But then, Finlay was one to lean upon me, so I suppose the both of us leaned upon Aeolmar. Add our weight to that of Aeolmar's mate, and his children, not to mention the many others who *look to him for guidance. How Aeolmar finds the strength to support so many, I will never know.*

Of course, Aeolmar's absence also meant that the duties of the First Hunter had fallen to the king. Logically, Aeolmar's second, Elkin, should have assumed the obligations, but Finlay had been Second Hunter not so long ago, and understood Aeolmar's mindset as First Hunter better than any of the other hunters, possibly better than Aeolmar himself. Besides, Elkin had his own work to do.

That left me, Queen of Parthalan and Lady of Tingu these last thousand or so winters, to my own devices. Not the best of plans, but there wasn't anything to be done about that, now was there? Luckily, I did have the younger Finlay and Attia to distract me, so on the whole nothing untoward had happened. Yet. Still, I was bored, and a bit lonely, being that the two women I associated with, Innetha and Latera, were both distanced from me in one way or another. I was uncharacteristically pleased when Mallia, the healer whom I occasionally despised, came to c all.

"How fares my queen?" was all she asked, and my true feelings burst forth as strong and fast as a tidal wave. I told her everything: how I resented being left alone in my chambers; how Parthalan was doing far too well without me; my loneliness without Innetha and Aeolmar; Latera's ridiculous hatred of me; my mate being too overwhelmed and my son too young to notice that all of this forced relaxation was driving me mad. I even mentioned the man in my dreams, he whom I knew but could not seem to recognize.

"Well, who would you like him to be?" Mallia asked. To anyone else I would have demurred, or possibly even ignored the question, but I told the healer the truth.

"Lormac," I whispered.

"*Ah.*" Mallia sat back and smiled that warm smile of hers, the one that usually preceded a bowl of steeped herbs and blissful oblivion. "It's not wrong to want to set eyes upon him again, even if only in a dream."

"I've always wondered why Lormac's spirit has never come to me," I said. I knew that Torim was well, since her spirit had at least interacted with Latera in the mortal realm. When I was of a mind to consider such things, I realized that I only began to fear for Lormac's spirit after my dearest friend gave her warnings for Parthalan's safety to someone other than me. "I worry that he hates me for his death. Blames me. I worry that... I worry that he may be wandering the underworld." I squeezed my eyes shut, imagining Lormac endlessly traversing a burning plain, lost and alone. "Gods, I hope he is not there."

"How could he be?" Mallia stood and approached the hearth, and picked up something from the ledge above it. It was the bundle of herbs she'd left with me during her last visit. "He is an elf; I don't think his spirit would go to the underworld on its own," she said as she tossed the herbs into the fire.

"But what if he's trapped?" I wailed. "What if... What if he's in my dreams because he's calling out for help?"

Mallia put a hand on my forearm, and I gasped at her cold and clammy flesh, as if she'd been in the bath until the water cooled and chilled her like a corpse. I was about to call for Attia, to ask her to bring Mallia a blanket or maybe some hot soup, but the healer spoke first.

"What is your heart's desire?"

"I..." I stopped, shook my head, and began again. "I want to know that Lormac is well. I want to know if he blames me for his death. I want... I need to tell him that I still love him." A hot tear freed itself from my lashes; my guilt over living while he was dead, taking men to my bed while his bones lay in the ground, nearly overwhelmed me. And Finlay... how could Lormac ever forgive me for taking another mate?

"Then tell him," Mallia said.

I looked up, confused as to why Mallia was suggesting I speak to a dead man, when I saw movement behind her shoulder.

There he was.

Solid.

Alive!

It's not him not him no it can't be him.

But the man before me bore the same soft brown hair and tall, wiry build. The craggy brow, merry gray eyes, lips twisted into a grin. The winters hadn't touched him, and he looked as well and hale as the last time I'd seen him alive.

"It can't be," I whispered, but it must be. It's him. After all this time, he has returned to me.

"Lormac," I cried, and threw myself into my mate's arms.

Chapter Forty-One

Aeolmar squinted up at the suns, cursed, then he fixed his glare on the muddy ground before him. The hunters had been following Mara's trail for the better part of a moon as it twisted, turned, doubled back on itself, and occasionally disappeared entirely. At times he felt like there was no trail and that he was leading his hunters blindly across the westlands, farther and farther away from Teg'urnan, and from wherever Mara was.

Inevitably, Innetha would find something; a broken twig, a bit of hair or cloth caught on a patch of rough bark, an upturned pebble. He lived for these tiny, tangible reminders that they were on the correct path, and while he did not doubt Innetha's tracking sense in the slightest, he was tired of crashing through the underbrush based on naught but her word. Aeolmar wanted a solid, clear trail; that, and to find his daughter.

Then he would take care of whoever had dared harm her.

"This way," Innetha called over her shoulder. Aeolmar didn't bother asking if she'd found a sign or if they were following more magically obscured tracks. He would not admit—not to the other hunters and certainly not to himself—that he was exhausted. He hadn't slept at all during the first few days of the hunt, his mingled excitement and terror keeping him wide awake while the others managed to rest, however fitfully. Once the initial exhilaration had worn off, he tried to sleep, but his thoughts flew in maddening circles around him; if he was not imagining some torment being visited on Mara, he was acutely aware of how much he missed his children, and his mate.

Latera... She'd been so angry with him, first over his past relationship with Asherah, then when she realized she could not join the search for Mara. Aeolmar wished he could have spent one more night with her before they departed, one more night to hold her as they watched the moon dance across the sky, one more night to convince her that he was nothing without her. That night was time that couldn't be spared, not with their daughter missing, so he had to hope that Latera would still love him when he returned to her.

To assuage his guilt, Aeolmar had been sending daily messages back to Teg'urnan, informing Latera of their progress, what sort of trail they were on, and the obstacles they'd encountered. At the bottom of each scroll he left small reminders of their time together. The first just said arena, an allusion to the night she'd chosen him; the last, written when he was achingly aware of her absence, said *nalla*. Aeolmar hoped that she appreciated the notes, and that those special memories gave her a bit of happiness during this horrible time.

"Aeolmar," rumbled Bron, rousing Aeolmar from his memories, "Innetha's got something she wants you to see."

The First Hunter nodded, then dismounted and approached Innetha. She was staring at an oak on the edge of a thick wood, the trees so dense that hardly any of the noon sun filtered through the undergrowth.

"What have you found?" he asked.

"It's here," she replied, not taking her eyes from the oak. "Whatever's hiding Mara's trail is here."

"In the wood?"

"In the tree." Innetha glided her hands across the bark, her brows drawing together. "It doesn't feel like bark, or bare wood. It's smooth, and... and a bit rough. Wiry, even. Fur?"

Aeolmar felt the bark himself, his own brow furrowing as he watched his hand touch a rough brown trunk, but he could not deny the feel of fur beneath his hand. "Get back," he warned, and in one fluid motion he drew his sword and struck the tree. He expected to hear a crack as he shattered the living wood, but instead there was a dull *thunk* as his sword made contact. The illusion dissipated, and the hunters saw that the oak was in reality a stag strung up by its antlers.

"Sacrilege," muttered Bron, but Aeolmar ignored him as he studied the stag. Other than the fact it was dead, it appeared to be in perfect shape, its coat only marred where Aeolmar's sword had scored its hide.

It must have swallowed a charm, he deduced. With a silent prayer to Olluhm, Aeolmar sliced open the stag's belly. After a bit of prodding a small pouch landed on the ground before his feet.

Aeolmar crouched down and poked the pouch with the tip of his sword. *Is that the same charm used on the innkeeper to poison Asherah?*

"That's it," Innetha stated. "Whatever's in the pouch is what's been hiding Mara's real trail. The stag was nothing but a decoy."

"The poor beast must have wandered with it for days before it died," Luth murmured. "No wonder we've been going in circles."

"No more." Aeolmar whispered the words for fire, and watched the flames consume both the pouch and stag. As they both crumbled to black, stinking ash the image of the wood ahead wavered, revealing a narrow but very present path. He glanced to Innetha, who nodded.

"We go on," Aeolmar announced, then he grabbed Myrnnhe's reins and led his horse into the wood. *And we'll keep going until we find her. Mara, be strong. I am coming.*

Chapter Forty-Two

Asherah Speaks

I *can't believe he's returned.*

Is it really, truly him?

It has to be.

Lormac is alive!

When I made that first leap into his arms I'd nearly expected to fall flat on the floor, and add a few bruises to my already damaged pride. But he caught me in those strong arms I had missed so, and held me and told me that he loved me. Over and over, he told me that he loved me.

"Where have you been?" I asked between kisses. "All this time..."

"Hush," he said. "I'm sorry it's taken me so long to reach you."

"But, your bones. I buried them myself!"

He laughed deep in his chest. "You didn't really think that would be the end of me, did you?"

"How can I know?" I whispered, tracing the severe, angular features of his face I knew so well. That I'd never forgotten. "How can I know it's really you?"

He could have said a hundred things, small anecdotes about our life together than only he and I had known. How we arranged the cushions on the bed, what he'd bring me for a late night snack, those silly wool stockings I insisted upon wearing because (as he said) I didn't yet have the thick blood of a northerner that was able to withstand the frigid cold. Instead, he said the one word that proved his identity beyond any doubt.

"Hillel."

My name. Only Lormac and Torim had ever known my true name.

"Oh, Lormac," I murmured, losing myself in his arms.

Later, he held me tightly, the cushions stacked up around us like a cocoon. It was how we'd always slept; well, except for when Leran had joined us and wedged himself between us. But now it was just Lormac and I. Me and my mate.

"I have to tell you something," I said. "I've taken another mate." I began the apology I'd rehearsed so many times in my mind, telling him that he was my one true love and that no man would ever compare, but I'd just been so damnably lonely, when he hushed me again.

"It doesn't matter," he said. "My star, you're mine. You'll always be mine. This Finlay is nothing to you."

"Who?" I blinked; I had no idea who he was referring to. Then I was staring into Lormac's eyes, those gray eyes I'd missed so dearly, and knew he was right. I was forever his.

As often happens when you're mated to a king, all too soon Lormac had to take his leave of me. Some matter in the north, or maybe it was the west. Or was it the mountain trolls? No matter, he promised he'd return soon. I just needed to be patient, and wait.

Waiting is easy. I can wait for him forever.

Chapter Forty-Three

Latera Speaks

Gods above, these have been the worst days of my life. I hated being apart from Aeolmar, I was sick with worry over Mara, and it was a wonder that I hadn't gone mad from my constant fretting. Aeolmar must have understood my rattled state, since he had been going to the trouble of sending messengers to the palace every day or so, advising those of us left behind of his progress. Indeed, his reports were so detailed I felt like I was there with him.

With trembling hands, I read that Mara's trail had gone cold not far from Teg'urnan. I had expected it might, but that didn't mean I liked reading about it. Luckily, Aeolmar had a secret weapon that the kidnappers either were oblivious of or had severely underestimated: Innetha.

She wasn't an elf or faerie, but a nymph from the northern woodlands. Innetha could lay her hand against the earth and tell you of every foot and hoof and cart that had touched it in the past season, in what direction they moved, and if they had been carrying anything. And while she could sense a spell from a league away, she was immune to the effects of most magic.

I was especially grateful for Innetha's help, since (according to Aeolmar) Mara's trail had been magically obscured. Aeolmar's messages detailed the types of spells used, if he was able to break them, and what sort of magic handlers tended toward using them. Grudgingly, I sent these messages on to Asherah, since the details Aeolmar had provided might help us discover the identity of whomever had abducted my Mara. Privately, I wondered if this was Aeolmar's way of reminding me that Asherah had always been my friend, even when I had been nothing more than a stable girl who had caught the First Hunter's eye.

I enjoyed his frequent messages, just as I understood that they were a costly and time-consuming endeavor. Aeolmar had warned me when the messages would slow to every other day; then a sennight past that, nothing had come for three days. At first dawn on the fourth day, a messenger arrived; his horse had foundered and he was thus delayed, but the good man delivered his scroll nonetheless. As soon as I had studied every brushstroke from that scroll (for Aeolmar does have a lovely script; I imagine that his fine penmanship is yet another legacy from his mother the priestess) that day's message arrived. The receipt of two messages in a single day had me beyond relieved, and I had overflowed with confidence that my mate and daughter would soon be returned to me. And, as a special treat only for me, Aeolmar had rendered a likeness of brambleberries across the bottom of the parchment.

The memory of him and me at the brambleberry patch, dodging snakes while we also dodged what was growing between us, almost made me smile.

That confidence was now gone, and it had been replaced by an ever-growing despair. No messengers had arrived for six days, and the waiting had very nearly driven me mad. I hadn't worried at all on the third day, and only a bit on the fourth, but by the time the child sun had set on the fifth day with no word from my mate, I was in a full-blown panic. If it hadn't been for Tor and Ember's care, I would have spent every moment staring out the palace gates, though I am ashamed to say that my younger children hardly received my attention. My mind was set on my eldest child and my mate, wherever they may be.

Aside from the messages, one thing that kept me grounded, kept me sane throughout that hopelessly endless waiting: Aeolmar's presence in my mind. It's hard to explain, but from the moment we were bound I've been able to feel him, almost like a warm fur drawn close about my neck, soft and comfortable and familiar.

Though he was far from Teg'urnan, our bond had retained its strength. I knew whether Aeolmar traveled on a road or across a bridge by the cadence of his horse, and when he slept, rare as those moments were, for his breathing slowed ever so slightly; I'd lay in our bed at night and pretend he was beside me, just beyond my reach. Whenever I'd managed to work myself up into a particularly frazzled state, I would close my eyes and concentrate on the warmth that was just so uniquely him, and know he was well.

Just before noon on the sixth day of with no word from him, I deposited Tor and Ember in Wren's chamber, and went to the top of the steps that led to Teg'urnan's grand entrance. I faced the dark iron gates with my eyes closed, bathing in Aeolmar's presence. He was riding through a forest, Myrnnhe carefully picking his way through the trees. After he'd first departed I had watched for messengers from the tower balcony, but yesterday I had begun standing watch here, for while the tower offered the farther view I would waste precious moments running down the stairs, and I wanted whatever scroll or foolscap borne by the rider as soon as possible.

I'd rip it from his cold dead hand if I had to.

"There is still no word, then?"

I cracked an eyelid and glanced to my left. Finlay, the older one, had joined me in my vigil. "There's not," I said softly. He quietly kept watch with me, and we both stared through the gates at the royal road beyond. It teemed with runners and carts bearing wares for market, but was devoid of messengers.

"I know he's well, though," I said after a time, more for my own benefit than for Finlay's. I'm the one who needed to hear it said, not him. "I'd know in an instant if he wasn't."

"You really can feel each other," he murmured, and I nodded. Aeolmar had told me that our binding was different from Asherah and Finlay's, but for the life of me I couldn't understand why. Shouldn't the same ritual produce the same results?

"Perhaps it's my elf blood," I ventured. Finlay cocked an eyebrow, and nodded. We'd been thinking the same thing.

"Or my troll blood," he said. It was difficult to remember that our king was descended from a creature like Grelk, what with his leaner form and head of dark curls, though he did retain some of the attributes of the great, lumbering smiths. One of the more obvious was the rough skin on his palms and the soles of his feet, meant to guard against the oppressive and ever-present heat of the forge. I remember when Aeolmar had first told Mara about Finlay's gritty skin, and in a short time the King of Parthalan had his boots off and was watching Mara giggle as she acquainted herself with his rough toes. She had been the age that Ember is now, so young and full of promise...

"Innetha and Elkin can feel each other, too," I said. If I kept remembering Mara as a child I'd end up sobbing in the public square.

"But they aren't bound. Are they?" Finlay asked.

"They're not," I replied. "According to Innetha, Elkin chose her when they first met, and they've been linked ever since."

"He chose her," Finlay muttered. "Have you asked Elkin how Innetha's faring?"

"I have. He... he says she's well, but he worries for her."

"They're going to be fine. All of them," Finlay said. I'd squeezed my eyes shut again, the image in my mind's eye having transformed from a little girl tickling the king's foot into something... other. I nodded, but must have been unconvincing, since Finlay placed his hand on my elbow and led me to the side of the entrance. "Aeolmar is nothing if not a stubborn lunatic, and a crazed man such as he will overturn every stone in the nine realms if he needs to." I laughed, since the description was accurate.

"Come," he said, extending his hand. "We can watch for messengers together from the royal balcony."

I resisted, since the royal chambers held the woman I'd been avoiding these past few sennights. "I'm fine here," I said weakly.

Finlay pursed his lips and sighed, then took both my hands. "Latera, I understand how you feel," he began. Well, yes, I imagine that he is the only one in Teg'urnan who would. "But I need you. Asherah hasn't been well the past few days, and I can't seem to help her. The healers can't, either."

"Why isn't she well?" I asked. Between my despair over Mara's fate, Aeolmar's absence, and caring for Ember and Tor, I hadn't even noticed. My mother always told me that my habit of holding grudges would only harm those I loved. "Is it an illness?"

"I don't know what's wrong," he replied. "She seems to be wasting away."

"How is that possible?" I asked, but Finlay didn't reply. For the first time in days I looked at him, really looked at him, and saw the dark smudges beneath his eyes, the fine lines of worry carved around his mouth. I cursed my pride that had made me avoid him and Asherah, and together we made our way to his rooms.

The royal chamber's public rooms were vacant, but what I saw there gave me cause for worry. Asherah's maps and scrolls were haphazardly strewn about, the colored inks she favored dried and flaking in their crystal wells. The queen was forever consulting one document or another, and treated each as if it were encrusted in gems. For her to leave her tools lying about was unheard of.

The disarray was even more evident in the royal family's private apartments. Clothing and furs were heaped up on the floor, plates and bowls were stacked in corners. If I'd left Ember alone in our chamber for a moon the mess wouldn't be so bad, yet this was the queen's bedchamber. Gods, where was Attia? I began to ask Finlay if the queen was merely ill or if she was drinking those blasted herbs again, when I saw her.

Asherah the Ruthless was sitting on the steps before her bed, singing softly. She was methodically smoothing her dress over her knees, and her once lovely hair hung in lank clumps around her shoulders. Her crystalline skin had lost its translucence, and was yellowed like old wool.

"What happened?" I whispered, but I may as well have yelled for all that she noticed our presence. "What is she saying?"

"It's a song. She claims she once sang it for Leran, when he was a baby," Finlay replied.

"Finlay, she didn't know Leran when he was a baby," I said, though Finlay was well aware of the fact. I hazarded a glance at my king, his face a mask of despair. I grabbed his hand, pulled him into the bathing chamber, and shut the door.

"Tell me everything that's happened," I demanded. "We need to determine if she was cursed, or has contracted plague, or—"

"She doesn't know me." His voice was hoarse and soft, as if he'd been shouting for days and his throat had gone raw. "She thinks Finlay is Leran, but she has no idea who I am. To her, I'm nothing more than a stranger."

I thought I'd been despondent being away from Aeolmar, but at least he knew I was his mate. Something had ripped Finlay's mate right out of his grasp, and he was forced to watch her waste away before his eyes. I didn't know what to do; I'm not Aeolmar, the mighty First Hunter with the blood of gods coursing through his veins, gifted since birth with an innate understanding of magic. He would know what to do, what to say... I wished he was here.

But he's not. There's just me, Latera Demon-killer, First Huntress of Parthalan, and I would drag them across the plains of hell before I'd let them—whoever they were—take my queen from me. I still didn't know what would fix this, so I did the only thing I could think of, and wrapped my arms around Finlay. Comfort, I could offer aplenty.

"We will fix this," I promised him. "Something—someone—has caused this. We will find out who did this, and we will stop them. We will get you your mate back." He nodded against my shoulder and made a noise somewhere between a snuffle and a grunt. I looked the other way, giving him a moment to compose himself.

"Let's go back," he said, drawing me toward the door, "before one of the saffira find us in here together." His tone was light, but his reddened eyes spoke of his pain. I nodded, but he grabbed my hand when I reached for the door. "No one can know of this." No, I imagine Parthalan at large shouldn't be made aware of its insane ruler.

"Luckily, we have our king to lead us," I said, then stepped out of the bathing chamber, and went to confront a madwoman.

"Asherah," I said, kneeling before her. Her eyes, heretofore always black and glittering like the finest gems, were coated in a dull film. I

wondered if some kind of a powder had been blown into her face, thus letting the enchantment take hold of her before she managed to blink it away.

She had been singing, but stopped and smiled at me. "Latera. How lovely to see you."

The fact that she recognized me, and not Finlay, made me wonder who the real target of this enchantment was. "You've a lovely voice."

"Leran likes it when I sing," she replied in those same musical tones. "He's cutting a tooth, and I need to sing him to sleep. Do you think I'm a good mother?"

"I think you're a wonderful mother," I replied. That, at least, was easy, since it was the truth. "As does Finlay."

"Is he here again?" She made a sweeping gesture, as if she could sweep Finlay from her presence. "When Lormac returns he'll not be pleased about that man hanging about my bedchamber!" Finlay looked as if he would weep; truly, he was suffering far more than I.

"Lormac thinks quite highly of Finlay," I said quickly.

"He does?" Asherah asked, cocking her head to the side like a bird. The film on her eyes shifted, and was now nearly opaque.

"He does," I confirmed. "Lormac sent him here to watch over you." Asherah looked at Finlay with her dull eyes as one would look over a horse at market. I half expected her to check his teeth. "Lormac knows that Finlay will care for you better than anyone else."

"Not better than Lormac," Asherah scoffed.

"Of course not," I agreed. "Would it be all right if he sat beside you?' I ventured.

"I suppose, if Lormac approves of him," Asherah murmured. I beckoned to Finlay, and he reluctantly took a seat next to the addled queen. I still had no idea of what I was doing, but I hoped that if Asherah was

close to her mate she would remember him. Of course, sitting there not touching him wouldn't do much good...

"Take his hand," I said suddenly. Both of them regarded me dubiously, so I blurted out the first thing that came to mind, "If he's to protect you, he needs to know the feel of you!" All right, that was horrible, but I soldiered on. I leaned in, and whispered as if the words were for Asherah alone, "As you know, Lormac has many enemies. The better Finlay is acquainted with you, he'll be better able to protect you."

"I don't know," Asherah murmured. "Lormac won't be pleased if he finds me holding another man's hand."

"He'll be less pleased if you're harmed." She pursed her lips, considering. "Here, take my hand first, then I'll place yours on Finlay's. It'll be but a moment."

I took Asherah's hand, the coldness of it startling me. She shouldn't be this cold, not indoors on such a warm day. I was so distracted by her chilled flesh I almost didn't notice it, the removal of that tiny weight, that bit of me that wasn't me fluttering away. Then I was flooded with an awareness that was all my own; I could no longer feel the comforting presence of a woodland, or sense a horse beneath me.

I couldn't feel Aeolmar.

I dropped Asherah's hand and crumpled to the ground, the loss of him having struck me to my core. I reached out with my mind, my hands, my heart, but he was gone.

Gone.

Please, don't let him be gone.

I felt hands on my shoulders, and cold water splashed onto my face. Finlay and Asherah were both shouting, I realized at me. "I can't feel him," I whispered. "My mate is lost to me."

The crazed queen gathered me into her arms, and we wept together.

Chapter Forty-Four

Aeolmar exited his tent, stretched, and glared at the elder sun. "If you truly are my grandsire, why don't you shine your light somewhere that will help me find my daughter?" he demanded. "Isn't she your granddaughter, too?"

The sun remained a glowing orb, a constant yet silent observer of his progeny. Unsatisfied, Aeolmar spat.

"Useless gods," he grumbled. Along with the usual tales of the All Father, Aeolmar had heard other, unflattering stories about Olluhm. Those accounts—usually relayed by those few who still followed the old gods—told of a petty, vindictive god who cared for no one save his newest child, and most recent bedmate. He never paid much attention to those tales, but now that he knew what Olluhm had allowed to happen to Aeolmar's mother—his own daughter—and now Mara, he wondered if there was any truth in them.

"Must be why Mama only prayed to Cydia," he said as he broke down his tent, loudly crashing about in order to rouse the rest of the party. They had been following Mara's trail for days—sennights, by now—since Aeolmar had destroyed the charm secreted in the stag's gut. What he had initially seen as a piece of good fortune had quickly degraded upon itself, and the trail, still charmed but now by another source, circled back upon itself like a serpent swallowing its tail. Innetha claimed that she was she was following the trail as it had been left, and, since she was the only one immune to the obfuscation spells, Aeolmar had no choice but to believe her.

He had no choice but to believe that his daughter was alive at the end of this endless spiral.

At least he was moving. Doing something. It had hurt him to leave Latera behind, but there again he had had no choice. Ember and Tor needed their mother, and Latera was still recuperating from Tor's birth. She claimed that she had regained her strength, but Aeolmar could still see the exhaustion in her eyes, feel how her muscles had weakened whenever he held her.

But she would have come, all the same; hells, Latera would tunnel through a mountain with naught but a wooden spoon if she thought that tunnel would lead to Mara. Aeolmar concentrated on that bit of his mate that was always present in his mind, willing her to know that he was safe, and that he would find Mara soon. One way or another, he would bring his family together again.

The hunters broke camp, far too slowly for Aeolmar's taste, and resumed following Mara's trail. Innetha rode at the front while Aeolmar brought up the rear, with those between scanning the landscape for something. Anything. Any sign, be it a bit of broken branch, or a disturbed patch of ground that might be a clue as to Mara's whereabouts.

Anything. Aeolmar just needed a sign.

To add to his misfortune, the wounds he'd sustained at Vilja's estate had ceased healing. They hadn't gotten worse—at least, he didn't think they were worse—but they showed no progress. Aeolmar had been scored by enough demon claws to know that by now the cuts across his chest should be fully healed, yes they remained red and angry. The puncture wound above his knee fared no better, and it was all he could do to hide it from the rest.

Aeolmar glanced up at the suns. He assumed there would be no godly assistance for his wounds, or anyone else's.

Hours later, Aeolmar was again staring at the elder sun when Innetha dismounted, and pressed her palms to the ground. "I can feel her," she said.

"Is she alive?" Aeolmar demanded, sidling up beside the tracker.

"She was when she walked across this earth," Innetha said, then adjusted her hands in the mud. "No, she was dragged."

Aeolmar growled. "Where?"

Innetha indicated a dense stand of trees, oaks of markedly wider girth than the surrounding evergreens. Noticing that the bark of one certain tree wavered in the bright sun, Aeolmar reached out and touched it, half expecting to find another sacrifice dangling from the branches. He found nothing but empty air, not bark or even stag's body, but the charged ether around his hand confirmed that an illusion was present. Aeolmar gritted his teeth, and walked straight into the tree.

The hunters gasped aloud as Aeolmar walked through what appeared to be a thousand-winter oak. Innetha followed him, crawling on her hands and knees in order to maintain contact with the earth Mara had moved across.

After both had passed through the image of the tree the illusion broke, and the forest dissolved away until the hunters stood at the edge of a clearing. In the center was a small cottage that appeared abandoned. Aeolmar glanced at Innetha; she nodded, which was all the confirmation he needed. The First Hunter drew his sword and strode toward the cottage that held his daughter.

Aeolmar hardly spared a glance at the weathered hide covering the doorway as he entered the cottage. The interior was dark and cold, the sort of empty chill that meant no one had inhabited the space for a long, long time. A thick layer of dust blanketed the few furnishings, and the hearth, caked with greasy soot, was devoid of kindling.

"You're certain?" Aeolmar demanded, not bothering face Innetha while he addressed her.

"Yes," she replied. "Mara was brought here. I have no sense of her being taken away."

What if only her body remains? He didn't give voice to the thought, and instead ran his hands over the dust-caked walls. *There must be another room*, he thought as he examined the walls, pulling and pushing on each tiny imperfection, studying every edge and join. *Mara, I am coming for you.*

"Aeolmar." He turned around, and saw that Bron had ripped down the door hide and spread it across the cottage floor. "Have you ever seen these symbols before?"

"*Nir si'lan.*" Flames licked at Aeolmar's hand, and he crouched down for a better look at the hide. He studied the runic characters for only a moment before he extinguished the small fire. He had seen those symbols before, scrawled inside a spell book bound with human flesh that his mate had discovered in the mortal realm. That spell book had belonged to Sarfek, Harek's brother and fellow traitor to Parthalan.

"This entire cottage is bound with illusions," he said as his gaze swept around the small room. "Mara's here, but not *here*."

The hunters began searching the cottage in earnest, with Bron going so far as to rip up the floorboards. Aeolmar didn't bother to tell them it was a wasted effort, being that Mara was concealed by magic rather than a wall or a door. Instead, he closed his eyes and called up the memory of how his mother had taught him to cast glamours, and of how one could see around them.

***

"But I can't undo a glamour done by someone else," young Aeolmar had whined. Aeolmar did not understand how he or anyone could see around a glamour. The whole point of a glamor was to trick people, wasn't it? He also couldn't understand why he and his mother had been confined to the barn talking about glamours on the first warm day of spring. None of his siblings had been made to suffer a magic lesson. In fact, he could hear the lot of them romping about in the sunshine.

"Now, Aeolmar," Alluria said in her soothing voice. Mollified, he sat up a bit straighter, and tried to be a good student. "There's my young scholar," she said approvingly while she patted his hand. On that day he had still been the youngest, being that it was many winters before his sisters, Linnea and then Enna, were to come, and he had been in desperate need of proving himself alongside his older siblings.

"Mama, I don't understand," he said, in a much less petulant tone. "If I can't undo a glamour, why are we learning this?"

"A glamour is naught but a trick played on your senses," she replied. "But the trick does not extend to one's mind." She tapped her finger against his forehead; it was the sort of gesture that, if performed by anyone else, would have resulted in bruised knuckles or a broken finger. When Alluria did it, Aeolmar only smiled.

"Then I can't rely on my hearing or sight?" he asked.

"Nor touch nor taste," Alluria added; Aeolmar wrinkled his nose at the idea of tasting things like trees or goats. "Tell me, my scholar, what is left?"

"Smell?" he offered, pleased with himself when Alluria nodded. "I can smell an illusion?"

"No, you can smell what's *not* an illusion," she corrected. Alluria closed her eyes and motioned for Aeolmar to do the same. "What do you smell?"

"Hay," he replied, exhaling heavily. "And that Fiornacht did a poor job cleaning out Myrnnhe's stall."

Alluria chuckled. "Wasn't it your turn to rake out the stalls?" Aeolmar felt his ears go hot, and he hoped his mother still had her eyes closed. "Now, what else is there?"

He took a few more deep breaths, all of which were rife with the typical smells of a barn, until he detected something sweet. "Is that... Are there sunbonnets in the barn?" he wondered.

"Tell me what you know about sunbonnets," Alluria prompted.

"They are bright yellow flowers on a long stalk. The stems have a sweet juice, like honey. The petals make good teas. They only open when the suns shine on them."

"Do the suns shine inside the barn?"

"No." Aeolmar opened his eyes, and he saw that were indeed in the meadow, not the stuffy old barn. "How did you do that?"

"With a glamour," Alluria replied with her warm smile. "And you, my brilliant boy, have broken it. Now, run and play."

***

Aeolmar remembered that lesson now, as he breathed deeply of the cottage's stale air and searched for what was hidden. He detected old wood, soot, and the sweet, sickly stench of rotted vegetables, all of which were expected odors. But there was something about that sweet smell, maybe there were some berries amidst the rot...

Kemen was shouting for the rest to search faster, and Aeolmar was fed up with ignoring him. Without opening his eyes, he reached out and grabbed Kemen by the back of his jerkin. "Quiet," he ordered, then dropped the man to the floor. Wisely, the other hunters stopped rattling around the cottage, and Aeolmar inhaled again.

Sweet...sweet...sweet...

After several more breaths he found it, that cloying scent that reminded him of the exotic flowers in Asherah's garden. There was one flower that only bloomed at night. It had tiny white blossoms that Latera would twine into her hair, and Mara...

When she had come to speak with him and Latera before leaving with Kemen, Mara had had white flowers in her hair.

It can't be the same flowers. They'd have dried to nothing by now.

Still, the scent was there. He recalled the flowers that Mara had tucked behind her ear; they were from the vine that grew near Asherah's favored stream, a plant that the queen called lover's wake. The vine had a fat, waterlogged stalk, which was one of the reasons Mara and Latera so favored them: they lasted for days, sometimes even a sennight or more, after they were harvested.

Aeolmar blindly walked toward the scent, stepping on Bron's foot and Surya's hand in the process. He heard Surya call out for him to mind his footing as he walked through an illusory piece of furniture, and heard the hunters' gasps as the glamour collapsed around him. Convinced he'd broken the glamour, Aeolmar opened his eyes and beheld his captive child.

Mara's wrists were bound with heavy rope, and she was hanging from a metal hook in the ceiling. Her head lolled forward, whether in exhaustion or lack of consciousness he couldn't tell. Her back and belly were striped with many long cuts, and what he initially thought were the tattered remnants of her leggings was in reality dried blood and streaks of black pitch that covered her from her waist down to her ankles.

"Aeolmar! Trap!" Innetha shouted as he strode forward to his daughter. He understood what she saw, that the floor below Mara was a viper's pit, but that was also an illusion, likely to keep his daughter terrified and compliant. He ignored the snakes as he cut Mara free from her bonds.

"Mara," he murmured, laying her out on the floor; as soon as her body made contact with the floor the snake illusion vanished. "Mara, Mara, Mara." She didn't answer, not that Aeolmar had expected her to. She was breathing, and that was what mattered to him.

Aeolmar took off his cloak and wrapped it around Mara, all the while murmuring soothing words, before he saw her face. Her eyes were open, wild and terrified, and her mouth was sealed shut with the same dark, sticky substance that coated her legs and back. Aeolmar moved to wipe it away, but Mara shook her head wildly. He let his hand drop; in the next instant, Innetha knelt beside them.

"Don't fear for me, little one," she crooned. "Their magic can't affect me." Innetha glided her fingers across the dark marks, then grimaced as she brushed a small wound. Aeolmar knew that Innetha could not only heal the wound, but read the bearer's memory of it being inflicted.

"What did they do to her?" Aeolmar demanded.

"They wanted her blood," Innetha replied. "We need to get this pitch off of her," she said as she stood. "Now."

Aeolmar lifted his daughter in his arms, and followed Innetha out of the cottage and to the adjacent well. While he settled Mara against the well Innetha hauled up a pail of water, and Surya produced a handful of clean cloths. As Aeolmar gently wiped the sticky resin off of Mara's mouth, he learned why Innetha had insisted on its immediate removal: it was caustic, leaving the flesh it touched red and swollen; he remembered similar wounds on Kemen's arms and chest. Grimacing, Aeolmar wiped his hand on the grass; at least the burn ceased when the pitch was gone.

Her mouth now clear, Mara gasped a lungful of air, then tried to throw her arms around Aeolmar's neck but only managed to fall against him. Innetha gently prodded Mara's shoulders, and confirmed what Aeolmar already suspected. "Her arms have been pulled out of joint," she explained.

"Gods," Aeolmar murmured, "how long were you hanging like that?"

"Four days," Innetha replied automatically, ignoring Aeolmar's sharp gaze as she coaxed Mara into a sitting position. "This will hurt, little one, but only for a moment," she murmured in Mara's ear. The girl cringed, but Innetha persisted, "You won't be able to use your arms until we do this. Forgive me."

Innetha braced herself, then she grabbed Mara's upper arm and shoved the bone back into its socket. Mara screamed, more in surprise than pain, and Innetha quickly took care of her other arm. Aeolmar glared at Innetha over Mara's head, but he knew it was best to get the task over with quickly. Surya chose that moment to reappear, this time bearing a satchel.

"Fresh clothing," she explained, then proceeded to dampen another cloth. "We'll get her cleaned up and dressed." That had always been Surya's way; bad things may happen, yes, but she always found something to do, some way to help, and moved onward. If only Aeolmar possessed those same attributes.

"Do you want me to leave you with them?" Aeolmar asked. Mara shook her head, so Aeolmar hushed her as he stroked her hair. "I'll stay, I'll stay," he whispered. He maneuvered Mara so her legs were uncovered to her knees, as well as one of her arms, doing his best to preserve whatever was left of his daughter's modesty. Surya immediately set to work on cleaning Mara's battered feet, but Innetha took a moment to ask permission.

"Little one, may I take your hand?" she asked. When Mara whimpered and pressed her face against Aeolmar's neck, Innetha stroked her hair for a moment, her fingers catching on the dried remnants of the lover's wake, and tucked a length of it behind her ear. "I'm sorry about your shoulders, but you know that you were better off with me doing it instead of your father. His hands are so big he'd have shoved one of your arms clear over to the other side." Mara made a small noise that might have been a laugh, and didn't flinch when Innetha took her hand, though her face remained pressed against Aeolmar's neck.

Innetha worked quickly and silently, her deft fingers removing every trace of blood and pitch from Mara's flesh. When she reached Mara's shoulder she took a moment to massage the sore joint, and Mara's sigh told Aeolmar that Innetha had absorbed a measure of her pain.

"Innetha," he warned, for while he wanted his daughter's pain lessened he also wanted his huntress well and hale, and able to help him kill whoever did this.

I just need her to help me find them. I'll kill them myself.

Innetha ignored his warning, and rearranged Mara's arms so the clean limb was tucked under the cloak and drew the other out into the light. While she did so, Aeolmar got his first good look at the wounds across Mara's back. Long strips of her skin had been peeled away, and the burning pitch rubbed into the wounds.

Whoever did this is a monster. Aeolmar grabbed the cloth from Surya's pile and began cleaning the wounds. Surya rummaged in her satchel, and produced a pot of salve and bandages.

"Tell me," Aeolmar murmured while he rubbed the salve across Mara's back. "Tell me what happened." Innetha looked up sharply and shook her head, which only made Aeolmar more determined to learn exactly what sort of torture his daughter had suffered. He turned Mara so that she faced him, and held her face between his hands. Her eyes were wide, tears freely coursing down her cheeks.

"I am going to take care of whoever did this to you," he declared. "But you need to tell me things so I can find them. Help me."

"Aeolmar, she might not be able to speak," Innetha said, then leaned forward to stroke Mara's neck just below her chin. Aeolmar felt magic ripple, and Innetha struggled not to retch as she absorbed whatever had been done to Mara's throat.

Innetha cleared her throat, then gulped some of the cold well water before holding the dipper to Mara's swollen lips, coaxing a few drops down her throat. "Not too much," Innetha warned, her voice having gone raw. "We don't want to add a sore belly to your list of ailments." Mara nodded, and laid her head against Aeolmar's chest.

"She wanted me to suffer like she had," Mara croaked. Her throat worked for a moment, and Innetha offered another sip of water. Thus refreshed, Mara continued, "She said she was burning for years. That ointment, it burns like fire. She made me swallow it. She put it... everywhere... Then she cleaned it off, so I could remember what it was like to not be in pain. Then she did it again." Mara paused, and drank more of the water. Innetha didn't caution her to sip slowly this time.

"Then she started cutting me," Mara continued, her words coming in a rush as she stared straight ahead. "She wanted my blood, because it's like yours. She wants all of your blood." Aeolmar recalled the sight of his daughter, hung up on a hook as one would hang a carcass. Whoever did this had wanted her to bleed out like a slaughtered pig.

"Were you hanging the entire time?" Aeolmar asked.

"No," Mara whispered, then she began to cry. No, she wailed as she hadn't done since she was small and had fallen from her horse onto a cobbled street and shattered her elbow. Aeolmar cradled his daughter against him, murmuring soft words in the old language while he wished Latera was with them. She was best at calming their children, with her soothing voice and silly songs. *Gods, I need her. Mara needs her.*

After a time Mara calmed, or perhaps she was too exhausted to cry any longer, and Innetha broached a tender subject. "There is more to be done," Innetha said with a pointed look at Mara's torso. "It might be easier if you leave for a moment." Mara stiffened and clutched Aeolmar's shirt.

"*Dea comora*, is it all right if I leave you for a moment?" he murmured. "I promise you, if Innetha harms you in any way I'll kill her, too."

Mara snuffled. "What about Surya?"

"Never Surya," Aeolmar replied. "She's the one with the bandages. We need to keep her around."

Mara smiled as much as her inflamed mouth would allow, and nodded. Aeolmar handed over his daughter to Innetha and Surya's care, and reentered the cottage.

CHAPTER FORTY-FIVE

AEOLMAR SPEAKS

I stood in the cottage's doorway and got my first good look at the interior. The true interior, not the glamoured mess I'd originally seen. The lower walls were dark stone that gave way to daubed timbers, and there wasn't a single window. A table comprised of the stump from a truly enormous oak was in the far corner, its surface covered with bundles of herbs and what looked to be scrying tools. Interesting.

My body blocked most of the light that filtered through the doorway, causing Bron, Luth and Kemen to leave off their search and look toward me. After a moment, Kemen spoke.

"Is she all right?" he asked hoarsely.

"No." I took in Kemen's face, the bruises he'd sustained during Mara's abduction having faded almost completely, and almost regretted my short response. Almost. While this current situation was not Kemen's fault, if he had just let Mara alone none of this would have happened. Gods, I wish I'd listened to Asherah and abjured him after Asgeloth's fall, rather than forgive him his misdeeds. I should have known any

hunter who could have been swayed by Harek was a hunter that would only bring trouble.

Kemen began some sort of babbling tirade, but I waved away his words as I approached the stump-table. I rifled through the herbs and various objects, hoping to understand why these foul acts had been done to my daughter.

I sorted through the herbs, all of which had been carefully tied with silken cords and organized with the precision of a priestess. In fact, they were arranged exactly as my mother had once kept her supplies. I noted the odd coincidence, and moved on to examine the scrying tools: a small mirror, a bell, and what I assumed was a ritual wand for piercing the ether, all forged of gleaming orichalum. They were quite fine, and obviously well cared for, their very existence a sharp contrast to the crude dwelling that housed them. I moved them aside and opened a small, roughly hewn wood box. Inside was a small bowl that was eerily fa miliar.

I took it to the doorway and examined it in the bright light. It wasn't made of orichalum like the other tools, but carved from a single bone, small enough to fit in my palm, with symbols incised on the interior in a spiral pattern. The whole of it stank of blood, which made sense since my own mate had once bled into this same bowl.

"Innetha," I bellowed. She came running, pot of salve in hand. I regretted taking her away from Mara, but she was the only one who could confirm my suspicion. "Is this the bowl the seer used with Latera?"

Her brows peaked, then Innetha handed me the salve and took the bowl. She'd been present when Asherah had brought a seer to Teg'urnan in order to determine if Latera was mortal; my beloved refused to bind herself to me unless she was certain she was also immortal, for she couldn't bear the thought of me suffering eternity alone after she grew old and died. I had offered to share my immortality with her, but Latera had declined, not wanting me to shorten my own existence for the sake of lengthening hers. Beginning on the day we'd met, Latera had always put my needs ahead of her own, no matter the cost to her. Is it any wonder I love her so?

Once the seer had arrived, she'd claimed to need a few drops of Latera's blood. In the next instant, a vortex had appeared and swallowed Latera, with me powerless to save her. She'd been taken to the mortal realm where she was born, but I didn't know it at the time. To me, she was just gone. Lost. I had no idea of who'd taken her, where she was... if I'd ever see her again. I'd searched for her my entire life, and in the blink of an eye, she was gone.

We had tried interrogating the seer, but she had disappeared on her way to the dungeon. I don't mean that we lost track of her, she actually disappeared; one moment she had been walking between Luth and a guard, and in the next she wasn't. With no other options, and no clue as to where Latera had been taken, I had gone west to Brennus, where Latera had worked as a stable hand after coming to this realm. I remember her description of being stolen from her home in Gannera, and ultimately appearing in a tiny cottage with a hag called Relle.

Latera had always speculated that the seer was Relle, and now I've found Mara in a tiny cottage filled with sorcerous implements and a bowl used to collect blood and open vortexes. My beloved is a canny, canny huntress.

I stared at Innetha while she studied the bowl, running her fingertips over the symbols. "One and the same," she said with certainty; Innetha never forgot anything, not the tiniest detail. "Why is it here?" she wondered.

"I've no idea," I stated as I took the bowl from her and stowed in my belt pouch. "We've never heard from that seer again?"

"No," she replied with a shake of her head, "but Latera has always maintained that the seer and Relle are one in the same." I grunted, mostly because I hated to agree with Innetha. It was just unnatural. I assumed that she felt the same when she pursed her lips, but then she drew me outdoors and away from the cottage.

"I need to talk to you about Mara," she whispered when I asked what she was after. "What was done to her was the vilest torment."

I swallowed the bile that burned the back of my throat. "That sticky mess, it was burning her?"

"Yes," she confirmed. "It feels like a nettle's sting. It was poured down her throat, and she felt as if her belly was burning from within."

"Hells." I raked my hand through my hair and leaned back against a tree. Mara was an innocent; never had she spoken a word against anyone, never had she committed an ill deed. For someone to do this to her, they were truly evil. "She told you that?"

"No," Innetha replied. "She won't tell me anything. When she realized I was reading her skin's memory, she asked for only Surya to touch her." She turned toward where Surya still tended Mara, and didn't look at me when she spoke. "There are many things that happened to her, here in this cottage and before. Things she doesn't want you to know."

"Then don't tell me." I wouldn't betray Mara's trust, not for anything short of saving her life. Innetha cocked an eyebrow at my declaration, but didn't question me.

"What I can tell you is that Mara was covered in that resin to make her feel like she was set afire in the underworld," Innetha said.

"The underworld?" I repeated, and she nodded. "This makes less and less sense. Why bother kidnapping my daughter, why make her feel like she's in the underworld? I've never been there, never sent anyone there as punishment."

"*Then perhaps this grudge isn't against just you,*" Innetha suggested. *If not just me, then who else?*

"*Who in the nine realms would seek to punish me—or anyone—by punishing Mara?*" I demanded. "*Who could even manage all of this?*"

Innetha shrugged. "Which of your enemies still breathes?"

I snorted. "None."

"*Then you must think about your family's enemies,*" Innetha said. "*Mara said they wanted her blood, because it's like yours. Who else has your blood?*"

I ran my hand through my hair. The only others that shared my blood were dead, but Cydia only knew who my father and mother had run afoul of. And my grandsire... I imagined that the former Prelate of Parthalan could have made a fair few enemies over the years.

"*This vendetta could be centuries old,*" I said. "*How will I ever find out who caused this?*"

"*You don't need to learn how all of this began,*" Innetha said. "*You need to find who is working against you and yours today, and end it.*"

Today... "Gods, Tor and Ember have my blood."

Innetha nodded. "Luckily, they're in Teg'urnan, behind Latera and Elkin and the rest of the hunters. With them safe, we have time to learn how all of this began."

Yes. This blood feud did not start with me, but I will end it.

Chapter Forty-Six

For the past sennight I had wandered about my chambers devoid of purpose, caring for Tor and Ember but doing little else. It had been seven days—seven days!—since my connection with Aeolmar had been severed. I was beyond panic and approaching abject hysteria. Horrible, dark thoughts kept skirting the edges of my mind, but I shoved them away.

Aeolmar would come back to me. Him and Mara, they will both come back. They had to.

Despite my anxiety, or perhaps because of it, my thoughts kept returning to a dream I had the night before. Whenever Aeolmar wasn't beside me, I had a hard time sleeping, and it had been well past moonrise when I'd finally drifted off. In my dream, I was in darkness so complete it was like a cave. Slowly, the darkness faded, and I found myself in a meadow. Aeolmar was standing on a rise before me.

"Mar," I shouted. I ran toward him, faster and faster until my lungs burned, but I couldn't get any closer to him. "Mar, why can't I reach you?"

"I am not your mate," the man said, laughing. His skin glowed, and I realized that he was taller than Aeolmar, and that his limbs were unnaturally long and slender instead of heavily muscled. But the impossibly blue eyes were my mate's eyes, and his long brown hair was identical to the strands I'd raked my fingers through so many times.

"Who are you?" I demanded of this imposter. "Have you done something to Aeolmar?"

"I watch over him, and his children." Not-Aeolmar made a sweeping gesture, and in the darkness beside him I saw Tor asleep in his cradle, and Ember nestled in bed. "And his children's mother."

Perhaps it was only the nature of the dream, but this vague declaration comforted me. "Will Aeolmar and Mara return?"

"Perchance they shall, but first there is something you must do." The glow intensified, pushing outward from Not-Aeolmar's skin, the white brilliance surrounding me until I was one with the light. When I woke a shaft of sunlight was streaming directly onto my face.

Olluhm. I had dreamt of Olluhm, the god who was both the elder sun and Aeolmar's grandsire. I didn't know if I should go to temple and thank Olluhm for visiting me, or bar my chamber door against whatever the gods might unleash upon me next. Despite that he is the faerie All Father I'd never accepted the claim that Olluhm is a kind god of love. What god of love kills his rivals and damns their people? What god of love would let his daughter, and her mate and children, be murdered by Mersgoth?

I shook my head. I was beginning to understand why we elves only worshipped our ancestors.

The morning light had burned away the strangeness of my dream, and I reluctantly got out of bed. Tor was still sleeping, although Ember was wide awake and busily rearranging my boots. I let her be as I wandered out to the balcony, feeling a twinge of guilt. I'd confined the children to our chambers since I learned of Asherah's strange malady, and Ember clearly missed her playmate, but what else was I to do? Asherah had well and truly lost her mind, and we needed to keep that secret while we searched for a cure. To that end, the elder Finlay had been tasked with ruling Parthalan with the younger Finlay as his only advisor.

The only other person who knew of Asherah's mental state was Elkin, but no one had suggested he take on additional duties. His connection with Innetha had severed as cleanly as my and Aeolmar's had. Publicly, he declared that he had the utmost faith in all the hunters and knew In-netha would soon return to him. Privately, he visited me every evening, and we wept together.

As for Asherah, she'd been given over to Mallia and Attia's care. Indeed, Attia had confided to me that she hadn't seen Asherah in such a state since Lormac's death, but then, that was the crux of our current problem. Asherah had forgotten that Lormac had died long ago.

Mallia hadn't left the queen's side for a moment, save to replenish her herbs or salves or whatever it was she toted about in that basket of hers. The healer's selfless actions had restored her reputation in my eyes, albeit minimally. Still, if she could peel away the layers of insanity from Asherah's mind, I would make sure she was lauded as the greatest hero Parthalan had ever known.

When I stepped onto the balcony, a basket in the eastern alcove caught my eye. It was filled with scrolls that Aeolmar had yet to read, and I'd been reluctant to move the basket. He'd want it in the same spot he left it, for surely he would read all of the scrolls upon his return. Moving it felt like an admission that he might not...

"Don't want these getting rained on," I muttered under a cloudless sky, then I picked up the basket and set it on the bench beside me. I wiped some wetness from my cheek, then I removed the lid and looked through the scrolls. The distraction helped me calm down, and I selected one scroll that had already been unsealed. It was about the former High Priestess, Sarelle.

The scroll listed her known family, and I learned that she was only one generation removed from Olluhm and Cydia. I read on, and discovered that her family was responsible for the red grape vineyards in the west, a large enterprise that had made them quite wealthy. Being that Sarelle outlived all of her close relations, she eventually became the sole owner of the vineyards, and once boasted a treasury that rivalled Teg'urnan's.

What happened to all of that coin? *I found a map of Sarelle's holdings, and realized that what were once her vineyards was now the Golden Knoll, Iruna and Avinor's lavish home. Finlay had recognized they lived beyond their means, but he'd thought they were taxing locals. Little did he know that Iruna's fortune was built on a traitor's legacy.*

I must remember to tell Finlay. *I set the scroll aside, then I stood and leaned my elbows on the short stone wall of my balcony, and gazed at the courtyard below. My gaze travelled the now-familiar route down the grand steps and through the gates, toward the village below. If I were as tall as Aeolmar, I could see the roof of The Swan, the last place Mara had been seen.*

By Kemen. The last place she had been seen by Kemen.

I will see her again.

I shook my head and let it droop between my shoulders. The lack of messages from Aeolmar was driving me to my wits end. The small, rational part of my mind knew that he likely hadn't come across anyone willing or able to carry word back to Teg'urnan, a simple, practical reason for the lack of messages. I couldn't feel him in my mind because of the great distance between us, nothing more. Never mind that I had felt him as clear as a summer evening every day since our binding, even when I was in Gannera and he had remained in Parthalan. No, distance was the sole cause of this momentary disturbance.

While those thoughts coursed across the front of my mind, the rest of me feared for Aeolmar and Mara's lives, along with the other hunters who had accompanied Aeolmar on his quest. If these warring thoughts kept up, my mind would fracture upon itself and I'd join Asherah in her madness.

A woman's voice hailed me from below, and I saw Asherah taking her morning walk on Mallia's arm. We couldn't keep Asherah sequestered in the royal chambers indefinitely, though our queen was content to wait on Lormac's return. Once we had discovered that her eyes looked almost normal in direct sunlight, Finlay and I decided that Asherah should take a daily walk across the palace square. The sunlight and fresh air had done her some good.

I waved at the pair below, narrowing my eyes as they turned to greet a few others. Asherah's people truly loved her, and our queen enjoyed nothing more than to interact with them. When she was in her right mind, of course. Now, we had to convince her that Lormac wanted an accessible queen, and she had been doing as she was told. For now.

But that wasn't why I was examining the scene below. Asherah was only supposed to take these short jaunts with Finlay or Attia, both of whom would keep her from divulging... well, anything. Between our missing First Hunter and insane queen, Parthalan held its fair share of secrets of late. It irked me that Mallia was walking with Asherah, only partly because the queen being seen on the healer's arm may lead others to question if she was well. The last thing we needed was for Asherah's delusions to become public knowledge before Aeolmar returned.

I sighed, having decided that Mallia was only trying to help in her own clumsy manner. I did appreciate Mallia's skills as a healer, but as a person she fell flat. More, she'd been trying to work her way into the queen's affairs for some time, since the very moment Asherah had announced that she was carrying Finlay. No matter the mess that had become of Tor's birth, I was glad the healer-witch had never had access to me at my most vulnerable.

The child sun had just crested the Eastern Tower, and a shaft of light illuminated Mallia's back. Her green healer's robes shimmered, and inexplicably darkened. I squinted and cocked my head to the side; her silken robes now appeared like gray sackcloth, worn and filthy.

Why would Mallia wear such a garment? *As matriarch of the healers, Mallia was always espousing cleanliness; why, one of the first arguments she and I had had was when I was heavy with Mara, and she had wanted me to boil my sleeping furs before I began my lying in. To sterilize them of any lingering contamination, she had said when I questioned why my bedclothes needed to be turned into so much soup. Contamination! As if Aeolmar and I slept in some filthy, flea-infested castoffs. My bedclothes were as fine as the queen's own, Aeolmar had seen to that from the beginning.* Then, a shaft of light sent directly from the elder sun alighted upon Mallia's head, and I forgot my inner meanderings about furs and sheets.

Consider that the child sun follows his father across the sky, and therefore the elder sun's rays are typically ahead of his son's. I've always found that a bit odd, but it's only noticeable at the very beginning and end of the day, when the suns are close to the horizon. But before my eyes, a ray of light shone from the elder sun directly onto Mallia, further illuminating what the child sun revealed.

She wasn't clad in a healer's robe at all, but a gray hooded garment. The hood was thrown back, and I could see her lank gray hair, and her rough, bark-like skin. Her shoulders were hunched forward, and the edges of her sleeves trailed in the dust. Then she laughed, a malevolent cackle I had only heard once before, but had never forgotten.

Mallia was the seer, the very one who had sent me back to the mortal realm. More, I now knew her to be Relle, the hag who'd stolen me from Gannera in the first place.

I do not pray, other than to utter an epithet now and then. Elves follow no gods, and my human gods abandoned me long, long ago. But I could not ignore the help that Olluhm and Solon had given me, their descendant's mate, and I thanked them both.

"Please, now help Aeolmar, and Mara," I whispered, then I went inside my chamber.

Olluhm's Balls. Now what was I going to do?

CHAPTER FORTY-SEVEN

LATERA SPEAKS

*M*y hands shook as I donned my hunter's gear, the once-supple leather stiff from lack of use. Other than the day of Aeolmar's left to follow Mara's trail, I hadn't worn any of my gear since I'd first suspected Tor's imminent arrival, the joy of a third child far outweighing the coming boredom of staying inside and forgoing riding and hunting. But then, I'd only really been a huntress again for a few short seasons after Ember had been weaned. I laughed to myself; here I am, the First Huntress of Parthalan, yet I rarely hunt demons.

"Mama?" Ember stood before me, her blue eyes wide. "Are we going somewhere?"

"We are, but we're not all going to the same place." I drew her onto my lap and held her, my little self. "I need you to do something very important. If you do, Papa and I will be very proud of you. Can I count on you?" Ember nodded; she was always eager to be in charge of any adult-oriented task. "I need you to take your brother and go to the king.

Tell him that he must take you, Tor, and the younger Finlay into the vaults beneath the temple."

"Why the king?" Ember wondered, with good reason. I had debated sending her to Wren, but I didn't know if Mallia-Relle also had designs upon the younger Finlay. By sending Ember and Tor to the elder Finlay, he was sure to keep all of our children safe. Besides, I needed to confer with my sister about the queen, and I couldn't do that in a room full of children.

"Because without Papa here, he's the only man I trust with you," I replied.

"But what if Tor gets hungry?" she pressed.

"Give him goat milk. Finlay can get it for you. Now come along. We need to get your brother ready." I set Ember on her feet and threw a few things into a satchel, then I began strapping on my troll swords.

"Mama, you're scaring me."

I turned around and saw Ember, white-faced and trembling, and felt like a fool. Of course she was scared, what with her father and elder sister missing, and her mother dressed for battle and leaving her and her younger brother with the king while she went off to do who knows what.

"I'm sorry, baby," I whispered, pulling her into my arms. "I don't mean to scare you. I have to do something that I'd rather not, and I want you and Tor to be safe until it's over with."

"What do you have to do?"

"I can't tell you, not just yet," I replied. "What if afterward I tell you how it went?"

"Will Papa be back soon?" she asked. "With Mara?"

I kissed the top of her head. "I hope so."

"I miss them."

"I do, too." I held her for another moment, then I pulled back and regarded her wide blue eyes. "We should go. Are you ready?"

Ember nodded, and let me lead her to Tor's cradle. I picked up my sleeping baby, then I picked up the scroll that detailed Sarelle's fortune and handed it to Ember. "Will you give this to the king?"

Ember accepted the scroll. "Yes, Mama."

I smiled at my smart girl, and the three of us left our chamber.

The corridor that led to the royal apartments had never seemed so short. All too soon, we reached the end, and I relinquished my son to my daughter's arms. Ember had hardly reached her eighth winter, and here I was giving her more responsibility that most adults could bear. I prayed for the second time that day, now asking Olluhm to make good on his word and watch over Aeolmar's children.

"Remember, stay with the king," I whispered, looping the satchel's strap over Ember's shoulder. She looked so tiny, my brave little girl.

"I will, Mama. I'll make you proud."

"You already have," I said. "I love you, Ember. I know you'll do well." I kissed her brow and then Tor's, then she was on her way. I watched them until they turned a corner and disappeared from view.

I squared my shoulders and walked in the opposite direction. The mother in me was gone, and the Demon-killer crossed the palace to Wren's chambers. I found her alone in her stillroom, mashing up herbs.

"Latera," she greeted. "Has there been word from Aeolmar?"

"How can a spell be cast upon a person in a room warded against unknown magic?" I demanded without preamble.

"A spelled item could be introduced to the room. As long as it didn't make direct contact with the wards, the spell would likely hold. Then, one would only need to ensure that the item made contact with the victim's skin," Wren replied; she knew me well enough to answer first and ask why I wanted to know such things later. "A liquid could be absorbed by the wearer and then transferred to the victim, but smoke or even a powder would likely do the trick quite well."

I recalled Asherah's cloudy eyes and wondered if such a powder had been blown into her face. "If the spell was cast by way of a powder, can such a spell be countered?"

"I don't see why not. Have you tried washing it off?"

"I think it's in her eyes," I replied. Wren raised an eyebrow, so I elaborated, "Mallia is Relle."

She nodded but otherwise made no reaction; my sister is not amazed by much. "Relle must be quite powerful, more so than we ever suspected." she murmured, now rattling about small bottles of this and that. "What has the spell done?"

"Made Asherah forget the Finlays. She thinks that Lormac still lives, and that her son is Leran."

"Mmm." Apparently that was what Wren needed to know, since she snatched two tiny bottles filled with liquids off a shelf, then grabbed third and poured the substances together. "It's likely not just in her eyes, but bound to her skin," Wren said. "Get her in a bath and add this to the water." I glanced at the smaller bottles; incised runes identified the liquids as 'remembrance' and 'clarity'.

"How am I going to get her in a bath?" I wondered.

"Throw her in if you need to." Ever practical Wren. "How did you learn that Mallia is Relle?"

I recounted the vision of Relle's true form under the crossed rays of light from Solon and Olluhm, a sign from the gods if there ever was one. Before I'd finished that tale, Wren was again shuffling through her odds and ends; for a woman with no magic to speak of, she could manage almost anything. Eventually, she produced a curved lens the size of her palm from a crate of glassware.

"This will concentrate the suns' light," she explained. "Perhaps enough to destroy the spell, or it might be able to make Relle's true self visible for a few moments. The children?"

"*With the king,*" *I replied.* "*I sent them to the vaults.*"

"*I will research memory spells,*" *Wren said.* "*If what I've given you doesn't work, try to locate the carrier for the spell, and bring it to me. If I have it, I may be able to neutralize it.*" *I nodded and turned to depart. Wren stayed me with a hand on my arm.* "*And, sister, be safe.*"

I smiled tightly, then departed. No, I wasn't going to be safe, not in the slightest.

***

"*Unseen, unseen, unseen.*"

I stood in the corridor outside the royal chambers, my body pressed against the wall. I chanted the words in the old language under my breath, hoping my glamour would hold. Never once had it failed me, not this or any other spell Aeolmar had taught me. Even so, though a lifetime had passed since I had been kidnapped from my home in Gannera, I still had a hard time trusting magic.

At last, the chamber door opened. I leaned forward, hoping that Mallia-Relle was finally taking her leave of Asherah, but it was only a saffira *bearing away a basket of laundry. I slumped back against the wall, wondering what the healer was doing in there. I'd already been standing at the end of the corridor for the better part of an hour, swathed in shadows and glamour, my mind spinning as I imagined what that hag was doing to my queen behind closed doors. Perhaps I should have brought a blanket and set myself up for the night.*

Then the door opened again, and Mallia-Relle stepped into the corridor. I debated dropping my glamour and walking past her as if unaware of her true identity, but decided against it. In my present state of mind,

I was more likely to strike her down rather than ignore her, and what if we needed her to break the spell upon Asherah? More, what if she was responsible for Mara's abduction, and was the only one who could bring my mate and my child back to me?

Mallia-Relle, haughty as ever, passed within a hand's breadth of me, her heavy silk skirts nearly brushing my boots. But then, her skirts weren't silk, were they? Her illusion was complete down to the soft rustle of fabric, so complete it amazed me. Had there ever been a healer in Teg'urnan called Mallia? Or just an abductress called Relle?

Whatever or whomever she really was, she turned a corner and disappeared, unaware of my presence. I held on to my glamour as I approached Asherah's door, which opened for me of its own accord; Aeolmar had charmed the door for me long ago, and a simple glamour wouldn't fool it. Once I was inside the chamber, I let the glamour drop, and called Asherah's name.

"Here," she answered. I moved deeper into the chamber and found Asherah staring into the hearth, humming a lullaby. Asherah's appearance had improved over the past sennight, but she was still more of an invalid than a queen. She was clad in a thin chemise, not one of her usual elegant gowns, her hair was stringy, and her feet were bare. Ember would have been appalled. "Have you news?" she asked.

She didn't mean news from Aeolmar, but of Lormac. Suddenly, I knew what I was going to do. "It's just come," I said, rushing forward to grasp her hands. "Lormac will be here before nightfall. Come, we must get you ready to receive him."

I dragged Asherah to her feet and pushed her toward her bathing chamber, shoving her past a startled Attia. "But I need to dress," Asherah protested.

"First, you need a bath," I said firmly. I held Attia's gaze for a moment, hoping she wasn't also bespelled. After a moment, she nodded

and called for water. A small procession of saffira readied the bathing chamber, and soon enough they left me alone with the queen, a tub of steaming water, and herbal concoctions of dubious origin. I uttered my third prayer of the day.

I got Asherah undressed and into the water, added the contents of the vial Wren had given me, and that's as far as it went for a moment. After a deep sigh, I grabbed a sponge and ball of soap and set to scrubbing the queen myself. Much to my surprise a gray, powdery substance sloughed off her skin; so Wren had been correct, the spell was bound to her skin. Suspecting that there was more of it in her hair, I forcibly dunked her, not that my rude treatment affected Asherah's happy mood. She was positively euphoric, chattering away about Lormac's return, of how pleased he would be when he saw how well Leran had grown, and of all the things the three of them would do together once they were reunited.

"Once more," I coaxed, and I dunked her head again. Her hair had regained the pale luster it previously bore, and her skin was no longer sallow and grayish. "What is your mate's name?" I asked.

"You know as well as I that he's called Lormac," Asherah replied. "You were there at our binding feast."

"Such a wonderful feast it was," I muttered. She turned to me and I saw what I most feared; her eyes remained coated in that gray film. Well, I couldn't very well take a soapy sponge to her eyes, now could I? I'd already emptied the vial Wren had given me into the bath, so I halfheartedly flicked the bathwater into her eyes.

"Latera," she admonished. "Have a care! I cannot receive Lormac with my eyes red and swollen."

"Forgive me, I am just excited for his return," I mumbled, and we talked about Lormac some more. If this went on for much longer, I'd be as insane as she was.

My hand absently touched my throat, and I felt the pendant Aeolmar had given me the day we were supposed to be bound, but weren't. On that day, Relle had wormed her way into the palace and sent me back to the mortal realm for a full turn of the seasons, and I'd spent most of that time struggling to return. Yes, I had been reunited with my family, but the painful truth was that I no longer belonged in Gannera. Sometimes I wondered if I ever had.

I had worn the pendant daily in Gannera, its weight against my skin a constant reminder of Aeolmar. After I had made my return to Parthalan, Aeolmar and I had learned that the pendant was in fact one of the tears Asherah had shed upon the Day of Sadness in her grief over Lormac and Torim's deaths. Aeolmar's mother had taken her tears and somehow transmuted them into two jewels, one of which she kept, while the other ended up in Asherah's temple in the mortal realm. Mindful of Asherah's past, I had stopped wearing the pendant, but after Aeolmar's presence had disappeared from my mind, I put it back on, desperate for any connection to him.

Asherah's grief over Lormac's death...

I unclasped the chain and tossed the whole thing into the bath, fully expecting nothing to happen. For a moment, nothing did. Then the water swirled and took on a bluish tinge. Asherah asked what was happening, then she rubbed her eyes. She murmured that they burned, then she was screaming and tearing at them; I hope I hadn't just truly blinded her. Was that treason, blinding an ensorcelled queen?

I shoved her head under the water again and shook her back and forth, rinsing away the evil that had coated her. Asherah spluttered to the surface, thick gray globules streaming from her eyes. I grabbed some fresh toweling and dabbed at her cheeks, fearing her reaction to such treatment. As I cleaned her face, I saw that in her terror she had shredded the skin around her left eye, and her pale skin was scored with welts. At least her eye appeared undamaged; it was still cloudy, but not as badly as before.

"He's dead, isn't he?" Asherah asked. Then a magical tear in the bathwater is the proper technique to remove a remembrance spell. I must remember to tell Wren.

"He is," I replied. "But you have the Finlays. They're alive and well, and they love you."

Asherah nodded, staring at the murky water. "Gods, they must hate me. What kind of a mate am I? What kind of mother?"

"None of this is your fault," I said. "You were spelled by Mallia." I grabbed Asherah's hands and hauled her out of the bath; I had no idea what that gray mess might do if I let it dry upon her skin, and I didn't want to find out.

"Mallia?" Asherah asked, and I proceeded to tell her what I'd learned about Teg'urnan's matriarch. It was plain that I was furious, and I set to drying her a bit more enthusiastically than necessary.

"I believe I'm dry," she said, staying my hands before I rubbed her skin off her bones. "A robe would be well appreciated."

I blushed at that, grabbed the closest robe, and helped Asherah into it. "Why are you helping me?" she asked as she fastened the stays. "I thought you hated me."

"I don't," I said. "I was just mad at Mar." Asherah laughed softly.

"He is quite insufferable, at times," she agreed, keeping her eyes downcast. "I like that you have a name for him. All those who are truly in love seem to develop names for one another." Her voice trailed off at the last, and I realized that she had the worst of fates. She'd lost Lormac twice now, and forgotten Finlay and their son in the process. I guided Asherah to a bench, and began combing the tangles from her pale hair.

"Did Lormac have a name for you?" I ventured.

"Star," she replied. "His star, little star... Many names, but all a variation of star."

"For your hair," I surmised, and she nodded. "What does Finlay call you?"

"Love, his maiden. Warrior maiden. And my least favorite, Sher." She was silent for a moment while I worked out a stubborn knot. "What does Aeolmar call you?"

"Beloved," I replied. "That, or nalla." I shouldn't have asked it, but I did. "Did Aeolmar ever call you anything?"

"Nothing that can be repeated in polite conversation," she replied. "As for myself, I recall referring to him as both imbecile and bastard, on occasion."

"So he's always been this bad?"

"No," she replied, the familiar glint having returned to her black eyes. Well, the right eye, at least. "He's much better now." I helped Asherah to her feet, then she grabbed my arm. "You won't break your bond, will you?"

"What bond? My bond with Aeolmar?" I asked. The one thing I truly couldn't imagine was a life without him; even the lack of his presence buzzing away in my mind was enough to drive me mad. Whether it was distance that had negated his presence or something more, I knew I would never seek another.

"I couldn't," I answered at last. "I don't think any man would ever compare to Aeolmar. Though you seem to have done quite well for yourself."

Asherah smiled at that, and my strife with the queen was over. Aeolmar had been right; his past with the queen didn't matter. He was mine and always would be. However, he was still going to tell me everything. In detail.

"Your eye," I murmured, touching Asherah's left temple. Streaks of gray still obscured her black gaze, and the many gashes oozed blood. Gods, I hope I hadn't permanently damaged her.

"It's nothing," she demurred, but I knew that she was lying. I let her get away with it, for now. Then she and I exited the bathing chamber and found Attia close to the door, no doubt eavesdropping. Attia loved Asherah like a daughter, and had been as distraught as Finlay these past days.

"Asherah, your face," Attia gasped.

"I'll be fine," Asherah said to her saffira-nell. *"We'll put some salve on it, but then I must dress. I cannot dispose of treasonous hags while barefoot and wearing naught but a robe."*

CHAPTER FORTY-EIGHT

A string of curses broke the silence, and Aeolmar yanked a splinter out from under his thumbnail. He had been examining the exterior of the cottage alongside Innetha and Luth, searching for something—anything—that would shed some light as to who had abducted Mara, and for what purpose. So far, the edifice had turned out to be thoroughly, maddeningly ordinary.

Aeolmar hadn't quite finished cursing when Surya approached him, supporting a pale but walking Mara. As Aeolmar dropped the offending bit of wood, he noticed that Mara was wearing Surya's extra gear. Under normal circumstances, Surya's clothing would have been far too large for Mara, but the heavy bandages made the size difference unnoticeable. Luth and Innetha watched her approach, but Mara ignored them as she walked directly to her father.

"Do you need to rest?" Aeolmar asked. He moved to put his arm around Mara's shoulders, but dropped it for fear of hurting her.

"I've been doing nothing forever," she replied with a smile that was more of a grimace. "It's good to move under my own power again."

Aeolmar nodded; he understood the need to be up and doing something. "At least the skies are cooperating," he said, indicating the sunny clearing. As he did so, he realized just how flawless the clearing was.

The small field that surrounded the cottage was a perfect circle, and the clearing was wide and the smooth, all errant stones and other obstructions having been long since carted away. The grass was lush and evenly shorn, and the perimeter was ringed with stately broadleaf trees. What undergrowth there was, thick vines and shy woodland flowers, politely kept its distance from the clearing and the sole trail that led to it. Indeed, whoever owned the cottage must be a master woodsman.

Or one adept at changing the appearance of their environment.

Suspecting the latter, Aeolmar looked closely at the flowers that dotted the tree line; they were flaedyne, one of his mother's favorites. She'd planted the tiny red flowers against the south side of their barn, and had enjoyed their profuse blooms every autumn. Only, it wasn't yet summer.

It's not right. He stared at the sky, clear blue with only the occasional cloud, then at the impeccable lawn, and the artfully arranged wildflowers. It was perfect.

Nothing real is perfect.

Aeolmar rounded on Surya and Luth, and demanded, "How long have we been here, in this clearing?"

"The suns say it's not yet midday," replied Luth.

"It wasn't yet midday when we arrived," Aeolmar said. "By now, it should be close to dusk."

"I've been in that cottage for four days," Mara said quietly. "Before that, I spent three in the back of a cart."

Aeolmar's brow furrowed, as much from his daughter's recent torture as to the disparity in time. "Mara," he began, but she shook her head.

"I'm fine," she said, then her mouth twisted. "No, I'm not. I'm far from fine, but I will be. I just want this to be done."

Before Aeolmar could continue, Bron and Kemen exited the cottage. Kemen stepped toward Mara, but she turned away. Aeolmar placed himself between Kemen and his daughter, ignoring the former's pained features, then he addressed all the hunters.

"How many days since we left Teg'urnan?" he demanded.

"Thirty-four," Bron replied. "Today is the thirty-fifth."

"Yet Mara has only counted seven days," Aeolmar stated.

"You're sure it has only been seven?' Surya asked gently.

"Yes," Mara replied. "Every morning, she would rail at the elder sun as he rose. She has done it seven times."

She. We are looking for a she. Aeolmar's gaze swept across the clearing, from the lush lawn to the nearly cloudless sky, and on to the rather imperfect cottage. He was certain that the cottage was real, and likely the center point used to anchor a web of illusion spells. That web stretched farther than he'd initially realized.

"We're still in the illusion," Aeolmar concluded.

"I thought you broke it when you found Mara," Surya said.

"I don't think I did," he said, running his hand over the cottage wall. "I believe I instead pulled Mara into the illusion alongside us. Or maybe we're in it with her." He walked away from the cottage and to the edge of the clearing, then slowly paced the tree line. They all appeared to be real trees, none of his senses telling him otherwise, and the woodland beyond was filled with the smells and noises one associated with such a land.

"Perhaps the illusion is only the sky," he murmured, casting his gaze toward the suns. "Surya, can you see any birds?"

The huntress tilted her head up and squinted, then she frowned. Slowly, she rotated where she stood, then shook her head. "No birds fly across this sky," she said. "What's more, I don't think the clouds are moving."

"By all the living gods," Aeolmar muttered. "Someone's stopped time."

"I still don't understand that saying," Mara griped. "Even the old ones still have followers. The gods are eternal."

"They aren't," Kemen replied. "There were two full pantheons of gods that once warred amongst themselves. Olluhm appeared and sided with the rebels, then he cast the old gods from the skies and took his place as the All Father. Once Cydia began bearing his young, he destroyed the race that once inhabited Parthalan, leaving the land free for his children."

"Olluhm did that?" Mara asked. "I thought he was kind, and loving!"

"He loves his children, and whomever warms his bed," Kemen stated, "no others."

Aeolmar completed his circuit of the clearing and came to stand beside Mara. "Kemen, tell us how Olluhm destroyed the prior race, and those that refused to worship him," he said, his eyes fixed on the far edge of the woodland. Kemen raised an eyebrow, but complied.

"Olluhm decreed that no woman less lovely that his mate should live," he began. In response to Surya's quizzical face, he continued, "It was a death sentence for every woman who lived on Parthalan's soil. None were lovelier than Cydia, so each perished before the eyes of their mates and fathers and sons. Without women to bear young, Olluhm had hoped that the race would die off."

"Couldn't the men have just taken women from a different race—elves, or nymphs—as mates?" Surya asked.

"Most did," Kemen replied. "When Olluhm learned of this, he cursed every man that his seed would only bring forth male children. He still expected the race to die off, but they held on. They hid in the underworld, where Olluhm couldn't follow, and kept seizing women of other races, who bore them their children. Hells, they used animals if it suited them."

"The way you're describing them, they sound like demons," Surya said.

"They are," Aeolmar said. He noticed the air shimmer near the tree line. "A filthy, disgusting race. Olluhm was right to banish them."

"But we stole their land!" Mara exclaimed. "How can—"

Aeolmar held up his hand, and nodded toward the far side of the clearing. "They did not deserve Parthalan," he said loudly. Whomever had kidnapped Mara had wanted her to suffer as if she burned in the underworld, and Aeolmar suspected that was the key to drawing her abductor out. Along the edge of the wood, the air about the trees trembled. "They deserve their torment in the underworld. It's a fitting end for such beasts." Aeolmar's gaze swept along the tree line, his face a mask of disgust. "Whoever resides in this place, they have the filthy stink of demons. Even the air is fouled by their presence."

A swirling vortex near identical to the one that had spirited Latera to Gannera appeared in response to Aeolmar's taunts, and a mass of dark matter began taking shape.

"She's coming," Mara whispered, clutching Aeolmar's arm, her knuckles white.

Aeolmar shielded Mara with his body and shouted, "Face us, you coward. Show yourself, so we can send you back to the plains of hell where you belong!"

"Where I belong?" The voice was rough and cold, a winter wind that promised a blizzard. "I belong here, upon the surface, with sunlight on my face and wind in my hair. I belong in Teg'urnan, serving my god and king. *She* sent me to the hells."

The ether twisted like heat waves rising from cobbles on a midsummer day, and a grotesque woman stepped into the illusion. Her flesh was thick and cracked, like the crust of an over-baked loaf, and her hair hung in grayish clumps about knobby shoulders. She wore a shapeless gray garment, the hood pulled low and obscuring her eyes. Aeolmar instantly knew her as Relle, as surely as if Latera had identified the hag herself. More, he also knew that she was the seer that had duped the queen, and sent his mate hurtling through time and space back to the mortal realm.

"I belong here, walking Parthalan's soil," Relle hissed. "What she did, she had no right!"

"Who is this woman you speak of?" Aeolmar demanded. "You've tortured my daughter, yet you must know that she is not the cause of your plight!"

"She's dead, but it is not enough that my master killed her," Relle replied. "I will punish her children, and their children."

"Foolish woman, whose children?" Innetha asked. "We're all someone's child." The hag laughed, cackled really, until the harsh noises eventually degrading into a cough.

"Not just anyone's children, *her* children," Relle wheezed. "Her line must be ended." Her fit of coughs and laughs over, she straightened and fixed Aeolmar in her muddy gaze. "You. Whoreson. Your line must end."

Aeolmar bellowed, shaking free of Mara's grasp as he lunged toward the hag, but the air around him thickened like quicksand. With a flick of her wrist, Relle held Aeolmar aloft as if suspended by invisible ropes.

"You think to harm me as she did? I've learned much since those days," Relle said. Innetha and Luth moved toward Relle, but she sank the hunters into the earth up to their knees. Surya and Kemen flanked Mara, but did not advance. "Oh, I was wise then, but my power has truly flourished under my master. Flourished in ways I couldn't have guessed."

"What wisdom?' Innetha sneered. "What sort of salves and philters do they teach of in the underworld?"

"No, you ignorant wench," Relle said. "I was High Priestess of the Sun God. Magic flowed through my veins, the ether bent to my will. Then *she* refused the honor we had offered her. Stupid girl! She would rather lie with an animal than become consort to a conqueror."

"Sarelle," Aeolmar whispered.

Chapter Forty-Nine

*H*er name was never Relle.

Aeolmar assumed that Latera, having only heard the seer's name once and under duress, hadn't remembered her full name. If she had, all of Parthalan would have searched for the rogue High Priestess who had, along with Sahlgren, betrayed the fae.

"Yes," Sarelle hissed. She unclenched her fist, and Aeolmar fell to the ground with a thud. "I was once called that, before your dim-witted mother ruined me. For years I burned, burned in a pit of cold fire that held back the mercy of death. She wished my mind and body to remain whole for my torment."

"You don't look intact to me," Innetha said in her haughtiest voice. "You seem little more than a dried out stump."

"Beauty is sometimes the price of power," Sarelle said. "My master taught me that, once he rescued me from the pit. He taught me everything."

"Who was this master?" Aeolmar demanded, having risen to his knees. "Pray, who taught you to harm children? Surely none of Ol-luhm's followers!"

"Those prostrating fools can hardly pluck a chicken, let alone make a proper sacrifice. My master is the most powerful sorcerer ever known to the nine realms. His brother would have been king, if not for the elf."

"Who?" Aeolmar demanded as Mara shouted, "My mother killed him!"

Sarfek, Aeolmar realized; he'd forgotten that Mara had read the scrolls as well. *Sarfek took Sarelle out of the underworld, and this is what he made of her.*

"He's long dead," Mara continued, "longer than I've been alive. Shouldn't you find someone else to follow?"

"Careful, girl," Sarelle warned, "I know what makes you scream." Mara cringed, and Aeolmar fought the urge to leap in front of his daughter. Sarelle was clearly mad, but he needed to know more about the illusion she had trapped them in. More importantly, he needed to know how to break it.

"Is that why you've built this little world, Sarelle?" Aeolmar asked. "Have you got Sarfek's soul trapped in a pot of honey so you may still share a kiss? Or is he inhabiting your walking stick?"

"Your taunts mean nothing," Sarelle said, followed by another soul-chilling cackle. "This place was made for you alone, whoreson. Your strength is too great inside the palace your grandsire built. I had to get you away from Teg'urnan to end your line."

"My line..." The words died on his lips as Sarelle's laughter grew ever louder. She had separated Aeolmar from Latera and Tor and Ember, his beloved mate and defenseless children. Images of his family's deaths played behind his eyes... He rose, pulling himself free of the dregs of Sarelle's spell, spun around and grabbed Mara by the shoulders.

"What did she do when she first had you?" Aeolmar demanded.

"I-I don't remember," Mara stammered. "When I woke, I was burning."

"Try," Aeolmar implored. "What else was there?" Mara's eyes widened, and she bit her lip. "Forgive me, Mara, but I need to know how she created this world."

"I'm sorry, Papa," Mara sobbed. "All I know is that I was burning and burning, but it wasn't hot. Then she would cut me, saying how she needed your blood."

Aeolmar gathered Mara against his chest, soothing her as best he could. *My blood. She wants my blood. What can my blood give her?* He gazed about the clearing, the small pocket of illusion so clearly formed it was identical to reality; for an illusion this complete, Sarelle's power must be vast. Unless she didn't have enough magic of her own…

Aeolmar released Mara and grabbed the knife he kept in his boot, and scored the blade across his forearm. The hunters looked on as he flexed his arm and let the dark liquid drip onto the soil. Sarelle screamed, gesturing wildly, attempting to thicken the air and hold the red droplets aloft, but she only slowed them. Aeolmar laughed, a wicked sound that chilled hunters and hag alike.

"You don't have the power, not like you used to," he said. "You can't accomplish an illusion such as this on your own. When you were his priestess, you wielded a measure of Olluhm's power, but now you're nothing more than a lonely hedge witch." Dark droplets splashed onto the ground, magic rippling outward like water. The illusion fractured apart as the power in Aeolmar's blood—only twice removed from Olluhm—shattered Sarelle's spell.

"Perhaps," Sarelle conceded as her illusion dissolved around her, "but my agents in the palace are stronger yet—but even they don't know the truth about Asherah."

Aeolmar went still. "What have you done to the queen?" he demanded.

"I made her remember, and I made her forget," Sarelle said around her cackling. "But best of all is something the queen herself has forgotten—her true name!"

Aeolmar remembered the many days and nights Asherah had searched for a clue about her life before the demons had taken her. "Tell me her name, and I might let you live."

Sarelle laughed until she wheezed and doubled over. "Ish h'ra," Sarelle replied. "The Deliverer herself, living right under Olluhm's nose. Imagine how pleased the All Father will be with me once I kill the one god he couldn't!"

Sarelle's hands disappeared within her robes, but never made contact with what she sought. Bron, who had been skirting the edge of the clearing, threw his arm around her neck and choked her unconscious.

"Don't kill her," Aeolmar warned. "We may need her yet." He gazed about the clearing, now stripped of Sarelle's influence. The cottage remained, along with the well, but the trees were no longer eerily similar, and birds and clouds could once again be seen overhead. The suns—the real suns—told him that it was early morning, and he wondered how long they had been trapped in time.

"Innetha," he began, but she had already thrust her hands into the soil.

"Less than half a day west of Teg'urnan," she replied. Beside her Luth pulled himself free of the ground. "We can be there by nightfall."

"You'll be faster on your own," Mara said.

Aeolmar looked toward Mara; surely she didn't think he would leave her? Reading his thoughts as well as Latera ever had, she continued, "I'll be all right. Mother and Tor and Ember need you. You've already rescued me. Go, and rescue them."

He nodded, proud of Mara's courage, then handed her his knife. "Follow closely. If you haven't reached the palace by nightfall, I'll turn back," he said as he closed her fingers about the hilt. Then he mounted up, and called over his shoulder, "Take Sarelle with you, but gag her and bind her hands and feet. Empty all her pockets and pouches, and keep her things on a separate horse. Once that's done, ride directly to Teg'urnan." He frowned, and added, "Do not speak of the Ish h'ra, not even among yourselves, until I learn if she was telling the truth." *And what that truth means for Parthalan.*

Orders spoken, the First Hunter rode off to save the rest of his family.

Chapter Fifty

Asherah the Ruthless, Queen of Parthalan and Lady of Tin-gu, sat upon her throne with her back straight as an arrow, appearing every bit the ruler. She was clad in a white silk gown cut close to her body, the high neckline and the edges of her sleeves and skirts embroidered with tiny clear crystals. She loved wearing white, the purest of colors, and always donned it for important occasions. Being that the day would likely see the healer's death, she supposed it was momentous enough.

"Are you certain you'd like to confront her here?" Latera whispered. The First Huntress of Parthalan, her wickedly sharp troll swords strapped across her back, stood in Aeolmar's place to the left of the queen's throne. "Innocents might be injured."

"Hells, you might be injured," Elkin said from his post at Latera's side. Attia had summoned him while Asherah dressed, and between the *saffira-nell* and Latera he learned exactly what Mallia had done. "Let Latera and me handle this. You need to rest."

"I appreciate your concern, but no," Asherah said. Her son and her mate were safe in the vaults beneath the Great Temple, along with Latera's younger children. Finlay didn't even know that his mate was no longer insane, or that she no longer pined for a dead man. *Gods, will he ever forgive me?*

"I will be the one to question Mallia," Asherah continued, effectively slamming the door shut on that thought. "Vengeance is my right, and I will have it."

Elkin shook his head. "They don't call you The Ruthless for your winning smile."

"What will happen when she arrives?" Latera asked. "What if she doesn't come?"

And thanks to my throne, she might not notice my eyes.

Asherah's throne, which had been a gift from Lormac at a Madoc'na held so long ago, consisted of white metal upon an orichalum base. The armrests and high back were encrusted with gems in varying shades of blue, carefully set so as to reflect a prismatic glow about the throne's occupant; when this unusual attribute had been revealed to Asherah, she had teased him that Lormac was loathe to share her, even her appearance. Now she hoped the glow was enough to obscure her clear eye and the red marks about the other. Asherah silently thanked her once-mate's spirit, wherever he may be.

"I hope you're right," Latera said. Asherah hoped she was right too, and had much less faith in her decisions that Latera did. Why, she had forgotten her mate and son for nearly an entire moon, forgotten that she was supposed to see to Parthalan's well-being... Forgotten everything, save for a dead man's face.

What's more, her left eye wasn't healed. When both her eyes were open, everything on her left side looked to be shrouded in fog, which was distracting enough, but if she closed her right eye the spell regained its hold on her. She would anxiously look about for Lormac, hoping for his swift return to her side. Every time she opened both of her eyes, she lost him all over again.

Gods. This dead man will yet be the death of me. If Latera has any sense, she'll behead me and take the throne this instant, and be hailed as Parthalan's true savior.

Then Latera set her hand on Asherah's shoulder, and their renewed friendship calmed her racing thoughts. *I can do this. I can be strong. As long as Latera and Elkin stand beside me, I can be a queen.*

Aloud, she only said, "I am glad you're here."

"Where else would I be?" Latera asked with a tight smile. Asherah had forgotten that Aeolmar and Mara's whereabouts were still unknown, but they must be all right. Of course, nothing had happened to them. If anything had befallen them while Asherah had been making her latest foray into insanity, she would never forgive herself.

Asherah's gaze moved on to Elkin. His mate, Innetha, was also missing. Hopefully, she was still with Aeolmar and the rest. If the hunters remained together, they had much better odds of returning, but if one of them had been separated from the others...

We'll deal with that later. Asherah put her hand atop Latera's and squeezed her fingers, then straightened her posture. She was still queen, regardless of competency, and was determined that she would at least look the part.

Acting the part was somewhat more difficult. Asherah's closest advisors were well aware that she had taken ill, though the details had been kept quiet, and they had been somewhat taken aback by the queen's sudden reappearance. Add to that King Finlay's conspicuous absence, and the whole of Teg'urnan was in a state of confusion.

The palace's *saffira* were nothing if not well trained, and after a few gaping stares the day went smoothly. Asherah had swiftly dealt with the matters brought before her, which mostly involved a disgruntled fisherman, until close to nightfall when there was a small commotion near the entrance of the great hall. Being that nothing is more fleet of foot than gossip, Mallia had already learned that the queen alone presided over court. Then the matriarch pushed her way through the throngs and stepped into the queen's view, and Asherah nearly gasped aloud.

"She really is the seer," Asherah murmured; somehow, this knowledge didn't surprise her.

"Wren has never disappointed," Latera said. Wren had instructed the court attendants on where to install the glass lens that amplified the suns' light, and it had illuminated the center of the hall as bright as day. Once Mallia stepped into the bright shaft of light, the truth of her was revealed.

The edges of Mallia's form wavered; Asherah initially blamed her clouded eye, but this was different. It was as if an illusion had been placed on top of an older guise, though why one wouldn't just remove the first Asherah couldn't fathom.

"Her true name is Relle," Latera said. "She is the one who kidnapped all those winters ago. She is the cause of all of this, and she will be its end."

With that, Latera straightened and stepped back from the throne, affecting a nonthreatening countenance. There was nothing unusual about Latera attending Asherah as First Huntress, since she had done it often enough before. At least, Asherah hoped that Mallia wouldn't find it unusual.

"Mallia," Asherah greeted. "I am so very pleased to see you."

"My lady," the healer acknowledged with a respectful bow. "And I am much pleased to see that you have recovered so speedily."

"Well, I wouldn't have without you," Asherah replied. The hunters who had not accompanied Aeolmar on the search for Mara moved to encircle Mallia, thus trapping her in the hall. "After all, if you hadn't bespelled me in the first place, Latera wouldn't have had the opportunity to cure me. Many thanks, Mallia. Or is it Relle?"

Relle made no response. Instead, she snatched a portal from her sleeve and threw it to the floor. Nothing happened.

"My dear, this hall is warded against portals and vortexes," Asherah said, rising to her feet. "Long ago, the old king used portals to bring demons into my hall. Naturally, I took precautions against similar occurrences. It was one of my first acts as queen." Asherah descended from the dais and stood before Relle. "Now tell me what you've done with my First Hunter."

"He is dead, along with his whelp," Relle replied.

"No," Latera shouted. "That is not true!"

"You know the truth," Relle sneered. "Isn't your bond broken? Can you no longer feel your precious mate? Oh, he is dead, as you well—"

A soft thud, and Relle crumbled to the floor. Latera had flung one of her swords at her, and it lodged deep in the woman's chest. The blow was swift and sure, and would have killed anything from a man to the *mordeth-gall*. Oddly, Relle was still speaking. Odder yet, sand, rather than blood, spilled forth from the gaping wound.

"That was unexpected," Elkin said.

"You think to kill me like I killed your man, and your babe?" the sand creature cackled. "You cannot harm me!"

"They aren't dead," Latera shrieked.

"They are," Relle insisted. "I cast a spell that would only break when Aeolmar's blood was drawn."

"That doesn't mean he's dead!" Latera shouted. "He could be wounded."

"Latera," Elkin cautioned. "Don't waste your breath arguing with her. She's built all of this on lies."

"I can show you his corpse," Relle taunted, making a few motions with her fingers. Latera ran down the dais, yanked her sword free of Relle's chest and hacked off her hands. On closer inspection, Latera learned that Relle's flesh wasn't blood and sinew, but clay.

"She's... clay?" Latera prodded the severed hands with the tip of her sword.

"She's a golem," Asherah said; she had risen from her throne and stood at Latera's shoulder and scrutinized what they'd all thought was Mallia. Instead of a woman, the healer was a manikin fashioned from clay and sand, and enchanted to behave a certain way. Asherah wondered who in the nine realms was powerful enough to accomplish such a feat. "Has she always been a golem?"

Her moment of wonder over, Asherah called for a bucket and brooms, then stood by as *saffira* and hunter alike swept and packed the still-speaking Relle into a barrel. As the lid was hammered shut, she turned her attention back to Latera. The First Huntress still held Relle's severed hand, and was staring at the clay palm. Asherah swallowed the lump in her throat, and hoped for Latera's sake, and her own, that the golem had lied.

Please, gods, let Aeolmar and Mara be alive.

Chapter Fifty-One

Sweat poured down Aeolmar's neck and back as he galloped toward Teg'urnan, restraining himself from pushing Myrnnhe harder. His mount was strong, yes, but despite what Innetha had told him, Aeolmar remained unsure of the true distance to the palace. And, if he pushed Myrnnhe too hard, and he foundered, they would both need to walk the rest of the way, keeping Aeolmar away from his family even longer.

Aeolmar glanced upward, fixing his ancestors in his glare. "Fat lot of good it does me, being descended from you," he growled. "Don't you care for your progeny? Or are we all just pawns in your game?"

His heart thudding in his chest, only in part from his outburst, Aeolmar lowered his gaze to the road before him. In time, the drudgery of the passing trees turned his thoughts to a memory he would rather forget.

***

Latera had been laboring with Tor for nearly two days, and Aeolmar had long since banished Mara and Ember from the chamber. Wren had been on the far side of the room preparing one of her concoctions, and Latera lay resting on her side.

"Soon," Aeolmar said, swabbing Latera's brow with a damp cloth. "He will be here soon." Slowly, her fingers slipped into his palm.

"What if he's not?" she asked, opening her fever-bright eyes. "You should take the baby."

"Beloved," Aeolmar murmured, gripping her delicate fingers. He'd had the same notion, but Wren quelled it at once. With the amount of blood Latera had already lost, she likely wouldn't survive if they cut into her. "We cannot."

"You must," Latera insisted. "This... this is too much for him."

"If we do that, we'll as good as kill you," Aeolmar said, his voice catching.

"But, our baby," Latera pleaded. "Mar, it's all right. Just let me go."

Another wave of pain had washed over her, rendering her silent. Aeolmar had offered her a small sip of water, then he resumed dabbing at her brow. Little comfort, yes, but it was all he could do.

"No," he said once her pains subsided. "When you bound yourself to me, I promised you that nothing would take you from me, not even death. I will keep my promise."

***

Not even death. The words rang in Aeolmar's ears, as did the dull thuds of Myrrnhe's hooves. Determined to never break that promise, he urged the horse faster.

CHAPTER FIFTY-TWO

*A*eolmar *and Mara... They're gone.*

Latera threw the healer's clay hand at the barrel and fought the urge to scream. Her worst fear—the fear that her mate and children would be harmed—had now come to pass, and she had been helpless to prevent it. She, the *deva'shi*, had failed her own family.

"Latera," Asherah began as the queen placed her hand on her shoulder, "she—it—is lying. We will find them."

Latera nodded, far too distraught to speak. She looked into the barrel that held what was left of the creature called Mallia and Relle, her mind's eye still fixed on its mangled chest. Beneath a thin layer of what appeared to be skin, fine white sand had spilled forth from the wound Latera had inflicted on it. This thing, this monstrosity of clay and dirt had plotted to kill her children and her mate. And, if it was to be believed, it had succeeded on two counts.

"Why... why all of this?" Latera murmured. She turned to the queen, her body trembling. "Why would anyone want to wipe out

Aeolmar's entire line? To go to such lengths... to make an entire person from sand, and... It doesn't make any sense."

"It doesn't," Elkin said. "Relle didn't mention the rest of the hunters. Innetha could be hurt, she could need me, and I'd never know."

"We will find them," Asherah vowed. "Innetha and Aeolmar and Mara and the rest. We will find all of them."

Latera nodded again, watching as the barrel that held the clay woman was hauled away by the guards. She knew that she should retrieve Finlay and the children from the vaults, but she could not bear the thought of telling Ember and Tor what had befallen their father and sister. They were safe with the king, and she needed time to think.

Abruptly, Latera turned and strode out of the hall; when Asherah called after her, she raised her hand in acknowledgement, but did not slow her pace. Latera walked through Teg'urnan like one possessed, hardly noticing where her steps took her. She didn't stop until she stood at the peak of the southern tower, her hand on the door of what was once Aeolmar's chamber.

He only took this chamber to watch for my return from the border.

She entered the dark, tiny room. As always, her gaze fell on the multitude of old boxes piled on the far side of the room. They were filled with a strange assortment of items her mate had collected over the years and could never bring himself to part with. For all of his posturing as First Hunter, the warrior of legend feared throughout Parthalan and the lands beyond, she knew he was nothing if not a sentimental, gentle soul.

Latera smiled, tears pricking at her eyes, as she approached the heap of mementos. For all that she teased her mate, some of these were her memories, too. There was the blanket they had wrapped Mara in when she was born, the knife Aeolmar had used to kill Mersgoth, Caol'nir's sword...

Who will teach Tor to wield a sword?

I will.

Latera stumbled backward and covered her face, the memory of Aeolmar's mindtouch too much to bear. She cried so hard she lost her breath, and blindly climbed the stairs to the balcony, and slumped against the stone floor. Latera reached out to caress the weathered old bench—how many times had she and Aeolmar sat upon that bench, huddled under blankets in the winter, nearly bare in summer's heat? And now, she would never sit with her mate or eldest child again.

We will be together again. Soon.

Latera rubbed her eyes, unsuccessfully rubbing away the words in her head. Without her mate, she was going mad.

Latera didn't know how long she lay prone on the balcony floor, her head propped up against the leg of the bench, when she heard the gatekeeper call out that a rider was sighted. Out of long habit, she rose and looked toward the horizon. The rider was approaching from the west, and the fool was pushing his horse so hard Latera worried it would injure itself. As the rider came closer, she could make out his blue jerkin, and long brown hair against it...

She turned and ran down the steps, heedless of where she put her feet, only knowing that she needed to reach that rider. Halfway down the spiral stairs Latera missed her footing and slid to the bottom; once she hit the floor, she leapt to her feet and ran toward the palace doors, ignoring and evading those she passed.

Latera did not slow as she crossed the square and passed through the dark iron gates and continued down the royal road, stopping directly in the rider's path. The gatekeeper yelled for the rider to ease up, and for Latera to get to safety, his shouts falling on deaf ears. As the gatekeeper called for the guards to intercept the madman, Aeolmar leaned from the saddle and snatched his mate into his arms.

They said nothing for long moments, their arms wrapped around one other as Myrnnhe slowed to a halt. Latera's tears mingled with the salty sweat on Aeolmar's neck as she clutched him, one hand thrust into his hair while her other arm encircled his waist. "I am never letting go of you," she whispered against his chest.

"Don't," he murmured as he tilted her chin up to his, "don't ever." He kissed her with the sort of passion he usually reserved for their bed, leaving Latera breathless.

"Mara?" Latera asked once they parted.

"Alive," he assured. Latera felt his relief through their shared bond, and she in turn was relieved that the bond had rebuilt itself. *It really was him in my head.* "Battered, but whole." Latera let the relief wash over her as she wept again, this time with tears of joy. She leaned her head against Aeolmar's shoulder, grateful for the solid warmth of her mate. "What of Ember and Tor?"

"They're safe in the vaults, with Finlay."

"Older or younger?"

"Both." Aeolmar buried his face in Latera's hair, relishing the sweet smell of her; he'd been terrified that her scent, like sun-warmed honey, was lost to him. His hands moved across her back, and he noted the thick leather she wore, the twin scabbards strapped to her back, and that one of her swords was missing.

"Beloved, why are you dressed for battle?"

"I had to kill a fake woman," she replied. "Mallia. Relle, really. Her body was sand and clay. She is still speaking, so I suppose she's not really dead. Or alive. Asherah called her a golem."

"A golem? Really?" he asked, as he kissed her hair. "They are quite rare, and difficult to control."

"She told me you were dead, that Mara was dead, that her master had killed you days ago." Latera raised her head and pushed the loose hair from Aeolmar's face, stroking his cheekbone. "Why would someone want to do this?" she asked; for all that battles and death were her birthright as the *deva'shi*, Latera could not comprehend why someone would want to kill her children.

"Mallia's real name isn't Relle. It's Sarelle," he murmured. Latera leaned back, her pale blue eyes meeting his dark ones.

The priestess your mother banished? Aeolmar nodded, then he tucked Latera's head against his neck. *I thought Sarelle would have died in the underworld.*

I did, too. He went on to share everything that had transpired through their mindtouch, from the endless spiral they followed to the cottage that held Mara, to the state their daughter was in when he found her, and finally to Sarelle's revelation that it was Sarfek who had freed her from the underworld.

"She was hanging?" Latera rasped.

"She was," Aeolmar replied. "But she is strong, like her mother. Our girl is a fighter, even without a sword."

Since neither parent wanted to reenter the palace without Mara, they waited on the royal road for the rest of the hunters to arrive. While they waited, Latera told Aeolmar all that had transpired in Teg'urnan, beginning with the queen's short bout of insanity and ending with Ember's bravery.

"I missed you," she said, once she had told him everything she could remember. "I liked your messages."

"And my notes?" he asked, his blue eyes gleaming.

Latera laughed. "I'm glad they were at the bottom. I had to tear them off before I gave the scrolls to Asherah and Finlay. I've got bits of parchment everywhere."

"Which was your favorite?"

She looked at him in that way of hers and whispered, "Gallery."

Aeolmar raised an eyebrow; he'd thought it would have been brambleberries. Instead of mentioning that, he remembered something Sarelle had said.

"What is it?" Latera asked when his face darkened.

Aeolmar shifted so he was holding Latera's shoulders, and gazing fully into her face. "Sarelle claims that Asherah is Ish hr'a."

"Ish hr'a?" Latera repeated. "Isn't that one of the old gods, the ones Olluhm killed?"

"He did not kill them," Aeolmar said. "He cast them from the sky and sent them to be punished, in the underworld or otherwise."

Latera frowned; she knew well the stories of how Asherah became queen, and that she was once called The Deliverer. "And Asherah remembers so little..." She looked up at her mate. "You don't think there's a chance Sarelle was telling the truth, do you?"

"I don't know," Aeolmar replied. "And I have no idea how we can learn the truth."

"Perhaps we should leave it."

Aeolmar gathered her close. "I don't know if we can."

The elder sun had gone to rest before the rest of the hunters, led by Bron, reached the mates. Latera craned her neck, and spied Mara riding behind Innetha. The huntress sidled close to Latera and Aeolmar, and Mara reached out to grasp her mother's hand.

"Mara," Latera began, but her daughter shook her head. Latera understood; Mara must have worked hard on appearing strong, and their reunion would undo all of her work. It was all right; now that Latera knew her daughter was safe, she could wait.

Once she was able to tear her gaze from her firstborn, Latera noted that Surya and Luth had doubled up and an unknown form was lashed to a horse. "Is that Relle's body?" Latera asked her mate. She could not reconcile that the hag was Sarelle, not quite yet.

"Yes, and she's not dead," Aeolmar replied. "I thought Asherah would want to see to that."

"I will challenge her for that right," Latera murmured. With that, the First Hunter kissed his mate's forehead, and led his hunters home to Teg'urnan.

Chapter Fifty-Three

Asherah Speaks

We still hadn't really talked, Finlay and I. Not since I forgot his face and his name, our son—no, make that our entire lives together—and, Cydia help me, I just wanted to run. I've felt the need to hole up and lick my wounds many, many times in the past, but I've always emerged ready to fight. Now, I couldn't bring myself to confront my mate, he whom I should be able to share everything with.

I fully realized that I was under a spell, and that my actions were not my own. Finlay seemed to be of the same opinion, and he didn't appear to be anything other than glad for my recovery. His kindness and understanding may drive me back to madness.

After Latera had hacked the healer's golem to bits, we sent word to Atreynha in the temple in order to release Finlay and the children from the vaults. When I arrived, they were just ascending the steps. I moved toward Finlay, but then I saw my son, saw him and knew that he wasn't Leran but mine and Finlay's son, and my heart nearly burst.

"Mama!" he cried, leaping into my arms. Then Ember was hugging me as well, knowing in the way that children do that if I was recovered, then her family must be safe as well. I felt a larger hand on my shoulder, and regarded my mate with my good right eye. His brows furrowed when he saw the state of my left eye, but his smile remained.

"My warrior maiden," he murmured, pressing a kiss to my temple.

"It's good to see you," I replied, then we all laughed at the absurdity of that remark. The five of us—me carrying the younger Finlay, the elder Finlay carrying Tor, and Ember leading the lot of us as effectively as any trained commander—had returned to the hall just as Aeolmar, Mara, and the rest of the hunters returned, and my mate and I hadn't had a moment alone together since.

Now I was hiding in my bathing chamber, staring at my newly scarred face. I was no stranger to scarred flesh, far from it in fact, but I'd managed to keep my face unblemished until earlier that day. My left eye was nearly an opaque white, and while things were blurry, I had retained most of my sight. We'd tried pouring more of Wren's concoction in my eye, holding Latera's pendant against it, but to no avail. And, gods, it burned.

More troublesome than the eye were the deep red gashes that scored my cheek and eyelid, self-inflicted when Latera had thrown that infernal piece of jewelry in the bathwater. Gods, if only she'd dispense with the foul thing. Perhaps I'll order her to burn it.

I leaned close to the mirror, and gently prodded the swollen red lines with my fingertip. It was the first mirror I'd ever allowed in my chambers, on account of my dislike of looking at my misshapen body. Then Aeolmar had come along and tried to convince me otherwise, and when I ignored him, he had this installed without my knowledge. It was a large, elegant piece, stretching from floor to ceiling and framed in gilded wood. I'd been furious with him, but once I got into the habit of seeing myself,

I had to admit it: Aeolmar was right. I didn't look so bad after all. As long as I let the mirror fog with steam, and carefully kept from looking at the still-red scars that crisscrossed my back, I wasn't that unattractive.

Not now. Now I truly looked like a monster.

I heard the door open and shut softly, then saw Finlay's reflection as he wrapped his arms around my waist. I shut my eyes and leaned back against him, enjoying his warmth. Gods, why ever would I want to forsake him for a dead man? I feared that I already knew the answer.

"Does it hurt?" he asked.

"Yes," I replied. I twisted around in his arms, but kept my face hidden. "Finlay, I'm so sorry."

"Hush." He tilted my chin upward, but I cocked my head and let my hair obscure my left eye. Not to be deterred, he tucked my hair behind my ear and kissed the gashes. "I'm not angry. I know it wasn't you."

"What if it was?" I whispered. "What if the spell just allowed my true nature to come forward?"

"I know you still love Lormac," he said. "Your heart is too big to do otherwise. I'm confident that there's room in your heart for all of us." I nodded; I do love my mates, both of them. And both of them would be better off without me.

"Did you know that bindings can be broken?" I asked. "If you aren't of pure faerie blood, it's not eternal."

"Who told you this?" he demanded.

"Aeolmar. He was worried that Latera might leave him." Finlay balked at that; truly, that fear was Aeolmar's alone.

"Worry not, love, for you are mine. I will never break our bond."

"I think you should." He was silent, but of course, what could he say? So I continued, "You shall remain king. I will step aside and depart from Teg'urnan."

"Asherah, no," he said, his arms tightening around me. "No."

"Yes." I stepped back, and faced him. "Look at me. I'm a disgusting, misshapen beast. I can hide the scars on my body, but not my face. No one wants such a woman for queen or mate."

"These few scratches?" Finlay gently touched my cheekbone, the tender pink wounds. "These will heal. Your eye will heal."

"What if it doesn't? Whenever it's the only eye open, I look for Lormac." Finlay pursed his lips, his brows low over his summer blue eyes. He may claim that my heart is big enough for him and Lormac, but will Lormac fit in Finlay's heart, too? "I cannot... You should not have to live like this. Your mate should not be always looking for another man."

"Then we'll get you an eyepatch." He stepped toward me, but I backed away, retreating until my back was pressed against the mirror. "Asherah."

"Can't you understand? I'm doing this for you!" I turned away, and caught a glimpse of my reflection in the mirror. How I hated Aeolmar for this gift!

"Then stay. For me." He caught me then, being that I had nowhere else to retreat. He murmured in my ear, his rough palms tracing their familiar patterns across my back. I was silent, which Finlay wrongly assumed to be acquiescence on my part.

If he won't break our bond, I'll find a way to do it myself.

Chapter Fifty-Four

"Get your hands off me," Iruna hissed.

"Queen's orders, my lady," the guard said unapologetically as he replaced his great paw of a hand on her elbow. "Also, your brother must remain here, at least for the time being."

Iruna and Avinor shared a panicked glance. Neither of them had any idea of why they had been called to Teg'urnan; certainly, Asherah had been content to ignore their existence in the past. Iruna had considered snubbing this unprecedented and unwanted summons, but Avinor had convinced her otherwise, mostly because he enjoyed the idea of spending a few nights gambling in the seedier sections of the village.

Now that she was being forcibly separated from her brother, she began to question Asherah's motives. "May I ask why?" Iruna asked coolly.

"My lady, I only know what the king and queen order me to do, and not a bit more," was the curt reply. Iruna debated leaving Teg'urnan altogether, but forfeiture would make Asherah the clear winner of this bout. Reluctant to concede, even when she knew not the prize, Iruna straightened her back and allowed the guard to escort her to the throne room.

Seated upon the velvet-wrapped dais were Queen Asherah and King Finlay, she on her ugly elfin throne, he on the regal seat her father had once graced. Next to Asherah stood the tall, muscular man who had caught her eye during her last trip to Teg'urnan. *Alluria's boy, the First Hunter,* Iruna recalled. *I'm surprised Mallia hasn't done away with him by now.* She took a moment to admire his very long, very shiny chestnut hair, and eyes of such a piercing blue she could make them out across the room.

Next to the First Hunter stood a small woman with flame colored hair that matched her badly concealed anger. Another male and female hunter stood on the king's right, with the rest of the queen's hunters having taken positions on either side of the dais.

But what held Iruna's attention, even more than the First Hunter's intense gaze, was lumpy, filthy bundle on the dais steps. It looked to be a heap of well-worn sackcloth and rope; then the heap moved, and Iruna realized it was a bound person. Next to the prisoner was a wooden barrel, trembling of its own accord. Her heart in her throat, Iruna tore her gaze from the prisoner and settled it on the royal pair.

"My king and queen," Iruna greeted, bowing low as per custom. The fools would not have cause to accuse her of disrespect before the whole of court. "To what do I owe the honor of this summons?"

"Oh, I doubt you'll consider this an honor," Asherah replied. "Tell me again how much you revere Sarelle's memory."

Iruna swallowed. "May I ask why?"

"It was an order, not a request."

Iruna felt cold sweat on her neck and thrust her hands into the folds of her gown. "Sarelle was always good to my brother and I. After Sahlgren sent us away to the westlands, she made a point of visiting us several times a season. I believe she took pity on two poor, parentless children, and attempted to make our world a bit brighter."

"Mmm." Asherah shifted on her throne, and Iruna saw an angry red wound on the queen's face. Uglier by the day, that one. "How long did these visits last?"

"She would often stay a sennight or more."

Asherah laughed mirthlessly. "No. I mean, when did you last see Sarelle's physical form? She visited you beginning when Sahlgren sent you away, until?" The prisoner shifted, drawing Iruna's attention. "Answer, Iruna."

"I-I'm not certain," Iruna replied, despising that the pretender queen had rattled her so. "Before you took the throne, surely."'

"Are you familiar with a sorcerer called Sarfek?" the king asked softly.

Iruna blinked. "The Prelate's brother?"

"Yes, he was Harek's brother." Finlay held the king's seal—her father's seal—as he continued. "Did he also make these goodwill visits along with Sarelle?"

"On occasion." The prisoner shifted again, and the bucket responded with an answering shudder. "Please, may I know why I'm being interrogated?"

"Please, could you explain how Sarfek and Sarelle visited you together when Sarfek only reached Teg'urnan the day Sarelle was banished to the underworld?" Asherah countered.

Iruna went cold. "He... They must have known each other before."

Asherah smiled at her hands, folded demurely in her lap, then nodded to the First Hunter. Gingerly, as if contact with the body repulsed him, he nudged the prisoner with his boot and rolled the body down the stairs. It came to rest on its back, staring blindly upward.

"Do you recognize this person?" Asherah demanded.

"I know no such filth—"

"Do you recognize her?" the queen repeated. "Come closer, if you must. It won't be your first experience with filth, of that I'm certain."

Hot blood stained Iruna's cheeks, but she quashed her anger and stepped toward the body. She craned her neck, ostensibly to get a better look at the prisoner, not that she needed to. She knew the prisoner's identity as surely as she knew her own name.

"Child," croaked Sarelle, "what is my girl doing here, of all the hellish places?"

"What have you done to her?" gasped Iruna. Sarelle's eyes were unfocused, spittle running down her chin. "You cannot harm a High Priestess of Olluhm! It is death to lay hands upon her!" Iruna turned around, shouting for Avinor to come and witness this most heinous act, and found herself surrounded by hunters. "What is the meaning of this?"

"I will tell you what I believe has transpired," Asherah said calmly. "You hate me. You believe I'm an unfit queen, and that you should sit upon my throne." Asherah laughed. "Well, that throne," she amended, indicating the king's seat.

"You have no royal blood," Iruna said.

"True, but that does not matter. Solon saw to that long ago. We have his descendant here, did you know that?" Asherah asked, now indicating the First Hunter. "Oh, and he's also Olluhm's grandson. If you would, Aeolmar, tell the Lady Iruna your mother's name."

"My mother's name was Alluria," he said, his deep voice reaching every nook and cranny of the great hall. "Alluria, herself once a priestess of Olluhm, she who rightfully sent Sarelle to the underworld."

Sweat dripped down Iruna's neck, pooling between her breasts in an icy puddle. "Sarelle deserved no such fate."

"I disagree," Asherah said, "but I'd rather not speak of deeds done so long ago. Let's talk about something more recent." The queen gestured again, and Aeolmar kicked over the bucket. Iruna danced backward from the bits of clay and sand that spilled forth and bumped into one of the hunters, who grabbed her arms as if she were about to flee. She would have, but was shocked into immobility when she saw Sarelle's own face worked upon the mangled clay.

"It seems that Sarelle made a golem of herself in order to gain entry to my palace," Asherah continued. "She's been pretending to be a healer for centuries. Or was there once a woman named Mallia? Did Sarelle kill her too?"

"Sarelle is no killer," Iruna whispered, tears coursing down her cheeks. "She is the kindest of souls."

"Why would a kind soul seek to harm my children?" asked an unfamiliar voice. Iruna looked toward the dais and learned that it was the red-haired woman speaking. "Why would a kind soul have my daughter abducted, beaten, and tortured for no wrong other than being descended from Alluria? Why would she bespell the queen? Why would a kind soul act in collusion with Sarfek, a known traitor to the realm?"

"Who are you?" Iruna countered. "I need not answer accusations levied by a baseborn warrior woman like you! I only answer to royalty!"

The woman laughed, the hollow sound chilling Iruna's blood. "You do not know me? Truly, your avoidance of Teg'urnan will prove your undoing." The woman descended the steps, carefully avoiding the spillage from the bucket until she stood directly before Iruna. "I am royalty. I am firstborn and heir to Gannera. I also claim descent from

Elvasla, once Lady of Thurnda." Iruna's eyes widened in comprehension.

"So you have heard of me?" the woman continued. "I am Latera Demon-killer, First Huntress of Parthalan, *deva'shi*. I am the one who took Sarfek's head, and then I killed the *mordeth-gall* himself. I played no small part in the deaths of Mersgoth and Harek. For what she has done to my family, I will kill Sarelle. Or Mallia, or Relle." Latera glanced at the pathetic body upon the ground. "I care not what she chooses to be called, so long as she's dead."

"What do you want from me?" Iruna whispered.

"Want? I want my family safe. I want my daughter to not fear walking alone, for the wounds on her soul to heal as cleanly as the wounds upon her skin. I want my king and queen to live long, happy lives. I want a world free of you." Iruna began to protest, but Latera grabbed her jaw.

"One must wonder, *my lady*, how Sarfek procured the resources to free Sarelle from the underworld? Once liberated, where did she go for shelter? What fool would take in one guilty of the worst treasons? Who hates Asherah that much?" Latera squeezed her jaw, so forcefully Iruna felt the huntress's nails pierce her flesh, her teeth aching in protest.

"You do," Latera hissed. "You are the agent behind these events. You plotted to destroy my family, and for that you shall suffer."

"You... you cannot," Iruna gasped. Latera relaxed her grip, but only slightly. "You have no proof of these claims. If you did, I'd be dead already."

"I have proof. Where did Sarelle's vast fortune go after she was banished to the underworld?"

Iruna went cold. "There is no way you could know that!"

"How could we not? The Golden Knoll was once Sarelle's family home." Latera released Iruna's jaw so suddenly she fell to the ground, the golem's detritus staining her fine gown. "You think you're so far above us, yet your arrogance is your end. Did you think us fools, that we were unable to read historical land titles? You didn't even have the sense to change the estate's name."

"For suspicion of crimes against the crown, I hereby rescind the titles and station of both yourself and Avinor," King Finlay announced. "You may not keep your manor in the west, since the archive confirms it was passed to you directly from Sarelle, herself guilty of treason and other crimes. Your *saffira* will be given stipends and sent from you. Your vineyards—forgive me, Sarelle's vineyards—and farmlands have been seized, and will be bestowed upon the surrounding villages. And the royal stipend the crown so generously offered following your father's demise has ended. Your treasury is now the crown's."

Iruna struggled to stand upright, her feet slipping on the wet clay. "You're taking everything from us! How are we to survive?"

"How is my daughter to go on after what Sarelle did to her?" Latera countered. "Do not mistake the boon you are being given. If we'd done things my way, I'd be torturing you myself."

Iruna looked from the furious huntress to Asherah and Finlay, unwilling to admit that Latera was right. The monarchs could easily take her head for far less than this. She also understood that she and Avinor were only being allowed to live to set an example.

"One more thing," Asherah said. "We need funds to pay for cleaning up after this sticky mess." Asherah made a dismissive gesture, as if shooing a bothersome fly. "Since you, Iruna, are being held at fault for these crimes, you must offer compensation."

"But you have taken everything from me!" Iruna protested. "I have no treasury, no lands! What am I to do, scrub it myself?"

"An excellent notion." Asherah's lips twisted into a smile, and Iruna realized her error. The queen murmured a few quiet commands, and in a moment a bucket of soapy water and brushes was brought before Iruna. "Once the floor is clean, we will need it polished as well."

Iruna gazed despondently from the brushes to the vast expanse of the hall's floor. She understood that she'd be scrubbing the whole of it, and that the task would likely take days. "Can I not pay for the cleaning? Will you not take my jewels instead?" Iruna extended her hands before her, displaying her glittering rings and bracelets. "I... I have never scrubbed anything. I do not know how. Surely, you would prefer one who understands the task at hand."

"What I would prefer is watching you suffer." Asherah stood and descended the dais, coming to stand beside Latera. "Have you never been humbled before? I have. In fact, Sarelle was behind those who did the humbling. For that her sentence is death." Suddenly a blade was passed from Asherah to Latera's hand, and before Iruna could react the First Huntress slit Sarelle's throat. Iruna moved toward Sarelle's body, but rough hands grabbed her and began unlacing her gown.

"My gown!" Iruna exclaimed as the rich velvet and lace was peeled from her form.

"You cannot scrub in such a garment," Asherah admonished. "It will become waterlogged and heavy, thus making your task much longer than it needs to be." A brawny hunter grabbed Iruna about the waist and lifted her out of her gown while another removed the silk slippers from her feet, leaving her shivering in her thin chemise. "While you scrub, I want you to think about what you've done," Asherah said in the condescending tone Iruna so often used. "Oh, and be sure to clean away all the blood from between the tiles."

Iruna nodded, folding her arms across her breast. "What of Avinor?"

"Your incestuous brother? He'll be spending his time mucking out my stable. Pity he tends not to wear undergarments. The horses will be quite offended."

Chapter Fifty-Five

"All this, because my mother sent a priestess to the underworld," Aeolmar mused, as he draped an arm around his mate's shoulders. He and Latera were seated on their balcony, but instead of facing the courtyard, they gazed inward at their children, sprawled about the chamber's central room. A sennight had passed since Iruna and Avinor had completed their punishment and left Teg'urnan, and their lives were slowly returning to normal.

Ember, who had taken Aeolmar's instruction of looking out for her mother and brother quite seriously, was determined to teach Tor to walk by the time the suns set. She had also grown adept at ignoring her sister's comments, most of which centered on the fact that a boy as young as he could not be expected to walk on his own.

"Don't forget, your father also castrated a *mordeth*," Latera reminded him as she nestled against Aeolmar's chest. "If only he'd cut off his head instead."

"If he'd done that, would we be here now?" Aeolmar wondered.

"I don't know. I would still be the *deva'shi*, my path destined to cross the *mordeth-gall's*, but would you be First Hunter? Or would you be a farmer in the west, mated to a meek fae woman and surrounded by children?" Latera teased.

"A meek fae woman? I wouldn't trade my feisty elf for anything, not in this realm or any other," Aeolmar murmured as he nuzzled her neck. The nuzzling became nibbling, and he kissed her to muffle her laughter. "I think if my father had killed Mersgoth, he never would have left the palace. He might have even become Prelate after my grandsire."

"So you would be here waiting for me, my mighty Prelate of Parthalan?" Latera asked, gazing at him through her lashes. "I disagree. I believe that given the choice, you would have left Teg'urnan and made a quiet life for yourself, which means that I would have had to go on a quest to find you, and get you out of whatever trouble you'd gotten into."

"You rescue me?" he asked incredulously. "Whenever you leave my sight, you manage to hurt yourself." He stroked her tightly bound arm; when Latera had seen his return from the tower, and fallen down the spiral stairs as she raced to meet him, she'd injured her wrist. Wren was confident that it wasn't broken, but she'd bound Latera's arm as a precaution.

Latera laughed, but Aeolmar's manner softened as he smoothed her curls back from her face. "You think I wouldn't find you?" he murmured, his endless blue eyes drawing her into their depths. "I will always find you."

"I know you would." Against forces beyond their control, forces both magical and mundane, many of which Latera hardly understood, Aeolmar had found her and given her life purpose, hope, love—everything she could have asked for, and so much more. With a lopsided smile, Aeolmar scooped Latera onto his lap and began covering her face with kisses. Mara, who'd caught sight of the pair, was about to express her disapproval when there was a knock at the door. Ember, who fancied herself not only in charge of Tor but the entire family, ran to open it.

"Mara," Ember called, since Kemen was waiting on the other side. The mates watched their daughter walk to the door and greet her guest, then Latera dropped her gaze.

"Why aren't you angry with me?" Latera asked, intently studying the edge of Aeolmar's sleeve.

He raised an eyebrow. "Should I be?"

"For Gannera. For not telling you." She rested her head against his shoulder, still expecting him to lash out. Instead, he waited.

"When Mara and Wren and I last crossed the veil, the king asked me when I wished to take my place as his heir," she began, her words rushing forth like a stream choked with snowmelt. "It made sense, being that I now have an heir of my own. But I told him I could do no such thing, because my place was in Parthalan. He put on this glum face and said he'd expected that response, so I left him with no choice but to marry Sasha off to Gannok."

"The idiot prince?" Aeolmar asked. "He's old enough to be Sasha's father!"

"Grandsire," Latera grumbled.

"Shouldn't Elia be the heir after you?" Aeolmar asked. "Or is Jannei the next oldest?"

"You're right. It should go to Elia." Latera shifted, now burrowing against his chest as she had done when she was younger, long before they'd ever been bound. "Apparently, Gannok has expressed some kind of interest in Sasha. I must have put him off redheads." She shuddered, and Aeolmar rubbed her back. "The filthy man."

"Mmm." They remained that way for a time, Aeolmar remaining silent while Latera curled against him. Most wouldn't have taken Aeolmar for a patient man, but he had all the patience in the world where it concerned his mate.

"What it really comes down to is that he's manipulating me again. He wants me in Gannera, and he knows how I love my sisters, so to get me to return, he'll marry off Elia and Jannei to some outlying kingdom, then give poor, sweet Sasha to that vile man." She made a noise against his chest, a small, mirthless laugh. "When I told him he was a cruel tyrant, he sneered and asked if I would bring the three of them here to Parthalan."

"Why didn't you?" Aeolmar asked, brushing her hair back from her brow.

"I cannot make their choices for them," Latera replied. "If they wish to join me, they can."

"Can they?" Aeolmar was surprised by this revelation, being that there were precious few ways to cross from one realm to another.

"The knowledge is within Asherah's temple. I made sure of it." Latera leaned back so she could look Aeolmar in the eye. "You think I'd leave them helpless?"

"I know you wouldn't," Aeolmar replied, his lips against her forehead. He gathered her against him, content that his mate was in his arms. For the thousandth time since he'd left in search of Mara, he vowed to never leave Latera's side again.

"I'm sorry."

Aeolmar tilted up her chin. "For what?"

"For not telling you what happened. For keeping it from you. I just..." She pressed her face against his chest. *I cannot believe my own father would use us to such ends. He is supposed to take care of us, not cast us about like dice. We're his daughters!*

Sobs overtook her, and Aeolmar held her until the trembling ceased. There was no love lost between him and the man who'd sired Latera, whom Aeolmar had always regarded as a cold, calculating ruler. *I would never let such things happen to Mara or Ember. Or Tor, for that matter.*

"I know. It's one of the many reasons my place is here. With you."

"You're right," he murmured, tightening his arms around her. "You belong right here."

"So." Latera twisted about, fixing her mate in her gaze. "About leaving Teg'urnan."

"We'll not be going anywhere." Latera arched her brow; this had taken her by surprise. "My family has always belonged here. *We* belong here. It would be wrong to leave."

"Would it?" Latera asked. "I thought you were concerned about our family's safety."

He knew she was baiting him, but explained himself anyway. "I'm of Solon's line. We are meant to guard Teg'urnan and the royal family. Father... My father ran from his destiny, and it cost him his life."

His voice trailed off at the end, and Latera reached up to stroke his cheek. Aeolmar captured her hand and kissed her palm, and pressed it against his heart as he continued. "He should not have run. Mother was marked by a *mordeth*, not just any *mordeth* but Mersgoth. They knew he could find her, but still they tried to hide."

"They wanted a life together," Latera said softly. "They wanted happiness."

"And they had it," Aeolmar conceded, "but at what price? Their lives. The lives of six of their children. Was that really worth a few good winters?" He fell silent for a moment, gazing at his children, Mara as she spoke with Kemen across the chamber threshold, Ember and Tor where they played on the hearth rug. Gods, how he loved them.

"No. It wasn't." Aeolmar kissed Latera's hand again, then tucked her head against his neck. "Father should have hunted down the beast and killed him. Instead, he ran from his problems. I did the same after Mersgoth killed them." *I only stopped running when I found you, beloved.*

Latera winced at his intense mindtouch, but didn't complain. "Then Teg'urnan will remain our home, and we will fight our battles together."

"Yes." Aeolmar tilted her chin upwards, gazing at the woman who was the center of his world. "Together. All our foes shall fall before us!"

Latera frowned. *Mar, what of Asherah? Could she really be The Deliverer?*

Aeolmar looked at the sky, and tried to imagine that the woman he'd known for so many winters—the woman who had once slept in his arms—might be one of the old gods. *I don't know. Asherah has always been strong, but is she as strong as a god? All the tales say that Ish hr'a was the strongest of them all, that she fought against Olluhm the longest.*

Stories? Are any of them here in the archive?

Yes. I must find them, familiarize myself with these tales.

I will help you.

He kissed her forehead. *I know you will.*

Aeolmar would have said more, but Latera bade him to be still. Mara had shut the chamber door, leaving Kemen alone in the corridor. The mates watched as Mara initially moved to rejoin her siblings, then changed her mind and walked out to the balcony. She said nothing as she leaned over the railing, letting the wind tousle her hair.

"And how is Kemen faring?" Latera asked at length.

"What? Oh, he's fine," Mara answered. "He asked if I am well. He apologized again, but I truly don't hold him at fault. He would never do anything to harm me. I'm sure of that." Latera murmured her agreement. Mara briefly studied something in the courtyard before she continued. "He has asked me to go to The Swan again," she added quietly. "Well, maybe not The Swan, but somewhere. Alone with him."

"And will you?" asked Latera. Mara was silent for a time, then turned to regard her parents.

"No, I won't," she declared. "You're right; I can't make him into the love of my life if he's not. If I really want the kind of love you two have, then I need to be patient and wait for it to find me. After all, Finlay waited for the queen, you waited for each other… I can wait as well, if the reward is as wonderful as love."

"My wise daughter," Aeolmar said as he extended his arm to her. Mara leaned against her father as if she were still a child, and Aeolmar remembered those long-ago days when he and his two girls would watch the stars together. "I always knew you would take after me," he continued, only to have Latera thump his shoulder. How he loved those thumps.

Aeolmar kissed his mate's forehead, and then his daughter's, but before he could speak, he was interrupted by a squeal from the central chamber. The three rushed in to find Ember pointing at Tor, who was standing upright and desperately clutching the side of a bench.

"You see!" Ember said. "I taught Tor to stand! Now he just needs to put one foot in front of the other!" She turned an indignant face to her older sister. "See? I told you I could do it!" she said.

Latera scooped up a shaky Tor and sat on the bench while Aeolmar settled Ember onto his lap. Mara sat on the floor before them and laid her head on her mother's knee. "Before you two met, did you ever think you'd be this happy?" Mara asked.

"No," the mates replied in unison, then they laughed. Aeolmar kissed his mate, then stroked her cheek with the back of his hand.

"No," Aeolmar repeated, "I never thought I would be so blessed as to have all of you."

Chapter Fifty-Six

Asherah Speaks

I was dreaming.

Not a dreamwort-induced plunge into blackest oblivion, not a foray into hallucinations and wishes. I was having a real dream. I didn't know I could still do that.

Of course, my present state likely has much to do with the fact that I'd fallen asleep naturally for the first time in... Well, let's not discuss that either. The fact that I'd been exhausted certainly helped matters.

I'd spent nearly the entire day in the archive, researching how a ruler may abdicate the throne, whether my bad behavior would also force Finlay to step down, and what all of this may mean to our son. What I'd ended up learning was that, as long as I made it clear that I was relinquishing my crown for the good of Parthalan, all should be well.

My second quest, that of releasing Finlay as my mate, wasn't as successful. It seemed that he was the one who could break the bond, not I, on account of this maddeningly pure faerie blood that courses through my veins. However, if I left, the bond between us would be stretched thin, hopefully thin enough for him to forget about it, and move on. Move on to someone who deserves him, not a woman who let a few dreams overwhelm her reality.

The suns had long since set before I returned to my chamber. My intent had been to leave that very night, before my resolve wavered, leaving nothing behind but two short letters; one to my mate explaining why I'd gone, to beg him not to look for me; and the other to my son, saying much the same. I had grabbed a satchel and started tossing items inside when I glanced toward my bed.

I could just make out Finlay's dark hair, the shape of him underneath the furs. My heart clenched; truly, leaving him would be the hardest thing I've ever done. Still, it had to be done. But did it have to be done right away?

I'd always been weak when it came to my man from the desert. I crawled into bed and lay beside him, only intending to stay for a moment, imprinting the feel of him onto my memory. I hadn't meant to fall asleep, but I did.

And now, I was dreaming. I was still in my bed, but my mate wasn't beside me. Well, that's not true; my current mate wasn't beside me.

"Is it really you?" I asked the man. "Or are you just another hallucination?"

"My star, you don't know me?" Lormac murmured. He pulled me into his arms, his warm embrace that I'd pined for, and whispered, "I would know you anywhere, Hillel."

"I can't trust that name any longer," I muttered. "Sarelle used it against me."

His brow furrowed, making it even craggier than normal. "That was a curse, twisting your memories to make you think you were with your heart's desire. This is truly me."

I watched him for a moment, my fingers tracing his jaw. "I want it to be you," I murmured. "I so want it to be you."

We sat together for a time, just like we'd done in the beginning of our days together, when I had been such a skittish fawn I wouldn't even look toward our bedchamber. After I time, I asked, "Why are you here, now? Why haven't you ever come to me before?"

"Ah, Asherah." He shifted so he was looking me in the eye. "You needed to live, if for no other reason so that I could watch you. If I'd come to you, you would have stayed with me until you were a spirit yourself."

He was certainly right about that. "You were watching me?"

Lormac chuckled. "I had little choice. Elves are bound to the earth, and our spirits are not meant to wander. My bones should have been interred at The Seat, but you buried me here."

"I couldn't send you back to Tingu," I whispered, my eyes welling with tears. "I couldn't lose all I had left of you. Forgive me, love."

"I am glad you did so. You've allowed me to wander between both Teg'urnan and Tingu, and keep watch over the two I love most." He kissed my forehead, and I settled into his arms. Any doubts that I'd have over this truly being Lormac's spirit were gone, since only I had ever known that his bones rested alongside the stream in my garden.

"I'm sorry," I said, when we parted. "I'm so sorry I wasn't with you. Forgive me, for letting you die."

"Treachery is treachery," Lormac said. "It wasn't your doing." Gods, Lormac was the kindest of men, not even holding a grudge over his death. I will never be half the ruler he had been. "Instead of talking about my death, I'd rather discuss your life. Specifically, your life with your king."

My heart fell to the floor. "Lormac, I'd never intended to take another mate, truly I hadn't—"

Lormac touched his fingers to my lips. "I'm glad you did."

I blinked. "You are?"

"You need to live, Asherah. You need to lead Parthalan, and he helps you. I could feel your happiness when you met him, so strong it warmed me in my grave."

"I've never been as happy as I was with you."

"Be that as it may, I am not here with you. Harek saw to that." Anger flamed inside me, only to sputter away. Somehow, I think I'd always known that Harek was responsible for Lormac's death, in one way or another. But the traitor was long since dead, having paid the ultimate price for his arrogance.

"Tell me, my star," Lormac murmured, holding both my hands in his, "why do you want to leave this man that loves you so?"

"I do not deserve him," I replied. "I bring him nothing but heartache. I tried to convince him to break our bond, but he refused. So I will leave, and let him have the life he deserves."

Lormac glided his fingers across my cheek, catching a tear on his thumb. "I believe he wants a life with you."

I had nothing to say to that. Lormac didn't press the matter, so I laid my head against his shoulder, taking whatever comfort he would give me. I hadn't felt so calm and centered since Lormac had been alive, when we used to have our late-night talks before the fire. I remembered once such talk, centered on our own mating.

"Do you remember when you asked me to bind myself to you?" I asked.

"Of course," Lormac replied, his lips against my temple.

"Why did you ask me?" I pressed. "Only those of fae blood are held by the bond. You could have broken it at any time."

Lormac laughed again, and smoothed my hair back from my face. "Only the fae are bound by blood, that's true," Lormac said. "Those of other races—elves, nymphs, trolls, even—are bound by love."

My gaze flew from Lormac's gray eyes to Finlay's sleeping form. "Love?"

"*That's why your mate won't break your bonds,*" *Lormac said.* "*His love for you is too strong. He's tied to you, as surely as if you'd thrown a rope about him.*"

I felt a tug at my heart; it was my bond with Finlay, pulling me toward my mate. Gods, I hadn't felt the bond in so long I'd almost forgotten what it was like, how wonderful it felt to have our hearts beat in unison. When had I last felt it? Before all the dreamwort, surely. Before Mallia had made herself such a fixture in my life. Before I'd executed Harek.

But Finlay, he'd felt it all along.

"*I love you, my star,*" *Lormac said.* "*Never forget that I do.*"

My eyes opened; I was awake, and Lormac was gone. I allowed myself a moment to mourn him, a moment to truly say goodbye, but only one. As Lormac said, I have a life to live.

I rolled onto my side, and nestled myself against Finlay. I toyed with the soft curls over his chest, listened to his heart. Even after all I'd put him through it still matched mine, beat for beat.

After a time, his eyes opened, and I gazed upon the summer blue of my mate's eyes. "*I love you.*"

"*I love you too.*" *He blinked, his eyes settling on my clothes.* "*Why are you dressed? Is something wrong?*"

I'd forgotten I'd been intending to leave last night. No matter, clothes were removable. "*Nothing is wrong. Nothing at all.*"

***

The story continues in...
Elfsong

The Chronicles of Parthalan, Book Five

Keep reading for a sneak peek!

Thank you so much! You, the reader, make all of this worthwhile.

***

Elfsong, Book Five of the Chronicles of Parthalan

The mountain troll's hide made a thick, tearing sound as Leran's sword pierced its flesh, followed by the wet crack of bone. Leran stepped back from the corpse, then braced his boot against the still-twitching corpse and wrenched his sword free. He looked up from the mess and saw Balthus approaching.

"Is that the last of them?" Leran asked.

"There's a few up by the ridge," Balthus replied, "nothing that won't be dealt with by day's end." Leran nodded and looked out across the rocky plain. A few days ago, it had been an expanse of frozen tundra punctuated by the occasional boulder. Now, it was littered with stinking troll corpses.

How did they come upon us so quickly? Leran wondered as he stepped around a congealed pool of ichor; while the bloodlike substance that flowed from mountain trolls was not nearly as caustic as that from an orc, it still left a nasty mark. Mountain trolls had long been an enemy of the elves, mostly because of the alliance forged between Nexa and Grelk that allowed the ground trolls to keep their dens beneath Tingu's soil. It was a reciprocal relationship; elves sheltered the ground trolls, and trolls supplied the elves with weapons unequalled in all the nine realms.

Even if the ground trolls offered the elves nothing in return, Leran would sooner die than enter into any sort of agreement with mountain trolls. They were vile, despicable creatures, as likely to war with neighboring lands as eat their own children. Nexa had proclaimed the mountain trolls enemies of the elves, and each of her descendants had followed her edict.

"Let's have at the stragglers," Balthus said. Leran grinned, despite his exhaustion. He was a warrior born, the thrill of battle one of the few pleasures he allowed himself. Good thing, too; he'd been fighting for his throne nearly his entire life.

"The elfsong is strong within you," Balthus said as he clapped Leran's shoulder. Leran could not fathom what would have become of Tingu without the steadfast Balthus; not only had he commanded the legions under Leran's father and grandsire, he served as Leran's regent until he grew to manhood. True, the lands surrounding Tingu saw Leran's youth as the opportune time to break away from Tingu's rule, but that was hardly Balthus' doing. Of the seven lands, four were again under Tingu's standard, and it was only a matter of time before Leran reclaimed the remaining three.

And, I'm still the Lord of Tingu. No matter whom the other lands called leader, it was Leran who was Nexa's last living descendant, Leran who was the ruler of the elves. Asherah still bore the title of Lady of Tingu, yes, but she left the elves to govern their own affairs, and it should be an elf to rule the elves.

Half-elf. Leran's parentage had always been an issue; some said his mother was a nymph, while others claimed she was fae, but it mattered not what sort of blood coursed through her veins. What mattered was that she was not an elf, and whenever Leran's leadership was called into question his half-blood status was raised. Normally, he railed at the fool who dared disparage his mother; while she had done very little mothering, she had been good enough for his father, and for Leran that was enough.

Of course, once the issues had turned to Leran's parentage someone invariably mentioned Asherah's continued rulership of both the elves and all of Parthalan, and that the only land she had ever expressly given to Leran was Nibika. Never mind that Leran now wore the Sala, never mind that Nibika was little more than a memory after Leran's thorough razing of it in the wake of Natraues' treachery, those who would question him claimed that Asherah was his faerie mother looking out for her boy. Nothing could be further from the truth, and Leran had spent his life rejecting the only parent left to him in order to prove his mettle.

Such had been Leran's life since his father died, too soon to have taught him the nuances of leadership, too soon to help him become the king he was born to be. Leran's time since then had been a struggle, but he wanted nothing more than to rebuild his kingdom, and preserve his father's legacy.

The mountain trolls were subdued, for now, and a new, unwanted task loomed on the horizon. He shouted for his men to regroup, then Leran turned to Balthus and uttered the words neither wanted to hear.

"We'd best return to The Seat, and make ready for our journey," he said to Balthus. "If we arrive to Thurnda late, I'd rather face a host of trolls than Senan's new mate."

***

Continue the story in Elfsong

About The Author

Jennifer Allis Provost is a native New Englander who lives in a sprawling colonial along with her beautiful and precocious twins, a dog that thinks she's a kangaroo, a parrot, a junkyard cat, and a wonderful husband who never forgets to buy ice cream. As a child, she read anything and everything she could get her hands on, including a set of encyclopedias, but fantasy was always her favorite. She spends her days drinking vast amounts of coffee, arguing with her computer, and avoiding any and all domestic behavior.

Find Jenn on the web here: http://authorjenniferallisprovost.com/

For up to the minute sale notifications, follow her on Bookbub here: - https://www.bookbub.com/profile/jennifer-allis-provost

For exclusive content, follow her on Patreon: https://www.patreon.com/jenniferallisprovost/

Friend her on Facebook: http://www.facebook.com/jennallis

Follow her on Twitter: @parthalan

Happy reading!

Oleander

Bleeding Hearts

Thornapple

Gallowglass, an urban fantasy set in Scotland and New York:

Gallowglass

Walker

Homecoming

Winter's Queen, an urban fantasy set in Scotland and Elphame:

Touch of Frost

Giant's Daughter

Elphame's Queen

Changes, a contemporary romance:

Changing Teams

Changing Scenes

Changing Fate

Changing Dates